THE KEEPER OF HANDS

Recent Titles in this series by J Sydney Jones

THE EMPTY MIRROR
REQUIEM IN VIENNA
THE SILENCE
THE KEEPER OF HANDS

THE KEEPER OF HANDS

A Viennese Mysteries Novel

J. Sydney Jones

severn House

This first world edition published 2013
in Great Britain and in the USA by
SEVERN HOUSE PUBLISHERS LTD of
19 Cedar Road, Sutton, Surrey, England, SM2 5DA.
Copyright © 2013 by J. Sydney Jones.

British Library Cataloguing in Publication Data

Jones, J. Sydney.
　　The keeper of hands.
　　1. Werthen, Karl (Fictitious character)–Fiction.
　　2. Murder–Investigation–Fiction. 3. Prostitutes–
　　Austria–Vienna–Fiction. 4. Lawyers–Austria–Vienna–
　　Fiction. 5. Vienna (Austria)–Social conditions–20th
　　century–Fiction. 6. Detective and mystery stories.
　　I. Title
　　813.6-dc23

ISBN-13: 978-0-7278-8269-1 (cased)

For old friends, Tom Ovens and Jim Barry

All Severn House titles are printed on acid-free paper.

Severn House Publishers support The Forest Stewardship Council [FSC],
the leading international forest certification organisation. All our titles that
are printed on Greenpeace-approved FSC-certified paper carry the FSC logo.

MIX
Paper from
responsible sources
FSC® C018575

Typeset by Palimpsest Book Production Ltd.,
Falkirk, Stirlingshire, Scotland.
Printed and bound in Great Britain by
MPG Books Ltd., Bodmin, Cornwall.

PROLOGUE

Vienna, May Day, 1901

Sometimes he fancied himself a character from one of Schnitzler's early dramas: Anatol, the Lothario who is ever on the prowl for a sweet young thing.

He sported a thin moustache and the neatly oiled and brushed hair of such a womanizer, carried a walking stick, and dressed to the nines even on days when he did not feel particularly compelled to join the hunt.

A fellow has to keep up appearances, even if there is no one to appreciate the effort.

Today, however, there most definitely was a woman to impress. It was May Day – and a bright and cheery day it was, he thought.

He had seen her throwing flowers to those red-nosed rowdies carrying socialist banners at the head of the parade. Silly young thing, she could hardly understand the politics she was thus espousing. He would take her in hand, educate her in the ways of the world, and get that socialist claptrap out of her mind.

The horse-chestnut trees were in full bloom along the Prater-Allee, their white-and-pink blossoms dazzling. Even the red sashes the paraders wore diagonally across their chests were luminescent today.

A fine day for the chase.

She was exactly the sort he fancied: petite, with luxuriant black ringlets spilling out under her hat. Her face was all expectation, a full-lipped mouth making an 'O', eyes open wide. Her nose was a pixyish thing, tiny and twitching like a small forest creature sniffing its way home.

He gave her a name: Gretchen. It was as good as any other, and Goethe might well approve. Gretchen's hands, holding the last of the carnations, were pink and chapped. A worker then; it was clearly her special day off.

He inched his way through the crowds to the kerbside, next to his chosen one. He could almost smell her now, feel the warmth coming from her young, ripe body.

It was as if this Gretchen sensed his presence. She turned slowly, and her face in silhouette was a thing of beauty – tiny ears like mollusc shells, small creases at her neck as she rotated her head.

Yes, he decided. She would be his before the day was out.

Her eyes fixed on him.

'Back off, will you?' she said in a croaking voice full of working-class coarseness and rebuke.

In the end, he settled for a woman not quite so lovely as his Gretchen, but fetching just the same. A few years past her prime, perhaps, but then his blood was up and the parade was winding down. He had to be quick about it or miss his chance.

He admired her hat and they struck up a conversation; he bought her an ice, told her of his travels and his important work. Actually, though he did travel a good deal, he had no work, important or otherwise. No need to, with his family annuity.

Anna was her name, out for the day from Brigittenau. Due back by five.

Yes, there was time, but not enough for subtlety and play.

He steered her towards the forested section of the Prater, taking her on a seeming nature walk, indicating a chestnut tree here, a linden there. He raised a manicured forefinger at a plover flying overhead; nodded at a delicate St John's wort underfoot, its yellow flower warding off evil.

Little good that would do his Anna, he thought.

They had left the paths now, and quite suddenly he wrapped his arms around her and kissed her on the mouth. She struggled for a moment.

'What sort of girl do you think I am?' she said with what he knew to be feigned outrage.

'This sort,' he said, giving her bottom a pinch.

That made her giggle; a bit of her spittle landed on his lower lip.

They were well out of sight of anyone, and he hurriedly tugged off his jacket, spreading it on the ground.

But she did not reciprocate.

'Quickly,' he urged. Then he added more coaxingly, 'My sweet dove.'

Looking at her face, he realized that she had no intention of pleasing him. In fact, she was about to scream; he saw it building on her face like an infant that has just injured itself. She was not looking at him. No; her eyes were diverted to his left. He followed the glance. And then, as her scream tore through the idyllic softness of the day, he saw it, too.

There, thrust under a low bit of brush, was the body of a young woman, the sort to whom he was normally attracted. She was quite naked, her limbs and torso of a startling whiteness in contrast to the deep woodland greens all around. The right arm was pinned under the body, the left thrown up over the head as if in abandon.

By the look of the purple bruising around her throat and the thick knot of tongue poking out of her mouth, she was dead.

PART ONE

ONE

Advokat Karl Werthen was surveying his demesne.

Only to himself did he dare think of this smallholding in the Vienna Woods as a manorial estate. Were he to use the word demesne with his wife, Berthe, to describe their summer home, she would of course voice full-throated laughter.

Yet, when she referred to it as their 'cottage', Werthen never thought of chiding her. Cottage was the term given to elegant villas on the edges of the woods by Viennese who identified too much with British understatement.

So, alone behind the old farmhouse in the village of Laab im Walde, Werthen surveyed his 'demesne', appreciating in particular the white and violet lilacs tumbling in natural bouquets of bloom in the overgrown bushes to the rear of the farmhouse. Their scent filled the air though he was a good thirty metres from them.

Behind him, at the limits of his property, which locals called simply 'the farm', he heard the chuffing exertions of Stein, finishing the rolling of the last section of fresh brown earth. A small man, Stein was strong as a mule, pushing the large roller in front of him over the tilled ground. He would plant the seed before leaving.

Stein was steward of Hohelände, Werthen's family estate in Lower Austria. In fact, this tennis court was the gift of Emile von Werthen, a show of approval for his son's purchase of a country home. Werthen's father had sent for special rye-grass seed from the All England Lawn Tennis Club and had also dispatched the invaluable Stein to create the court, or at least see to its planting.

Of course, Werthen's father had never asked if such a gift might be appreciated, or indeed if it were even appropriate. Stein had merely showed up at Werthen's door earlier in the week, his wagon full of hoes, shovels, pick axes, measuring sticks and twine, and the large roller. He'd even brought along a tent to camp out, but

Werthen would not hear of that, establishing him in the spare bedroom in the farmhouse instead.

It was as much an embarrassment for Stein as for Werthen that his arrival was unannounced.

Werthen, not one for organized sport, intended to let the grass grow knee deep on the prospective court, to become a wild part of nature again once Stein departed.

A hawk overhead caught Werthen's attention, and then looking down the lane leading to the farmhouse he saw a man approaching. He was a slight figure, dressed all in white on this warm late-spring day. He wore a straw boater and carried a walking stick, using it like a baton as he strolled down the lane – as if keeping time to music. As the man drew nearer, Werthen could hear that he was, indeed, whistling as he walked, at one moment a tuneless mimicry of birdsong, then abruptly transformed to a snippet from Wagner and then one from Mozart.

Another figure now came into view, his daughter, young Frieda, toddling towards the stranger on sturdy legs, with Berthe close behind her. The child was dressed in a white pinafore, but went hatless in the strong sunshine. Her auburn curls were below her ears now.

It was as if his daughter knew this stranger, for she picked up speed on tumbling legs, staggering downhill. She was pulling away from Berthe, who seemed to be amused by this display of independence. As Frieda neared the man in white, Werthen felt a sudden and inexplicable panic. What did he know of this man? What if he were to sweep up Frieda in one arm and abscond with her?

He dropped the secateurs he was carrying and began running round the side of the farmhouse, built in a square around a central courtyard. He wanted to call out to Berthe, to warn her, but he could not find voice. The man in the linen suit was leaning down to one knee, actually beckoning to Frieda, who began giggling insanely as she tottered towards him.

In desperation Werthen leaped over a watering can, catapulted himself over the fence, and found himself face to face with Berthe, who was startled at his arrival.

'What are you on about?' she said as he stood panting in front of her, gesticulating towards Frieda.

'Did you forget?' she said. 'Salten. He's come to see you about a case.'

God! He had forgotten.

He looked at his daughter and now realized that she was not attracted to the man in white, the journalist Felix Salten, at all. Nor was Salten beckoning to Frieda. Both of them were trying to gain the attention of a long-haired dachshund that was happily chasing butterflies and cavorting among the red poppies, pale-blue liverwort and yellow sassafras in the fields.

Salten took three cubes of sugar in his tea, watching with a keen parental eye the antics of Mimi, his beloved dachshund, playing on the flagstones of the kitchen floor with Frieda.

'I do appreciate you letting me meet you like this,' the journalist said.

'Not at all,' Werthen said, though somewhat abstractedly. It was his habit to try to determine the nature of the commission that prospective clients were bringing him, and that was the mental exercise he set himself now.

Theater critic of the *Wiener Allgemeinen Zeitung,* Salten could have earned himself a number of enemies for the biting satire of his reviews. In fact, several years back he had got into a famous altercation with Karl Kraus at the Café Central that led to Salten giving the other journalist a cuff on the ear. A threatening letter, then?

Or was it a missing person? A lover, perhaps? Werthen, via Berthe, who kept up with such matters, knew Salten had a rather complicated love life. On the other hand, Salten might have come on behalf of his current mistress, the Burgtheater actress Ottilie Metzel.

'Is it appropriate that I speak of business here?' His eyes trailed to the frolicking pair on the floor.

'Shall we finish our tea? Then we can retire to my office.'

Berthe cast her husband a reproachful glance.

'Actually,' Werthen quickly added, 'there's no reason we could not discuss matters here. My wife is part of the agency, you know.'

Salten, small and courtly-looking, sporting a rather jaunty, self-satisfied moustache, nodded at Berthe, who was rearranging glasses in the cupboards. They were still settling in for the summer months when the family would spend more time in the country.

'I didn't know. Quite an unconventional family.'

Werthen was unsure how to take this comment. Was it a compliment or an insult? A man like Salten – part of the Jung Wien group of writers and an up-and-coming literary man who had, the year before, published his first collection of stories – might very well expect Werthen to be a staid old bureaucrat; a wills and trusts lawyer despite his sideline in private inquiries.

'I of course mean no slight with that description,' Salten hastily added, as if sensing Werthen's discomfort.

'None taken,' Werthen said, but he traded glances with his wife once again.

'For me, unconventional is a word of respect. A high compliment, in fact.'

Werthen smiled at the comment.

'I know your work,' Salten said.

'I have had some small successes, to be sure,' Werthen said. 'The Mahler case among others.'

'No, no,' the other interjected. 'I mean your literary work. I edited one of your pieces for *An der schönen blauen Donau*. I rather liked your boulevardier . . . What was his name?'

'Maxim.'

'Right,' said Salten. 'Rather a nice tip of the hat to our friend Schnitzler, I thought at the time.'

'How so?' Werthen asked, feeling suddenly protective of this short story he had written a number of years ago.

'There is a certain resonance to the name,' Salten said, obviously enjoying a discussion of the subject closest to his heart. 'First there is the association with the establishment of that name in Paris. Maxim's restaurant and cabaret caters to the rich and powerful of the world.'

'I hadn't really thought of that,' Werthen said, thinking better now of his character, who was something of a silly skirt-chasing fop.

'But how does Schnitzler come into it?' Berthe inquired.

'Well, there's Schnitzler's beloved Anatol, of course, the subject of his early plays. The constant playboy, forever in love and forever changing partners. You might recall that his best friend and sometimes advisor was named Max.'

Salten leaned back in his chair with a sigh. It was a physical gesture Werthen knew only too well from his years in the courtroom. The prosecution rests, your honor.

'Those are indeed interesting associations, Herr Salten. And I am flattered that you, a well-known writer yourself, should remember the scribblings of an amateur.'

Salten made no immediate reply. He stirred his tea, blowing over the rim of the cup though the contents were long since cooled.

'I am hardly the well-known figure you describe, Advokat Werthen. In my mind's eye I am still poor little unhealthy Siegmund Salzmann from Budapest toiling away in my cousin's insurance office. Those days are not so very far behind me.'

He looked wistfully at his dog and Werthen's daughter. 'It must be wonderful having a child.'

About to respond in the positive, Werthen was silenced by Salten's next remark.

'But enough of socializing. To the matter at hand. I come about murder, sir.'

The word resounded in the cosy kitchen like a blasphemy.

'Whose murder, Herr Salten? A friend?'

'I represent another in this inquiry.'

'But surely the police—'

'The victim is of too low a status to warrant their concern.'

'And your client?'

'Frau Josephine Mutzenbacher. I am currently engaged in writing her life story.'

'A literary figure?' Werthen asked, not recognizing the name.

Which comment brought a low chortle from Salten. 'Hardly! In point of fact, the woman runs a brothel. Rather high-class, mind you, but a brothel all the same.'

'A madam?' Berthe said, now joining them at the table.

Salten pursed his lips in assent. 'Frau Mutzenbacher is a rather amazing woman. Born in Ottakring, of course. Her father was a saddler. She herself was initiated into the world of Eros at a most tender age.'

He quickly cast his eyes Berthe's way, not wanting to cause embarrassment. Seeing none, he proceeded.

'They called her Pepi. She entered the brothels at the age of twelve, as a licensed prostitute. But by cunning, and sometimes sheer disarming honesty, she worked her way up in her chosen profession. Now, at the age of fifty, she operates one of the finest houses in the Empire. And what is most incredible about the woman is that she has not an ounce of bitterness about her hard life. On the contrary, she is quite humorous in the detailing of her various liaisons.'

'And the victim is therefore one of the good lady's working ménage, one assumes,' said Werthen. 'The person deemed of too low status by the police?'

'Exactly.'

'Does this have anything to do with that unfortunate girl found in the Prater on May Day?' Berthe asked.

The death had made the headlines in an otherwise dull news climate, but had been just as quickly forgotten when supplanted by a much bigger news story: the death of Count Joachim von Ebersdorf several days later, victim of bad shellfish. An absurd way to die, Werthen thought. Eating oysters in land-locked Vienna.

'Very good, Frau Werthen.'

Werthen waited for his wife to correct Salten. Instead, she smiled wanly at his compliment.

'Meisner, actually,' she said after a pause. 'Frau Meisner. I kept my maiden name.'

This made Salten sit up in his chair. 'My apologies, Frau Meisner.'

Werthen was tiring of all this toing and froing. 'The murdered girl, Herr Salten. What is Frau Mutzenbacher's interest in her, other than commercial?'

'You'll have to ask her that, Advokat. That is, if you accept the commission.'

'Frieda, dear,' Berthe said to their daughter. 'Don't pull the doggie's ears. She doesn't like that.'

'Sof ears,' the child said.

'They are that,' Salten said. 'Like silk.'

Frieda, squatting by the rather impatient animal, craned her neck Salten's way.

'Sill,' she said.

'Silk.'

'And how is it you have come to me?' asked Werthen, redirecting the conversation once again.

'Well, it was over a game of Tarock, actually. I enjoy a hand or two at the Café Landtmann now and again, and two days ago my usual partners and I were joined by Gustav Klimt.'

'I would never credit Klimt with the patience for cards,' Berthe said, but her eyes were still on Frieda and the dachshund.

'True,' said Salten. 'It is my considered judgment that he would be better off with a more physical pastime.'

'Such as lifting dumbbells,' Werthen said. 'I mean it quite literally. He is very much the one for exercise.'

'And for cream pastries,' Berthe added. 'Please, Frieda. Not the doggie's ears.'

Salten eyed his beloved Mimi warily. 'Perhaps I should tie her up outside.'

He got up and did so. Meanwhile, Berthe took Frieda to another room.

Once Salten returned, the dog began whining outside.

'Quite a social animal, the dachshund. They don't like being left alone.'

'I'm sure she'll survive,' Werthen said. 'So it was Klimt that put you on to me?'

'I mentioned quite casually the intentions of Frau Mutzenbacher, and he immediately came up with your name.'

'Most kind of him.'

'He also mentioned you are quite zealous in your billing. I don't believe there will be a problem with Frau Mutzenbacher.'

'Did you know the girl in question?'

'Mitzi? I'd seen her about. As I say, I am engaged by Frau Mutzenbacher on her memoirs.'

'I mean in a professional way.'

'You are a direct one, aren't you?'

'I like to know where I am in a case.'

'No. Not that I haven't been known for dalliances. I am, of course, now engaged to Fräulein Metzel of the Burgtheater.'

Werthen nodded at this information, but remained silent.

'She was not my type,' Salten added.

'How is that?'

'I do not know how familiar you are with such establishments as Frau Mutzenbacher's, Advokat.'

'Educate me.'

'Well, there are usually young women to satisfy almost every taste. Including the hard-pressed woman of good birth who takes up the trade to pay off her father's debts.'

'A fabrication?'

'Generally so. At Frau Mutzenbacher's, always. Her premises are the home of illusion. The high-class lady fallen low appeals to the sensitive trade – the talkers rather than doers, if you understand?'

Werthen nodded. He'd had some experience of the trade during his years of criminal law in Graz, but thought it better to let Salten play the *magister ludi* in this regard. No telling what a fellow might blurt out when in an educative mood.

'Then of course there is the pale young thing who never says a word, the mute of the boudoir. And the tough woman with the heart of gold, the soft woman with the harsh voice and tendency toward discipline. I'm sure you understand.'

'And what was Mitzi's role?'

'The child virgin. Don't get me wrong,' said Salten quickly, seeing Werthen's look of disapproval. 'She was neither. But she was quite young-looking, a diminutive young woman who could and did easily pass for thirteen. In point of fact, she was nineteen.'

'So her clients believed she was a child?'

'I would assume so, though I'm hardly privy to their thoughts. Really, you must put these questions to Frau Mutzenbacher. I only saw the girl in passing a few times. Bringing tea to us as we worked during the day. That sort of thing. She seemed to be a special favorite of Frau Mutzenbacher.'

The whines grew more insistent from outside.

In the end, Werthen, deciding prostitutes also deserve justice, agreed to the commission and set up a time for an interview with Frau Mutzenbacher the following Monday. The case was already over two weeks old, so there seemed no need for undue haste, and Werthen and his family had planned a weekend in the country.

Salten said his goodbyes to Berthe and Frieda and went off down the lane, with Mimi trotting along quite proudly in front.

That evening Berthe experimented with a new spaghetti recipe. They waited for these breaks from Vienna and their housekeeper, Frau Blatschky, and her traditional Austrian cooking, to try more exotic fare. Werthen had noticed that of late his wife had taken more of an interest in cooking. He doubted very much that it was merely a sign of increased domesticity. Instead, he supposed that she was finding variation, and a sense of discovery in whatever way she could, for as a new mother she had been tied more closely to home since Frieda's birth.

Stein, freshly scrubbed after his day's exertion building the tennis court, looked at his plate of pasta with a degree of suspicion. Then, watching Berthe twirl a bit round the tines of her fork, followed suit and was soon slurping along with the rest.

They had moved on to the meat course, veal, which for Stein was more recognizable, when he said, 'The rye grass is experimental at best.'

'Pardon?' Werthen said.

He was watching Frieda, who was lingering over her pasta, busily painting her cheeks a brilliant orange with the sauce.

'We're not really too sure about how well it will do in this loamy soil. Your father and myself, that is.'

'I did not expect you were referring to your own father,' Werthen said with a smile. Stein senior had long since been pensioned off, though still living on the von Werthen estate. 'Young' Stein, as he was called although he was a bit older than Werthen, had taken his place a number of years ago.

'He still misses the work,' Stein said ruefully.

'Why the experiment?' Werthen said at length.

'Well, to see what grass will be best for your father's new place.'

'New place?'

Stein laid down his fork. 'You didn't know he is purchasing land near here?'

Werthen felt his entire face sag in dismay, then hurriedly got control of his emotions.

'I expect he was planning it as a surprise.'

'Yes,' Berthe chimed in. 'Very much a surprise.'

'I must apologize,' Stein said, his face reddening at his perceived *faux pas*.

'Not at all, Stein,' Werthen reassured him. 'One assumes he is not creating a tennis academy to rival the All England Croquet and Lawn Tennis Club?'

A polite demi-laugh issued from Stein. 'It's to round out the new estate. I believe there's to be an equestrian ground, as well. It is the sole topic of conversation at Hohelände.'

'It's only natural they want to be near their only grandchild,' Berthe said.

They were lying side by side in bed, gazing up at the darkened ceiling.

'Perverse, not natural. Stein says the property is near here. Just a bit of breathing room, that is all I require.'

'They probably assume that now we have a summer home they would not see much of us at Hohelände.'

'And they would be right. I do not have the fondest memories of that house.'

'Even though that's where we met?'

The bed boards underneath the cotton mattress creaked as Werthen rolled on to his side to face his wife.

'You are being awfully conciliatory about this. It affects us both, you know. They'll be constantly underfoot, or expect us to be their guests. This is my little piece of heaven and I do not appreciate interlopers.'

'It's the Burgtheater for you, Karl. So dramatic.'

'Have you forgotten how difficult my father and mother are to be around? And I repeat, why are you suddenly the peacemaker?'

She said nothing for a moment. A fly had got into the house and was now busily buzzing in the dusk of the room.

'It *is* only natural for grandparents to want to be near their grandchild.'

She continued staring at the black expanse overhead.

'Is there something you've been wanting to tell me?' he asked.

'Father mentioned that he might be moving to Vienna. Well, not *moving*. Perhaps a *pied-à-terre* to begin with.'

'Wonderful!' Werthen groaned. 'They've got us boxed in on both fronts.'

'It doesn't have to be like that,' Berthe said.

'Don't you remember the argument over christening?'

'That was settled amicably enough,' Berthe said.

'Yes. But I had to threaten to bring Frieda up a Buddhist unless they stopped intervening. The hypocrisy of it. We're all Jews – it doesn't matter whether they are assimilated or not, or if they were baptized Christians or not. Yet they go about playing at being German aristocrats.'

'It's their lives, their hypocrisy.'

'Not when it has an impact on our lives. And let us not forget your father's insistence on an *aliyah* naming ceremony for Frieda.'

'But he finds her name so Nordic.'

'Better Ruth? That is fine, though. I understand his position. After all, he is a leading Talmudic scholar . . .'

'It's not about religion. It's more about tradition for him.'

'Fine. So now he will be in Vienna part of the time to be close to Ruth.'

'There is a silver lining,' Berthe said, turning to him now and placing a kiss on his nose. 'There is a certain widow he has met . . .'

'Nuptials in the offing? Sorry. I don't know why I am being so difficult about all of this. I enjoy your father. I even enjoy seeing my parents with Frieda now and again. It just feels suddenly like the world is crowding in on us.'

She moved against him, putting a soothing hand around the hair at the base of his head. Her fingers felt cool to the touch. Her lips touched his.

'Not the world,' she said, moving closer. 'Just me.'

In the middle of the night Frieda woke them with a cry. Berthe

went to her and then came back to their bed with the little bundle
of their daughter cradled in her arms.

'It's still a strange room to her. She'll get used to it.'

'I don't mind,' he said. 'A couple of hours ago, maybe. But
now —'

'There,' Berthe cooed to the infant as she lodged Frieda between
them. She was asleep again in a matter of minutes.

'I've been wondering,' Werthen began.

'No more discussion about our parents tonight. Please.'

'No. About Salten. Was he hiding something, do you think?'

'You mean when you asked him about his personal contact with
the unfortunate young woman?'

'So you overheard our conversation?'

She ignored this question. 'Definitely defensive.'

'Why, one wonders?'

TWO

On Monday morning Werthen set off for the office first, and
would leave from there for his eleven o'clock appointment
with Frau Mutzenbacher.

The day was glorious: a shimmering blue sky overhead and a
soft warmth already at eight as he made his way down the
Josefstädterstrasse. On the opposite side of the street he noticed the
same military man he had seen for the past few months. Tall and
thickly built, his moustache finely waxed, the patent-leather visor of
his peaked cap shiny and without a smudge, as if the fellow put it
on only after he had donned the fawn-coloured suede gloves he
invariably wore. The greatcoat had long since been relegated to moth-
balls, Werthen imagined. The captain – for the three stars on his stiff
collar indicated that rank – looked resplendent in the green tunic of
the General Staff. His meticulously creased blue pantaloons were
tucked into low black boots, as gleaming as the visor of his cap. A
sword swung from his belt, and on his chest he wore the 1898 Jubilee
Medal presented by Franz Josef in honor of the Emperor's fifty years
of service to his country.

This General Staff officer had interested Werthen from the first
time he had seen him during the dark grey days of winter. Like

Werthen, the officer was an inveterate walker. He stood ramrod stiff yet moved with a seeming casual elegance despite his size. Werthen, who still fancied himself a short-story writer in the odd moment, thought this officer would make a splendid character in a tale of love and regret. He secretly looked for a flaw in the captain as they continued to make their way down towards the Inner City on opposite sides of the street. A gambler, perhaps? There were enough of those in the military; forced to live on impossibly small army pay, many a young dandy had ruined his career attempting to supplement his income at the *vingt-et-un* tables of Baden bei Wien.

Soon Werthen lost interest in this game, however; and also lost sight of the officer as they approached the Volksgarten, since the other man headed off to the Ministry of War offices in the Hofburg while he, Werthen, continued through the park to his law office on Habsburgergasse. He was in an elated mood, looking forward to a new commission, wondering what to expect from Frau Mutzenbacher.

His orders from Berthe before leaving this morning were clear enough.

'Eyes forward, Karl,' she had teased.

'I'm sure the working members of the establishment will still be sleeping, dear,' he assured her.

Prostitutes were not his style. He neither fancied them nor frowned upon them. They had their job, and he had his. Quite simple, really. He had never sought their services, though once, when Werthen was sixteen, his father had made a clumsy effort at initiating his son into the ways of the world by a visit to a Viennese brothel. One look at the ghoulish eye makeup, however, at the sullen expression of the woman his father intended for him, and Werthen ran out of the place and all the way back to the hotel where they were staying, up from the country for the ball season.

His father never mentioned the incident.

The Habsburgergasse was bustling with activity when he arrived at No. 4. Down the street, Waltrum, the booksellers, had wooden boxes out on the street with second-hand books for sale. The flower shop next door was alive with bunches of lilac in large metal buckets of water, the heavy scent attracting honey bees. The *Portier* of his office building, Frau Ignatz, was out sweeping the cobbled sidewalk in front. The day was so splendid that he would not allow her presence to dampen his spirits.

'Good morning to you, Frau Ignatz,' he said, tipping his Homburg as he entered the door.

'I am not so sure what's so good about it,' she said. 'The refuse that's left behind on this street is something awful.'

He ignored her remark, taking the stairs at a fast clip until he reached his office. As usual, Fräulein Metzinger had preceded him. She was already at her typewriter, beating out a staccato rhythm on the keys. A far cry from the forefingered typing that was all she had been capable of when she first came to his office. She looked surprised when she saw him.

'I thought you had an interview this morning.'

There was a small sound of reproach to her comment.

'I thought I would get some work done here first. The Herbst trust is still in need of that codicil.'

'It's been taken care of.'

'Wonderful. I'll look at the papers, then.'

'Sorry to be so curt,' she said as he was about to walk into his inner office. 'I feel rather abashed at being caught out.'

'At what?'

She swept her hand at the typewriter and the stack of letters next to it.

'This is not office work.'

'Ah,' he said, nodding his head. 'You really do not need to explain, Fräulein Metzinger.'

'It is for the cause.'

'I assumed so. You do more than your share here. The Herbst codicil, for example.'

'Still, it is perhaps not right.'

She was waiting, he knew, for his approval. 'It is a noble cause,' he said.

'The keeper of hands . . .'

'I beg your pardon?'

She shook her head in disgust, looking at the paper in the carriage of her typewriter.

'That is what they call the Belgian officer in charge of keeping the cut-off hands of natives deemed too indolent at gathering rubber.'

'Why ever would they do that?'

'Cut off their hands? As punishment, of course. King Leopold must have his slaves industrious at all costs.'

'I meant *keep* the hands. Collect them like that.'

She sighed. 'Those in charge of discipline make their living by keeping track of punishments. So many crowns for each hand.'

He felt a shiver pass over him.

'Of course they take the hands of those who have done no wrong, as well. They must make a living, you see. It's all been documented in Mary Kingsley's book on Africa and by the reporting of Edward Morel. Even in the novel of that Pole, Conrad.'

'British now, actually,' Werthen said. '*The Heart of Darkness*.' Werthen had read it in the English original, in instalments in *Blackwood's Magazine*, and found it a powerful indictment of the horrors being perpetrated in Africa.

'But people do not listen. Letters need to be sent to those with power and conscience all over the world, in order to end this savagery in the Congo Free State.'

Werthen swallowed hard. 'It is a noble cause, Fräulein Metzinger. Keep up the good work. Spread the word.'

But she had already gone back to a furious clacking of keys, quite ignoring him. It had been like this ever since she lost the street urchin whom she had hoped to adopt, a tragedy that set her to fighting for noble causes wherever they might be, from pacifist campaigns to ones against European barbarism in the Congo.

In his office, he sat down at his desk, looking forward to the morning edition of the *Neue Freie Presse*. As per arrangement, Frau Ignatz's younger brother Oskar should have already delivered the paper, but there was nothing on his desk. Oskar was slow – some would say disadvantaged mentally – but dependable. It surprised Werthen that the man had failed in his duties today. He was about to go and inquire about it with Fräulein Metzinger when he heard a commotion from that direction. There was a low mumbling and a higher voice. Surely that of Frau Ignatz? An argument seemed to be ensuing.

Poking his head out of his office, he saw his secretary, Frau Ignatz and Oskar in a tug of war over the *Neue Freie Presse*. Frau Ignatz saw Werthen and sighed.

'There you are, Advokat. Will you please tell this stubborn man to hand over the paper and go back to bed? He has a temperature of a hundred and two.'

Looking at Oskar, Werthen saw that he was as pale as *Semmel* dough.

'It's my duty,' Oskar countered, his usual booming voice a weak imitation.

'I heartily agree with the ladies, Herr Oskar,' Werthen said, approaching the stand-off. 'I much admire your sense of duty, but you clearly belong in bed.'

He took the newspaper out of the man's sweaty hand, clapped him on the back, and announced, 'Back to bed with you. Have you seen a doctor?'

Frau Ignatz snorted at this suggestion. 'Oskar won't let the white coats near him. Had a bad fright with one when he was a child.'

'Well, Oskar, you're in luck. My friend Doktor Kramer wears a dark coat and knows more about stamps than anyone I know.' This was Oskar's passion, and it drew an instant response.

'He'd know about the Basel Dove? First time they made a three-colour stamp.'

'Absolutely,' Werthen said. 'Now let your sister put you back to bed. And Fräulein Metzinger, could you call Kramer's office and see if he can pay a visit?'

She nodded, and reached for the telephone even as Werthen was returning to his own office with his prized, but somewhat battered, newspaper.

Werthen spent the better part of an hour perusing the paper. He skimmed over the lead article on Hungary – yet another question about that unwilling partner in the Austro-Hungarian empire. Then read a feuilleton from Pretoria on the war in South Africa, and finally settled into the sports news dealing with the Traber Derby. It seemed much the saner choice, but there was no safe ground today. Details of the Derby simply reminded him of his father, Emile, and his plans to create his own estate in the Vienna Woods with an equestrian area.

Werthen wanted to feel more kindly towards his father, but found it a difficult task.

Looking at the standard clock on the wall in front of him, he saw that he had managed to squander the better part of an hour. He grabbed his Homburg and left. In the reception, Fräulein Metzinger was still at her pile of letters. She did not notice his departure.

The establishment in question, the Bower, was located in a narrow lane in the First District near the Danube Canal. A narrow three-story baroque building, its exterior could have been that of a fashionable men's club – for, compared to its bleak and dour neighbors, the façade of the Bower was newly repainted in a shade of buttery gold several tones lighter than the Habsburg yellow of Schönbrunn that continued to infect the imperial world. Multi-colored putti frolicked about the heavily shuttered street-level and second-floor windows that housed Frau Mutzenbacher's establishment. It was clear the brothel was closed, but Salten had told him to simply ring at the front door.

He would be expected. He let himself in through the street door and, as Werthen went to the door of the Bower in the vestibule, he heard a tssking of tongue: descending the stairs was an elderly woman about her shopping, reminding him that the third floor was still given over to apartments. She was not too busy to scold him for illicit behavior.

He read the small brass plaque on the door to ensure he was at the right place, pulled the bell, heard it jangle behind the oak doors, and was soon greeted by a man of about forty in suspenders and shirt collar. He looked as if he could use a shave.

'You'll be the investigator, then,' he said.

Werthen had no chance to reply. The man turned and began heading down a long, darkened hallway. Werthen stood uncertainly at the door.

The man turned and waved to him. 'Come on. She's expecting you.'

Entering the hall, Werthen was struck by the heavy blend of aromas: cigar smoke, talcum powder and, from deeper inside, the smell of fried food. He followed the man down the long hallway with some difficulty. The world outside was iridescent in the spring light; here, inside the Bower, it was eternal night.

Finally they came to a door at the end of the hall. The man tapped gently and from inside a voice mumbled something. Werthen could not make out what was said. The man turned the knob, opened the door, and gestured Werthen inside with the wave of a hand.

'In you go.'

Werthen found himself still in the gloaming; he could barely discern a figure sitting in an armchair at the far end of the room.

'You may be seated on the divan,' this figure – a woman by the tone of the voice – said.

Werthen did as he was bid. The divan was across the room from the woman.

'Frau Mutzenbacher, I presume?'

'Is this Salten's idea of a clever detective?'

Werthen felt himself stiffen at the jeer. 'May we have some light?'

'No we may not, thank you very much for asking. You're here so that I can determine if I want to hire you. What do you know of my business?'

The question took him aback for a moment. 'I'm not sure what you mean. Salten tells me that you operate a house of . . .'

'Say it, man. A house of ill repute. A brothel. A whorehouse.'

'Indeed.'

'Have you any familiarity with such establishments?'

'Very little, I'm afraid.' He tried to focus on her face in the darkness. It seemed she was wearing a veil.

'Good. I want someone with fresh eyes. No assumptions. Would that be you?'

'Madam, I must admit I am unaccustomed to this sort of interview.'

'Too many words, Advokat. Speak plainly.'

This remark suddenly endeared the woman to Werthen, for it was an echo of what his wife Berthe had said to him when they first met several years before. She had accused him of sounding like someone running for mayor. 'Pompous' was the word she chose, and she was right.

'Plainly said. I am quite good at what I do, as you are at your job. However, I am not a miracle worker. Neither do I have a bias against prostitutes. If you wish to employ me, fine. If not, I have other matters at hand.'

She said nothing for a moment. Then stirring in her chair, she nodded.

'That's better spoken, Advokat. With some feeling.'

'What is it exactly that you want?' Werthen asked.

Another long pause.

'The young woman's name was Mitzi, as I understand,' Werthen began.

'My girls are expendable,' Frau Mutzenbacher said, as if not hearing him. 'I can give you a list of Mitzi's customers, but they surely use assumed names when coming here. Society spits on us, yet we hold the social fabric together. How many marriages do you think would survive, Herr Advokat, if we were not around to service oversexed husbands? How many marriages would be torn asunder by affairs with married women? How many ignorant youths would blunder on the wedding night were we not there before to train and gently guide? You ask what I want. I want justice for whores, that is what I want. I want society to finally acknowledge us. Barring that, I want to see the bastard who killed poor Mitzi rot behind bars in the Liesel for the rest of his pitiful days.'

'Justice for all whores is a tall order. But I can try my best to find who killed this one young woman. And yes, I would like that list of names. It is a place to start, though the killer need not have been one of her clients. Do you have any suspicions?'

'I'm not the detective.'

She sounded defensive; he did not bother to correct her choice of titles. 'Private Inquiry Agent' is what was listed on the brass plaque at his office below 'Wills and Trusts' and 'Criminal Law'.

'Was Mitzi close to any of the other women here?'

'Fräulein Fanny.' Said without an instant's hesitation. 'I will have her brought to us.'

'In other words, you wish to engage my services?'

'It appears so, no?'

'Then I need to know something before we begin. Why do you care? You must have lost girls before. This can be a dangerous business for young women.'

She uttered a mirthless laugh. 'Don't I know!'

Suddenly, she turned up the wick on the kerosene lamp at her side and he could see her more clearly: a woman of ripe middle age, somewhat dowdy and matriarchal in appearance, thick in the middle with feet squeezed into lace-ups perhaps a size too small for her. She removed the veil covering her face and he saw the jagged line of a scar along the right side of her face.

Frau Mutzenbacher jabbed a finger at it. 'That is what one of my clients left me as a going-away present. Did me a favor, actually. I couldn't work the houses anymore, not even the streets, not with this. So I started using the other end of my body to make a living.' She tapped her temple. 'And it brought me all this.'

Werthen suddenly remembered what Salten had said about Frau Mutzenbacher: that she was not bitter about her former life.

Not a very discerning witness of human character, Salten.

'You haven't answered my question,' Werthen said. 'Why the concern for Mitzi?'

'Well, take it as an old woman's fantasy, but I looked on the girl as the daughter I never had. She was special. You never met her, you could not know. But she was attentive to one's needs. Thousands of little kindnesses. I really don't know how to explain it. She was also the living likeness of my younger sister, Theresa. Dead these twenty years from consumption.'

She paused for a moment, working the embroidered black silk of her skirts between thumb and forefinger as if searching for imperfections.

Werthen said nothing, allowing the silence to gather around them in the muffled room.

'I was planning to adopt her,' Frau Mutzenbacher said, looking up from her skirt. 'This was all going to be hers.'

'But she continued working?'

'That was her decision. She was stubborn. Swore that she would keep working, that otherwise the other girls would think she had wormed her way into my affections and was using me.' She permitted herself a sniffle.

Now she fixed Werthen with a look commingling ferocity and pleading. 'She was special. You see?'

'I am beginning to,' he replied. 'And as for my earlier question regarding any suspicions you might have. I cannot help you if you are not absolutely forthcoming with me.'

She touched the scar and then shook her head. 'Everyone loved Mitzi. She had no enemies.'

He watched her carefully as she said this. After all, Frau Mutzenbacher was a woman paid handsomely for dissembling, as were all her employees.

'No one client who was exceptionally attached to her?'

Another abrupt head shake. 'As I said, she was beloved by all.'

'Except for one,' said Werthen. 'The person who killed her.'

THREE

He met Fräulein Fanny in the parlor, and not in the company of Frau Mutzenbacher. He wanted candor from this young woman.

Fanny looked amused rather than concerned; her chalk-white face was still puffy from sleep, her black hair untidy but partially hidden under a shawl wrapped dramatically around her head. She held a cup of morning tea daintily between forefinger and thumb as if trained to do so.

'Frau Mutzenbacher tells me that you and Mitzi were fast friends,' he said, as the major-domo – still in his suspenders – left the room after delivering the young woman.

'Well, aren't we all working girls together?'

'Did you know her well?'

'I found her. If that means I knew her well, then yes.'

'Found her?'

She nodded, giving a chirrup of laughter.

'I saw her working the corner near the Naschmarkt. Bright-looking little pigeon she was, as I told Frau Mutzenbacher. She'd be tarnished soon enough working that corner, though. Obviously not very experienced in the trade.'

'And you told your mistress about this young girl on the streets?' Werthen said.

'Of course. That's part of the job, you know. Finding new girls, fresh girls. Mitzi had that look on her. The kind men like.'

She did not look away as she spoke, as if daring him with her frankness.

'How long was she here?'

She wagged her head as if attempting to shake order into her thoughts.

'Seven or eight months, I'd say.'

'She must have been an extraordinary young woman, then,' Werthen said.

'How so?'

'To have so impressed your employer, that is. To have charmed her and earned her love.'

He got the reaction he was waiting for. Fanny pursed her lips and narrowed her eyes. She set the teacup down.

'She knew what she was about, despite all her ignorance of the trade. Knew which side of the *Semmel* is buttered.'

'I take it you were Frau Mutzenbacher's favorite once?'

A knowing look transformed her face like wind on water.

'Oh no you don't. I see what you're doing here, Advokat.'

'What am I doing, Fräulein Fanny?'

'You're trying to make it look like I might have done for Mitzi. That I had some grudge. A motion.'

'Motive,' he corrected, and quickly regretted having done so. Fanny's face grew sullen, her eyes hooded in defiance.

'I assure you, Fräulein Fanny, I am not attempting to associate you with this murder. I only want to get to know the victim, to understand her workings. Knowing that might lead me to the person who committed this barbarity.'

She adjusted herself in the chair. Holding her head haughtily, she sniffed.

'Truly,' he added. 'You must believe me. Whatever your true feelings for Mitzi, you must feel compelled to help. The person who perpetrated this outrage is still at large, perhaps hunting other poor young women at this very moment.'

She shivered at this pronouncement.

'Did she have special clients? Any man who paid unusual attention to her? Someone she might have met off the premises?'

'No, that is strictly forbidden. If Frau M found out, she would take the hide off your backside and you would find yourself on the street.'

'Did she confide in you at all? What of her background, her family? Do you know where she came from?'

'We shared a room, that's all,' Fanny said. 'We weren't friends. We just talked about the usual things. The new Paris fashions, what we would do if we found the right man. She was not very talkative. She saved that for her customers.'

There was an ironic edge to the last comment.

'How do you mean?' he asked.

Fanny shook her head. 'She had that way about her. Used her mouth as much as what she sits on. And not in the way you are thinking, either. She came across the innocent young girl, and men loved that. They liked to talk to her, to confide in her. She talked to them and seemed to listen.'

'Her clients shared secrets with her? Did she tell you that?'

'Not in so many words.'

'Any names? Of clients, I mean.'

Another sniggering laugh.

'Oh, plenty of names. Loads of names. And all of them false, to be sure.'

She hesitated, thinking.

'What is it?' Werthen asked.

'There was this one old duffer,' she said. 'He would sit and wait his turn if it took all night. Had a particular fancy for the young girls, even if they weren't really so young. Funny-looking old guy with flowing moustaches, and sandals sometimes – even in winter. He would sit in the second parlor all on his own, writing in this little leather notepad he carried. Even drawing pictures. I saw him doing a face one time. Not a bad likeness of one of the other gentlemen swilling his champagne.'

'You don't recall his name?'

'I told you, we're not much on names here. They have the crowns or florins, what do they need with a name?'

'Is there anything out of the ordinary you can tell me about Mitzi? Any sudden change in her emotions, for example?'

'That's exactly it,' she said, suddenly excited. 'A change in her emotions. Like she was worried. I thought at first it was because of her relationship with Frau M: that she was feeling, I don't know, somehow strained by it. By what Frau M expected of her. But that wasn't it.'

'Did you ask her about it?'

'Like I told you, we shared a room, not secrets.'

'When did this change begin?'

'Two, maybe three months ago. Not so you would notice it in public; but in our room, I would sometimes come in and she would be looking in the mirror at herself like she was searching for something, someone. I came across her writing a letter not long ago, and she hid it under her skirts like a schoolgirl.'

The major-domo – now wearing a morning coat – showed Werthen to the room Mitzi had shared with Fräulein Fanny. It was on the second floor of the old building, reached by a backstairs so narrow you had to walk single file and so dark a candle was needed at midday.

They had no candle.

The room, once they reached it, was dark and spare. The major-domo, whose unlikely name was Siegfried, lit the spirit lamp on the small deal table between the two beds. Werthen could now see that, despite being cramped, there was nothing squalid about the room. Rather, it was clean and functional like a dormitory at an all-girls school. The irony was not lost on Werthen, who could not suppress a smile when he was ushered in.

'You find something amusing about our establishment, Herr Advokat?'

Siegfried was now standing close enough for Werthen to discern the aroma of the man's sausage breakfast.

'I believe I can carry on without your assistance,' Werthen said by way of reply. 'I shall call if I need you.'

'Shall you, then? Very good, m'lord.' Siegfried said this archly, like a comic performer at the German Volkstheater, and tipped a non-existent hat as he left.

Focusing his attention on the room, it was immediately clear to Werthen which bed was Mitzi's, for the bedding had been removed and the mattress rolled up as at the end of term. He half expected to see hockey sticks, or perhaps a blue ribbon from the local riding club. There was indeed an element of unreality about this affair. Fräulein Mitzi had thus far been the stuff of plays and fantasies: a newspaper article read by Berthe; a proposal passed on by the writer

Salten; and the misty-eyed remembrances of a madam. At least young Fanny had offered a piece of real information regarding Mitzi. She had been troubled by something lately and had been seen putting her thoughts down on paper. To Fanny it had appeared to be a letter, but Werthen knew that it could just as easily have been a journal or diary.

But where would the young woman have kept it? The room afforded a distinct lack of privacy, furnished as it was by two metal-framed beds, the deal table, one straight-backed chair, and a pair of wardrobes along one wall. According to Frau Mutzenbacher, all of Mitzi's things had been left untouched in her wardrobe.

Werthen opened the curtains on the room's one window in a vain attempt to allow in more light, for the glass was hard upon the building next door. A bit of dull daylight came into the room. Instead, he turned up the lamp on the table, and then went to the wardrobe across from the foot of Mitzi's bed. Here he found the tools of her trade: several blue schoolgirl uniforms with high starched white collars hung on the left side of the wardrobe, with embroidered crests on the left chest to enhance the fantasy for aged voyeurs. Suddenly the awful truth of Mitzi's life and death struck Werthen. No longer was this a second-hand death. The pitiful reality of these school uniforms touched him in a way an autopsy report could not. He was surprised to find his eyes misting as his thoughts went to his own daughter, Frieda. How did a young woman come to this?

Mitzi had to have a history, but according to both Fanny and Frau Mutzenbacher the girl was a blank slate as far as her past was concerned. According to them, Mitzi never offered the least piece of information about her parents, where she came of age, any of it.

On the other side of the wardrobe hung what was presumably Mitzi's off-duty clothing: an assortment of risqué low-slung evening wear mixed with domestic dresses in black and gray of the distinctly conservative nature a housekeeper might possess. It was as if Mitzi were herself cleaved into two separate lives. Hats, some with feathers, some with veils, lay on the top shelf of the wardrobe. Werthen stood on tiptoe to make sure there was nothing else of interest on the shelf. In the end he had to fetch the one wooden chair in the room to examine the top of the wardrobe, but his efforts were rewarded with a thin layer of dust and nothing more. There were very few areas in this Spartan room that would function as hiding places had Mitzi been keeping a diary or anything else of a personal nature. Werthen examined the back of the wardrobe as well, but found nothing.

He was about to give up when he noticed that there was a space under the wardrobe, as it stood on four rounded feet. Crouching, he was rewarded with a bit of dust, nothing more. Yet something was amiss here. It took him a moment to see what it was. The front of the wardrobe stood on two feet, one at each corner. However, at the back there appeared to be three. On more careful inspection he saw that the one in the middle was not rounded like the others, but was in fact more rectangular and was not made of wood. In fact, once he maneuvered the wardrobe out from the wall, he could see that this object was covered in dark oilcloth. It was wedged rather tightly under the rear frame of the clothes-press, and when he finally retrieved it and began unwrapping the cloth he discovered a Bible.

Not the sort of thing one expects to find in the room of a prostitute.

He opened the flyleaf and found nothing. If it had been a family Bible, then it might have provided a lead to Mitzi's true identity. This Bible was an 1860 edition; nothing to learn from it.

Inspecting the book, he noticed a bit of paper sticking out of one of the pages. He opened the Bible at this page – the Old Testament, *Joshua: 2* – and found a beige envelope with no address. He opened it and discovered what appeared to be a brief letter, with the date *12.4.1901* written at the top. But beyond that, he could not read a word. It was in some foreign language he could not make out at all. He scanned the letter again, looking for anything familiar, and found the phrase '*Nök Hieronymus*' repeated a couple of times.

Hieronymus. A name that he could make out, yet one hardly in use in the modern world.

There was what also appeared to be a salutation: '*Löfik Mot & Fat.*' Mother and father?

Some of the words seemed to have a Latin base to them; others to be Germanic or even English in origin. He could make nothing of this note other than that it appeared to break off in mid-sentence.

Perhaps it was at this point that Fanny interrupted her room-mate and Mitzi never had the chance to complete the note. He folded it and put it back in the envelope, and then returned the envelope to its original place in the Bible.

'What have you got there?'

It was Siegfried, standing at the door.

'Looks like a Bible.'

'It is,' Werthen said. 'I don't remember calling for you.'

'The Madam says you are to stop and see her before leaving. Something about a retaining fee.' He nodded at the Bible. 'Doesn't surprise me she had one of those hidden some place. She wasn't what she seemed, our little Mitzi.'

'What *was* she like?' Werthen asked, suddenly realizing that he had been antagonizing a possible source of information.

Siegfried's eyes squinted at the question.

'The more I know about her the more it aids the investigation,' Werthen said, trying to reassure the lanky man.

'They're just whores to you.'

'Not if you tell me otherwise.'

The squint slowly relaxed. 'What's in it for you?'

'It's my job. I like to do it well.'

Siegfried drew closer. 'She wasn't a whore. Not up here.' He tapped a dart-like forefinger against his temple.

'Where did she come from?'

'Christ knows. Fanny picked her up off the street. The Madam took a shine to her right away. We all did. She wasn't like the others. She cared about people. Really cared.'

Werthen could see emotion cross the tall man's face like the shadow of a fast-moving cloud in the Alps.

'Were you a personal friend?'

Siegfried crossed his arms over his chest, scowling at the question. 'See what I mean? They're all whores to you.'

'I meant a friend, not a lover.'

A jaw muscle twitched. Siegfried rubbed his nose between thumb and forefinger. 'I guess you could call us that. We talked.'

'About religion?'

'Jesus, Mary and Joseph, no! I gave up fairy tales when I was a kid growing up in Ottakring.'

'About what then?'

He cast his face downward. Snorted through his nose.

'It's in the strictest confidence,' Werthen said.

'Food, that's what we talked about,' Siegfried said, raising his face and looking defiant. 'I always wanted to be a cook, but never had the chance. Too busy surviving day to day. So here I get to finally do it. I make the coffee in the morning, fetch the fresh rolls from the bakery down the street, and do a sit-down lunch for the whole house. And not some bit of boiled sausage and cabbage, neither. Proper food from a cookbook. Mitzi, she appreciated the meals. Told me so, told me they reminded her of her mother's home cooking.'

'Did she talk about her mother, her parents?'

He shook his head. 'No, just that once. Then she shut up about them. I got the feeling she wouldn't want them to know what she was up to here.'

'When you came in, you said it didn't surprise you that Mitzi had a Bible. Why?'

'Well, she just seemed that kind of girl. You know? Proper.'

It seemed to be Siegfried's favorite word; a strange choice for the major-domo of one of Vienna's most famous bordellos.

'Do you have any idea who would want to kill Mitzi?'

Siegfried bit his lower lip, shaking his head. But his eyes squinted in suspicion.

Frau Mutzenbacher received him once again in her sitting room. Now, the curtains were drawn open and dusty daylight poured in. She was still ensconced in her chair. She nodded at a slip of paper on a side table near her. Werthen picked it up; it was a cheque for one thousand kronen drawn on the Austrian Länderbank.

'Sufficient, I assume, to begin?' she said.

He nodded, placing the cheque in the inside pocket of his jacket. It was more than some laborers made in a year. The Bower was obviously doing well for itself.

'Did my brother fill you in on the doings of our little establishment?'

He was confused for a moment. 'You mean Siegfried?'

'Yes. Always was a chatty little monger, Siggy. Could talk the teeth out of a hen. Looks like you found something.'

She nodded at the Bible he was carrying.

'It was hidden under the wardrobe. I checked just now with Fanny and she said it does not belong to her.'

She was silent for a time, then let out a sigh.

'I didn't know Mitzi was religious.'

'Did she speak another language?'

'I don't think so. Why do you ask?'

'No reason,' he said, deciding not to mention the note he discovered in the Bible until he could get it translated.

Only now, with the daylight coming into the room, did Werthen notice some photographs on the side table near her. One, in a silver frame, showed a young girl with eager, innocent features, holding a stuffed bunny. Another, framed in black lacquered wood, appeared to be a photo taken at a graveside with various mourners. The photographer caught Frau Mutzenbacher just releasing a handful of blossoms on to an ornate coffin still suspended over an empty grave.

She saw his glance. 'That was her.' She picked up the silver frame. 'Had an outing at the Wurstelprater, we did. Played all the silly games and even went on the Ferris wheel. She won that bunny at the ring toss. Slept with it every night, just like a child.'

She took a handkerchief out of her sleeve and brushed dust from the glass, replacing the photo on the table.

'And that is from the funeral?' he asked.

She nodded. 'Gave her the best farewell I could. She would have liked that.'

'May I?' he asked. She handed him the funeral photograph. Werthen looked closely at the graveyard scene, at each of the mourners in turn.

'You recognize somebody there?' she asked.

'Perhaps.'

'You're a close one, especially as I'm paying.'

'You will receive regular reports from me,' he said handing her the photograph.

She placed it carefully back in the same position on the side table.

'Mitzi's body was found on May Day,' he said. 'Which means she must have been . . .' He hesitated for a moment, not knowing how strong Frau Mutzenbacher was, despite her crusty façade.

'Murdered,' she said. 'Say it, man. Damn it all, say the word.'

'She must have been murdered the night before. What was she doing out that evening? Was it her day off? Did she have an appointment?'

'That is a mystery to me. The first I knew she was gone was when Siegfried told me she had missed an appointment with a valued customer.'

'Did she have regular days off?'

'I don't run a prison, Advokat. My girls are free to come and go as they like, in *their* time.'

'And April 30 was not Mitzi's day off?'

She shook her head. 'Never missed a shift before that day. Always working, even if she felt sick. Her days off came close together every month. Same as for all my girls.'

It took Werthen a moment to register this. Of course. No work when the girls were menstruating.

'I see,' he said.

'You find him, Advokat. Find the man who killed my Mitzi.'

Her voice broke on the girl's name.

'Now please leave.'

FOUR

Werthen took a list of names away with him, but did not expect much from it. As Frau Mutzenbacher herself had noted, it was highly unlikely Mitzi's customers would use their real names. But a quick perusal of the list once he was outside on the street showed him he was wrong. One of the customers had actually scrawled his real name: Richard Engländer. A joke, perhaps? Few in Vienna knew him by that name.

Werthen had recognized him from the funeral photo and from Fanny's description of the unusual customer who wore sandals and had flowing moustaches.

The impressionist coffee-house poet Engländer had, like Salten, eschewed his Jewish roots and taken a pseudonym, Peter Altenberg. He had also recently become a Catholic, if Werthen remembered rightly. Son of a prosperous Viennese businessman, the young Altenberg managed to avoid the family business when a psychiatrist declared the excitable youth medically unfit for employment.

Altenberg's prose poems and vignettes – he called them extracts from life – caught the flavor of Vienna on the fly: faces at a coffee-house, a bear act at the Ronacher theater, a mouse on the loose in a hotel, and girls. He wrote reams of paeans to the female sex – usually the younger end of the spectrum. These works celebrated pubescent girls not yet affected by male lust; they spoke of shop girls, prostitutes, actresses, maids, nannies, even young frustrated middle-class wives with elderly husbands. A new work of his was out this very year – *What the Day Brings Me,* a collection of fifty-five such impressionistic concoctions.

Werthen was not one of Altenberg's champions, though his friend Karl Kraus was. It was Kraus, in fact, who had first got Altenberg published with the premier German publisher, Fischer Verlag.

Werthen found Altenberg's musings self-indulgent; he agreed with the grammar-school teacher who declared the youthful Altenberg a 'genius without abilities'. Altenberg was a showman, Werthen thought. His strange clothing – sandals and flowing cloaks – and his generally bohemian lifestyle, living out of hotels, spending his days at the Café Central, drinking away the nights in the company of other writers and painters, was no substitute for writerly talent.

As Werthen turned away from the Danube Canal and followed Rotenturmstrasse back to the centre of the First District, he thought of some of the apocryphal tales surrounding Altenberg. One of his favorites – and what was said about Altenberg was always better than what Altenberg said himself – was the story of how he failed his *Matura*. Taking the all-important exam to graduate from the exclusive Akademisches Gymnasium, Altenberg had supplied a one-word response to an essay question on the importance of the New World. 'Potatoes' was Altenberg's laconic reply.

The examiners were not amused.

Soon Werthen passed the Stephansplatz, with the cathedral to his left. He resisted the impulse to dash into the cool darkness for a moment of solitude in the pews. It was a pleasure he had too long neglected, but he knew Altenberg's daily routine and wanted to talk with him before he left for the Café Central – his office and home away from home.

He and Altenberg were neighbors, of a sort. The hotel where the man lodged in Wallnerstrasse was only a couple of streets away from Werthen's office in Habsburgergasse. Werthen stopped off at the office briefly to put away the Bible he had found in Mitzi's room. Walking the streets of the city with it in his hand, he felt like a missionary doing the rounds; and by the quizzical look Fräulein Metzinger gave him as he entered, he obviously looked the part, as well.

'Don't ask,' he said, briskly moving to his office and placing the book on his desk.

'I may be out the rest of the day,' he said as he returned through the outer office to the main door.

'His work is done in mysterious ways,' the assistant said to him deadpan as he departed. Glancing back from the door, he saw the hint of a smile on her face.

The Hotel London was not to be found in Baedeker, for it was more a brothel than a lodging house, the rooms – except for a few such as Altenberg's – being rented by the hour.

Happily, there were no women outside the hotel at this hour. Going through the portal, with yellow paint peeling on the sign, Werthen was assaulted by the cloying fragrance of day lilies, the first of the year. They could be the last, for all Werthen cared; he hated the noxious objects, their six yellow stamens and dusty anthers curled like beckoning fingers.

It was destined to be one of those days, he decided. A day when he was poor company even for himself.

'What brings you to this fine establishment, Advokat Werthen?'

He looked with a mixture of surprise and recognition from the vase of day lilies to the man standing behind the front desk. He saw a thin man, in shirtsleeves, with sunken eyes, gray complexion, and hair plastered to his abnormally large skull like wet paint. The man wore a celluloid collar that was at least one size too large and a chartreuse tie with a pearl stickpin; in his left hand he held the latest racing sheet for the Freudenau track, in his right a pencil.

'Herr Fehrut! You've changed your place of employment.'

The man shrugged as if to say that was self-evident. 'On your advice, Advokat.'

True. Last time Werthen had unsuccessfully defended Herr Fehrut against pandering charges, he advised the man to find a new occupation.

'No more *Zuhälter* for me. I'm on the up and up now, a concierge.' He visibly puffed up as he said this.

Werthen looked around at the shabby foyer – dusty potted palms and aging notices tacked to the walls – and stopped himself from reminding the man this was a *Stundenhotel,* after all, and that he was still in the procuring business one way or the other.

'I see you like my flowers,' Herr Fehrut said, nodding towards the vase. 'Grow them myself. I've got a little plot of land in a garden settlement in Penzing. Spend the occasional day off there. Nothing like a bit of fresh air.'

'Especially after the stale air of the Liesel,' Werthen added.

'They're not getting me back in there, again. No more iron bars for Fehrut. I'm a reformed man.'

'Glad to hear it,' Werthen said without enthusiasm. 'And to return to your question, I wish to speak with one of your guests.'

'Advokat, you surprise me!' He made a tssking sound.

'Not that kind of guest. Altenberg, is he still in?'

'I think maybe you should visit one of the other rooms. That fellow's strange.'

'Is he in?'

'Oh, he's in alright – insane.'

'Room number?'

'Thirteen. And no, we didn't have a room number thirteen before he came here. He paid us to change the number of room twelve.'

Werthen wasn't listening now, though. Instead, he was making his way to the narrow staircase leading to the upper floors. Room thirteen was on the third floor, at the end of a dimly lit hall. A notice was posted on the door: *I am not available to speak with anyone today. No exceptions!*

Werthen rapped his knuckle on the notice.

Nothing for a moment, and then an irritable high-pitched voice from inside:

'Can't you read?'

'Advokat Werthen here. I have come from Frau Mutzenbacher's.'

Now a shuffling of feet. The door was drawn open inwards with force. Altenberg stood in the doorway, a short, stocky, disheveled man whose half-bald pate was camouflaged poorly with wings of hair from the sides brushed forward Roman-style. He was wearing a silk dressing-gown of indeterminate color that had clearly been around since the 1848 Revolution; his tortoiseshell pince-nez dangled from a crimson cord around his neck.

'Do I know you?'

He peered at Werthen as if measuring him for a new suit.

'We met once,' Werthen said. 'Kraus introduced us at the Café Central. But briefly only.'

He grunted at this, smoothing his drooping moustaches with the top edge of his right forefinger. It drew Werthen's attention to the brown nicotine stains on both finger and moustache.

'Frau Mutzenbacher, you say. Do you mean you have come from there?'

Suspicion showed around his rheumy eyes; they were red-rimmed as if he had been crying recently. Now Altenberg's breath reached him, a raw ferrous mixture of tobacco and alcohol.

'Perhaps I might come in,' Werthen said. 'It is about Mitzi.'

The mention of the young woman's name struck Altenberg like a body blow. He grabbed his middle, sucked in air.

'Mitzi.' The name was uttered in a whimper.

Altenberg looked as though he might fall. Werthen took his left arm, holding him up.

'You should sit down.' He shuffled the small man into the

cluttered room, its walls filled with postcards and photos of young women and girls, many of them nude, some of them framed, others merely pinned to the wall. A central table held two large black Japanese lacquer boxes, assorted writing paper, a Mont Blanc pen, a half-empty bottle of gentian schnapps, a packet of Sport cigarettes, and a tumbler overflowing with the crushed ends of partially smoked cigarettes.

Altenberg allowed himself to be steered to one of two straight-backed chairs, and then at the last moment said, 'No. On the bed.'

Werthen helped him to the bed in the corner, its surface covered with newspapers, soiled food wrappers, and a drawing of a woman that Werthen recognized from Frau Mutzenbacher's photo. Mitzi.

Altenberg slumped on to the bed, thrust his head into his hands, and began weeping.

Werthen did not know what to do. He tentatively patted the man on his heaving back, but this did no good. Finally he said, 'You can cry your eyes out or you can try to help me find her killer. The choice is yours.'

This seemed to reach Altenberg, who looked up at Werthen, snot dribbling from his nose. He wiped at it with the sleeve of his dressing-gown.

'How?'

'Tell me about Mitzi.'

'She was a sweet innocent.' Altenberg noticed Werthen's lips pursing. 'No, I mean it. I know innocence when I see it. Mitzi was pure. She and I, you see . . .'

'You were not intimate with her,' Werthen finished for him.

'Is it that evident? No, we were not intimates. I paid her fee, but we talked. We shared a higher form of intercourse.'

Again, Werthen could not help feeling skeptical. He looked around at the photos of naked girls plastering the walls: gamboling Alpine maidens; a saucy young harem miss; a view of the back of young legs, a petticoat showing above, boots below.

'This is my gallery of beauty. They are all my sweet innocents. As fresh as air off the Semmering. Nothing sordid. Nothing tainted.' He got up and crossed to the table. Opening the lacquer boxes there, he showed Werthen the contents: thousands of postcards. Pictures not only of his adored pubescent girls, but also photos of Beethoven, Tolstoy, Hugo Wolf and Klimt; and numerous Japanese woodblock prints. 'I put these in order in my spare time,' he said, flipping through the cards and photos as if they were a deck of Tarock cards.

Werthen ignored this. 'What did you talk about?'

'Her life. Her ambitions. Her disappointments.'

'Can you be more specific? Was there anybody threatening her? Something or somebody she feared?'

Altenberg squinted at him and then put his pince-nez to his eyes, and inspected Werthen for a full minute before answering.

'You ask a very pertinent question, Advokat. Something was obviously bothering Mitzi in the last few months.'

Werthen was reminded of a similar observation by Mitzi's room-mate at the Bower, Fräulein Fanny.

'Did she mention what it was?'

Altenberg shook his head. He motioned Werthen to a chair now, and they both sat. Altenberg picked up the bottle of schnapps, uncorked it, and took a long draught as if drinking from a mountain spring.

The drink revived him. 'No. She wouldn't say. Not that I didn't ask. I am a sensitive man, Advokat. After all, I had known her since she first came to the Bower early last fall. Fresh from the country, she was. You could still smell the hay on her.'

'Do you know where she came from?'

Altenberg stuck out his lower lip. 'She wouldn't say. But I have a feeling her name was not really Mitzi. At first when I would address her by that name, she would appear not to hear me. No, I think our Mitzi had a secret about her past. But I watched her develop over the months. When she was first at the Bower, there was a certain sadness to her. She once told me someone had betrayed her. Nothing more specific. But soon she adapted to the life there. You could see it in her face, she felt at ease, in control. She had a place and she was admired. Even Frau Mutzenbacher was taken by her.'

'She was planning to adopt her. Did you know that?'

Another shake of the head, another swig from the bottle.

'I would have adopted her if they'd let me.'

Werthen interrupted before Altenberg grew maudlin again.

'So, in a way, she blossomed at the Bower, you are saying?'

'Yes, most definitely. A changed young girl. Everyone wanted to be with her. Sometimes I had to wait half the night for my turn. But then two or three months ago a change came over her. She seemed fretful, worried about something, but grew angry if I questioned her. 'Mind your own business, Bunnykins,' she would say. She loved calling me that name. Such a sweet young thing.'

Werthen could see the tears welling again, but Altenberg surprised him, shaking his head as if to fight off the sadness and sitting up straight in his chair.

'I am not always such an old woman, Advokat. I had my period of mourning directly after Mitzi's death. I was perfectly fine this morning, ready to make my way to the Café, and then I came across a drawing I made of my little angel.' He nodded at the drawing Werthen had noticed earlier. 'And then, you see, the tears once again, the schnapps once again. I'm afraid I appear a silly goose to you, but I did love her. In my way. It was real love. Nothing asked in return. The only tragedy in this world is not to love at all, don't you agree?'

'Yes, Herr Altenberg, I agree. And I am sorry if I have appeared less than sympathetic. Accept my apology, please.'

Altenberg extended a slight, puffy hand, and they shook.

'Now, to the business at hand,' Werthen said. 'You mention that Mitzi was popular. Did she have any other regular customers?'

'Oh, yes. Several. She was a popular young woman. Mostly they were the usual sorts after the usual pleasures. But there was one even more persistent than myself. And Mitzi confided in me that this particular customer was less than appealing. It seems he wanted her to play the naughty girl so he could punish her. Well, it takes all kinds, I'm sure.'

'Do you know his name?'

'No. Mitzi was discreet about such things. You think this fellow could be involved in her death?'

'You mentioned punishment. Perhaps he was a violent sort.'

'But it is all theater at the Bower.'

Werthen said nothing.

'I see what you mean. But perhaps play-acting got out of hand? Perhaps he hired her for a private meeting, even though such things were strictly forbidden?'

It sounded to Werthen as if Altenberg had firsthand experience of such attempted assignations.

'But wait. I do have something that might help.'

He went over to the single chest of drawers in the room, rummaged about in the second drawer, and then pulled out a small leather notepad, examined the first page for the date, threw it back in the drawer and found another, read the date, and then leafed through the pages.

'There. That's the fellow.'

He came back to the table and thrust the notebook at Werthen.

Drawn on the graphed paper was the likeness of a middle-aged man with furious Franz Josef side-whiskers and a full head of curly hair.

'I drew this while waiting one night. He was ahead of me, you see. I never did get to see Mitzi that night.'

'It's well drawn.'

'It's actually also a very good likeness of the man.'

'May I take it with me?' Werthen asked.

'If you think it might be of help, of course.'

He ripped it out of the notepad and handed it to Werthen, who in turn placed it for safe keeping in the pages of his own notebook.

'You never mentioned how you discovered Mitzi, Herr Altenberg. Did you simply pick her out of the new arrivals?'

'Not at all,' Altenberg said, and then seemed to grow wary.

'Herr Altenberg?'

'I wouldn't want to bring trouble to a friend.'

'There will be no trouble if your friend has nothing to hide.'

'True. But there is the matter of his new paramour . . . No, you are absolutely right, Advokat Werthen. Suddenly I develop bourgeois values. I was told about Mitzi by my dear friend Arthur Schnitzler.'

'The writer?'

'Yes. I was not aware of another.'

'And he was a client of Mitzi's?'

'That you will have to ask Schnitzler.'

They talked for a few more minutes, but there seemed nothing more that Werthen could discover from Altenberg.

As he prepared to leave, the poet fixed him with a searing gaze: 'I would do anything to help find Mitzi's murderer. But, Advokat, I wonder that you do not suspect me.'

Werthen returned his gaze, pausing a beat. 'Who said I don't?'

Fehrut was still inspecting the racing form as Werthen came down the stairs.

'Glad to see you survived.'

'He's eccentric, not insane.'

'What's the difference?'

'A matter of class, Herr Fehrut. A simple matter of class. The lower classes are insane. The upper are eccentric.'

'So what does that make us?'

'Employed and relatively well adjusted, Herr Fehrut. But next time try growing carnations instead.'

FIVE

Thus, Werthen, in the course of a morning on the job already had a handful of suspects. Fräulein Fanny, despite her protestations, had much to gain by the death of Mitzi. In all probability the lonely Frau Mutzenbacher would turn to her again for comfort and support. And Mutzenbacher's brother, Siegfried, though he attested to pure friendship for the girl, might have done her in during a fit of pique – perhaps she rejected his advances? After all, he only had the man's word for it that he and Mitzi were friends rather than lovers. There was also the mysterious client of Mitzi's who enjoyed doling out punishment. As Altenberg said, perhaps play-acting got out of hand. And finally there was Altenberg himself. Werthen was honestly moved by the man's declaration of love for Mitzi, but who can tell what dark places lie in each of us? Perhaps he grew weary of waiting in line – or perhaps, worse, he grew jealous.

Now, as Werthen searched out a gasthaus where he could take his midday meal, he thought of his next steps. First was the caricature of Mitzi's client sketched by Altenberg. He would take that back to the Bower and see if anyone there recognized it. Perhaps they could even put a name to the face. Then, if that proved unsuccessful, he would take the sketch to Detective Inspector Drechsler of the Vienna constabulary. Perhaps the face would match that of someone on the police registry. Short of inserting a personal ad in the newspaper – not, to Werthen's mind, a wise move as it would possibly alert the man if he were actually the guilty party – this was all he could think of doing with the sketch.

The Bible next. Werthen was unsure about that. He assumed it belonged to Mitzi – as well as the note interleaved in *Joshua: 2*, for the date at the top of the note fitted into the timeline of Mitzi's occupancy. It had the appearance of a letter; but until he could determine what language it was written in, he could not be sure. However, it might very well cast some important light on what had been troubling her recently, a fact that more than one witness thus far had commented on.

As he walked, Werthen remembered a wine house in Fürichgasse that he had not frequented lately. They served a passably spicy *Bohnensuppe* along with a *Kalteteller* of cheese and wurst that would be perfect for today. He was there in less than three minutes, found a single table in the corner under a dusty pair of stag's horns, and settled in for his lunch, which he accompanied with a glass of chilled Welschriesling.

Eating, Werthen decided that the next obvious step was to pay a visit to Arthur Schnitzler, the man who had led Altenberg to Mitzi. How was Schnitzler involved in all this, Werthen wondered, other than in the most obvious ways?

Salten, Altenberg and now Schnitzler. Half the literary establishment of Vienna seemed to be connected to Mitzi. Werthen speculated how many more men of Vienna's literary world would be included in his investigation.

Werthen finished the last of the wine with a chunk of nutty-tasting Emmenthaler and decided now was a good time to talk with the playwright.

Werthen stayed on foot. Though Schnitzler had not practiced medicine in almost a decade – ever since scoring his first dramatic success with *Liebelei,* a play that defined flirtation and was the first in Viennese dialect to be performed at the austere Burgtheater – the writer still lived in the medical quarter of the Ninth District. His flat was on Frankgasse, just behind the Votivkirche.

In a way, Werthen felt an affinity for Schnitzler. There were similarities in their lives. An assimilated Jew, Schnitzler had been forced against his will into a suitable profession. In his case, as the son of a famous laryngologist, he had gone into medicine, becoming an ear, nose and throat specialist, a much-needed profession among the numerous singers in Vienna. In Werthen's case it had been the law, despite an inclination toward writing. But there, it seemed, the similarities ended. Schnitzler had more than a mere inclination to the literary life. He was fast becoming one of Vienna's most respected writers. As mentioned by Salten, the man's early plays featured the playboy Anatol; and Schnitzler had single-handedly created the trope of the *süsses Mädel,* the sweet young thing from the lower classes and the suburbs who has sexual adventures with aristocratic or upper-class men before settling down to a quiet life with an honest husband of her own station. Schnitzler's plays and stories examined sexual love in all its aspects, focusing on the psychology and outcomes of passion.

By all accounts, Schnitzler himself was an Anatol character, finding love where and when he wanted. It was said that he had been initiated into the sexual world by an actress at the age of sixteen; and that he kept a journal tallying the exact number of his orgasms with various mistresses.

This year he had created a sensation with *Lieutenant Gustl*, a short play about a military officer, the lieutenant of the title, who gets into an altercation with a baker following a concert. The baker goes so far as to grab the lieutenant's sword, but Gustl fails to challenge the man to a duel, fearing that he might indeed lose to this burly fellow below him in class. Instead, he hurries from the concert hall, hoping that no one has witnessed his shame. He spends the rest of the night worrying about his lost reputation – only to discover in the morning that the baker has had a stroke and is dead. His guilty secret is safe. Recovering, Lieutenant Gustl resumes his aggressive ways and makes plans for a duel that he is certain to win.

Werthen read this play when it was first published as a serial in the special Christmas editions of the *Neue Freie Press*. It had caused a firestorm of protest from the military-loving conservatives, who pilloried Schnitzler for depicting the army in a bad light. The gutter press had resorted to their tried-and-tested theme: anti-Semitism. A writer for the satirical journal *Kikeriki* asked what more one could expect from such a "Jew writer." In fact, the same writer averred, the cowardly lieutenant of the title was most likely a Jew himself.

For Werthen it was not this implicit indictment of the military that made *Lieutenant Gustl* interesting; instead, it was the manner in which Schnitzler told the tale. 'Interior monologue,' the critics were calling the device. The entirety of the story was told from inside the mind of the lieutenant, a bold new method Werthen thought.

Werthen had now reached Frankgasse 1, where the portal was guarded by three putti-like stone warriors, seemingly Roman legion-naires, on the façade overhead. The street door remained unlocked during daylight hours; he checked the name-plates to see which was Schnitzler's flat before entering. He noticed that Schnitzler had never bothered to change his brass plaque announcing him as an ear, nose and throat doctor.

Several minutes later he found the flat on the second floor and was about to ring the bell when suddenly he was gripped from behind by a pair of thick and exceedingly strong arms. He tried to struggle free, but the man had him in an iron grip.

'*Gott in Himmel*, if it isn't Advokat Werthen!'

Werthen would have recognized that choirboy's voice anywhere. And now, as the owner of the voice appeared, he saw he was right. A week for reunions with the criminal class, it seemed: first Fehrut and now Herr Prokop.

'Let him go, Meier,' said Prokop, in that high sweet voice which ran counter to his pugilist's appearance.

Released, Werthen was able to gather his breath again. 'What are you doing here, Prokop?' He swung around and the hulking Meier smiled down at him sheepishly. Both of them were dressed in their usual work clothes: tattered suits and dented bowler hats. Prokop, Werthen noticed, had not had dental work done since their last meeting – he was still missing a front tooth. And Meier's left little finger had now healed, its stub missing the last joint. Hazards of the trade.

'I suppose I should be asking you the same question, Advokat,' Prokop said. 'Herr Doktor Schnitzler described everyone he knows who might pay him a visit. You were not on the list.'

'You're working for Schnitzler?'

The two of them nodded in unison.

'Whatever for?'

'Half-crown a day each,' the literal Meier answered.

At which Prokop merely shook his head in disgust. 'Ah, then you haven't heard, have you? The Herr Doktor suffered a vicious beating not three days ago. We have been engaged for protection.'

'Klimt recommended you?'

A smile appeared on both their faces.

'Herr Klimt never forgets a favor,' Prokop said.

Indeed, Werthen and the painter Klimt had earlier secured the services of these two toughs when their lives were endangered by an *eminence grise* at the Habsburg court; Werthen had also later employed them to watch over the composer Gustav Mahler when someone was trying to kill him.

'It is good to see you both again,' Werthen said brightly. 'But how is Schnitzler? Can he receive a visitor?'

Meier and Prokop exchanged glances, puffed out their lips and stared at Werthen.

'Perhaps you could ask,' Werthen suggested. 'You might tell him it is important.'

'I suppose I could do that,' Prokop said. 'His fiancée is out. She's been a terror, I can tell you. Won't let a soul in. Terrified, she is, his attacker will come back. His mother has the adjoining apartment. You would think she'd be the one hovering over the wounded son – but no, she's off to a spa somewhere. Something tells me she and Fräulein Olga don't get along very well. She can't be twenty, but she's already got the makings of a real Viennese wife, if you know what I mean.'

Werthen nodded, though he was not sure what Prokop meant, other than that the said fiancée must be a strong-willed woman. Anybody who could get Schnitzler to propose marriage must have special talents.

Werthen waited in silence with Meier on the landing as Prokop went to Schnitzler. Meier was not one much for talking. Prokop made up for that deficiency; they made a good team.

Another minute of silence and then Prokop lumbered back out on to the landing.

'He'll see you. Seemed almost eager, I'd say. Gentleman like Herr Doktor Schnitzler, I don't think he's used to being cooped up.'

Prokop led the way down a long dark hallway to double doors that opened on to a large and bright study, its walls covered in bookcases. A massive potted palm stood in a brass pot near the floor-to-ceiling windows, through which he could just make out the spire of the Votivkirche.

Schnitzler lay on a divan, a white bandage round his head. A boyish lock of hair stuck out of the wrapping, dangling over his forehead. He was a good-looking man, despite a somewhat pained expression on his face. He wore a beard, closely trimmed on the cheeks and longer at the chin. As he looked up, his eyes were inquisitive and sparkling. Dressed in a royal-blue velveteen suit with kid slippers, he held a book in his hands. As he approached the divan, Werthen could see that this was a volume of the works of Lessing.

'Advokat Werthen,' Schnitzler said as he drew near. It appeared he was struggling to get up to welcome his visitor.

'Please Herr Schnitzler, stay recumbent. What a nasty state of affairs.'

Schnitzler leaned back against a mound of white pillows, giving up all thoughts of *politesse*.

'Isn't it just?' He motioned to a chair near the divan. 'Please, bring it over here next to me and sit.'

Werthen did so, and sat close to the divan. 'Who did this? Have the police caught the blackguard?'

'Well, I assume that is why you are here.'

'I'm sorry, I don't quite understand.'

'I assume Klimt sent you. He talks much about your deductive powers.'

'No. Sorry for the misunderstanding. I have come about a completely different matter. I had not heard of your unfortunate circumstances.'

Schnitzler closed the volume of plays, setting it on his lap. 'And what matter would that be?'

'I have just come from Altenberg. He tells me that you introduced him to a young woman . . . Mitzi is, or was, her name. From the Bower.'

Schnitzler's eyes suddenly grew larger. He looked around the room as if fearful someone might overhear.

'That part of my life is past,' he said in almost a whisper.

'I understand that you are recently engaged,' Werthen said. 'I do not wish to create any difficulties—'

'Hardly engaged,' Schnitzler interrupted. 'Fräulein Gussman and I have a certain understanding. Still, it would be better if she did not learn of my visits to the Bower.'

'I understand,' Werthen said. 'You know, of course, of Mitzi's death?'

Schnitzler nodded rather vigorously; the motion seemed to cause him pain. He put a hand to his bandaged head.

'I sent flowers to the funeral. Anonymously. Such a sweet young girl, she was. A pity. But then, it does come with the profession, doesn't it?'

'How do you mean?'

'Well, servicing all sorts of men. One can never be sure of the type of client, can one? It appears she broke the golden rule and met one of her clients after hours.'

'That is one possibility.'

'Might I inquire as to your interest in the matter?' Schnitzler said.

'Frau Mutzenbacher has employed me to find the murderer. She was very attached to Mitzi.'

'I see. And you suspect me?' He said it with arch humor.

'Hardly. But I was hoping you could tell me something about the young girl. I visited Herr Altenberg earlier today and he indicated that you had introduced him to Mitzi. I thought perhaps you might have known her and could somehow help in the investigations.'

'Sorry to disappoint you, Advokat. But ours was strictly a working relationship. I discovered her at the Bower before she was too much tainted. I grew bored with her services after a couple of months and passed her on to Altenberg. He has, as I imagine you discovered, a penchant for the young ones. Though Mitzi was not the schoolgirl she pretended to be.'

'Did she mention other clients? Anyone she was frightened of?'

'We didn't speak a great deal, Advokat, as I am sure you understand.'

Werthen did not appreciate the man's tone, but then it was not the most comfortable thing to be interviewed about one's sex life. He himself might be equally defensive if questioned like this.

'Sorry to be of so little assistance, Advokat. She was a good girl. I too would love to see the murderer brought to justice. At the moment, however, I have my own concerns.'

'You thought initially that Klimt had sent me. Why should he have? And why are you employing bodyguards?' Werthen asked. 'Surely the police should be able to provide protection if necessary?'

Schnitzler sighed. 'I see now why Klimt speaks so highly of you, for you have hit exactly on it. The police are not involved.'

'Why is that so?'

'You have heard of my recent play?'

'*Lieutenant Gustl*?'

Schnitzler nodded, more slowly this time.

'What does that have to do with the attack on you?'

'Everything, I believe. It has angered a great many people, some of them very powerful. That play cost me my Senior Physician status in the army reserve. I believe it also brought on this beating. The man who attacked me did so just outside the door of my flat in the middle of the day. He made no attempt to steal anything, made no demands. He merely struck me to the floor with a powerful blow to the head and then kicked me until I was almost unconscious. Thank God he was scared off by the arrival of Fräulein Gussman, who raised an alarm, screaming her head off. In addition to a slight concussion, I suffered two broken ribs and severe contusions. The man who did this to me is a professional. They were sending a message.'

'They?'

Schnitzler shrugged. 'I am not a paranoid sort of individual, but I do know how the military works. It defends its honor.'

'You think it was a lone wolf or someone recruited for the job?'

'That is what I would dearly love to discover, Advokat. But, why not take on the job yourself? Find the man before he returns to finish the job.'

Schnitzler put out his hand, touching Werthen's arm.

'Please, I implore you.'

'I would gladly, Herr Schnitzler, but as I told you I already have a commission.'

'Understood. But I am sure a man with your abilities could find a bit of time to spare for my case as well. I and Fräulein Gussman can both provide you with a description of the man. The *Portier* also saw him flee. A rather nondescript man of medium height. Compact and efficient in his movements.'

'You really should go to the police.'

'I can't, Advokat. If my instincts are correct, they will be of little help.'

Schnitzler fixed him with eyes at once piercing and soulful. 'Please.'

Werthen paused a moment. 'Alright, then. But I cannot promise full-time commitment. I suggest you continue to retain the services of Herr Prokop and Meier. Now tell me about this assailant.'

SIX

They sat amidst the ruins of Frau Blatschky's dinner. They had done justice to her *Beinfleish,* roasted beef shank with potatoes done to a golden brown. This was accompanied by a chilled white wine from Gumpoldskirchen and followed by *Germknödel* for dessert, a light yeast dumpling filled with plum jam and covered in vanilla sauce with a sprinkling of poppy seed. They were still lingering at table with their coffee. Frieda was sleeping peacefully in the nursery; Berthe had just returned from checking on her.

Their unexpected guest, Doktor Hanns Gross, suddenly blurted out, 'If I were not already married to Adele, I would ask Frau Blatschky to marry me.'

This was said just as the lady in question – Werthen's cook and housekeeper, Frau Blatschky – entered the room to begin clearing the dishes. Her face turned a brilliant red, contrasting with the starched white apron she wore.

'Doktor Gross,' she said. 'You are a wicked man.' But it was clear she loved the attention. In fact, since Berthe had taken to experimenting with more international fare, Frau Blatschky had sallied even deeper than before into traditional Viennese cuisine.

'Wicked I may be,' the criminologist said, 'but I feel perfectly angelic when eating your meals, Frau Blatschky.'

At which the housekeeper raised her eyebrows and continued with her clearing.

When she was out of the room, Werthen turned to his former colleague.

'Well, Gross, I must say you do make a habit of turning up at the most propitious moments.'

Gross, the famous criminologist, had been Werthen's mentor at one time and had been responsible for bringing him back into the realm of criminal law and establishing himself in private inquiries, in addition to the more prosaic field of wills and trusts. They had collaborated on three previous cases; it was as if Gross had antennae that alerted him to the fact that Werthen had a new case.

The head of the first department of criminology in Austro-Hungary, for the past two years Gross had been posted to the Franz Josef University in Czernowitz, the capital of Bukovina. Gross was, of course, elated to develop his department of criminology, but neither he nor his wife was fond of Czernowitz. Gross had more than once termed the city a dusty, dirty claptrap of dodgy buildings, many of them gussied up to look like the Austrian homeland, but largely a Potemkin village. He had also dubbed that metropolis of a hundred thousand souls an overgrown *shtetl*.

Gross was no anti-Semite, but he did not shy away from using any language he cared to, despite the fact that both Werthen and Berthe were of Jewish background. They were too accustomed to such comments to even attempt a response. And at any rate, Gross meant no harm by such comments; for him, they were merely statements of fact.

Now, with the spring term finished and his wife off to visit friends in their former home town of Graz, Gross had come to Vienna en route to the University of Prague, where he was to interview for a new lectureship. He was full of excitement at the prospect of living once again in a 'civilized' environment.

'It does appear you have your hands full, dear friend,' Gross said as he filled his coffee cup again.

'How was I to turn Schnitzler down? He seemed quite desperate.'

'Well,' Gross said. 'I do have some few days before I am due in Prague. If I could be of assistance . . .'

Usually Gross's intrusion in his cases irritated Werthen. The renowned criminalist had a way of taking charge of things. But in this instance his assistance would be greatly appreciated and Werthen was quick to tell him so.

'Perhaps it is doubly fortuitous your being here, Herr Gross,' Berthe added. Sitting next to her husband, she put her hand over Werthen's. 'I didn't tell you earlier as you were so involved with relating the day's events, but I had a telephone message earlier today—'

It was as if Werthen could read her mind. 'Not another case!'

She nodded. 'I believe so.'

'You're making quite a name for yourself, Werthen,' Gross said. 'Soon you'll have to be taking on help. Perhaps I should put my application in now.'

Which comment Werthen chose to ignore.

'You *believe* so?' he said to his wife.

'Well,' Berthe said. 'I highly doubt that Bertha von Suttner wants to see you about her will.'

'Von Suttner!' Werthen said with amazement.

'That peace woman!' Gross muttered it like a dubious epithet.

'Yes, Herr Gross,' Berthe said in her best schoolteacher voice. 'That woman who very sensibly advocates diplomacy over fighting.'

'The woman's an adventurer,' Gross thundered. 'Look how she wrapped poor Alfred Nobel round her finger, getting him to endow that idiotic prize.'

Berthe merely shook her head at this, squeezing Werthen's hand. The first Nobel Prizes – in physics, chemistry, physiology or medicine, literature and peace – were to be awarded this upcoming December 10, the fifth anniversary of Nobel's death.

'A sad day for his family, that is all I can say. Left in poverty.'

Again, Gross's impolitic remarks were met by silence from Werthen and Berthe. Nobel, the Swedish-born inventor of dynamite, had hired the young and impoverished Countess Kinsky, as Frau von Suttner was then, as a private secretary. Although she worked for him for only a matter of days, the two had remained in contact over the years. It was she, more than any other person, who convinced Nobel to do something grand with his wealth. Dubbed 'the Merchant of Death' by the tabloids, Nobel lived with great guilt, knowing that his invention had been turned to such destructive purposes.

'They should damn well have sued,' Gross rambled on, unaware or uncaring that his words caused offense.

'They did,' Werthen said, for he had studied the situation when Nobel died in 1896. He had left almost the entirety of his vast estate to establish the prizes in his name. The relatives were of course shocked and dismayed. 'They've been in and out of the courts for the last five years battling the will and making no one rich but estate lawyers such as myself.'

'I think it was a wonderful thing for him to do,' Berthe added.

'I'd like to see how wonderful you think it would be had he been *your* relation.'

'You are in a foul mood tonight, Gross,' Werthen finally said. 'Even more reactionary than usual.'

Gross touched his moustache, a nervous tick that meant he had something on his mind.

'It's my son, again. Always that son of mine. We've had to put him in the Burghölzli Clinic near Zürich. Drugs, drugs, damned drugs!' He slammed his fist on the table.

'Gross, we're so sorry to hear it.' Werthen meant it sincerely.

'It was all the fault of that voyage to South America as a naval doctor. We were so excited for him, but he has never been right since returning. It's the cocaine – the coca plant thrives in South America. He is so brilliant, you see. A psychiatrist and assistant doctor, but this cocaine has a grip on him. Blames me, of course.'

'I'm sure he doesn't,' Werthen said, but did not believe his own words. He had been intimate with the Gross household during his years in Graz. He knew the bitter feud between father and son. He had thought, however, it was past. Otto Gross, brilliant and erratic, had finally studied medicine; his first monograph on psychology had been published earlier that year.

'Says I ruined his life. Calls me an anachronism. An unwanted patriarch.'

As he said these words, he visibly winced.

'Sorry,' Gross said after a pause.

'Don't be,' Werthen said. 'We are your friends. You don't have to be merely polite around us.'

'He doesn't?' Berthe asked with a smile.

Her comment broke the oppressive air in the room, bringing laughter from Gross.

In the event, they decided that Berthe would meet with Frau von Suttner, her long-time idol. She had read the woman's famous work of fiction, *Lay Down Your Arms,* more times than Werthen liked to count. At the same time, Gross would take the sketch of the mystery client at the Bower to Detective Inspector Drechsler at the Police Praesidium and would also begin seeking information on the Schnitzler beating.

When Werthen handed him the drawing Altenberg had made, for a moment Gross thought he recognized the likeness, though he could not put a name to it. Not so those at the Bower earlier in the day: when Werthen showed them the drawing they were unanimous – they had never seen the person before. No hesitation. Not a second glance from any of them. A bit too sure, Werthen thought.

'And now, Werthen, why not show us this mysterious note you've sequestered?'

'Hardly sequestered, Gross. I merely returned it to the location in the Bible in which I originally found it.'

'Well don't be coy, man. Let's take a look at it. Wouldn't you agree, Frau Berthe?'

'I'm always eager to agree with you, Doktor Gross.'

'What a wife. Could you please give my Adele a lesson in empathy?'

Meanwhile, Werthen left the table and went down the hallway to his study to fetch the Bible. On the way, he peeked his head into Frieda's room: she was sleeping peacefully, a stuffed bear from Steiff that Frau Blatschky had given her last week tucked in her arms. His housekeeper had been excited about the purchase, for it was the newest design from the company, and now Frieda would not be parted from it day or night.

Back in the dining room, Gross and Berthe were deep in conversation about Herr Meisner, her father, who would soon be moving into his small flat in Vienna.

Werthen opened the Bible and retrieved the note, taking it from its envelope and unfolding it for the others to see. Gross, however, seemed more interested in the Bible at first. Berthe picked up the note, turning it front and back and looking at the light through it.

'No watermark,' she said.

Werthen smiled at this. She had been reading Gross's landmark criminalistics handbook, *Criminal Investigation,* again.

'Yes,' he said. 'I noticed that, too.'

'It does look like a letter,' she said.

'May I?' Gross said, tiring of his inspection of the Bible.

He also looked closely at the paper before examining the writing.

'I see what you mean,' Gross said after an interval. 'I can't place the language, though it has aspects of Latin, German and the Romance languages, and, I suspect, a goodly dose of English.'

'Could it be one of those new universal languages they're talking about?' Berthe said.

'My thoughts exactly,' Gross added.

'I thought perhaps Afrikaans,' Werthen said. 'But then there is too much of a Latin influence. You may well be right, Berthe.'

'Esperanto, perhaps?' Gross said. 'But really, what young girl working in a bordello is going to write a letter in Esperanto?'

'That, Gross, is what I hope to ascertain once we translate this message.'

Gross nodded, putting the note down on the table and once again picking up the Bible.

'Why so interested in the Bible, Gross?'

'It would seem that we are investigating the death of an uncommon young woman. Someone who writes in a created language and someone with, I believe, a sense of literary allusion.'

'How so, Doktor Gross?' Berthe asked, with real interest.

'Her choice of hiding place – *Joshua: 2*. I do not believe it is accidental. If you look here,' Gross said, lifting the Bible, closing it, opening it again at random, and showing its bottom edge to Werthen and Berthe. 'This is a relatively unused Bible. The book itself is not new, but its owner has not spent a great deal of time or study with it. That is not to say that your Fräulein Mitzi was not religious. Indeed, I think she was. Otherwise how would she have known which passage to choose? So she must have purchased this Bible during her residency at the Bower. Now, do you see how the pages, fanned out as they are, show a slight bulging at one particular spot?'

Werthen did see what Gross meant.

Turning to that bulge, Gross again came to the hiding place, *Joshua: 2* in the Old Testament

'Almost as if it were bookmarked,' said Berthe.

'Precisely.'

'I'm sorry to admit my ignorance, Gross,' Werthen said. 'But what exactly does *Joshua: 2* talk about?'

But Berthe answered instead. 'It deals with the spies that the children of Israel sent into the land of Jericho, and how they were saved by the harlot Rahab in the harlot's house.'

Gross nodded in agreement. They sat in silence for a time.

'Coincidence?' said Berthe. 'Mitzi the prostitute and Rahab the harlot?'

'Maybe,' Werthen suggested, 'that's something else we'll find out once the note is translated.'

SEVEN

F rau von Suttner arrived punctually at eleven the next morning and was now seated in the sitting room overlooking Josefstädterstrasse. The former Countess Kinsky carried herself with a regal attitude. She was dressed in a somewhat outmoded black silk gown, and she seemed as nervous as Berthe felt.

Frieda, wearing a pinafore, was standing next to her seated mother, gripping the precious stuffed bear in one arm and putting her head in Berthe's lap and then lifting it again, playing peekaboo, auburn curls bouncing as she did so.

Meanwhile, Frau Blatschky bustled about the room getting the tea things in order. Berthe picked Frieda up, placed the girl on her lap, and then smiled at Frau von Suttner as the housekeeper fussed.

Berthe was familiar with the woman's history. Born into an impoverished military family, the Countess took a job as governess in the von Suttner household. It was there she and the youngest son of that family, Baron Arthur Gundaccar von Suttner, fell in love. Ten years his senior and without a dowry, the Countess Kinsky, despite her title, did not seem an appropriate catch for a scion of the von Suttner family. She left the household and went to Paris, where she served as Nobel's secretary for a short time. But the young Baron von Suttner would not be thwarted; he and the Countess eloped to the Caucasus, where they made a precarious living for a decade as writers and language teachers. It was during this time that both of them began to focus on the cause of peace.

Eventually, in 1885, the von Suttner family relented in their opposition and the couple returned to Austria, taking up residence in the Suttner family's summer home, Harmannsdorf Castle in the Waldviertel. It was there she penned her famous books on pacifism. Berthe admired the woman for her work as much as for her fairy-tale life.

Frau Blatschky finally finished her ministrations and nodded at Berthe.

'Go to Frau Blatschky,' she told Frieda.

The little girl crawled off her lap. 'Baba,' she said.

'Yes, come to your Baba,' Frau Blatschky said.

Left in peace, the two women began speaking at the same time, filling the sudden vacuum.

'Sorry,' said Berthe, motioning for the older woman to begin.

'I just wanted to thank you for receiving me at such short notice. Frau Mayreder speaks very highly of you and your husband.'

Rosa Mayreder – the author, painter, musician and feminist – was a Renaissance woman who was connected to many of the new movements in art and thought in Vienna. Berthe counted her among her friends, having met her through her work helping the less fortunate children of the working class gain an education.

'How is Rosa?' Berthe asked, for it had been months since she last saw her. Indeed, since becoming a mother, her time was no longer her own.

'Well,' Frau von Suttner said. 'Very well and hard at work on a new book.'

'As you are yourself, I assume?' Berthe asked.

Frau von Suttner sighed. 'Oh, yes. Always scribbling away. I've got to keep a roof over our heads. The problem is it's a vast castle roof, always in need of repair.'

She laughed slightly at her own little joke, but Berthe had the feeling there was no mirth in it.

'It must be wonderful living in the country, as you do, and devoting yourself to writing and just causes.'

'Wouldn't it be, though?'

'How do you mean?' Berthe asked.

'May I have some tea?'

'Oh, please excuse my manners. Of course.' She made to serve the tea.

'I can serve myself, that's fine.' And she did, pouring a cup for Berthe, as well.

'Rosa tells me you are a sensible young woman. And a person to be trusted. I feel I must disabuse you of some notions you have of my life. Harmannsdorf Castle still belongs to my husband Arthur's family, many of whom are continually in residence. The estate farm and its quarry have shown no profit in more years than I care to talk about. The von Suttners have been on the verge of bankruptcy

for years, and it is only my literary efforts and Arthur's that have
kept the place solvent. Novels and serial stories have become my
ball and chain, stealing valuable time from important work in the
peace movement. To be honest, there are times when I cannot even
afford to travel from the Waldviertel to Vienna.'

She set her cup down.

'I hope I'm not shocking you.'

'Not at all,' Berthe said.

'Because what I have come about is family business.'

Frau von Suttner paused as if offering Berthe a way out.

'I work with my husband on private inquiries. Whatever you have
to tell me will be in the strictest confidence.'

The other woman nodded.

'I mentioned that there are many von Suttners in residence at the
castle. One of them is my husband's niece, Marie Louise. She came
to us as an orphan at fourteen. Such a lovely young girl and so
devoted to Arthur.'

Another pause.

'I am sure you see where this is going,' Frau von Suttner said.
'So tawdry. Human, all too human. Marie Louise is no longer a
sweet young girl. She is now a quite handsome young woman. And
one of means, I might add, for she attained a contested inheritance
two years ago. She continues to live with us, and continues to be
the devoted companion of her Uncle Arthur. She even paid for him
to visit a spa last year. I could not visit him more than once a week.
The cost of the rail ticket, you see. But Marie Louise took rooms
nearby to keep him company.'

She stopped speaking, shaking her head. 'This is so embarrassing
and I feel such a fool. I have devoted my life to the cause of peace
and cannot even assure peace within my own family. You see, Arthur
is younger than I am. A good deal younger. And Marie Louise is
so vibrant, so full of life.'

'What is it you would like my husband and me to do, Frau von
Suttner?'

'Arthur has taken to educating Marie Louise in the world of art.
To that end they have been coming to Vienna quite regularly. Oh,
she pays for the trips. Quite the *grande dame*. And when they come
back there is a charged atmosphere in the castle. Something
unspoken, but manifest nonetheless.'

Berthe was trying to make it as easy as possible for Frau von
Suttner.

'And you would like us to follow your husband and niece when they come to Vienna? To ascertain . . .' Berthe paused, not knowing how blunt she should be. 'To discover where they go and what they do when in town.'

'Precisely. I need to know. It is destroying me. Jealousy is a terrible thing.'

'You're looking well, Gross,' Detective Inspector Drechsler said. They were sitting in his office in the Vienna Police Praesidium.

The pictures of Drechsler's family, Gross noted, had changed since he was last here. Growing up all too fast.

'Feeling fit,' Gross responded. 'And I assume the same of you and your good wife?'

Drechsler brightened at this comment. 'Yes, she is doing marvelously. Had you heard?'

Gross simply nodded at the photograph of her on the desk as a reply. Frau Drechsler was looking portly and radiant.

'Ah, yes. Always the detective at work.'

The previous year Drechsler's wife had badly needed an operation, which she refused to have. Gross and Werthen, while engaged in their last investigation, had been able to put her in the hands of one of Vienna's top surgeons. With positive results.

They chatted for a time about Gross's visit to Vienna and his coming interview for a new post in Prague. But finally Drechsler had had enough of small talk.

'It's clear from your good humour that you're on a case, Gross. Are you working with Advokat Werthen again?'

Gross beamed at him. 'You see, never too late for a dog to learn new deductive tricks, Inspector. I am not my usual bearish self; ergo I must be investigating something. Yes, the matter of the death of a prostitute in the Prater. And my good friend Werthen seems to be gaining a reputation as a private inquiries agent. I am also assisting him on a case of bodily assault.'

'Sounds like police business to me,' Drechsler said.

'Well, in the case of the prostitute, our client appears to believe the police have better things to do than search for the murderer of a lowly prostitute. And in the matter of the assault, our client . . . Well, shall we say our client is hesitant to come forward for personal reasons.'

Drechsler wrinkled his nose at this. 'Don't sound very promising, either of them. Though I believe I know of the one case. A girl from the Bower, Frau Mutzenbacher's establishment?'

'That's the one.'

'A very popular place the Bower is. Exclusive clientele.'

'And that exclusive clientele wish to keep their identities secret, one assumes.'

'Besides, the girl wasn't killed on the premises. It was in the Prater. There may very well be no connection to the Bower at all.'

'Surely you don't believe that, Inspector?' Gross said.

Drechsler shrugged. 'Maybe, maybe not. But our friend Meindl indicated the investigation should be given low priority.'

Though elfish in size, Drechsler's superior, Inspector Meindl, was a force to be reckoned with. He had once worked with Gross in Graz, before he moved to the Police Praesidium in Vienna. Punctilious in his efforts to secure his rise in the police force, Meindl had made a specialty of protecting people in high places.

'The case is still open,' Drechsler added.

'I am sure it is, and that is why, in part, I have come to see you.' He drew the sketch out of his inside jacket pocket and placed it on the desk.

'We have come into possession of this likeness. A witness tells us this man was a frequent client of the unfortunate young woman.'

Drechsler picked it up, squinted at it closely, and then placed it back on the desktop.

'That's not going to do you much good.'

'Why would that be, Inspector? It seems a rather good likeness.'

'Oh, it's a good likeness alright. Problem is the man's dead. Food poisoning incident. It made quite a stir a few weeks ago. Ate some bad shellfish, it seems. We investigated, had to. An important man. Count Joachim von Ebersdorf, from the Foreign Office. But there was nothing to it. Just as suspected, some bad oysters.'

Gross nodded. That was why the sketch looked familiar. He had once met the Count. At the opening of Gross's new institute at Czernowitz, von Ebersdorf had been an emissary of the government.

'When exactly did this occur?' Gross asked.

Drechsler exhaled, focusing on the ceiling as if the answer might lie there. 'Must have been the first week of May. Perhaps the fourth or fifth. I would have to check.' He paused, fixing Gross in his gaze. 'You're not going to try to tie these two deaths together, are you? Just because the prostitute was found on May Day and von Ebersdorf died a few days later?'

'He was, after all, her continual client.'

'Says who? This "witness" who made the sketch? And who would he be, another of the girl's clients?'

Drechsler seemed to be gaining interest in the case now, but then a sudden change came over his face.

'As I say, we are still looking into the matter. If you have evidence, you should share it with us.'

And with Inspector Meindl, Gross thought.

As Gross was about to leave, a few minutes later, Drechsler tapped a finger on his desk. 'And this other case, Gross. Since when have you been working on a mere assault? Somebody important, I assume?'

'Yes, he is,' Gross said. 'If you must know, it's Schnitzler. The playwright. A fellow beat him senseless. Schnitzler thinks it is on account of his new play.'

'Well, I heard it was bad, but that's taking criticism to the extreme!'

Gross smiled at this weak attempt at humor.

EIGHT

They conferred again over dinner. Gross was dining with Berthe and Werthen again, though he was staying at the nearby Hotel zur Josefstadt in the Langegasse, where Werthen's parents stayed when visiting. But now, with the construction of an estate in the Vienna Woods, they would soon be part-time residents of Vienna. Werthen had tried not to think of that little complication. It only served to bring on feelings of guilt and extreme frustration. Guilt that he should feel so churlishly toward his parents; frustration that they could not let him have his own bit of turf. Werthen would much rather focus on the investigations under way.

'So, Frau Berthe,' said Gross, laying his fork down after finishing his second serving of Frau Blatschky's *Backhendl,* golden and crispy fried chicken, which she always paired with parsley potatoes. 'What of your countess?'

'I'm afraid it's the sort of thing you do not much care for, Karl,' she said to her husband, ignoring Gross and his ironic tone.

'I sense a straying husband,' Gross said playfully.

'That seems to be the case. It was most difficult for her to talk of it. She is a proud woman.'

'I hope you politely told her we do not do domestic cases,' Werthen said.

Berthe remained silent.

'Berthe?' he said. 'You did tell her we couldn't take her commission?'

'Well . . .'

'Ah, you may soon want to add another line to your professional card, Werthen – divorce lawyer.'

'Please, Gross. You are being rather too full of yourself tonight.'

'With good reason,' Gross said. 'I have discovered the identity of the mystery man in the sketch.'

Berthe and Werthen both said at once, 'You have?'

'Not a matter of great detection,' he said. 'Inspector Drechsler recognized him immediately. In fact I actually met the man myself once – which is why I thought he looked familiar.'

'Well, don't keep us in suspense,' Berthe said.

'Count Joachim von Ebersdorf. Seems he died just a few days after our Fräulein Mitzi. Bad oysters.'

'Yes,' Werthen said. 'I remember reading about it in the papers. 'So he was the customer. Wasn't he something in the government?'

'Foreign Office,' Gross said. 'But the details of his employment there seem to be rather sketchy.'

'*That* kind of sketchy, you mean?' Werthen said.

'It appears so.'

'Wait. You two are talking in riddles,' Berthe said. 'What do you mean by sketchy?'

'As in indefinite, unclear, unspecified.'

'I know what the word means, Gross.'

'Espionage,' Werthen said. 'If one's title at the Foreign Office is not entirely clear, then it's safe to assume one is involved in espionage. After all, the Foreign Office is our major information-gathering agency.'

'I thought that the General Staff had such a role,' Berthe said.

'In fact they do,' Werthen told her, 'but it is something of a newcomer. One hears of competition between the two. Frankly, I find the concept of military intelligence to have internal semantic contradictions.'

Gross remained silent through this, smiling to himself like a satisfied cat.

'You think there is a connection between von Ebersdorf's death and Mitzi's?' Werthen finally said to him.

Gross folded his hands over his paunch. 'Possibly. I have never been one to subscribe to the powers of mere serendipity.'

'First the biblical reference to spies,' said Werthen. 'In *Joshua: 2*. And now Mitzi's foremost customer turns out to be involved in espionage. Do you actually think Fräulein Mitzi—'

'We should not speculate at this point,' Gross said. 'It is, however, a possible avenue of investigation.'

'And what does Drechsler think now that he's seen the sketch?'

Gross imparted to them what the Inspector had told him that afternoon.

'Meindl again,' Werthen sighed. 'The man is insuperable.'

'But it does make how we should proceed with our investigation clear,' Gross said.

The three of them sat in silence for a moment, considering this information.

Gross suddenly said, 'But do excuse me, Frau Berthe. I interrupted you.'

Werthen also refocused. 'Yes, Berthe. I really hope you did not accept Frau von Suttner's case.'

'I did accept. And you will not have to be involved. It is all settled. Frau von Suttner merely wishes to see where her husband goes and what he gets up to when he comes to Vienna with his niece.'

'She suspects his niece?' Werthen said.

'I thought you were not interested in domestic cases? But yes, she does. So I and Fräulein Metzinger will take turns following the pair when they come to Vienna.'

'But Fräulein Metzinger is needed in the law office,' Werthen said to his wife. 'And you have a child to care for.'

'Don't worry, Karl. I talked with Erika – Fräulein Metzinger – on the phone this afternoon and she thought it was a wonderful idea. You know how efficient she is; and it is only once or twice a week, I assure you. It is something I very much want to do.'

He could see it in her face: she was committed to this.

'Of course, then, if you feel that way. But I do not want you putting yourself in harm's way.'

'Karl, it is a domestic case. Frau von Suttner's husband is a baron. I think the danger factor is rather low.'

Such a comment was like wishing for bad luck, but none of them said anything.

'Besides, we can hardly turn her down now,' Berthe added. 'Frau von Suttner has helped solve the mystery of our missing language.'

'You don't say!' said Werthen, who – having copied the note out longhand for fear of losing the original – had spent the better part of the day at the Hofbibliothek fruitlessly looking for linguistic sources to match the original. Esperanto had been a complete washout, as had Solresol, an artificial language developed about seventy years earlier.

'Yes. You know Frau von Suttner travels in international circles, promoting peace and a sense of a shared destiny on this planet.'

'Watch out, Werthen,' Gross intoned. 'I fear you may have a convert on your hands.'

It was Berthe's turn to smile knowingly now. 'If I may continue,' she said. 'Such international languages are integral to world peace. No more need for the tower of Babel to separate humankind.'

'Perhaps we can dispense with the propaganda,' Gross said.

'The long and short of it is that I mentioned the note to Frau von Suttner and she examined it briefly.' She paused dramatically just to annoy Gross.

'And?' Werthen said.

'Volapük,' Berthe replied.

'I beg your pardon?' Gross said.

Werthen thought the word sounded familiar.

'Volapük. It is a language developed by a Catholic priest in Germany.'

'Schleyer,' Gross said, snapping his fingers. 'Yes, that makes sense.'

'Johann Martin Schleyer, to be exact,' Berthe said.

'The man thought that God spoke to him in a dream and gave him the idea of the language.' Gross looked well pleased with himself.

'It was the first widely accepted universal language, according to Frau von Suttner. Its name actually means "world speak", or "world language". Frau von Suttner studied the language for several years, and went to the 1889 Volapük convention in Paris. The entire proceedings were conducted in that language. But the movement fell apart thereafter.'

'Too damned complicated,' Gross announced. 'Thousands of declensions and inflections and verb forms, which make Latin seem like child's play.'

'Yes,' Berthe said, 'but the basic vocabulary is quite simple, as Frau von Suttner demonstrated. I think she was happy to concentrate on something other than her domestic problem.'

She produced the note from Mitzi's Bible. 'If, as we assumed last night, this is a letter, then the first line, *Löfik Mot & Fat*, should be a salutation.'

The others agreed and Berthe, referring to another sheet she was not as yet sharing with them, said, 'It translates as "Dear Mother and Father".'

'Excellent,' Gross said. 'Is that the complete translation?' He nodded at the other sheet.

Berthe ignored this and went on for a time, taking them through the steps Baroness von Suttner had followed in making her translation. The phrase *Nök Hieronymus*, which appeared twice in the letter, became Uncle Hieronymus. And then, Berthe explained, they were also able to trace place names. First came the name of a village, *Bukbel*.

'As Frau von Suttner explained, Volapük is an agglutinative language, building new words by joining smaller ones together. Thus, "*buk*" is "book" and "*bel*" is "mountain". So *Bukbel* translates as Buchberg.'

'But there are hundreds of villages in the empire named Buchberg,' Werthen said.

'Yes,' Berthe said. 'But the very next line reduces the possibilities.' She pointed at the word *Vinfoldil*.

'That translates as the Weinviertel,' she said with a smile.

'Buchberg in the Weinviertel. Sounds a lovely place for a visit, Werthen,' Gross said. 'Sample the lovely white wines of the region.'

'Let's see the complete translation,' said Werthen, finally losing patience with the game.

Berthe placed it on the table in front of them and they read it together:

Dear Mother and Father,

   It has been too long since I last wrote, but I am very busy in Vienna, as you can imagine. Uncle Hieronymus has a busy household and I must attend to many duties. If I wrote my daily schedule for you, Father, you would laugh and no longer call me the seagull, the bird who just comes for the food and then leaves. Uncle Hieronymus says that young people should have a busy life to keep them out of trouble.

   I hope to make it home to Buchberg for a visit soon. The Weinviertel must be lovely at this time of year. But as I say, things are very hectic for me here . . .

And that was where the letter broke off.

'No family name,' Berthe said, disappointed.

'But how large could the village be? And how many of its families have a daughter in service in Vienna?'

'You're right, Werthen. A brief chat with the local postmaster or the *wirt* at the village gasthaus should do the trick. Everyone knows everyone else's business in such a place, I am sure.'

Berthe looked at the letter again. 'Makes you wonder, though, doesn't it.'

'About Uncle Hieronymus?' Werthen said.

'Mitzi had obviously left the man's home months before she wrote this letter, but she could brazen out the lie to her parents of still living there instead of at a bordello.'

'Which means Uncle Hieronymus did not alert the parents of her departure,' Gross said. 'One assumes that he actually was an uncle, and it was not simply a term of affection. If so, why would he not write to the parents and tell them?'

'I intend to find that out tomorrow,' Werthen said. 'When I take the train to Buchberg.'

NINE

The next morning the Nordbahn was slower than usual. It followed the course of the Danube for a time, through Klosterneuburg and past the castle of Greifenstein. Just beyond that castle lay the village of Altenberg an der Donau. It was from this place that the writer Peter Altenberg had taken his pen name. The story, well-known in literary circles, was indicative of Altenberg's proclivities and sentimentality.

A school friend – son of the publisher of the *Neue Freie Presse* at the time (an edition of which Werthen had purchased at the station before departure) – had invited the young Richard Engländer to the family home in Altenberg during the summer break. The family had three sons and four daughters. The girls were all younger than the boys and suffered the nicknames their brothers saddled them with. The youngest of these girls – an adolescent with thick auburn braids – was jokingly called Peter. Altenberg's sympathies were with the young girls, whom the older brothers treated like servants, expecting them to fetch their shoes and bring them food.

Thus was born Peter Altenberg.

Although the train rumbled slowly through the countryside, Werthen was comfortable enough, ensconced in a first-class compartment that he did not need to share. The commission he had received from Frau Mutzenbacher was handsome enough for him to afford the little luxury of first class. He turned his attention to his newspaper and discovered he had been cheated by the vendor at the train station. This was yesterday's edition. No matter. He avoided the news articles and instead read a feuilleton by the Hungarian-born playwright and critic Rudolf Lothar entitled *From India to the Planet Mars*. This piqued Werthen's interest, as it was the title of a book by the Swiss professor Flournoy recounting, and mildly debunking, the claims of the French-speaking Swiss psychic Hélène Smith. She held that in séance she was able to communicate with Martians and, using the process of automatic writing, had written out bits of hieroglyphic-like Martian language which she later translated into French. Mademoiselle Smith – born Catherine-Elise Muller – further claimed she was able to communicate with Victor Hugo and averred that she was the reincarnation of a Hindu princess and also of Marie Antoinette. Flournoy's book, published the year before, was a huge success and had stirred interest in the occult around the world.

Without ever stooping to mockery, Lothar managed a searing indictment of such paranormal fluff, making the French psychic appear a well-meaning spiritual naïf. Reading the lengthy feuilleton took Werthen all the way to Tulln, where the train crossed the Danube, heading directly north into the Weinviertel.

Now they were passing into a region of gently rolling hills, with strips of vineyard laid out like a chessboard. As the name suggested, it was a wine region, and the vines were in full leaf now, glistening green under a high spring sun. Hollabrunn was the next large stop, and Werthen found himself growing hungry; breakfast of coffee and a *Kipferl* was not sufficiently sustaining. He treated himself to the guilty pleasure of a wurst *Semmel*, purchased from a vendor on the platform at Hollabrunn.

The train jerked out of the station and in another half hour had reached the small town of Haugsdorf. Werthen gathered his paper and briefcase from the overhead rack and descended to the deserted platform. The smell of the country struck him at once, a mix of damp earth and manure. He inquired with the stationmaster – a tall rail of a man with a continual snuffle – about finding transport to take him the several kilometers to the village of Buchberg. The man stared open-mouthed at Werthen, as if not hearing him, and sniffed several times.

'A cart, a trap, perhaps a fiaker?' Werthen repeated.

'You must be from Tulln,' the stationmaster finally said, in an accent that sounded as if it might have come from the Mars of Hélène Smith.

'From Vienna, actually,' Werthen said and instantly regretted it.

His interlocutor squinted at him, for Werthen was now a frightening and potentially dangerous emissary from the cosmopolitan capital.

'That explains it then,' the man said. 'You know, people work around here. We've got no time for such things.'

'I could pay a fair rate.'

At this, the man's expression immediately changed. He was full of sudden goodwill and *bonhomie*.

'Well, why didn't you say so in the first place? Follow me. I've got a little rig by the side of the station.'

'You're going to take me?'

'You want to go to Buchberg or not?'

'But the station . . .'

The man waved away this suggestion. 'Ach, there's not another train through here for four hours.'

Thus Werthen arranged for the stationmaster – Herr Platt the man's name was, as he discovered during the course of the uncomfortable ride – to take him to Buchberg and wait there for the return journey. The train in four hours' time would be just right for going back to Vienna.

'What business brings you to the Weinviertel, if you don't mind my asking?' Platt said as they plodded along the dirt track.

'No, I don't mind the question,' said Werthen, as he sat next to the man on the board seat of the trap, pulled by one emaciated pony. 'I'm looking for a family.'

Platt laughed at this. 'Got plenty of those around here and that's a fact.'

'This particular family would have a daughter in service in Vienna and would also have an interest in universal languages.'

'Oh, you mean Jakob Moos. Locals say he's a nutter with that language of his. Always saying "Glidis" instead of good day. He's a good enough man, though.'

Platt thought a moment. 'Their daughter.' He shook his head. 'No good will come of that, you'll see. Sent off to Vienna like she was. Pardon my saying so, but that city's a sin hole. Father Bernard says so. And the girl was a handful here already, I can tell you.'

Werthen did nothing to encourage Platt's loquaciousness.

'There were stories about that one.'

Werthen could imagine. Any beautiful young girl such as Fräulein Mitzi would be considered, *a priori*, loose in the conservative environs of a place like this.

Finally noticing Werthen's silence on that issue, Platt took another direction.

'What business do you have with Jakob?'

'It's a private matter. Do you know where they live?'

'Well I guess I should. I worked for Moos when I first came to this district from the Waldviertel. Looking for opportunities. Always looking to better myself. Moos, he's got a few hectares and needed help at harvest time. I lived in one of their outbuildings, but took my meals with the family. Four daughters. Each prettier than the other.'

He flicked the reins at the pony, which had slowed to chew milkweed at the side of the narrow rutted track.

'They would talk with one another that funny way. At first I just thought it was Weinviertel dialect, me coming from the Waldviertel. But nobody else around here talks like that. Still Jakob Moos is a hard worker, an honest man, always pays on time and goes to mass like clockwork – though, once in a while, he does go on about Marx and workers' rights. I got the feeling, though, that Frau Moos didn't really approve of all that language or political stuff. She comes from a real religious family. Brother's a priest and all. Strange what love makes us do.'

Werthen looked sideways at Platt. He hadn't taken him for a philosopher.

They travelled the rest of the way to Buchberg in silence. Moos had his small farm on the north side of the village. The house was low and whitewashed with a slate roof. Early geraniums in pots stood in front of recessed windows, making the house seem cheerier than it was. A pump stood outside the front door, a sheaf of wheat hung over the door for good luck. They would need it, Werthen thought, as he rapped at the door. Platt remained in the rig.

A short round woman answered the door. She wore an apron and was using it to brush at a streak of flour on her cheek. She had an expectant look on her face, but when she saw Werthen this turned to suspicion.

'Oh, I thought you were the mailman.'

'Gentleman from Vienna to see you, ma'am,' Platt called out from his rig.

'Vienna.' The woman said it like an incantation. 'Thank you, Herr Platt. Won't you come in, have a cup of tea?' This was directed to Platt, not Werthen.

'I'll just wait here, Frau Moos. Thank you anyway.'

Werthen had paid the man extra to decline any such invitations.

'Could I have a moment of your time, Frau Moos?' Werthen finally said.

'Of course,' she said. 'Where are my manners? Come in, please. From Vienna. What a long way.'

She spoke quickly, obviously nervous.

The door opened directly into the kitchen. Three young girls sat at a large table in the center of the room. They were dressed in simple home-made clothing: colorful vests over white blouses and pleated skirts that matched the vests. Each girl wore a scarf over their long tresses, as did their mother. The girls were busy sewing; a lump of gray dough lay on the other end of the table.

'I am sorry to interrupt your work, Frau Moos, but I need to speak with you and your husband.'

'Jakob? He's out back. Shall I get him then?'

'Yes, please.' He noted that she did not ask him his business. It was as if she were afraid to know.

The girls whispered among one another while their mother was gone. The middle one, perhaps twelve or thirteen, with rosy cheeks had a close resemblance to Mitzi. She looked up shyly at Werthen and then quickly back down at her sewing, giggling as she did so.

Frau Moos came back in, leading her husband, a large man dressed in a soiled white shirt and black trousers held up by black braces. He took off his hat as he entered the room.

'What's all this, then?' he said. 'A visitor from Vienna. Whatever for?'

'My name is Werthen. Advokat Karl Werthen,' he said, handing them a card he took from his coat pocket.

Moos examined the card closely. 'Says here wills and trusts, criminal law and private inquiries. Which is it today?'

'Could we speak privately?'

Frau Moos said quickly, 'Girls. Outside. Get some fresh air and sun.'

The girls looked up in surprise, hesitating.

'Now, girls,' she clapped her hands.

After they shuffled out of the door, Moos offered Werthen a chair at the table.

'Now, what business do we have with you?' Moos asked.

Werthen felt his throat contract as he pulled out the photo of Mitzi he had got from Frau Mutzenbacher: the smiling young woman in the Wurstelprater hugging her stuffed bunny. He placed the picture on the table in front of the parents.

'Is this your daughter?'

Moos glanced at it and put a thick hand over it, shoving it back to Werthen.

'No. Never seen that face before. All made up. That's not our Waltraude.'

'Why do you ask, Advokat?' Frau Moos inquired, her voice trembling.

There was no kind way to say what had to be said. 'The young woman in the picture is dead. Murdered several weeks ago. I am making inquiries in an attempt to apprehend her murderer.'

Frau Moos breathed in deeply, her hands clutched together at her chest.

'Doesn't concern us,' Herr Moos said. 'Like I say, that's not our Waltraude. Now, if you'll excuse me, I've got work to do.'

Werthen and Frau Moos sat in silence for a moment after her husband lumbered out.

She sighed. 'That's our Waltraude. I knew something was wrong, we hadn't heard from her in so long. Such a good girl she was. Always writing and letting us know about her life in Vienna.'

She reached for the photograph, picked it up, and stared at her dead child.

'My little baby,' she said and began weeping.

Werthen weathered it. He needed information. But it did not last long, as Frau Moos made a final determined sniff and wiped her eyes with her apron.

'You say she was murdered. Why? Who would want to harm my Traudl?'

'That is what I am trying to ascertain, Frau Moos.'

She sat up straight staring into his eyes. 'How did she die?'

'She was strangled.'

The word shocked her into silence for a moment as she considered what kind of death that meant to her child. Then, 'At her uncle's? Why didn't he let us know?'

'Her body was found in the Prater. It's a large park in Vienna.'

She sat in silence, looking at the image in the photograph.

'Who is her uncle, Frau Moos? I will need to speak with him.'

'But I don't understand. She was living with Hieronymus. Keeping house for him.'

'Not since last fall. I would like to speak with him. Could you give me his address?'

She rose and went to an open cupboard near the front door. She kept letters in a batch on one of the shelves and brought back a bundle of correspondence bound with a pink ribbon.

She pulled one out from the stack, removed the letter from the envelope, and passed the empty envelope to Werthen.

She pointed at the return address. 'That's where you can find my brother.'

Werthen read the address twice to make sure he had understood correctly. 'Your brother lives at the rectory of St Johann?'

She nodded. 'Yes. He's the priest there.' The priest brother that Platt had mentioned, Werthen suddenly realized.

She gathered her thoughts, attempting to be cogent despite her grief.

'But if she wasn't living with Hieronymus, where was she living? Not with that writer, I hope? My poor Waltraude. Why did we ever send her to Vienna?'

'Which writer would that be, Frau Moos?'

'His name is here somewhere. It was all she could talk about in her letters for a time, how Uncle Hieronymus had introduced her to this famous writer and he was giving her lessons in composition.'

She riffled through the stack of letters, opening one and discarding it then moving on to the next one.

Finally, 'Yes, here it is. Man named Schnitzler. Our Waltraude was so proud to know somebody so important. Sounds like a Jewish name, though. Have you heard of him?'

Werthen ignored the question. 'And when was this, Frau Moos?'

She looked at the date of the letter in her hand. 'Last summer. Her letters were full of him – Herr Schnitzler this, Herr Schnitzler that. My husband was concerned, I can tell you. But I convinced him that Hieronymus would make sure she was a good girl and come to no harm. And then, last fall there was no more mention of the man.'

At this, she began sobbing again.

In other words, Werthen thought, no more mention of Schnitzler just before running away from her uncle's home.

Looking up through her tears, Frau Moos asked, 'Why didn't Hieronymus tell us?'

It was a question Werthen wanted an answer to, as well.

Sudden suspicion filled her face. 'Why are you here at all?' she said. 'Why not the police? Private inquiries, the card says. So who's paying your bills?'

He said nothing for a moment.

'Is it this Schnitzler fellow?'

She was filled with confusion and sadness, and Werthen let her assume whatever was comforting.

'The police have given the crime a low priority, you see,' Werthen began.

'So Herr Schnitzler hired you to get to the bottom of things? Perhaps he is a real gentleman then, despite the name.'

He did not disabuse her of the notion.

She looked at him with a sudden thought. 'Several weeks ago, you said. Our daughter's been dead for several weeks? But we must fetch her. Bury her.'

'She was given a proper burial, I assure you.'

'This Schnitzler again, was it?'

He responded only with a tight smile.

In the end, Frau Moos allowed Werthen to take one of the letters mentioning Mitzi's 'education' at the hands of Herr Schnitzler and also retrieved from the cupboard a more recent one from the time when she would already have moved into the Bower. While at the cupboard, she placed his card next to the pile of letters. The letters he now had in hand were, like all the others, written in Volapük – which, Frau Moos went on to explain, the father, an ardent socialist, had religiously taught his children in hope of making the world a finer place.

Werthen assured the woman that he would do everything in his power to bring her daughter's murderer to justice. He knew that once she composed herself she would have further questions about where her daughter had lived for so many months and where she was buried. These he did not want to impart to her today. Instead, he told her to feel free to write to him with any further questions; they had his business card.

Let her keep an untarnished memory of her daughter for the time being, he thought.

As he left, the three girls came back into the kitchen, gathering around their grieving mother. Outside, he saw Herr Moos stacking wood, stopping occasionally to wipe his eyes.

'You've brought happy news then, haven't you?' Herr Platt said sarcastically as Werthen climbed on to the seat of the rig.

'No discussion now, Herr Platt. Just take me back to the station. I have a train to catch.'

'I said no good would come of the girl going to Vienna.'

'Just drive, Herr Platt. Please.'

'It appears that Herr Schnitzler has been less than forthcoming.'

They were gathered in the restaurant of Gross's hotel for late-afternoon coffee. A generous portion of *Schwarzwalder Torte* sat in front of the criminologist.

'He lied to me,' Werthen said, choosing not to mince his words. 'There could be more than one possible reason for the lie, or course, but the fact is that he knew Mitzi quite well prior to her being established at the Bower.'

'You said he was in a close relationship with a young woman now,' Berthe offered.

'Yes,' Werthen said. 'But from what I have heard, that has never stopped Schnitzler from dalliances before. It appears the man has no conception of monogamy.'

'I knew a fellow like that in Graz once,' Gross said. 'Convicted him of multiple murders.'

'I hardly believe Schnitzler is our man.' Werthen took a sip of his *mélange*. 'A womanizer he may be, but a killer? Perhaps Berthe is right. Maybe he is simply in love for the first time and does not want the lady to know about his sordid past.'

'All she needs to do is attend one of his plays,' Gross said.

'So what next?' Berthe asked.

'I visit Herr Schnitzler again and confront him with Mitzi's letter. I will, however, make certain that Fräulein Gussman is not in attendance, so we can speak frankly. After that, I believe it is time to pay the mysterious Uncle Hieronymus a visit and find out why he did not notify Mitzi's parents of her departure from his care.'

'Go softly, Werthen. The man's a priest.'

Werthen bristled at this, staring at his colleague. 'But I am not Catholic.'

'You mistake my meaning. I am not saying that his office auto-matically disqualifies him as a suspect. What I meant was that if cornered, he could hide behind the robe. It's been known to happen before.'

'I expect you had a case once in Graz,' Berthe joked, dispelling the slight tension. It was always like this when Werthen and Gross worked together, she thought. The competitive tension, the misun-derstandings. Like bristling father and son.

TEN

The spring weather broke suddenly and Thursday dawned wet and cold. Werthen decided to go to Schnitzler's apartment directly from home, instead of walking to his office first. He closed the door of the house behind him and breathed in an aroma that confused his sense of time, for once more the smell of burning coal was in the air, as if it were the first raw days of autumn and not almost summer.

He called ahead before leaving the house. Prokop with his angelic voice had answered. Werthen ascertained that Schnitzler would see him and that Fräulein Gussman would not be in attendance that morning. He thought about walking, as he had his umbrella with him and was wearing stout walking shoes, but then thought better of it as the needle rain increased to a real downpour.

He was in luck, for Bachmann, his favorite driver, was at the head of the fiaker queue up the street – seated on the bench of the fiaker, huddled under a black umbrella, and whistling his usual Strauss tune. Bachmann, known to the other cabbies as 'the Count', had been a great friend of Werthen's ever since the Advokat assisted him in a delicate matter a couple of years before. Fact was, Bachmann was actually the son of a Habsburg count, but because of a deformity he had been, in effect, traded for a healthier specimen, who, upon growing up, had entered the military and got himself killed. The Countess had then wanted her real son back, but Bachmann – the name he had grown up with – would have none of it. He renounced the title and stayed true to the only mother he had ever known.

At any rate, Bachmann was eternally grateful for the bit of legal work Werthen had done to effect the renunciation, and had proved a valuable and valued acquaintance ever since. Most particularly, he did not ask too many questions.

'Advokat,' Bachmann greeted him as he approached the fiaker. 'It takes unseasonable weather to see you again. How is the young one?'

Bachmann doffed a battered bowler at Werthen as he spoke. His thick frame was covered chin to boot top in an ancient and somewhat moth-eaten woollen greatcoat.

'She's lovely, Herr Bachmann. A fine young sprout.' Werthen climbed into the cab and then, speaking out of the window, supplied the address.

Other cabbies might have inquired as to the Advokat's health, as the address was in the medical quarter, but not Bachmann. He moved his single-horse fiaker out into the slow-moving traffic and made his way towards the ninth district.

Schnitzler was again lying on the divan when Werthen was shown in to see him. He looked expectantly at the lawyer.

'Progress already, Advokat?'

'Yes, in a sense.'

Schnitzler indicated the chair as he had before, but this time Werthen placed it at a distance from the divan.

'I paid a visit to the Weinviertel yesterday,' Werthen said.

Schnitzler continued to stare at him expectantly as if awaiting good news.

'Perhaps you don't know why I went there,' Werthen said.

'I have no idea, Advokat, but I assume you will tell me.'

'It's where Mitzi came from. Her real name was Waltraude Moos.'

'Oh.' The disappointment showed clearly on his face. 'That young girl from the Bower again. I had rather hoped you'd come about my case.'

'They overlap, it seems.'

'I don't follow.'

'You've been less than forthright with me.' He handed Schnitzler the letter he had taken from Frau Moos.

Schnitzler opened it and looked quizzically at Werthen.

'It's in Volapük,' he explained. 'The family used it in communications with each other. Mitzi didn't tell you about that?'

Schnitzler shook his head. 'But what does this have to do with me?'

'Look at the underlined part. Your name is mentioned several times. As it was in other letters from last summer. She was so proud to tell her parents of the grand writer in Vienna who had taken her under his wing.'

Schnitzler, realizing he was caught in a lie, tried to brazen it out: 'Well, I thought it only right to help the young girl to better herself—'

'Herr Schnitzler, I have not come to listen to more prevarications. I very much want to help you with your difficulties, but if you can not be open and honest with me regarding Fräulein Waltraude, then I do not see how I can be of any assistance to you.'

'Ah, so lawyers are not above a bit of extortion, I see.'

'Call it what you will, but I know for a fact that you were familiar with the young woman long before she went to the Bower. Would you care to explain?'

Schnitzler lay back against the pillow as if exhausted or disgusted.

'Fräulein Waltraude, as you call her, and I were known to one another before the Bower. That is correct. You must understand, I do not want any official inquiries about our . . . relationship.'

'The police have given this very low priority, Herr Schnitzler. It is highly doubtful they would interview you. The affair can be kept from Fräulein Gussman, if that is what troubles you.'

'I see. Then, why not?' He sat up on the divan looking quite bright and chipper once again, making Werthen wonder how badly injured the man really was.

'Well, you see, Mitzi – that was my name for her, Waltraude is an impossible name for an insouciant young thing like her – she and I met one day last summer in the Volksgarten. She had been shopping for combs and dropped her packet. I helped her with it. Such a sweet-faced young woman she was, and so impressed to meet a famous author. I am sure you will not believe this, Advokat, but going out that morning I had not the inkling of desire for another conquest. Indeed I had just left the bed of one. No, it was Mitzi who made the advances. I could sense she was an unhappy young woman, troubled even. Lonely. I took her for afternoon coffee at an out-of-the-way place I know and I found a young woman who wished to improve herself.'

'You became lovers,' Werthen prompted.

'Not that first meeting, no. But she arranged to meet again in the park. It was regular as clockwork on Thursday afternoons. I assumed that was her free afternoon, a young woman in service.'

Werthen did not bother to confirm this.

'Yes, we soon became lovers and our affair followed the usual trajectory.' Schnitzler smiled at Werthen knowingly.

'I am not a man well versed in such things,' Werthen said. 'Perhaps you could describe the trajectory . . .'

'Initial infatuation grows to passion as the young woman gives more and more of herself, opens with more abandon until she becomes totally smitten and obsessed. The sweet early days of dalliance are soon replaced with demands and recriminations. She actually thought we would live together. I had to disabuse her of that notion, but in such a way that our physical union was not disrupted. Delicate maneuvering.'

'But you have had a good deal of practice at that, no?'

'Advokat, I do not appreciate your tone. If you do not approve of my life, that is your prerogative. You asked for the truth. You are getting it.'

Werthen was silent for a time. Then, 'But you finally parted ways?'

Schnitzler nodded. 'She came to me saying she had run away. That we had to be together now. She had nowhere else to go. I told her in no uncertain terms that such a situation was an impossibility. I sent her away.'

'Yet she has an uncle in Vienna,' Werthen said.

'You know about him, then?'

'From her parents.'

'Oh – then you really don't know about him yet.'

'Herr Schnitzler, full disclosure please.'

Werthen had requested Bachmann to wait. The parish church of St Johann was near the Meidlinger Haupstrasse; behind the church was the rectory, and a graveyard surrounded the whole. It took Bachmann forty-five minutes to drive there, following the Gürtel most of the way.

The rectory was built on the plan of a small hunting lodge, its exterior walls painted the same creamy ochre as the nearby Schönbrunn Palace. Again Werthen asked Bachmann to wait for him, even though the weather had begun to clear up.

He took the miniature hand of a doorknocker in his and rapped it on the front door. An elderly housekeeper answered his fourth attempt. She opened the door with the timidity one might use opening a coffin. She was small, pinched and desiccated, the corners of her mouth turning down through a gullied landscape of chin wrinkles.

'Who is it?' she said in a voice barely more than a whisper.

Werthen drew out one of his business cards and handed it to her.

'The name is Advokat Karl Werthen. Could you tell Father Hieronymus that I have come to talk to him about his niece.'

She took the card, holding it carefully between thumb and forefinger as if it were infected, squinted at it a moment, and then closed the door.

Werthen waited patiently outside for several minutes, but was just about to use the knocker once more when the door opened.

The housekeeper was there again. 'He says to come.'

Werthen followed her into the rectory, which smelled strongly of furniture polish. There were three different crucifixes hanging from the walls of the long hallway they traversed. Passing a suite of rooms whose doors were open, Werthen saw that the windows had been thrown wide open and that furniture had been pushed against the wall, the large rugs in the center of the rooms rolled up.

He better understood the housekeeper's surly mood now; he had interrupted her spring cleaning.

They came to a room at the end of the long hallway and the woman tapped on the door lightly.

'Please enter,' a voice at once sonorous and self-satisfied said from the other side.

She nodded her head for Werthen to enter and walked back down the hall to resume her cleaning.

Inside, Werthen found himself in a study made almost unbearably hot by a white-and-green ceramic stove in one corner. The walls were covered with bookshelves filled with books that had impressive leather bindings.

'Advokat Werthen?'

Werthen followed the voice, and finally found its owner seated at a desk partially hidden behind the door.

'Please do close the door. Draughts, you know.'

Werthen did so and approached the desk, taking measure of the priest.

He had expected someone of the stature of an uncle and a priest, assuming that he was most likely Frau Moos's older brother. In the event, Father Hieronymus was obviously her younger brother, much younger. He looked, in fact, as if he still belonged in the seminary.

'You say you have word from my niece,' the priest said, not bothering to rise to meet his guest.

'May I?' Werthen tapped the back of a chair across the desk from the priest.

'Please, please.'

Seated, Werthen again assessed the man. Ash-blond hair, thinning on top and brushed off a high forehead. Features fine, almost fragile. Eyes watery blue, delicate hands spread out in front of him on the desk. A fresh manicure. He wore a black cassock and in front of him on the desk lay a Bible and some foolscap.

'Sorry to interrupt you,' Werthen said. 'It appears you are planning your sermon.'

'You mentioned my niece?'

'Yes, of course. My apologies.' On the way here he had thought long and hard about how to handle the questioning. In the end, he took Gross's advice to heart. Go easy at first; save the accusations for later.

'From your remarks, I fear that I am bringing you bad news. Your niece is dead. She was murdered over three weeks ago.'

Father Hieronymus leaped out of his chair as if set on fire. Standing, he was tall and thin as a wraith.

'My God, man! What do you mean? She can't be dead. She's just a child.'

'I assure you, such is the case. I visited her parents yesterday; they had not heard the news either. Your sister rather thought you would know, seeing that she lives with you.'

'Lived,' Father Hieronymus said. 'She ran away months ago. I did not have the heart to tell her parents. I did my best to find her, but what could I do? If a young lady wishes to hide herself in the metropolis, there is nothing a simple parish priest can do.'

'Did you notify the police when she left? Perhaps someone stole her away.'

He sat again, the shock beginning to wear off. He brusquely dismissed Werthen's suggestion. 'Waltraude? Unlikely. She was not the type to be stolen away.'

Then he looked at Werthen with suspicion.

'What business, Advokat, is any of this to you?'

'I have been retained to look into the death of the young lady.'

'By whom? And are not the police already investigating? Murdered, you say?'

It was entirely possible that Father Hieronymus was being honest in his avowal that he did not know of his niece's death. After all, the newspaper accounts identified the unfortunate young woman merely as 'Fräulein Mitzi,' not Waltraude Moos.

Werthen considered this quickly, then took the priest's questions in reverse order. 'Yes, murdered. Strangled and left naked in the

Prater. And no, the police do not concern themselves over much with the death of a prostitute. Lastly, I have been retained by a good friend of the deceased who wants to see justice done.'

'Are you mad? Waltraude a prostitute? Impossible!'

'After she left here – left you – she was discovered on the streets by a recruiter for a well-known bordello. Until her death, she made her living playing the role of an innocent schoolgirl.'

Definitely past the time for going easy now, Werthen thought.

'Which role she appears to have learned from an excellent teacher.' From what Schnitzler had related to him of Mitzi's story, such abuse had begun almost from the beginning of her stay in Vienna with her uncle.

Father Hieronymus cast Werthen a look of such animosity that the lawyer was happy the man was just a priest and not a shaman.

'What are you insinuating?'

An innocent man would tell me to get the hell out, Werthen thought.

'I know why your niece ran away from here,' he said. 'There are witnesses.'

'Get out of my rectory this instant.'

Too late for that now, Werthen thought.

'And the police might also be interested in knowing the background of the young woman so brutally murdered. As well as the whereabouts of those close to her on the night she was killed.'

The priest looked as if the air had suddenly been sucked out of him. He visibly slumped in his chair, his eyes darting this way and that as if looking for an escape.

Werthen kept applying the pressure. 'The archdiocese might also be interested in such information.'

'What do you want from me?'

'The truth.'

'I didn't kill Waltraude. I couldn't have harmed her. She was my niece and I cared deeply for her.'

'Not enough to keep her safe, it seems. Sounds more like lust than love.'

'I've given you the truth, now please leave. I have no idea who killed my niece, but if you find him I should like to know. Such a creature would be in need of the succour of confession. What more can you want from me?'

What in fact did he want from the man? A confession? By the looks of him, Uncle Hieronymus was not a killer. He had preyed on the helpless, had taken advantage of family trust; but he appeared too weak to kill. He did not have the blood for it. However, there was that moment of terror that made him leap from his seat; the evil glare he sent Werthen's way.

Even if guilty, though, it was doubtful the priest was going to confess.

Did Werthen want contrition? Perhaps. But he knew instinctively that this was not the sort of man to admit sins. Revenge for Mitzi? Again, perhaps.

Werthen had spent only a few days dwelling on the life of Fräulein Mitzi, but already he felt empathy and compassion for her, farmed out from her home as one mouth too many to feed and sent off to her uncle in Vienna, a man of god who should have made a safe haven for her. Instead, he took advantage of the young woman in the vilest way – threatening, according to Schnitzler, to send her to an orphanage if she did not satisfy him sexually. And then there was Schnitzler, whom she looked up to and adored. Her first love, in all likelihood. But he too betrayed her, sent her away in her hour of need to make a living on the streets. The only one in this sorry mess to really love the girl, it seemed, had been the madam who sold the girl's flesh to the highest bidder.

Yes, revenge, vengeance, justice, call it what you may. Mitzi, Werthen thought, deserved it.

In his mind he saw again the two contrasting sides of the wardrobe in her room: the virginal schoolgirl clothes of Waltraude and the vampish nightwear of Mitzi.

Why had she died? For the sins of Waltraude or of Mitzi?

'Now I beg you to leave,' Hieronymus said. 'There is a group of parishioners due here any moment to discuss the *Pfingsten* decorations for the church.'

Whit Sunday, Pentecost, would take place in just a few days' time. Though not a religious man, Werthen was angered to think of this sham priest officiating at such a service.

Leave the anger and outrage for later, he finally told himself. For now, focus on procedure.

'Did she have any friends when she lived here?'

'Of course not. She was my housekeeper. There was no time for such things.'

'Would it surprise you to learn that she had a lover during that time?'

'Why do you wish to torment me? I have answered your questions . . .'

'I would like to see her room.'

'There is nothing to see. I have a new housekeeper and she now has the room. The few pieces of clothing Waltraude left behind when she ran away I threw into the bin.'

'And you did not introduce her to any of your colleagues?'

'She was my housekeeper!'

'And your niece. And your lover.'

This time when Hieronymus leaped out of his chair, he had a mission. He strode to the door and held it open.

'I am finished with this interview, Advokat. And if you dare threaten me again with allegations of impropriety, I shall have the full power of the church come down upon you. The diocesan bishop is a personal acquaintance of mine. Now good day to you.'

Werthen figured he was lucky with the information he had got and did not wish to push his luck.

'I am sure we will see one another again,' he said as he was leaving. 'You might also try to establish your whereabouts on the night of April 30.'

Hieronymus slammed the door behind him. Werthen did not wait to be shown out, but made his way to the front door and outside, where Bachmann was waiting, nibbling on a wurst *Semmel.* The sun had come out.

'Where to now, Advokat?'

'The office, Herr Bachmann, if you please. And take it slowly. I need some fresh air.'

ELEVEN

'Just what is it you want, Gross?'

'I thought you would never ask.' Gross eyed Minister Brockhurst, and told him plainly his request.

Brockhurst pursed his lips and raised his brows in silent denial, feigning surprise in the same way he had as a boy when they were growing up together in Graz.

Even back then, Brockhurst had been a bully, the leader of a band of lower-middle-class children who followed him with abject obedience. The son of a local magistrate, he had attempted to recruit Gross into his ranks, but Gross would have none of it. Already at the age of eight Gross was an avowed leader, not a follower. And he distrusted Brockhurst, who seemed to speak out of both sides of his mouth; sweetness and light one moment, a brow-beating tyrant the next.

Brockhurst would dispatch his crew of true believers to follow cooks on their shopping rounds, in order to find the secrets of the kitchens of the wealthy or discover which maids were taking kickbacks from shops, unbeknownst to their employers. In this manner, Brockhurst became a veritable font of both valuable and downright silly information on the doings of the top twenty families of Graz. These families laughingly referred to themselves as the 'kilo': as compared to England's élite society, referred to as the 'ton'.

Brockhurst could tell you what the von Dresslers were having for dinner that night or what toiletries the Kneizler family favored, or which domestic might have something to hide in any of these great houses.

What he did with such information on Graz's society families, Gross had no idea. But the servants were another matter. Brockhurst lost his virginity to one such young maid, who feared for her position lest the young master tell her employers of her secret arrangement with the poulterer, who paid her five crowns every quarter for bringing the family custom his way at slightly inflated prices.

All in all, this had been a perfect training ground for the future spy – for that is what Brockhurst was, despite his protestations to the contrary.

'After all, I am only a simple bureaucrat,' he finally said in response to Gross's request. 'I hardly have access to such information.'

'Let us cut through the blather, Brockhurst. Life is too short for it. We both know what the other is about.'

'What does it matter to you whether the unfortunate von Ebersdorf was a diplomat or up to his eyes in espionage? He is dead. Full stop.'

'It matters because it figures in our investigation.'

'Into the murder of this prostitute of yours?'

'Of von Ebersdorf's, actually. He was her regular customer. Does that not raise any alarm bells for you?'

'My God, Gross. Are you suggesting that a man of von Ebersdorf's quality, whether spy or diplomat, would indulge in pillow talk with a tart? That he would divulge state secrets in between bouts of bedroom callisthenics?'

'The thought had crossed my mind.'

'Because of the coincidence in timing of their deaths?'

Gross said nothing, knowing that Brockhurst was surely experiencing the same suspicions.

There followed a long silence, punctuated only by the ticking of the baroque *cloisonné* clock on Brockhurst's fastidiously organized walnut work table.

'Russia desk,' Brockhurst suddenly said. 'But you didn't hear it from me.'

'Chief?'

Brockhurst nodded. 'A family man,' he added.

Gross understood the veiled threat: do not publicize the dead man's connection to the Bower.

'We were aware of Joachim's peccadilloes, of course.' He fixed Gross with eyes as grey and unforgiving as granite.

Gross felt a sudden chill, wondering if he were asking Brockhurst about the wrong death. Had he and his minions eliminated the source of the peccadilloes?

He returned the stare, and finally decided to lead the interview in a different direction.

'Seeing that you are sharing secrets, perhaps you can aid me in another investigation – involving Herr Schnitzler.'

'Our national treasure.' Brockhurst said it with dripping sarcasm. 'What's your connection?'

Gross briefly explained the attack on the playwright.

Brockhurst appeared unmoved. 'And what do you expect me to tell you? That Austria's power structure has lashed out at the man who betrayed his own officer class? Hardly. More likely some cuckolded husband took long overdue revenge on that Lothario.'

'Officer class?'

'You didn't know? The man was a reserve officer. As I understand it, the General Staff used his services from time to time.'

'If I understand you correctly . . .'

'Yes. Schnitzler has the perfect cover. As an artist he has access to many influential people across national boundaries. He can travel without raising suspicion. In short, the perfect courier. A pity he had to ruin such a mutually profitable relationship by penning that worthless play.'

The kitchen at the exclusive Hotel Excelsior was in the basement, a cavernous space filled with the bustle and hum of lunchtime activity.

Finicky in his daily habits and hygiene, fussy about his bath and his application of bay rum, Gross was appalled by what presented itself before his disbelieving eyes.

A scurrying in the bags of rice left open in one murky corner could very well have been a rat in search of lunch. He twice witnessed a sous-chef drop bloody cuts of veal on the filthy sawdust-covered stone floor, then calmly pick them up and lightly brush them off with his soiled apron before delivering them to the chef to dip into egg batter for breading. Another kitchen helper (what rank does one have if attired all in gray stripes?) appeared to have a cold and was happily sneezing all over the cucumber he was dicing.

Marcel – not his real name, he was actually Felix Kolowitz from Hernals – stood majestic in his tall white chef's toque, a commander in charge of spatula-wielding troops, dispatching his forces with a sang-froid that bespoke indifference to human suffering: the hallmark of all great leaders.

'Herr Gross, this is not the most opportune moment for your queries.'

'Doktor, actually, and Herr Direktor Mautner would beg to differ with your assertion. It is a simple query, actually.'

'I will have to examine my records. There were a number of extra kitchen hands and stewards laid on for the von Ebersdorf banquet.'

A dramatic pause. Then, 'Such a terrible occurrence! Nothing of the sort has ever happened in a kitchen of mine.'

'I'm sure Count Joachim von Ebersdorf would be equally appalled,' said Gross, 'were he here to complain.'

The comment went unremarked upon by Marcel.

'None of the other guests were affected?'

Marcel shook his head so forcefully that his toque cracked its starched confines and seemed to melt on his head like a pat of butter.

'The rest of the guests were quite pleased with the feast.'

It was this very fact that made Gross wonder.

She was early. She was always early. She also still had dreams of oversleeping for her *Matura* exam.

It was the train that was late. The Franz Josef Station was hardly the place she would have chosen to spend an idle fifteen minutes; a cavernous and chilly mausoleum. Outside the weather had left behind the morning's rain and gloom, and had changed to glorious summer-like warmth. In here, however, it was as if yesterday's clouds had never dispersed.

The Franz Josef Bahnhof was, Berthe decided, a perfect example of the usual graceless, tasteless architectural pomposity that characterized monuments to the Habsburgs – this one thrown together hastily about two decades earlier.

Berthe found herself in a foul mood. The train from Krems was delayed, and she was twitchy.

You should be enjoying this, she counseled herself. It is what you have been requesting for months: direct involvement in a case. Not just lending a charitable and informed ear to after-dinner discussions of the progress of a case, but actual personal involvement. Like this bit of surveillance at the Franz Josef Bahnhof.

So stop being so impatient. Take a cue from Frieda, she told herself.

Indeed, her child was cooperating marvelously, making little bubbling sounds as she napped. And why shouldn't she be content? Bertha thought. Like a little pasha, she was nicely bundled atop a feather mattress inside the wickerwork of a Richardson Carriage. A gift from Karl's parents, of course, and almost as expensive as a landau. It really was quite a marvelous bit of engineering, though, she had to concede. Unlike other children's carriages, in which the child always faced backwards, the Richardson Carriage's bassinet could be reversed so that the child faced forward. All one needed to do was loosen an axle under the middle of the enlarged bassinet and turn the bassinet around. And thanks to the enlarged bassinet, one could even use it for toddlers like Frieda.

American, of course. It was as if they had invented inventing.

Berthe pushed the carriage along Platform 12, momentarily casting her gaze towards the exit, where Erika Metzinger had taken up her watch. They exchanged glances but made no hand motions. It was only now that Berthe finally inspected the man under the clock. He had the unmistakable military stature, though he was dressed in a linen suit and straw boater.

He also had the unmistakable look of a watcher. Of course, train stations were full of those waiting and watching for passengers, anxious to greet friends or relatives or business associates. But this man was different, Berthe felt. He was, she fancied, not the sort to personally meet someone at a train station.

She had noticed him earlier but paid him no attention. Now she realized that trains had come and gone and still he waited. Could he be waiting for the delayed train from Krems?

She chuckled to herself, thinking that she had only been on the job half an hour and was already an expert at surveillance, if not counter-surveillance.

Her attention was brought back to the task at hand, hearing the hiss and thump of a train pulling into the station.

She watched as the 11:15 from Krems snaked into the station, and wheeled Frieda's carriage to the front of the platform, steps ahead of the engine. She knew Baron von Suttner would be in the first coaches, the first class.

Sure enough, second off the coach immediately behind the engine was the Baron, looking expectant as he arrived in the capital. He turned back to offer his hand to a young lady descending from the coach, who seemed awfully pleased with herself in a frilly summer dress, a perfect shade of robin's-egg blue to show off her blue eyes.

The young woman had, Berthe thought, exactly the sort of self-satisfied expression that needed slapping.

The Baron carried a walking stick, his niece a parasol. They could be father and daughter come up from the provinces for a day in the city.

Except that it was evident they were not. Not the way the young woman wrapped her arm through his, nor the way she kissed him as she joined him on the platform, lingering with a playful peck just by the ear. She whispered something that made him blush and then break into laughter. They passed by Berthe unmindful of her, laughing together like young lovers meeting behind their parents' backs.

Berthe felt her stomach sink as they passed. It did not take a private inquiry agent to know those two were having an affair.

From a telegram Frau von Suttner had sent earlier, Berthe knew they were coming to Vienna ostensibly to visit the Reinthaler Collection of Flemish art and porcelain.

The only problem with that was that the small private museum was closed on Thursdays for cleaning.

And today was Thursday.

Erika Metzinger was making her way out of the exit, one step ahead of the love birds. The pair would doubtless take a fiaker to their destination – and Berthe, with Frieda in tow, would hardly be able to keep up with them. Outside, Herr Bachman, Karl's prized driver, was waiting for Fräulein Metzinger to follow wherever they might go.

As Berthe watched Erika climb into Bachman's fiaker and drive off after the one the Baron and his niece had taken, the man in the boater came running out of the station, squinting in the noontime sun after the darkness of the train station. He hailed the next fiaker in line and headed in the same direction as the others.

With Fräulein Metzinger on assignment with his wife, Karl Werthen was acting as his own secretary; so when Hermann Bahr knocked at the office door without appointment, it was Werthen himself who greeted the writer.

Bahr, one of the luminaries of the Jung Wien literary movement so much in fashion, was an intimate of Altenberg, Schnitzler and Salten. Werthen figured it was no coincidence that Bahr should appear at his office, but was prepared to allow the usual platitudes to issue forth before his visitor got down to what really mattered.

Not so Bahr. Once the outer office door was closed behind them and they were ensconced in Werthen's office, Bahr said, 'This Bower business is a farce.'

Bahr, a lapsed Catholic, had the beard of a Jewish elder. He squinted at Werthen as he spoke, as if he suffered from astigmatism.

'How so, Herr Bahr?'

For a man so loquacious on the printed page – Bahr had already penned numerous plays, novels and volumes of theatre criticism – he was oddly terse in his spoken communication.

'One prostitute more or less . . .'

He spluttered it out like a caricature of a stolid conservative landowner from Styria. The implication was clear.

'I visited the young girl's parents, Herr Bahr. I can assure you her death was not inconsequential to them. And what business, if I may inquire, is this affair to you?'

'Schnitzler's being hard used.'

'Some might say he used the girl rather hard.'

'You're a literary chap, I'm told.'

Werthen made no response to this seeming *non sequitur*.

But that did not bother Bahr, who seemed to have his lines memorized.

'It's all experience. We store it up and later transform it into art. For a higher purpose. Schnitzler is a man of genius. Surely you see that?'

'No one is accusing him of murder. Indeed, he is one of my clients.'

Bahr, rather inelegantly, snorted at this.

'And,' Werthen added, 'it was your friend Salten who commissioned the case to begin with.'

'Salten is too involved with the woman's memoirs. Hardly an appropriate subject matter for his talents.'

'You did not answer my question, Herr Bahr. Why are you interested? Were you perhaps also one of Mitzi's customers?'

'I am a married man, Advokat.'

'Many are.'

'Altenberg said you are a perceptive sort.' Bahr suddenly shot him a winning smile. 'Jung Wien has its detractors.'

So that was it, Werthen thought.

'Scandal? Is that what you are worried about? One would think a hint of scandal would be *de rigueur* for the literary set.'

'I have worked long and hard to achieve the respect our movement justly deserves.'

'I assure you, Herr Bahr, I do not wish to bring public disapprobation to Jung Wien.'

Bahr looked into his folded hands as he next spoke. 'You are a friend of Karl Kraus's, I understand.'

'Yes. We have shared information from time to time.'

'A villain if there ever was one.'

Things were crystallizing now for Werthen. Bahr and Kraus were no friends, for Kraus thought Jung Wien was precious and febrile and lacked *gravitas*. In fact such opinions put into print in Kraus's journal, *Die Fackel,* had led to that infamous altercation at the Café Central which ended in an *Ohrfeig,* a slap in the face for Kraus, administered by Salten. The feud had continued into the courts, with Bahr suing Kraus for defamation. The case had just been settled, in Bahr's favor, but Kraus vowed not to be silenced.

'What might your point be here, Herr Bahr?'

'Kraus is the sort that will go to extraordinary lengths to avenge himself. He would like nothing better than to see scandal attached to the members of Jung Wien.'

'Extraordinary lengths, such as killing Mitzi?'

'You said it, Herr Advokat, not I.'

'You're delusional.'

'You know the man's penchant. He is forever writing about prostitutes.'

'In their favor,' Werthen pointed out. 'He wants to protect their rights, not oppress them.'

'The man is a sexual cipher. A monk. Repressed sexuality will find an outlet.'

Werthen was not prepared to continue this discussion. He stood up abruptly.

'I wish I could say it has been a pleasure, Herr Bahr.'

For a moment, Bahr did not budge.

'I am merely trying to be helpful, Advokat.'

Then he nodded, as if in defeat, and hands on thighs pushed himself up and out of his chair.

As he prepared to leave, Bahr cast one more crow-like remark: 'I fear our Viennese Svengali has bewitched you, Advokat Werthen. You might want to ascertain Herr Kraus's whereabouts for the night of April 30.'

As arranged, Bachman returned to the train station to pick up Berthe and Frieda.

'Hotel Metropole,' he said as she lifted Frieda into the fiaker. Bachman stored the Richardson Carriage on the luggage-rack at the back and then nodded for her to take her seat.

Berthe shuddered when she heard the destination. She had spent the last fifteen minutes, since the Baron von Suttner and his niece left the station, correcting her initial impression. Perhaps she was reading too much into a kiss on the cheek. The grateful niece giving her stodgy uncle a peck in appreciation for her day out. Perhaps the Baron had simply made a mistake about the opening days of the Reinthaler Collection. Perhaps it was nothing more than that.

She had almost accepted this revision, but now Bachman put paid to that. It seemed the Reinthaler Collection had not been on the Baron's itinerary, after all.

Berthe did not want Frau von Suttner's fears to be proved true; she did not want to be the one to tell her idol that her husband was conducting a tawdry affair with his own niece.

The hotel was only a few streets distant, not in the best neighborhood and definitely not known for its rooms or restaurant. Instead, it was known for the discretion of its staff.

As the fiaker pulled up to the kerb, Frieda peeked out of the window and then stared back at Berthe, grinning widely and showing off her two bottom teeth.

'Dah,' she said.

'Mutti,' Berthe corrected.

Erika Metzinger came up to the coach.

'Are they still there?' Berthe asked.

Erika nodded. 'It appears they have taken a room.'

Berthe's stomach knotted.

'The stupid man.'

'Dah,' Frieda said.

'Yes,' Berthe agreed.

And then, across the street, she noticed the man in the straw boater from the train station, so intent on watching the front of the hotel that he seemed unaware of Fräulein Metzinger or of Berthe's arrival.

Berthe motioned for Erika to join her in the fiaker. 'Are you sure about the room?'

'In truth, I cannot be absolutely certain. Through the glass front doors, I could see the Baron speak with a concierge at the desk. I can only assume . . .'

'Yes. But we have to be sure.'

She turned to Frieda. 'Will you stay with Tante Erika for a moment? Mutti needs to talk to someone.'

'Tan-tan,' Frieda said.

Erika's face brightened at this. 'Clever girl.'

Berthe slid along the leather bench and let herself out of the door of the carriage.

'What will you say?' Erika asked.

'I'm not sure,' Berthe confessed. 'But a bit of fresh air always helps activate my brain cells.' Then, from the pavement, 'Has anyone entered the hotel since they did?'

'No.'

'You be sweet with Tan-tan,' Berthe said to her daughter, but Frieda was already delighting in the examination of the outdated lorgnette that Erika insisted on wearing.

Berthe made her way to the entrance of the hotel. Out of the side of her vision she could see that she had finally attracted the attention of the man in the linen suit and boater. He watched her closely as she walked up the steps to the hotel and entered.

Berthe experienced a momentary *frisson* of delight in the precincts of this hotel so well-known for illicit assignations. The gray-faced, jowly man behind the desk looked up at her as she entered. He appraised her with rheumy eyes that had seen it all. She stopped for a moment, then straightened her back and strode to the front desk.

'Madam,' the concierge said.

'Good day to you.'

'May I be of assistance?' He managed to insert a large dose of nuance into those five words, so that Berthe felt she must bathe at once upon returning home. He spoke with a heavy Italian accent, and his eyes went up and down her body.

'Yes you may,' she replied. Opening her handbag, she extracted a lace handkerchief that Karl had just purchased for her. He enjoyed surprising her with small gifts: flowers, a special book, this lacework handkerchief.

'I am playing the Good Samaritan. This was left in the fiaker I am riding in. The driver says he dropped his fare here. I thought—'

'Very nice of you, Madam, I'm sure.'

He reached for the handkerchief, but she pulled it back from him.

'Don't you want to know which guests?'

He puffed his lips. 'Of course. How silly of me.'

'My driver tells me he deposited the young woman and a man here not fifteen minutes ago.'

'Ah,' the concierge nodded knowingly. 'That would be Herr and Frau von Tilling. They make a point of staying with us when they come up from the country. It must be the young lady's.'

He thrust his meaty hand palm upward across the desk. 'I would be happy to return it.'

Karl will understand, she told herself as she relinquished the prized lacework.

'Von Tilling, you say?'

'Yes, Madam. Perhaps you know them?' He turned for a moment, stuffing the prized handkerchief into one of the pigeon-holes behind him. Room 205.

She shook her head, wanting badly to get out into the fresh air once again. 'No. But I have done my good deed for the day.'

'Indeed you have, Madam.'

She made her way out of the hotel and back out on to the sunny street. The man in the boater tipped his hat at her as she walked back to the fiaker.

Inside the carriage, Erika and Frieda were happily engaged in a game of *schnick, schnack, schnuck*. Frieda had just made the scissors sign with forefinger and middle finger, while Erika's hand was outstretched as paper.

'Oh, you win again,' Erika said.

Berthe got in and took a deep breath.

'You look as if you've seen a ghost,' Erika said. 'What did you discover?'

'They are there. As husband and wife.'

'Registered as Suttner?'

'Worse. As von Tilling.'

Erika looked puzzled.

'More, Tan-tan!' Frieda pleaded.

'Just a moment, love,' Erika said. Then to Berthe, 'Who is von Tilling?'

'It's the name of the protagonist in Frau von Suttner's *Lay Down Your Arms*. This is a double betrayal! How sad.'

PART TWO

TWELVE

She had a bad feeling about this one. He did not smile, did not look her in the eye.

'I was expecting Herr Forstl.'

The man did not respond.

'Did he send you?' She looked around the park. The other walkers had disappeared.

'He was busy,' the man said in German that was curiously devoid of accent. The voice was without any distinguishing characteristics, like a face that has been badly burned.

'Did he send the money with you?' Her eyes darted down the empty pathway. She forced herself to keep calm. After all, it was mid-afternoon in a public park. She had arranged the meeting place with her own safety specifically in mind.

But this man's gray eyes made her shiver. Like his voice, they were totally without expression.

'Herr Forstl regrets to inform you that he cannot meet your conditions.'

There was a momentary twitch of his lips, almost a smile. And though his message enraged her, the lip movement made her relax her guard for just an instant.

It was long enough.

She did not even register his right hand coming up to her face, palm open. The ball of his hand smashed into her nose with enough force to crush bone and cartilage, driving shards into her frontal lobe.

She was dead before she hit the ground.

The emissary bent over her body, quickly putting his forefinger to her carotid artery. Then he made a rapid movement with his right hand, sighed, and stood up straight once again.

Satisfied, he strolled back down the path, past the UNDER

CONSTRUCTION sign he had earlier placed to block the path and keep other pedestrians away.

'You know her?' Detective Inspector Drechsler said.

Werthen nodded.

'Fräulein Fanny,' he said.

Flies buzzed around the corpse's left nostril, feasting on a dried trickle of blood. He averted his eyes.

'An assistant at the Bower,' he added.

Drechsler leaned down on one knee, careful to place a handkerchief under it to avoid soiling his suit. He looked closely at the dead body.

'We'll know better when our friend Todt at the morgue does his work, but I'd say this is the work of a professional. Blow to the nose sending bone to the brain.'

'Why contact me?' Werthen asked.

Drechsler drew an evidence envelope out of his jacket pocket and from it produced a business card. Werthen immediately recognized it as his own.

'She must have taken it from the Bower.'

Drechsler made no reply, replacing the card in the envelope and stuffing it into his pocket once again.

'No other identification on her?' Werthen asked.

Drechsler, again examining the ruined nose, grunted an assent. He wore his usual serge suit, the same clothes summer and winter, and Werthen wondered that he wasn't sweating under the strong morning sun.

The tall, thin inspector stood again, picking up the handkerchief as he did so.

'Professional,' Werthen said. 'As in professional killer?'

'It has the hallmarks. The single blow. The UNDER CONSTRUCTION sign blocking the path. Maintenance says it is not Turkenschanz Park property.'

Werthen's mind raced, trying to think of reasons Fräulein Fanny would be the victim of a professional killer.

'She's a long way from her turf,' Drechsler said.

Werthen agreed. The park, located in the eighteenth district, was quite a distance from the Bower and the First District.

'Makes you wonder what would bring her here,' Drechsler added.

'And when,' Werthen said. But he knew where to find the answer to that question at least.

'Our same man,' Drechsler said in an undertone, as if fearful any of the beat gendarmes at the scene might overhear.

Werthen was not sure he had heard correctly. 'You mean the man that killed Mitzi?'

Drechsler nodded. He looked dyspeptic today.

'I confess, Inspector, that I was considering the same notion. It seems too much of a coincidence that two women from the same bordello should fall victim to murder in such a short time. But, as you well know, prostitution is a dangerous game.' Gross's dictum – 'Never eschew the simple solution, but always follow the evidence' – played through his mind.

'Besides,' Werthen added, 'Mitzi was strangled, whereas Fräulein Fanny suffered a blunt-force trauma.'

'Heel of the hand to the nostril region of the nose, actually,' Drechsler said. 'But it's our man.'

Werthen squinted at the detective. 'Would you care to share, Inspector?'

Drechsler brought out the handkerchief once again, placed it next to the body, then leaned down on one knee. He dragged the dead woman's left hand out from under the body and held it up in the bright sun. Bile caught in Werthen's throat as he looked at it.

'Fellow's a pro, you must give him that. Sliced that left pinkie off just at the base knuckle. Clean as a butcher chopping a joint.'

Werthen sucked in fresh morning air, averting his eyes from the gore of the ruined hand.

Finally he spoke. 'And it was the same finger with Mitzi? That's why you figure it was the same killer? His signature?'

Another grunted assent came from Drechsler as he stood up and folded the handkerchief.

'You kept it from the newspapers, of course.'

'Just like your Doktor Gross advises. We don't want any emulators.'

'Copycats,' Werthen corrected. 'It's from the English. Gross's American colleagues.'

Werthen said this almost as an apology, but Drechsler was not listening.

'Fifth finger, first joint. Same on both women. That's no coincidence. And there was no trace of the finger at the scene. Our man's a collector.'

A sudden chill gripped Werthen, remembering his secretary's mention of 'the keeper of hands'.

*   *   *

'She was here for lunch yesterday,' Siegfried said.

The major-domo looked shaken, his face still bloodless as it was when Werthen told him of Fanny's murder.

'Was she supposed to be working last night?' Drechsler asked.

Siegfried did not look at the detective. Shaking his head, he addressed his response to Werthen.

'Her time of the month.'

'Did she tell anyone she was going out?' Werthen asked.

Siegfried sniffed at this, as if it were unworthy of comment.

Instead, he said, 'Lot of good you've been.'

Werthen bristled at this.

'I was hired to investigate Mitzi's death, not to be a bodyguard to your staff.'

'And you don't think there's a connection between their deaths?'

Werthen and Drechsler exchanged glances at this query.

'There may well be,' Werthen said. 'But one does not wish to jump to conclusions.' No reason to share the information of the harvested fingers.

The door to the sitting room opened and the proprietress entered, her shoulders slumped, eyes red-rimmed. Siegfried had dispatched one of the young women to give her the bad news. It seemed to have taken its toll. Werthen assumed that, with the death of Mitzi, Frau Mutzenbacher had once again bestowed her affection and attention on Fanny. And now they were both dead. What must she be thinking?

'I am not a religious woman,' she said, as if conscious of Werthen's silent question. 'Yet I cannot help but feel it is a kind of judgment.'

It was, in a way, a shocking admission, as if she was condemning her entire life as sinful.

'You wouldn't know who Fräulein Fanny was meeting at the park, would you?' Werthen asked the madam.

She sank into her armchair like a deflated balloon.

She shook her head. 'I cannot believe this is happening again.'

'Which park?' Siegfried asked.

'Turkenschanz,' Drechsler said.

Siegfried glanced at his sister.

'Is there any significance to that?' Drechsler asked.

'There are many parks in Vienna.'

Frau Mutzenbacher was more forthcoming. 'It was once her precinct, shall we say. Before she came to us at the Bower.'

There was a garrison near the park, Werthen remembered. Thus Turkenschanz would offer rich pickings for working girls. Obviously Fanny had chosen the location because she was familiar with it. She was not on the job; she was meeting someone. And she had suggested Turkenschanz Park because she knew it, because she felt safe there. Which implied whoever she was meeting was not necessarily trustworthy. In the event, her fears were sadly confirmed.

It also meant that whoever she met was, as Drechsler indicated, a professional. He had outsmarted Fanny on her home ground.

They would know more about the time of death when Todt got his report in, but Werthen guessed they would find that, concerned for her safety, Fanny had insisted on meeting during daylight hours. This time of year, that could mean up to eight o'clock in the evening.

'Does this change the direction of your investigation, Advokat?'

Like her brother, Frau Mutzenbacher ignored Drechsler, an unwelcome presence.

Realizing little information would be forthcoming while he was there, the inspector stood up.

'I'll confer with you later, Werthen,' he said and stalked out of the room without a good-bye for Frau Mutzenbacher or her brother.

They both watched his progress out of the room, and then turned their eyes on Werthen.

'I had meant to come here today anyway,' he said.

'Is there progress to report?' she asked flatly.

He briefly outlined his investigation to date, noting the roles Altenberg and Schnitzler had played. He also discussed the letter he had found in Mitzi's room and its subsequent translation. Then he hesitated, unsure how to broach the next steps in his investigation.

Aware of his hesitation, Frau Mutzenbacher looked at him firmly.

'Whatever you have learned, Advokat, I have paid for. I have a right to know everything.'

'The letter led me to her parents,' he said, knowing that the statement would hurt. Indeed, she jerked back at the news as if struck.

He explained their ignorance of their daughter's death. Then Werthen came to the priest-uncle and accusations of sexual abuse.

She made an audible gasp and Siegfried pounded his right fist into his left palm. Werthen wondered if he had given too much information.

'An animal,' Frau Mutzenbacher muttered. 'Hypocrite.'

There was silence for a moment.

'And what of the mysterious customer you asked about?' Siegfried finally said. Werthen sensed real interest despite Siegfried's seeming nonchalance.

'We have traced him, as well. One Count Joachim von Ebersdorf of the Foreign Office. He seems to have died only days after Fräulein Mitzi.'

More silence met this announcement.

'So many deaths,' Siegfried said after a few moments.

Werthen nodded, locking eyes with him. Siegfried was the first to break eye contact.

'Perhaps it is time we dispensed with all this,' Frau Mutzenbacher said.

'All this?'

'Your services, I mean,' she said. 'With the death of Fanny, the police are now bound to investigate.'

'You wish to terminate my services?' He could hardly believe his ears.

'I believe my sister made her intent clear.' Siegfried suddenly puffed out his chest.

The sitting room door opened and one of the young women stood there.

'Madam,' she said. 'A visitor. He said he has an appointment.'

Behind her, Felix Salten entered without further introduction.

'Dear Frau, sorry to be late—' he began, and then noticed Werthen.

'Apologies. Have I interrupted?'

'Not at all,' Frau Mutzenbacher said. 'The Herr Advokat was just leaving.'

Then to Werthen: 'You can send me your final bill.'

THIRTEEN

He made his way from the Bower through a tangle of streets in the First District to his lunch meeting with Gross at the outdoor restaurant in the Volksgarten. He was going to be late, but Gross would just have to wait. The shoe had been on the other foot enough times in that regard.

As he walked, he tried to collate a plethora of facts, but what stuck out primarily was what had just transpired at the Bower: he had been sacked. But why?

He meant to find out.

Entering the Volksgarten, he saw the officer from the General Staff whom he had often noticed on his way to work. He was ramrod stiff in demeanor today as always, perhaps even more so. Again, the patent-leather visor of the captain's cap was faultless, glistening in the sun, his high boots resplendently polished, the brass buttons on his green tunic twinkling like little stars. They passed one another on the path to the garden restaurant, but the officer's eyes were fixed straight ahead; a muscle in his jaw twitched, the only sign that he was human and not a moving wax figure or automaton.

Once again, Werthen was struck by the notion that here was a figure out of fiction, here was a fellow that could take center stage in a short story. This was no Lieutenant Gustl out of a Schnitzler play, but a man on a mission.

'Werthen.'

Gross called to him from a table at the rear of the restaurant's terrace, diverting his mind from such ruminations. Werthen tipped his Homburg in recognition, and picked his way through the crowded slalom of tables and diners.

'I thought you'd never get here,' Gross said as Werthen took a seat opposite him at the small table. The bread basket was depleted; flakes of crust, a salt crystal or two, and a scattering of caraway seeds let him know that Gross had not gone unfed while waiting.

'I have the most extraordinary news for you,' said Werthen.

Meanwhile, the General Staff captain Werthen had just seen – having taken an early lunch – made his way into the interior courtyards of the Hofburg, saluted a sentry on duty at the main door to the War Ministry, and then cantered up four flights of broad marble stairs, his boots clacking against the stone. At the top of the stairs another sentry returned a smart salute. Then he took his seat at his desk in the Operations Section of the General Staff's Intelligence Bureau.

Looking through the midday dispatches, Adelbert Forstl used all his strength of will to maintain a calm exterior. Inwardly he was in turmoil: this day might well be the most important in his career, indeed in his entire life. He had come such a long way from his humble origins in Lemberg, the son of a freight clerk for the railway. One of six children, Adelbert knew early on that his only escape from brutal poverty would be a military career. There was no money for

higher education; but because his father Franz had served as a lieutenant in the Austrian army for a decade, Adelbert was eligible for
free entrance to the Cadet School Karnovsky in the center of Lemberg.
And that is where he went when he reached the age of fourteen.

Though Galicia and Lemberg had been under Austrian rule for
over a century, the overwhelming number of citizens were still
Polish speakers, then came Ruthenian, and only about one percent
of the population were true German speakers. After the compromise
Emperor Franz Josef struck with his far-flung territories in 1867,
there was no pretense at all at making German the official language.
Polish, with its harsh gutturals, was the language of commerce and
government in the region. Adelbert, born in 1860, thus grew up
learning a Babel of languages and hating all but German, as he
was an ethnic German and a Catholic. Now, however, he was happy
that he had had such an upbringing; his languages (he had since
learned Russian as well) were in part what had secured him his
present position as Chief of Operations and head of the Russian
desk at the Bureau.

Separated from the empire by the Carpathian Mountains and a
non-Germanic culture, Adelbert had slowly made his way from
junior officer to captain, serving in various outposts of the empire.
Through diligence and good luck, he saw his value rise in the army,
not an easy task for the son of a freight clerk. Now, after twenty
years of hard work, he was delighted to have finally arrived, even
surpassing some of those who had a 'von' before their names. He
was at the very seat of power of the empire – no longer posted to
the fringes but at the heart of things, in the same constellation of
buildings the Emperor called home.

He looked at the pendulum clock on the wall of his small office.
Still fifteen more minutes until his meeting with Colonel von
Krahlich, chief of the Bureau. He needed to get his thoughts in
order – so much rested on the way he presented his case to von
Krahlich. He unlocked the bottom right-hand drawer of his desk,
took out two thick gray-covered files, and placed them on the desk
in front of him. Bombs about to be dropped.

Von Krahlich's adjutant poked his head in the door without
bothering to knock.

'Captain, the Colonel would like to see you now. There's been
an alteration in appointments.'

Forstl was dragged out of his ruminations, annoyed that the
adjutant had not first announced himself.

That was something he would fix later when he was in charge.

'If you don't mind,' the adjutant, Captain Johann von Daum, added with a barely discernable tone of irony.

That was also something Forstl would fix later.

'Not at all,' Forstl said, hiding his pique. 'Now?'

'This moment,' von Daum said.

Forstl straightened his green tunic as he stood up, careful that no evidence of his paunch should show. He picked up the two files from the desk as he left.

Von Krahlich had the largest office on the fourth floor, with tall windows looking out over the parade ground below. Daylight filtered through lace curtains at the windows; the lace was embroidered all over with the Imperial-Royal *K und K* insignia. Von Krahlich, a large, florid man with thick white hair brushed off his forehead, sat at his inlaid rosewood desk enjoying an after-lunch cigar.

'Ah, Forstl, just the man I wanted to see – or who wanted to see me,' von Krahlich said as Forstl and the adjutant entered. This was followed by a mirthless laugh and then the colonel waved away his assistant, laconically returning Forstl's crisp salute.

'Sit, sit,' said von Krahlich insistently as if this were the third time he had offered.

The room smelled of tobacco, leather and the pomade the colonel used. The scent of power; Forstl had longed for that aroma all his life. He sat on the edge of the offered Biedermeier chair, his back held ruler-straight.

'So, settling in are we?'

Although Forstl had already been at the Bureau for six months, von Krahlich still viewed him as a newcomer. Forstl had planned it that way: it gave him the advantage of surprise. Von Krahlich expected little of him; in fact, from Forstl's months there, the Bureau seemed to be a graveyard. Soldiers went there to end their careers, rather than begin them. Forstl had no such intentions. Quite the reverse, in fact.

'Yes, sir.'

'Come to see me about that little love nest at the Hotel Metropole, have you?'

Damn silly action, Forstl thought. A waste of manpower to catch a husband *in flagrante* with his niece, and then use it to blackmail the activist wife into silence. But it was von Krahlich's operation; Forstl inherited it when taking over the section. He had to appear enthusiastic about it.

'Actually, no, sir. That goes according to your excellent plan. I have, in fact, come to see you about an entirely different matter. I feel I've become familiar enough with Operations to offer some suggestions for improvement.'

Von Krahlich, who was appreciating a blue trace of cigar smoke as Forstl said this, cleared his throat at the suggestion.

'Improvements?'

'Yes, sir.'

'We've got a long tradition at the Bureau, Forstl.'

'I know, sir. That is part of the problem, if I may say so, sir.'

The mouse that roared; that was Forstl's tactic. Quiet as a mouse he'd been for the first six months. Now the roar of the bombshell.

Von Krahlich carefully placed the cigar in a cut-glass ashtray. But before he could speak, Forstl charged ahead.

'We're not getting the results we should, sir. I think I can tell you how to change that. And how, in so doing, to bring more honor to the Bureau and to yourself.'

Von Krahlich puffed his cheeks, about to speak, then thought better of it. He motioned with his hand for Forstl to proceed.

'First, we are not gathering information in the way a modern intelligence agency should.'

'Back to the Black Chambers and opening the citizens' mail? Is that what you are suggesting? Gentlemen do not open gentlemen's mail, sir.'

'That is where I come in, sir. I am no gentleman. I am the son of a freight clerk in Lemberg. I have no such restrictions on my actions. I do not have to play by the rules.'

At which von Krahlich let out a blunderbuss of a laugh.

'By damn, son, you do speak plainly.'

Forstl cocked his head at this. 'Half our so-called agents are running paper mills, making up their reports out of thin air. Fabrications, pure and simple, yet we are paying them for it. We have only one successful agent in the field, number 184.'

'The German Intelligence Service,' von Krahlich said.

'Yes. Without their cooperation, we would be sorely pressed to make assessments of potential enemies and their armies.'

'And you suggest?'

'That we reassess our agent lists. As it is now, we have people working for us who are unpaid patriots, spying for the love of country. We have foreign nationals that we pay to pass on information on their country of origin. And we have professionals that we send out from Operations to gather information. We need more of the latter. And we need to train them in the arts of intelligence. This is not and should not be a gentleman's club, sir. At the top, of course. But not those making the day-to-day decisions, such as myself. We should play the game by the modern rules of intelligence and be willing to take public disapprobation if that results from our actions.'

'And where do you suggest we get the funding for such agents, Forstl? Our budget is smaller now than it was a century ago—'

'And the Foreign Office detests us because we threaten their stranglehold on espionage in the empire. Yes, I understand those limiting factors. However, I believe we can turn that around if we have some successes.'

'Such as?'

'We catch some spies. After all, that is part of my mandate as Chief of Operations. Counter-intelligence falls within my purview. I think you may be interested in some files I have been compiling.'

He placed the two gray-covered files on the desk in front of von Krahlich.

Werthen and Gross had partaken of the particularly fine *Wiener Schnitzel* the garden restaurant served; all that remained on Gross's plate were the squashed remains of two lemon wedges. Werthen had been unable to finish his: a chunk of cutlet the shape of Styria remained on his plate. Gross eyed it as he sipped a small strong black coffee, what the Italians – who had just invented it – called an espresso.

Gross absorbed Werthen's news of the murder of Fräulein Fanny almost as if he had expected it to happen. He saved a show of emotion for the fact that Drechsler had kept back the detail of the cut-off finger from the newspapers; this seemed to please him no end.

'Finally,' he said. 'Light in the wilderness. My investigatory principles are taking hold.'

They then proceeded to review the progress of their various cases: Gross's findings at the Foreign Office, Berthe's discoveries regarding the Hotel Metropole and the von Suttner matter, and Werthen's own confrontation with the writer Bahr.

'Spies seem to be figuring rather prominently in our investigations,' said Werthen. He felt like having a cigar; he did not smoke, but suddenly a cigar seemed exactly the right complement to this heavy meal.

'Precisely what I was thinking,' Gross said, setting his small cup down with rather too much gusto, making a loud clanging sound against the tiny spoon on the saucer that drew attention from the next table.

Gross glared back at the middle-aged couple with a stare as dour as a dead carp's. They quickly returned to their strudel.

'Von Ebersdorf, Schnitzler.' Werthen ticked them off on his fingers. 'And let's not forget about the cryptic placement of the unfortunate Fräulein Mitzi's letter in the Bible at *Joshua: 2*. We thought at the time the reference about Rahab the harlot was the important one, that it was meant to signify Fräulein Mitzi. But I have been thinking more about this. The spies saved in the harlot's house might very well refer to von Ebersdorf.'

'Very good, Werthen.'

Gross seemed actually pleased, surprised even, at this feat of memory and deduction on Werthen's part.

It was the note of surprise that rankled.

'I have been known to have an original thought, Gross.'

'No reason to be so touchy. It was meant as a compliment. I was leaning in that direction myself. One wonders if Fräulein Mitzi knew of von Ebersdorf's true profession?'

They both allowed that query to linger for a moment.

Then Gross charged on. 'Nor should we forget the mysterious man in the straw boater your wife encountered yesterday.'

'That's a bit of a leap.'

'I assure you, it is not. Frau von Suttner has proved herself a most irritating thorn in the side of both the military and the Foreign Office with her damnable pacifist sentiments. I am sorry, Werthen, but your good lady wife is not present and that is what I call the Baroness when not forced to be polite. She's a nuisance and a traitor to her class.'

'Your point, Gross?'

'As obvious as the bit of breading on your tie.'

Werthen automatically looked down and brushed the crumb away.

'I am sure both the General Staff and the Foreign Office would like nothing better than to find some juicy scandal involving Baroness von Suttner or her family. A bargaining chip, you might call it.'

'Soften her tone towards the military or face public humiliation?'

'Exactly.' Gross swivelled his coffee cup on its tiny saucer. 'Ergo the watcher of her husband.'

'But in that case, they surely have their ammunition?'

'It would seem so from what your wife reports of the assignation. But that is not our concern. Not our case.'

'Berthe has taken it on in the name of the agency. It is my case just as surely as it is hers.'

'I should rather have said, not our *focus*. Most definitely not, after what you tell me of this second murder. Someone is very intent on covering up something.'

'Not a simple matter of a multiple murderer at large, you mean?'

A heavy nod from Gross. 'Our man is not killing willy-nilly. He has picked his victims carefully, both from the Bower, both confidantes of the madam of that establishment—'

'Frau Mutzenbacher.'

He waved away the name as if it were a gnat. 'Both victims of a killer who leaves a signature.'

'That part of it seems to me to put these murders in the realm of psychopathology,' Werthen said.

'Perhaps our killer wants us to believe so. Or perhaps he needs proof of the deed, needs to keep a tally of sorts.'

Again the thought of Fräulein Metzinger's 'the keeper of hands' ran through his mind.

'We are left to wonder,' Gross continued, 'exactly what is being covered up. A professional killer – one therefore assumes a professional motive.'

'Not necessarily,' Werthen said. 'Professional killers can be hired. Who is to say that the priest, Mitzi's Uncle Hieronymus, did not have a sudden fear of exposure? Perhaps his niece even threatened to expose him and he needed to silence her.'

'And Fräulein Fanny's murder?'

'Perhaps Mitzi shared her secret with Fanny and she was blackmailing Hieronymus.'

Gross raised his eyebrows.

'Or Schnitzler,' Werthen went on. 'He silenced his former lover to keep her from telling his betrothed about their affair. Fanny could have pursued the same scheme of blackmail in that scenario.' But even as he said it, he disbelieved it. Schnitzler's Lothario reputation preceded him: he would hardly kill to protect against something everyone assumed to be true.

'And I assume you could say the same for Altenberg,' Gross said, joining in the game. 'Perhaps he was lying about the platonic relationship he had with Mitzi. The man has a fondness for young girls. Maybe their tête-à-têtes were more about deeds than talk.

Something seriously neurotic. And perhaps Fräulein Mitzi was not the saint-like girl everyone says she was. She threatens to go public with his base desires.'

Remembering the evident grief displayed by Altenberg, Werthen somehow doubted this as well; but it was in the realm of possibility.

'The same could be true for Salten,' Werthen added. 'After all, he was frequently at the Bower for his interviews with Frau Mutzenbacher. Perhaps he also formed an association with Mitzi that he was not proud of? Like Schnitzler, he is engaged to be married.'

'Why stop there?' Gross asked. 'Herr Bahr seems so protective of the image of Jung Wien. Might that be sufficient motive for him to get rid of bothersome young things who threaten his writers' reputations?'

Werthen's head was beginning to spin with the possibilities.

Then after a pause, 'I do not understand Frau Mutzenbacher's reaction to this latest outrage. One would think she would redouble her efforts to find the murderer, having lost two such close . . . friends.'

'That is something we shall ascertain,' said Gross. 'All in good time. It does, however, present a certain difficulty.'

Werthen shrugged at him. 'What?'

'Well, we have no client. Ergo, we have no reason to investigate the deaths of the two young women.'

'I have no client, Gross. You, on the other hand, are the eminent criminologist out to aid and abet the constabulary in their investigations.'

It was said in levity, but Werthen meant it. 'We will not give up on this, Gross. Not until justice is done.'

Leaving the Ministry of War that evening, Captain Forstl exited the Hofburg through the Michaeler Tor and strolled along the fashionable Kohlmarkt. He had changed into a civilian suit that he kept at his office: gray serge with the barest hint of stripe. He did not want to attract attention with his green General Staff tunic.

Forstl stopped in front of Rozet's, the jewellers, seemingly to look at their window display. It was said that the Emperor himself purchased his presents here for Katherina Schratt. Die Schratt, as the Viennese affectionately called her, was the Burgtheater actress who played the role of surrogate wife to Franz Josef both before and after the assassination of his wife, the Empress Elisabeth. Peering in the window, Captain Forstl examined a pearl-encrusted pendant in the shape of a miniature doorway flanked by classical columns in gold and surmounted by a design like a fanlight made of mother of pearl. He momentarily fantasized about buying it for his mother. She had never had a piece of jewelry apart from her silver wedding band. And wouldn't that make the others in Lemberg talk, gossiping about how well Adelbert had done for himself?

Of course, the last thing Captain Forstl needed or wanted was people gossiping about how successful and wealthy he must be. Nor had he any real intention of buying such a bauble for his mother. The gesture would be wasted on her.

In fact, he was not interested in jewelry at all, but was more conscious of the reflections he could see in the window of others on the street who had stopped to gaze into the windows of the fashionable shops. He did not want anybody following him this evening.

Captain Forstl had trained himself well in the covert techniques of tradecraft. He lingered in front of Rozet's a moment longer, and then made his way along the Kohlmarkt to its intersection with Graben. Here it was all bustle and activity, with fiakers carrying passengers, the carriage tops down in the mild evening air, the horses' hooves clopping against the cobbles. Shops were closing and people were heading home or to their favorite café or gasthaus. Handsome women in full-skirted silk dresses carried parasols, though the sun was already slowly setting. Some few younger women wore less formal clothing, dresses that seemed to cling to their bodies. A few of the men on the sidewalks wore boaters, though it was still a month until summer. Forstl wore a more conservative bowler. There was the smell of horse dung, coffee and perfume all mixed together on the Graben: a heady mixture that for Captain Forstl never failed to evoke the metropolis.

Graben soon intersected with Kaertnerstrasse, where he turned right, lingering for a moment in front of Lobmeyr's to inspect the crystal and check once again for any followers. Then he made his way through a warren of small First District lanes, ducking into two different churches and quickly back out again by the same entrance, before he finally emerged on to the broad Ringstrasse at Park Ring. He crossed the thoroughfare and went into the Stadtpark, past the large pond and on to the quiet area around the Schubert Memorial where the meeting was scheduled.

Much simpler than their initial meeting. Then Forstl had been led a merry chase up and down the Vienna Woods at Mödling, following the hand-drawn map of an anonymous correspondent who had sent Forstl a letter threatening to expose him for certain irregularities. And those he had to keep secret at all costs.

That day had been foggy, and Schmidt had appeared suddenly out of the mist as if a phantom materializing in front of Forstl's very eyes. One moment Forstl was alone in the woods, the next he was joined by a specter.

The anonymous letter-writer called himself Schmidt, and spoke to him in German, though Forstl could hear what he thought was a Polish or Baltic accent. A small, compact man with a physiognomy and face that were nondescript, Schmidt could easily blend into any background, any surroundings, and not register in the mind of others.

That was a gift, and Forstl recognized it at once as one of the hallmarks of a true agent. Schmidt was also obviously a master of tradecraft, for he had planned that first meeting perfectly. On the high ground in the Vienna Woods, he could easily follow Forstl's progress to the meeting point, ensuring that he was not being followed and had not brought unwelcome accomplices.

At that first meeting Schmidt, or whatever his real name was, had been brutally blunt: he had proof of Forstl's secret activities. He also knew that Forstl was living far beyond his means and had run up ruinous debts. Unless Forstl cooperated, he would send such evidence to Forstl's superior, von Krahlich, at the Bureau. Cooperation in this case meant obtaining the plans for three Austrian fortresses in Galicia: Cracow, Halicz and Zalesczyki. In return, Schmidt's employers would be happy to remain silent about certain facts and also to begin paying off his debts.

'And just who are your employers?' Forstl had asked.

'I think you know,' Schmidt said.

'The Russians?'

'Naturally.'

'I could make it worth your while to turn that evidence over to me.'

At which point Schmidt emitted a mirthless laugh. 'Captain Forstl, I hope you do not play cards. You could never run an effective bluff. First, I know the miserable state of your finances. And secondly, I am a professional. As such, I would never be stupid enough to double-cross my employers. I want to live to enjoy my retirement.'

That had been five months ago, not long after Forstl's arrival at the General Staff. It had been easy enough to secure the designs for the fortresses, but that, of course had not been the end of it. Rather, it was only the beginning. For then Schmidt had announced the long-term plans of his employers: they would help to build Forstl's career by feeding him low-level Russian spies in Austria that he could capture and prosecute, making him the *wunderkind* of Austrian counter-intelligence. He would become their agent in place.

These recollections were interrupted by a voice from behind him.

'You're sure you weren't followed?'

Forstl swung round to find that Schmidt had, once again, appeared seemingly out of nowhere.

'Jesus! You don't have to sneak up like that.'

'Let's walk. Did you have your meeting?'

Forstl could not help himself; he smiled at the thought of the bombshells he had dropped that afternoon. One of the sacrificial lambs the Russians had supplied was a member of the Austrian Foreign Office who had outlived his usefulness. Mathias Kohl had been in the employ of Russian Espionage Center West, Warsaw, for the past eight years. The Russians cashed in their chips with him, looking for a better man on the inside. A long money trail connected Kohl to his Russian paymasters.

The other, Major Hugo Tallenberg, was a retired Army Officer from the War Ministry. He had never been in the employ of the Russians, but because of his access to War Ministry documents he had been selected by the Russians to take the blame for stealing the plans for the fortresses of Cracow, Halicz, and Zalesczyki.

Colonel von Krahlich's jaw had dropped when he began going through the dossiers on those two men. The Kohl dossier was sure to put the Foreign Office in disrepute, while Tallenberg, though a former member of the War Ministry, was not connected to the Intelligence Bureau of the General Staff. Thus both cases were guaranteed to raise the profile not only of the Bureau, but also of Forstl.

'I had the meeting.' He quickly told Schmidt of von Krahlich's initial reluctance to believe the documents before him, and then his gradual acceptance and understanding of what a coup this could mean for the Bureau.

'He will proceed against them?' Schmidt asked.

'He turned the dossiers over to the State Police and the Ministry of Justice late this afternoon.'

'Excellent. You should be well on your way to promotion. Herr Major would sound well, no?'

Forstl again found himself smiling as he walked along the pathways of the park.

'Yes,' he said.

'And on that other front,' Schmidt continued, 'there will be no fallout. You will, however, in future, seek guidance before striking out on your own like that. Agreed?'

Schmidt reached into his jacket pocket and took out a small leather cigar case. He handed it to Forstl, who shook his head.

'Take it. Add it to your collection. And learn from it.'

Forstl took the case and thrust it into the breast pocket of his jacket. He fervently wished at that moment that he could kill Schmidt. He knew that would not rid him of his problems – there would only be another Schmidt to take his place – but it would feel so good. It was his, Forstl's, personal initiative on 'that other front' that had given the Russians the idea of sacrificing agents in the first place. How was he to know that his agent in place would grow weary of her duties?

'Agreed?' Schmidt said again.

'Yes, yes, of course.'

'Work together and we all prosper,' Schmidt said as they came to a fork in the path.

Forstl said nothing.

'And now for your next assignment.'

'Shouldn't we proceed more slowly? Wait for the conviction of Kohl and Tallenberg?'

Schmidt ignored this. 'They want the mobilization plan for the Imperial and Royal armies in case of war with Russia. You have two weeks. I will be in touch about where to meet.'

Schmidt took the left fork, towards the Ring; Captain Forstl went along the right fork, curling back into the park. The cigar case felt as if it was burning his chest. He feared what was inside it. He should throw it away in the nearest receptacle.

But that was not good tradecraft. Perhaps it would be found; perhaps the purchase of it could be traced to Schmidt.

Finally, reaching a deserted stretch of pathway, he could no longer resist. He pulled the cigar case out of his pocket, took a deep breath and slowly removed the top half of the case. There was nothing to be seen at first; it was empty, a mere bluff on Schmidt's part. But then he saw the white half moon of the tip of a fingernail and felt the bile rise in his throat. He could not help himself: he tipped the case until the entire finger was visible. The slender little finger – of a woman, obviously – cut off precisely at the bottom joint.

He wanted to scream, but stifled the sound in his throat. How had it all come to this?

But Forstl felt a *frisson* of delight, as well. A sly feeling of power: that he could make Schmidt keep such a perverse tally. No, he would not dispose of the finger. He would, as advised, add it to the other present from Schmidt. His little collection.

FOURTEEN

It was Saturday and, cases or no, Werthen was determined to spend time with his family at his country home in Laab im Walde.

The morning dawned with clear skies, and the smell of fresh earth coming through the open bedroom window. Werthen got up early, leaving Berthe and Frieda to sleep in. Donning his lederhosen and a linen shirt, he took a walk around what locals referred to as 'the farm'. The rye grass that Stein – his father's steward at Hohelände – had planted several weeks earlier was shooting up through the black soil: eager green spears of life so fragile-looking yet so hardy. The sight of the grass growing filled him with a sudden pride in his property.

Perhaps a lawn tennis court would not be such a bad idea after all, he thought. Perhaps his parents building nearby would also be less than the disaster he feared.

The warm sun was making an optimist of him. He filled his lungs with morning air, and walked back to the house to prepare breakfast. He was becoming a dab hand in the kitchen with these weekends spent away from the ministrations of Frau Blatschky. A five-minute egg was his specialty; and coffee that was surprisingly drinkable.

Fresh *Semmeln* were waiting, nestled in a gingham napkin in a basket on the doorstep as he came back to the house. He put his hand to the crusts: they were still warm. The local gasthaus at the crossroads delivered the breakfast rolls each morning they were in occupancy.

Life was good, he thought, as he picked up the basket and went inside.

For the next ten minutes he occupied himself so thoroughly with breakfast preparations that he was quite unaware of the arrival of visitors, until an insistent knocking at the kitchen door brought him out of his reverie. He wiped his hands on the apron he loved to wear, a gift from Berthe purchased from the kitchen of the Hotel Imperial.

He opened the door and there stood Gross, cheeks flushed red and bowler in hand. His balding pate glistened in the morning sun.

Gross's discerning eyes went from the lederhosen to the apron, and a wry smile appeared.

'Sorry to interrupt this lovely domestic scene.'

'Good morning to you, too, Gross. What brings you to the countryside? I thought you were allergic to fresh air.'

'Invite me in, Werthen,' he replied. 'I need a cup of coffee.'

Over Gross's shoulder Werthen could see a *pferdelose Kutsche*, horseless carriage, chuffing exhaust in the early morning air.

'Nor did I think you were a fan of modern transport.'

'Coffee, Werthen, please. I will explain.'

They sat at the pine table, both sipping at the coffee. Gross, learning that Werthen had brewed it, eyed it with suspicion, but was soon won over.

'I have a feeling you are going to ruin my weekend,' Werthen finally said.

'It was not my intention. Events, however, outpace us.'

'I thought I heard voices.'

Werthen and Gross turned to see Berthe standing in the doorway between the sitting room and kitchen, wearing a fashionable Japanese kimono as a bathrobe.

'Frau Meisner.' Gross stood and nodded his head at her.

'Please sit, Gross. You haven't come to ruin our weekend, have you?'

Accused twice of the same crime, Gross was human enough to hang his head guiltily.

'I assure you—'

'It's alright, Gross,' Werthen said. Then to Berthe, 'Coffee?'

'Mmm.'

He took this as assent, and filled a cup for her. A sleep wrinkle scarred her left cheek. She yawned as she sat to join them.

'Frieda could sleep through a hurricane,' she said, taking the cup happily. 'Whatever are you doing riding in one of those machines, Gross? The stink woke me up.'

Gross sighed. 'I am simply the messenger, good folk. Please do not kill me.'

'The messenger of what?' Werthen said. 'And how are we outpaced by events, as you say?'

'All will be explained,' Gross said. 'But meanwhile we have been summoned.'

'The weekend, Gross. I will have a weekend with my family.'

'Archdukes do not respect weekends.'

'No.' Berthe said it as if it were an expletive.

'Franz Ferdinand?' Werthen said in wonder.

'The very same.' Gross once again eyed the apron and lederhosen. 'You might want to change for the occasion.'

Their driver turned out to be the loquacious type, which was fine by Werthen, for even though he and Gross sat on the back bench of the open carriage, anything they said could be overheard. Instead, they listened to Private Ferdinand Porsche as he extolled the virtues of the machine carrying them at a brisk pace along the dirt roads of the Vienna Woods towards Vienna.

'She's a beauty of a vehicle, and that's for sure,' the young man enthused. 'What we call a hybrid. Runs on both gas and electricity.'

'Ingenious,' Gross said through tight lips as he held on to the side rail of the bench with a fearful grip.

'The very word, sir,' Porsche said, glancing back at them from time to time, his youthful face made to look older by a wide hussar's moustache. 'She'll do upward of sixty kilometers an hour if I let her loose.'

Which statement made Gross audibly gulp.

'Perhaps we can save the high speeds for the race track,' Werthen advised. 'This is a comfortable pace.'

Werthen soon understood why Gross's cheeks were red when he arrived this morning. Sitting high above the road as they were, the wind played at their faces as they sped along the lanes. A pair of goggles would not go amiss, he thought. They both soon took their hats off, to stop them blowing away.

'I was none too pleased when I got my call-up notice,' Porsche said. 'That's not to say I am not a loyal Austrian, born in Bohemia. "Ferdinand," I said to myself when I saw the notice, "Ferdinand, you're off to the Balkans to some lonely outpost for two years." Instead, I became the chauffeur to the Archduke himself. Quite an honor.'

'It is indeed,' Werthen said, enjoying the young man's enthusiasm. 'Had you much experience with such vehicles?'

This brought a honking laugh from the private. 'Sorry, sir. Not to be rude, but yes, I have a fair amount of experience. I designed this little buggy myself.'

'*You* did?' Gross spluttered.

'The Lohner-Porsche system, it's called. Porsche. That would be yours truly.'

Werthen had, of course, heard of Jacob Lohner, who produced carriages for Franz Joseph as well as various other European royals. Lohner had also begun production of an electric horseless carriage in his Floridsdorf factory. Lohner was naturally the name one remembered. Just as with Martini & Rossi's vermouth. Who ever remembered the Rossi part? Poor Porsche, Werthen thought. Destined to obscurity because his name came second.

'Bravo for you,' Werthen said with gusto, as if to make up for the man's eventual anonymity.

'It's the future, I always say. We are riding into the future.'

Gross, Werthen noticed, closed his eyes briefly at this comment, as if he desired a time machine traveling in the opposite direction.

Before they realized it, they had reached macadamized roads leading to Vienna's fourth district and the Belvedere, where Franz Ferdinand made his office. They had made the Archduke's acquaintance once before, in 1898, when investigating a case that took them to the very doors of the Hofburg, the Habsburg seat of power.

Werthen wondered what the Archduke could have in mind for them this time.

Soon their vehicle pulled into the long circular drive of the Lower Belvedere. Franz Ferdinand, as heir apparent to the Austrian throne, was eager to assume some leadership position and impatient with his uncle, Franz Josef, who seemed to be living for ever; the old man had already been ruling for over half a century. The Archduke had therefore installed at this former palace of Prince Eugene of Savoy what was often referred to as 'the Clandestine Cabinet' – a sort of shadow General Staff, formally known as the Military Chancellery, ready to assume power when his uncle stepped down or died. Thus, he kept his hand in both military and diplomatic matters, often at odds with his uncle and with the General Staff, and always an enemy of the Court Chamberlain, Prince Montenuovo, who protected court etiquette and greatly disapproved of Franz Ferdinand's morganatic marriage to a 'commoner'. The Archduke's wife, Sophie von Chotek, was a mere countess with just sixteen quarterings of major nobility in her blood line, far too few to make an adequate Habsburg match, according to the Court Chamberlain, who himself was the product of a less than appropriate marriage between the Habsburg Archduchess Marie Louise and an officer of her guard. All of Vienna followed this enmity with the eager expectancy of an audience at a Lehar operetta. What new indignity would the Court Chamberlain submit the Archduke and his wife to next? Would Franz Ferdinand ever get his own back on Montenuovo? Thus far, the Archduke had sought revenge simply by spending as much time away from Vienna as he could, ensconced in his Bohemian castle of Konopiste.

A liveried servant awaited them at the columned entrance to the Lower Belvedere. They descended from the horseless carriage, bid adieu to the resourceful Private Porsche, and followed the servant not inside to the Archduke's offices but along the side of the massive building to the gardens. Just as with their first meeting with Franz Ferdinand, they once again met in his rose garden. The Archduke, in addition to being a frustrated heir apparent to Franz Josef's extreme longevity and an ardent hunter, was an enthusiastic gardener; and roses were his specialty.

Just as last time, Franz Ferdinand was at work in the rose beds, in a light-blue cavalry tunic and red breeches. His secateurs snipped at the long-stemmed tea roses while a liveried servant gathered the stems into a basket for bouquets.

Missing today was the array of medals the Archduke had worn last time, Werthen noticed as they approached. He was still amazed at the diminutive size of the man; in photographs he always appeared larger than life.

As they drew nearer, Franz Ferdinand turned to face the pair. His rather bulging oversized bright-blue eyes twinkled as he recognized them.

'Ah, so you have accepted my invitation.'

'One hardly refuses an Archduke, your Imperial and Royal Highness,' Gross said.

A sardonic grin softened the Archduke's features, making his moustache quiver. 'So you know the proper address for a Crown Prince? Court etiquette from a criminalist. Bravo, Doktor Gross. And you, Herr Advokat,' he said, turning his glistening eyes on Werthen. 'None too worse the wear I see for your duel.'

'No, your Highness.'

'An interesting solution to our little problem,' Franz Ferdinand said, referring to Werthen's desperate gambit several years ago.

A tall, lanky figure appeared out of the shadows deeper in the garden.

'Yes, Duncan. Please join us. You two remember my bodyguard, I am sure.'

Both Gross and Werthen nodded.

Duncan had saved their lives more than once in that earlier adventure. The scar down his cheek gave the Scotsman a ferocious appearance, though in actuality it was merely the result of a terrier bite and the subsequent ministrations of an incompetent surgeon when he was a boy.

'Gentlemen,' Duncan said, tipping his hat to them. He managed to place a thick glottal stop into the English word, imbuing it with a heavy Scots accent, which reminded Werthen that Duncan came into the Archduke's service after saving Franz Ferdinand's life on a Highland hunting expedition.

'I never had a chance to thank you for your service,' Werthen said.

'No need to mention it, sir,' the wraith-like Scot responded.

'But to business,' Franz Ferdinand said, handing the secateurs to a servant, who departed, leaving the four of them alone in the garden.

Franz Ferdinand waited until the servant was well out of earshot. He cleared his throat. 'Feels like rain.'

The sky overhead was still radiantly blue.

'The weather can be changeable this time of year, your Highness,' Gross replied. There was, however, a sarcastic edge to his voice that did not escape the Archduke.

Franz Ferdinand smiled again. 'Yes, quite right. I should get to the matter at hand. After all, it is the sacred weekend, is it not? I understand that the populace has grown quite fond of its weekends. Leisure time, I believe it is called. I shall soon return you to your weekend, never fear. But, as with the last time we met, I have information that you might want.'

Which meant, Werthen translated, the Archduke wanted to use them to do some of his own dirty work.

'I understand that you are looking into the death of the unfortunate Count Joachim von Ebersdorf.'

'That we are,' Gross said.

'May I inquire why?'

Both Gross and Werthen paused a moment, glancing at one another.

'Is it such a great secret?' Franz Ferdinand asked.

'His death pertains to inquiries we are making, your Highness,' Gross said.

'That is self-evident. What inquiries?'

'The death of a young . . . woman.' Gross was obviously searching for a euphemism appropriate to an archduke's sensibilities. 'Of a certain persuasion.'

'You mean a tart,' Franz Ferdinand said bluntly.

Werthen continued to let Gross take the lead; he enjoyed seeing the great man stumble.

'Yes,' said Gross, as if confessing to a crime.

'Should I surmise that the connection between Joachim and this girl was of a professional sort?'

The Archduke's use of the Count's Christian name did not go unobserved by either Werthen or Gross.

'That would be a sound surmise, your Highness.'

Franz Ferdinand sighed, returning to his roses for a moment and gently cupping an elegant bud as one might lovingly lift the head of an infant.

Turning back to them, he said, 'The death was reported as natural. Why do you suspect foul play?'

Gross had regained his equilibrium, and puffed out his chest as he replied. 'I find it quite curious, your Highness, that no one else at the banquet was afflicted by this tainted shellfish. I also question the propinquity of events. The Count died just days after the murder of the young woman in question.'

'Propinquity and causality are two quite distinct things, Doktor Gross.'

Gross thumped his sternum, a most uncharacteristic thing for him to do.

'I feel it. Here. The result of decades of working with murder and mayhem. One has an instinctive sense of these things, your Highness.'

It was a surprisingly impassioned speech for Gross, Werthen thought. This case was affecting them both in a most personal way.

'If I may,' Werthen said. 'There is a straightforward way to determine this.'

'Exhumation,' Gross added.

'Was there no autopsy done at the time of death?'

'None,' Gross said. 'The medical chaps took it as a clear case of food poisoning from tainted shellfish. Arsenic poisoning exactly mimics acute gastroenteritis.'

'But it's been what – a month?'

'Three weeks, your Highness,' Gross said. 'Count von Ebersdorf died three weeks ago today. Because arsenic is a metallic poison, it can be detected in the body even years after death. There is a test—'

'Yes, the Marsh test,' the Archduke said, amazing them both. 'A method for converting arsenic in body tissues and fluids into arsine gas. I had my suspicions, as well, you see.'

Franz Ferdinand paused to consider this information. As with the first time he was in the presence of the Archduke, Werthen was impressed with the difference between the man's mannered, thoughtful behavior and his reputation for bellicosity and posturing. Those at Court who did not like him, Prince Montenuovo foremost among them, had done their work well, filling the press and the people's imagination with a caricature ogre of a man, a slaughterer of animals and a warmonger to boot. Werthen saw no traces of such characteristics, mostly left behind in the Archduke's youth.

'I sense the Count was a personal friend,' Gross said, interrupting the Archduke's ruminations. 'I assure you, I do not make these assertions lightly.'

'I wish to spare his family unnecessary distress.'

'I am sure you also wish them to see justice done.'

'The young woman . . .'

Again, Werthen spoke up. 'This can be handled delicately.' But he knew such a promise was impossible to keep; once an investigation was initiated, there was no controlling the direction it would take. One thing only was certain: the Count was not Fräulein Mitzi's killer. He was long dead by the time of Fräulein Fanny's death, and it was abundantly clear that both deaths were by the same hand.

'I sh-shall see about permission for exhumation,' Franz Ferdinand finally said.

The Archduke was clearly moved, Werthen could see, even reverting to the stuttering of his youth, a condition that he had largely cured, along with tuberculosis, as a young man during the course of an around-the-world voyage.

'You say you had suspicions of foul play, your Highness,' Gross said. 'May I ask why?'

'Of course,' the Archduke said, seeming to find cheer now that a decision had been made. 'That is part of why I brought you here today.

You of course know that our empire is protected by two intelligence services, one military and one, shall we say, civilian.'

Werthen and Gross nodded.

'One would hope that such services would cooperate with one another, would act in the best interests of the country. Unfortunately, that is not always the case. Petty jealousies and feuds intrude.'

'You mean,' Gross said, 'there is a battle for primacy between the General Staff's Intelligence Bureau and the Foreign Office.'

'Precisely,' Franz Ferdinand said. 'Only, the Foreign Office officially has no such agency.'

'A deadly battle?' Werthen asked.

'I was hoping you gentlemen could answer that question. If, as you suspect, Joachim was poisoned, then I hope you will follow all possible avenues of inquiry.'

The Archduke's response sent a chill down Werthen's back. It was one thing to jockey for position and pride of place, but quite another to kill a member of the opposing side and fellow countryman simply out of interagency pique. Treason might not be too harsh a word to describe such actions.

'I shall once again provide quiet support,' Franz Ferdinand said, nodding toward the stoically silent bodyguard, Duncan. 'But you of course understand that such an investigation is not without risk to those asking the questions.'

Neither Werthen nor Gross spoke for a moment.

'I would quite understand if you refused such a commission. In which case, this conversation never took place.'

'But of course we accept—' Gross began.

'I need to consider this,' Werthen said quickly, interrupting him.

'Sensible of you, to be sure,' Franz Ferdinand said. 'With a child and wife, a man has responsibilities. Perhaps you wish to discuss it with Frau Meisner first. I would do the same with my wife.'

Franz Ferdinand's knowledge of his private life did not surprise Werthen. Indeed, there was most probably a third intelligence network at work in Austria that the Archduke did not mention: his own.

'I will have my driver return you to your respective abodes. Shall we say Monday, then? That should give you sufficient time to make an informed decision. At that point we can discuss your fee.'

'Fine,' Gross muttered, obviously displeased at Werthen's delay.

'Yes, most obliging, your Highness,' Werthen said.

As they were about to take their leave, Franz Ferdinand fixed them again with his startlingly blue eyes.

'As a sign of trust, I would like to pass on certain information. I am sure it will go no further.'

'Yes?' Werthen said.

'It concerns your wife, Herr Advokat. It comes to my attention that she has been keeping watch on one Baron Arthur Gundaccar von Suttner.'

Werthen felt a sudden protective heat at this and blurted out, 'And just how has this come to your attention?'

Werthen's sharp tone made Duncan stir.

'Do not misunderstand me, Advokat Werthen. This is not some sort of veiled threat. Rather it is offered more in the hope of reciprocity, tit for possible tat. I know what your wife and her young friend – I believe she is your legal secretary? – are doing because, as I understand it, our intelligence service is also thus engaged.'

Just as Gross had surmised, Werthen thought.

'Baroness von Suttner is a client,' Werthen said flatly.

Franz Ferdinand raised his eyebrows. 'And has engaged you to investigate her husband?'

'That is privileged information, your Highness.'

'Werthen,' Gross began, 'perhaps—'

'No, your colleague is correct, Doktor Gross. Private Inquiries is the business you are engaged in, and such inquiries should remain private.'

'Are you warning us off von Suttner?' Werthen said, tired now of *politesse*.

'Not at all. I simply supply this information. You do with it as you see fit.'

'Is Frau von Suttner such a threat to the empire?'

'Pacifism is a powerful message. For my part, I rather like it that she organizes for peace, that there is a voice against the rush to war. But there are others who are not quite so broad-minded.'

'Thank you for this information, your Highness. It confirms what we already suspected. You might also tell whichever intelligence service is at work that their man needs a refresher course in tradecraft. My wife spotted him within ten minutes.'

'What do you make of that?' Gross said, as they climbed on to the passenger bench of the Archduke's horseless carriage.

But Private Porsche then joined them and there was no further chance for discussion.

'Where to first, gentlemen?' the driver asked.

'You had best come to the country house for the weekend,' Werthen said. 'We need to talk things over.'

Gross did not demur at this invitation. After stopping briefly at Gross's hotel, where he packed a valise, Porsche drove them, mostly in silence, back to Laab im Walde.

En route, Werthen had time to mull over their meeting with Franz Ferdinand. It was apparent to Werthen that the Archduke had a special relationship with the Foreign Office, or at least with Gross's old schoolmate, Minister Brockhurst. It was obviously Brockhurst who let Franz Ferdinand know about their investigation of von Ebersdorf's death. But it also appeared that Brockhurst was perhaps prudishly less than forthcoming about the reason for their interest: Werthen did not think Franz Ferdinand was feigning surprise when he learned that Fräulein Mitzi was a prostitute.

'Beautiful countryside,' the private said once they reached the farm. 'I intend to buy myself such a place once I have made my first million.'

Standing in the drive, Gross clucked disapprovingly as Porsche put the motorcar into gear and sped off back down the country lane.

'Jumped-up carriage driver,' he muttered.

'Ambition, Gross. The mainspring of the new century. I'd put my money on that private making a million.'

Another plosive sound of disgust from Gross.

They were not able to discuss matters until Frieda had been put to sleep at eight that evening, complaining that it was still light outside and time to play. The complaints were short-lived.

Now they were gathered at the dining table.

'Why would he tell you that?' Berthe said, for out of all the startling information imparted by Franz Ferdinand, she had fixed on his revelation that Frau von Suttner was being watched.

'He made it fairly clear,' Werthen said. He poured himself a measure of slivowitz and offered the bottle to Berthe and Gross, both of whom declined. 'It was a sort of fair exchange. He hopes we take the von Ebersdorf matter forward.'

'Well, hadn't you planned to anyway?'

'On a practical level,' Werthen said, 'we have no reason to. After all, Frau Mutzenbacher has dispensed with our services, and the death of von Ebersdorf was important to us only as it might or might not be connected with that of Fräulein Mitzi.' He paused, and added, 'Also, we were unaware of certain facts before – such as the possible involvement of feuding intelligence agencies.'

'Such an investigation can be dangerous,' said Gross, 'just as the Archduke implied.'

During the course of the day Gross had obviously given some thought to the matter and now saw it somewhat more from Werthen's point of view and the need to protect his wife and child. It pleased Werthen to see his old friend taking others into consideration and he cast him a warm smile.

'After all,' Gross added, 'my good lady wife, Adele, must be consulted. She relies on me. I must think of my safety as it affects her.'

Werthen's smile disappeared. 'How good of you, Gross,' he said with a sarcastic edge that made Berthe raise her eyebrows.

'Are you holding back from taking the Archduke's commission on my account?' asked Berthe.

'Yes, of course I am. And Frieda's. She hasn't asked to be involved in such matters.'

'So,' Berthe said, stiffening her back, 'if von Ebersdorf actually was poisoned and the Intelligence Bureau of the General Staff was responsible for it, they would not like people nosing around making accusations, is that the theory?'

'In a nutshell,' Werthen said. 'Though we cannot be sure it was the Intelligence Bureau at work.'

'It stands to reason,' she said. 'If there are internecine battles, that means the Foreign Office is pitted against the General Staff. Von Ebersdorf worked for the Foreign Office, ergo—'

'Ergo nothing,' Werthen interrupted. 'It could just as easily be some competitor in the Foreign Office eager for advancement.'

'Then we give ourselves insurance,' she said, 'just as we did in the Grunenthal case.'

She was referring to Werthen's first case involving those close to the Emperor. In that instance, Werthen had let it be known that the information he gathered was waiting to be sent off to the foreign press in case anything untoward happened to him.

'They may very well decide to strike before we have damning proof,' Gross said.

Which comment brought a pall of silence over the table, punctuated only by the ticking of the pendulum wall clock. During this pause, Werthen recalled how that first case had put Berthe into deadly danger. How could he do the same again?

Berthe finally broke the silence. 'But what if it really was just a case of bad shellfish? Aren't we getting ahead of ourselves? First the exhumation and autopsy, and then the wringing of hands.'

Another moment of silence.

'I for one say we proceed,' she added. 'I know that I am going to go ahead with Frau von Suttner's investigation. And Karl, you know that you are not going to give up investigating the death of that poor young girl. Not after what you have found out. Not after visiting her family.'

Werthen felt a surge of pride in his wife, a warmth that engulfed him and made him want to embrace her.

'Most persuasive, Frau Meisner,' said Gross. 'I shall let you put the case to my dear wife, as well. And indeed, you are right. Though my instincts tell me otherwise, von Ebersdorf's death may turn out to be from natural causes.'

'And even if it is not,' Werthen added, in turn infected by Berthe's fighting spirit, 'who is to say that these deaths involve the intelligence agencies or even that they are connected? We still have a basket full of suspects who need vetting.'

'That's my man,' Berthe said.

'One concession,' Werthen said.

Berthe nodded. 'Yes, I know. Next time I shall leave Frieda with Frau Blatschky.'

They lay in bed later, haunches touching through their thin linen night apparel. She placed her head on his shoulder, threading her finger through the neck opening of his nightshirt and teasing the few hairs on his chest. The steady thrum of Gross's snores rattled through the house from the distant guest room.

'I'm awfully proud of you,' Werthen said.

She placed a forefinger on his lips.

'But I am,' he insisted.

'And I am proud of you – we're a proud family, and by the sound of the good Doktor's snores we could be a pride of lions.'

'Just how do you intend to proceed with the von Suttner matter?' he finally asked. 'It would seem you have accomplished what you set out to do.'

'I haven't notified her yet.'

'Are you going to warn her?'

She breathed in and then let out a warm sigh of breath on his chest.

'If you reported the conversation correctly, the Archduke requested that his information go no further.'

'But I've already told you—'

'That was before you decided to take him on as a client. Now it seems we have an ethical conundrum – clients with competing needs.'

'I didn't know I married a philosopher.'

'It must be my father's Talmudic influence at work.'

'I don't think we need to let that worry us too much,' Werthen said. 'After all, Franz Ferdinand also said he appreciates her work.'

'Amazing that he of all people should think so!'

They said nothing for a time.

'Well?'

She ignored this for a moment, then sighed again. 'I will deal with it – though it may take some thought.'

'She is the client. She has a right to know about her husband.'

FIFTEEN

The 7:00 a.m. train left the Nordbahnhof five minutes late. He was not overly concerned with such things today. A Sunday. The family would be at home all day.

He was a traveling salesman for the Viennese cologne-maker Heisl today. He carried a case with the brand name blazoned on the side in white lettering to prove it. Sunday was an odd day for a traveling salesmen to be doing his rounds; but he was also Jewish, for today.

In Vienna he was Schmidt, representative of the Heisl Parfumerie; in Berlin he was Erlanger, the rail engineer from Budapest; in Warsaw he was de Koenig, the agent of a Dutch mining concern; in Zurich he was Axel Wouters, rubber merchant; and in Prague he was Maarkovsky, an importer of Polish vodka. He had posed as policeman, actor, wine grower and noble. Sometimes he had diffi-culty remembering his true identity: Pietr Klavan, an Estonian who at one time had prospects of a career as a concert violinist. But that, he reflected, was so long ago . . .

Schmidt was a cautious man, a man who did not like loose ends dangling. Loose ends could unravel an entire operation; and they could cost a man of many identities his life.

The train followed the course of the Danube at first, and then traversed flat farmland. Schmidt stared out of the window at the fields of spring wheat, and orchards in full bloom.

He was not sure what he expected from this trip; he knew only that he needed to see for himself. Schmidt was not merely a chameleon: he also possessed an uncanny ability to see into and through people, to instinctively read their emotions and fears. These were skills that had made him an invaluable asset to Russian Army Intelligence. These and certain other talents with his bare hands, and with knives and pistols.

A compact man, he took up not two-thirds of the window seat; the rest of the third-class compartment was empty. Later in the morning, after church services, there would be far more traffic. That was one reason for his early start: Schmidt liked to be alone with his thoughts.

Soon the train entered rolling hills striped with vineyards. They pulled into the station of Hollabrunn, and a family got on to the train, entering his compartment with eager energy that made him purse his lips and focus more diligently on the view out of the window. But he was processing all the time. Schmidt was never simply around other people: he analysed them, dissected them, searched for fault lines.

A farmer and his wife, dressed in Sunday best by the looks of them. Two gangly boys in knee pants, smelling of hay and incense. Just out of church, he registered. An infant in the red-cheeked wife's arms. The man was carrying a basket covered over with a blue-and-white checked cloth. Off to the grandmother's for Sunday lunch, bearing what? No yeasty smell of baking. More likely the freshly slaughtered Sunday chicken.

The boys began squirming on the wooden bench opposite him. One was pinching the other. The father barked a command in a strong local dialect that Schmidt barely made out to mean 'Enough!' and the boys sat still once again. The older one, the one initiating the tickling, turned his attention to Schmidt, but tried to act as if he was gazing about the compartment or out of the window as he glanced at the valise in the overhead rack and examined Schmidt's reflection in the window.

All so obvious, Schmidt thought. He would kill the father first, of course. This was a game he played, a game of survival when around strangers. A blow to the thorax should do it. He smiled to himself: most would go for the older boy next, but he was not most. It was the wife second, for her full-throated screams would prove more of a threat to him than anything the adolescent boy could muster. A quick twist to break her neck. Then the older, curious boy.

He would use a knife for him and his younger brother. Which left the baby. It would be crying by then. And that meant . . .

But these thoughts were interrupted as the train pulled into the small station of Haugsdorf, his destination.

As the engine lurched to a stop, Schmidt stood, removed his hat and valise from the overhead rack, and nodded at the family as he left the compartment.

They had provided a few moments of amusement.

The day was beginning to heat up as he descended from the train to the platform of the tiny station. Only one person on the platform, a tall stick of a man who wore a station master's uniform too short at the wrists. He waved the train on.

Schmidt waited for him to finish his duties.

'Don't suppose there would be a trap for hire to Buchberg?'

The man looked at him queerly for a moment as if he did not understand German. Schmidt was about to rephrase the request when the man said in a thick country accent, 'Two in one week. Don't tell me you want to visit Jakob Moos, too?'

The trap jogged along the rutted dirt track, the sun growing higher in the sky. Schmidt was in luck, for the station master – Platt was his name – could be hired for several hours. On Sundays train traffic was light, so he could take Schmidt on his 'rounds' and drive him back to the station. Happily, Platt demonstrated little curiosity about a perfume salesman making the rounds of rural Weinviertel on a Sunday. Who could account for the ways of big-city people?

Instead, he unwittingly filled Schmidt in on the latest tragedy to befall Jakob Moos.

'We all said it would come to no good when she left. But Jakob always knows better. Sent her off to play housekeeper to her uncle and see what's happened.'

Schmidt waited an instant. Then asked, 'What did happen?'

'Murder, that's what the man who brought the news said.'

Schmidt's antennae instantly lifted. 'A policeman?'

Platt shook his head. 'No, a fancy one from the city like yourself.'

'But I'm a simple country man, actually,' Schmidt said, putting on an ingratiating voice now. 'Like yourself. Grew up on a farm and hope to get back to it once I've saved enough money.'

It seemed his fabrication was wasted on Platt, for the man ignored the comment and continued from where he left off.

'Come from the city just like you and asked for transport to Buchberg. Come for the Moos family.'

'Well, actually,' Schmidt said, 'I've never heard of the Moos family. But my superiors want me to introduce our new product line to citizens of the region.'

'Not a lot of use for such fancies out here, I can tell you that.'

Platt went silent, tssking at his horse from time to time.

'And the city man?' Schmidt finally prompted.

'Comes with the bad news and leaves right after. Frau Moos took it bad. Jakob, too, but he won't let on. Says the working classes are always the victims.'

Schmidt filed this bit of information away.

'Man's an investigator, I hear,' Platt added. 'One of those private inquiry agents you read about. As if the constabulary isn't enough. Some fancy city fellow has to stick his nose into it, too.'

'Do they know who killed the poor young woman?'

'No. Just that some big writer fellow in Vienna is paying for this agent. What a world we live in. I'll never leave Haugsdorf, I can tell you that. And if I had children, they would never set foot outside neither.'

As they approached the small hamlet of Buchberg, Schmidt could see a scattering of low farm houses, their white plastered walls glistening under the strong sun.

'Where to first?' Platt asked.

'You know, I've been thinking,' Schmidt said. 'My heart goes out to that family that lost their daughter. Maybe it would cheer the wife up if I left some samples for her.'

'Your funeral,' Platt muttered.

He directed the trap to a distant homestead on the north side of the village with a slate-roofed house and whitewashed exterior walls. Schmidt noted the geraniums in pots already in bloom in the low recessed windows. Showed care, he noted. Somebody tending the flowers indoors during the winter to get a bit of color in the spring. A good-luck sheaf of wheat hung over the door. A woman's touch.

Schmidt descended from the trap, sample bag in hand, and knocked on the front door. There was a shuffling of feet inside and it was opened by a young girl with rosy cheeks.

'What do you want?'

'I wonder if I might speak with the lady of the house?' He looked beyond the girl and saw a plump woman seated at the kitchen table, with two other young girls gathered about her. The woman's eyes were rimmed in red. Her face was haggard as if she had not slept in days.

'Good day to you, Madam,' Schmidt said in his most pleasing voice.

'Mother is sick,' the rosy-cheeked girl said.

'That is a pity,' he said, stepping around the girl and coming into the room uninvited. 'Because I have some samples in my case sure to cheer up the darkest day. Perhaps I could just leave them here . . .'

'Mother does not want to talk with anyone,' the girl at the door said.

But he hoisted his case on to the table, opened it, and pulled out several sample bottles of cheap perfume.

'And something for the young ones, as well,' he said, as he surveyed the room and quickly searched his own mind for some gambit by which he could trick information out of the family and learn something of this mysterious visitor who had brought news of the daughter's death.

His false cheer succeeded only in making the woman cry harder.

He heard footsteps behind him.

'What's going on here?'

Schmidt turned to see the man of the house standing at the door, looking like an enraged bear.

'Who are you and what are you doing here?'

Schmidt's eyes continued to scour the room for clues. And then he saw it: a professional card sitting on the shelf of a cupboard by the door.

'Just giving the ladies some samples, sir,' Schmidt said. 'A nice bit of perfume.'

'We don't use such things in this house,' Moos thundered. 'Now get out of here before I throw you out.'

'But of course. My apologies. Just trying to do my job.' He hurriedly put the bottles back in the case, and closed and latched it. Then made sure to sidestep Moos to the right, so he came close to the cupboard as he departed.

He paused for a moment at the door and tipped his hat. 'Good day to you, then.'

'Out of here!' Moos barked.

The door slammed behind him.

Schmidt made his way to the trap. As he walked, he fixed the information from the card in his memory: *Advokat Karl Werthen, Wills and Trusts, Criminal Law and Private Inquiries.*

'Told you so,' the dour Platt said as Schmidt regained his seat on the trap.

'Just trying to be a good Christian,' Schmidt said.

At which comment Platt flicked the reins and set the old horse on its way.

SIXTEEN

Werthen again made his way on foot to Frankgasse. The morning was beautiful and clear, a sweet scent of lilac in the air. Werthen was happy to be back in Vienna after the weekend cooped up at the farm with Gross, who had insisted on going over and over the accumulated evidence, completely destroying any sense of calm the countryside could impart. It was a relief to be strolling the cobbled streets again, hearing the clop of horses' hooves. Even the occasional growl of a motorcar was like a blessing to him now.

They had neatly apportioned their separate tasks this morning: Gross to confer with Franz Ferdinand, Berthe to begin her plan *vis-à-vis* Baroness von Suttner, and he, Werthen, to visit another neglected client, Arthur Schnitzler.

The house door was open at Frankgasse 1, and he went up the stairs to the apartment. Having telephoned in advance, he was expected by Prokop and Meier, who greeted him with more than usual *bonhomie*.

'At long last, Herr Advokat,' Prokop said as he reached the landing. He took Werthen's hand and shook it mightily.

'We are glad to see you,' he said, continuing to pump his arm. 'Didn't I just say that the other day, Meier? How good it would be to see the Herr Advokat again?'

Meier grunted something unintelligible that passed for agreement.

'What is it you want, Herr Prokop?' Werthen said, finally retrieving his hand.

Prokop put a hand dramatically over his heart as if pained.

'Ah, Herr Advokat, you misunderstand. I—'

'We want another job,' Meier interrupted.

Prokop glared at his burly partner.

'Is Herr Schnitzler dispensing with your services, then?'

Prokop shook his head violently at the suggestion. 'No. Not that. But it is more than a man can tolerate sometimes, Herr Advokat. Between the fiancée and Schnitzler, we're turning into bloody servants. It started off innocent enough, like. Just get a housecoat here, if you please, Prokop, or perhaps fetch a cup of tea there. But the here and there add up, they do. Soon enough they've got me running errands for them at the butcher's, taking a dress coat to the tailor's.'

'Go on,' Meier said. 'Tell him or I will.'

Prokop again shot Meier a withering look, his lips locked.

'Flowers!' Meier said. 'This morning it was the flower shop for Prokop.'

He let out a snort that sounded awfully like a bull breaking wind.

Prokop squared his shoulders, finally finding his voice again. 'We're strong-arm men, Advokat. Not liveried servants.'

'Well, just tell Schnitzler that.'

Prokop sighed. 'It's the fiancée. Fräulein Gussman. She's the real terror.'

'It can't be that bad,' Werthen said, stifling a laugh.

'She's got a tongue on her sharp as a razor.'

'Roses!' Meier said.

The vision of Prokop in greasy bowler and tattered jacket carrying a bouquet of roses was too much for Werthen, who had to cough into his hand to hide his amusement.

'Not funny, Advokat. And we are asking – no, begging you – to find another situation for us. You know what we do best. We're a trustworthy team. Just no cups of tea or bloody flowers!'

'I'll see what I can do, gentlemen. Perhaps a word in Schnitzler's ear?'

'You know best, Advokat,' Prokop said, opening the door for him officiously like a head butler. 'They are expecting you.'

'They?'

Prokop shrugged, ushering Werthen into the flat.

A small greeting party was awaiting him. Schnitzler himself was no longer bed-ridden, dressed today in frock coat and tie, the bandage still on his head. He stood uneasily in the hallway. Accompanying him were Altenberg and Salten.

'What news, Advokat?' Schnitzler asked by way of greeting.

'Good day to you, as well. A conference, is it?'

'Salten brings us news from the Bower,' Schnitzler said. 'But I'm forgetting my manners. Let me take your hat. I instructed Herr

Prokop on the proper etiquette for announcing visitors, but the man is rather slow on the uptake.'

'He's a bodyguard, Schnitzler, not a footman,' Werthen replied almost testily, removing his hat, but seeing no outstretched hand to relieve him of it, continued clutching it himself.

'To be sure,' Schnitzler replied, as if not hearing the criticism.

'They are quite a pair,' Altenberg said, eyes twinkling. 'Surprising that Klimt should know them.'

'Klimt is full of surprises,' Werthen said.

'Shall we?' Schnitzler waved an arm towards the sitting room and to a group of chairs around a low cherry-wood table. Werthen was left to dispose of his hat on a side table as the others sank into their chairs.

Werthen joined them and three pairs of eyes fixed on him.

'News from the Bower?' Werthen said. 'I assume that would be the murder of the unfortunate Fräulein Fanny.'

'Such a trusted helper for Frau Mutzenbacher,' Salten said. 'She is devastated. First Mitzi and now Fanny. I am not sure she will recover.'

'She was rather distraught,' Werthen allowed.

Altenberg took a soiled handkerchief out of his jacket pocket and blew his nose. Even the mention of Mitzi's name seemed to afflict him. He daubed a corner of the graying linen at his eyes.

'I expect you see a connection between the two murders?' Schnitzler said.

'What I see or do not see is no longer relevant, gentlemen. I am sure Herr Salten apprised you of the fact that I am no longer employed by Frau Mutzenbacher. This is now a police investigation.'

'Frau Mutzenbacher had mentioned as much, yes,' Salten added.

'Where will it stop?' Altenberg suddenly said, his voice breaking. 'Are we to be the next victims? Look at poor Schnitzler. Perhaps whoever beat him is also responsible for these heinous crimes. Perhaps whoever it is will attack me next.'

'I find that rather doubtful, Herr Altenberg,' Werthen said.

'Exactly what we have been telling him,' added Salten. Then to Altenberg, 'Peter, it is quite alright. It's the poor women who are the victims here, not the customers.'

Werthen thought of von Ebersdorf and wondered how accurate such an explanation was.

'But you surely will not leave it at that?' asked Schnitzler.

'As I said, Herr Schnitzler, it is now a police matter. On the other hand, I do have news for you regarding your assailant. My colleague, Doktor Gross, has ascertained from a person of some position at the Foreign Office that there is nothing to fear from that quarter or from the military. Whoever attacked you must be a private individual with a private grudge. We are still making inquiries on your behalf – but for now, rest assured that the injuries you suffered were not ordered by any arm of the government. Indeed, I might recommend that you lodge a formal complaint with the police. A man of your prominence, I am sure they will take the matter seriously.'

Silence greeted this report. Werthen cleared his throat.

'And now I must excuse myself. Monday is a busy day for me.'

'It won't do, you know,' Schnitzler finally said. 'I appreciate what you have done, Herr Advokat, but there is more to this than meets the eye. If you will not proceed with the investigation, then there is nothing left for us but to carry on ourselves.'

'By carry on, do you mean investigate these murders?'

'Yes.'

'The three of you?'

'We have been considering the possibility,' Salten said.

'Well, then I wish you good luck, gentlemen.'

Which comment deflated the trio. Their bluff had been called.

'But do not muddy things for the police. They take a rather dim view of amateurs, I can assure you.' Werthen stood. 'I really must apologize for making this so brief.' Then to Schnitzler, 'I will keep you informed as to any progress.'

'Had you thought of Mitzi's uncle, the priest?' Schnitzler suddenly let out. 'He had something to hide.'

'It's an area the police will investigate, I am sure.'

'And what of this Count von Ebersdorf that Frau Mutzenbacher mentions?' Salten said eagerly. 'His death seems an extraordinary coincidence.'

'Who will be next?' Altenberg moaned.

'I think you should all take three deep breaths, gentlemen.'

He left before they had a chance to present more theories.

Out on the street, Werthen headed back towards his office, once again on foot, enjoying the freshness of the day.

He did not notice the small, compact man who stepped out of a doorway to follow him.

Back at the Werthen flat on Josefstädterstrasse, Berthe was serving *Jause,* a mid-morning snack. Gustav Klimt, Berthe's guest, had already breakfasted heartily on his usual fare at the Café Tivoli: pots of strong coffee laced with hot chocolate and creamy white peaks of *Schlag Obers*, along with fresh rolls piled with mounds of butter and jam. His ten-kilometer circuit walking to the café and then back to his studio began at six o'clock sharp and usually left him with a ravenous appetite by ten. He greedily tucked into the selection of sliced wurst, liver pâté, cheese and rolls, supplemented by a pitcher of Styrian pilsner just fetched by Frau Blatschky from the Golden Cuckoo gasthaus at the corner. With the warm weather, the artist had returned to his usual fair-weather costume of caftan and sandals. The material of the caftan was, Berthe thought, exquisite – obviously designed by his mistress, Emilie Flöge. She had managed to bring Klimt's palette to the silk brocade.

Klimt remained silent as he tucked into the repast, punctuating it with large draughts of beer. He wiped his mouth on the swirling gold design on the sleeve of the caftan. Satisfied for the moment, he set down the knife he gripped in his meaty left hand and the stein in his right, and burped under his breath.

'Marvelous.' He managed to invest the word with both enthusiasm and awed respect for excellence, as if viewing a masterpiece.

'Glad you enjoyed it, Herr Klimt.' Berthe sat primly on the edge of her seat in the dining room, but did not feel at all prim. She wanted to get on with it, but knew Klimt had his own pace for such things. She marveled at the artist's seeming lack of curiosity as to the purpose for this requested visit.

'Not sure the past tense is quite correct, Frau Meisner.' He eyed a roll encrusted with caraway seed and salt crystals, then sighed. 'But for now, it should do.' He patted his stomach hidden beneath the veil of the flowing caftan.

Once again Berthe was struck by the thought that Klimt looked more like a navvy than an artist, his wide fingers meant to wield a pick axe rather than a paintbrush.

'It was most kind of you to invite me for *Jause*. I was desperate for it today. Amazing that we are just blocks away, yet we see each other so seldom.'

'Karl does seem to run into you more than I do.'

Klimt chuckled at this, for it was he who had brokered several of her husband's investigations – including his own, when he was arrested for murder.

'Glad to be of service, ma'am.' He gave into his baser desires and snatched the salted roll from the basket, tearing it in two and putting a piece to his nose to appreciate the yeasty aroma. Then he set it down on his plate for later.

'I have a feeling the roasting spit has spun round.'

'Perceptive of you, Herr Klimt. Indeed, I believe I have a commission for you, for a change. A portrait.'

He winced at the word. Half the female population of Vienna were eager to have their portrait done by Klimt. Portraits were his bread and butter; too much so, it seemed.

'My dear Frau Meisner, I much appreciate your efforts, but if I painted nothing but portraits from now until my eightieth birthday I would not come to the end of the requests already on my desk.'

'A very important person,' Berthe added as bait.

Klimt shrugged like a bear waking from winter hibernation. 'They are all important personages.'

'This commission involves intrigue . . .'

He squinted his eyes at her, saying nothing for a moment. 'As in your husband's investigations?'

'Mine in this case,' she said, 'but it comes to the same thing.'

Klimt picked up half of the torn salted bun and began spreading a thick coating of pâté on it.

'Well, perhaps I should hear you out, then.'

He loved his fine clothes. After his miserable youth in Lemberg, sharing cramped space with his five rowdy siblings, as the third son never having a new suit of clothes and always wearing tattered hand-me-downs, Forstl now luxuriated in his ability to buy whatever he fancied in the way of couture.

He looked at himself in the full-length glass on the inside of the door of his wardrobe and liked what he saw. Very nice indeed.

He had left the Bureau early today specifically to prepare himself and his apartment for tonight's assignation. A beautiful young thing, to be sure. Forstl felt his pulse quicken in expectation. He glanced at the clock by his bed. Still half an hour to go.

In the sitting room, all was in readiness. Several large bouquets of roses stood in place in solid crystal vases; there had been an ice delivery today and he had carefully chipped some, which was now beading the outside of a silver champagne cooler with moisture. A bottle of Veuve Clicquot was nestled in the ice – not Austrian Sekt, but the real thing. On the sideboard were delicacies ranging from caviar to truffles. Candles were ready to be lit.

He surveyed his small empire. Yes, he sighed, perfect.

The knock at his apartment door startled him. He had left word for the *Portier* to show his guest up. But so early?

No matter. Forstl did not want to keep his guest waiting. Must be as anxious as I am, he thought, as he went to the entrance hall and opened his apartment door.

He was momentarily shocked by the sight of his uninvited visitor. He quickly gathered himself, looked about the corridor to make sure no one else was around, and forced a smile.

'Arthur. How good to see you.'

'Were you expecting someone else, Adel? Or is this frock for my benefit?'

Forstl ignored the comment. 'Please come in.'

His mind was racing. What had Schmidt been talking about? He had told Forstl well over a week ago that this little matter had been taken care of. But the man seemed to be in fine fettle.

'A new wig?' Arthur asked from behind him as he closed the door. 'Oh my, and such a lovely repast laid on. You are expecting someone, aren't you Adel? Naughty boy!'

Forstl felt rage rush upward from his belly. It poured out in a hiss. 'What is it you want?'

'Blood pressure, Adel, remember your blood pressure. It will not do to excite yourself. Save that for later.' This was followed by a snide laugh.

Forstl fumed. How could he have ever found this creature interesting? How could he have taken him into his heart?

'The rouge is a bit heavy, don't you think, Adel?'

'I asked you a question.'

'Well, it must be patently obvious, don't you think? Our little agreed-upon sum has not made an appearance in my bank account. A man setting up practice in Vienna needs a helping hand. We agreed on that.'

'No.' It came out as a low growl. 'You requested, and I said I would give it some thought.'

And now what? Obviously Schmidt had lied to him. He had not taken care of this little problem at all. There was a pistol in a drawer in the side table. Perhaps he could say he surprised an intruder.

But just as quickly the calming voice of reason forbade such a wild move. It would all come out then, for Arthur had nursed him in Bohemia. It would surely be in the records. Someone would uncover it if the killing took place here in his own apartment. The connection between the two, perhaps even barracks gossip would be exhumed. And then the tidying up to be done in the flat. All his lovely frocks and delicate slippers, the wigs in four different shades. Those would have to be hastily disposed of. Prying eyes would examine his private empire.

'Such a small amount for such an important man,' his guest said.

Suddenly he knew what must be done.

'Yes, you are right, Arthur. I should be happy to help you.'

'And my wife,' Arthur said.

'Goes without saying. And your wife. After all we shared together.'

'That's the spirit, Adel.'

No bargaining with the man as he had attempted the first time, telling him that exposing their affair would destroy his own chances of success as a new doctor, as a new husband. But Arthur had only laughed that threat away, telling Forstl that he had so much more to lose as a member of the General Staff. Hence Schmidt's warning beating – though Schmidt had obviously failed him in this regard. Which called for a new tactic.

'I shall have the amount remitted to your account in a week at the latest.'

'I have been patient, Adel. But patience can wear thin.'

'I understand. But I need to withdraw a sizeable amount like that in dribs and drabs so as not to call attention to myself.'

'So careful in business, so careless in relationships.'

Neither said anything for a moment.

'Well . . .' Arthur nodded, and surveyed the champagne. 'Shall we toast to it?'

Forstl felt his anger rising.

'Only playing the fool, Adel. I must meet my wife for dinner. Tickets for the theatre, tonight. Vienna is a wonderful place for a professional man.'

From orderly and nurse in the army to a full doctor in less than a decade. Forstl had to give it to Arthur. He had ambition, just as Forstl did. But sometimes a man could overstep himself.

'I shall take my leave now, before your intended guest arrives. Let me guess. A subaltern? No, not in Vienna. Too many prying eyes at the General Staff. Not someone in uniform then . . .'

'Goodnight, Arthur.' Forstl began leading him to the door.

As he was leaving, he looked back with that wan smile that had first attracted Forstl.

'Sorry about this, Adel, but a man must get on in life.'

He almost felt sorry for Arthur. Then the fellow added, 'I'll be waiting. Next Monday at the latest.'

Which wiped out any trace of empathy Forstl felt towards him. He closed and double-bolted the door.

There would just be time before his nephew arrived. Well, not actually his nephew, in fact a distant cousin, but he had taken the young man under his wing, acting like an uncle towards him. Tonight was to have been a gala event, an initiation of sorts, but Forstl was no longer in the mood now. He quickly changed out of his beautiful new dress and silken underwear and into his green tunic and blue pantaloons. Once again an officer of the General Staff. He would take the boy out for a night on the town. Perhaps cards in a private room at the Sacher, then a visit to one of the finer Inner City brothels. Not the Bower, of course, as that was strictly Foreign Office territory. Tonight he would initiate the young man into sexuality of one sort or another. That thought cheered him up. A manly evening out.

He would need to contact Schmidt about this turn of events. He was one up on the bastard now; at least some good had come out of this. The meticulous agent had not done his job for once – which should serve to make Schmidt even more eager to rid them of the nuisance of Arthur Schnitzel, newly-wed doctor.

Moreover, this oversight on Schmidt's part might just buy Forstl more time to obtain the mobilization plans.

Meanwhile, it would be best if he delayed the début of his pretty frock. Time enough for that later.

SEVENTEEN

Fräulein Metzinger kept the grey-faced concierge occupied looking in vain for a parasol she insisted she had left in the breakfast room, while Berthe hurried up the stairs to the second floor.

As she climbed the stairs, she tried to rehearse what she would say, but words would not come. Her heart was racing and her handbag knocked against her hip. The bulky little box camera sat inside her purse – a Pandora's box as far as she was concerned, but simplicity itself to use, Fräulein Metzinger had assured her.

Erika – they were on first-name terms now and addressing each other *per du* – was a great fan of photography. A great fan of the twentieth century, in fact. Indeed, she often touted the wonderful advances that society would make in the next generation: in science, labour practices, women's rights. According to Erika, this inexpensive cardboard box camera with the comical name Brownie was another example of such progress. It took not photographs but what were, using the American vernacular, dubbed 'snapshots'. Although no snob, Berthe could not help being irritated by the creeping Americanisms now current in her country and culture.

Which thoughts served only to take her mind off the difficult matter at hand.

She stood in front of the door of Room 205. It was the pigeon-hole for that room into which, several days before, the concierge had placed the handkerchief that Berthe had used as a ruse. The Baron would, she guessed, be a man of habit about such things – using the same hotel repeatedly and the same room, as well.

At least she hoped that was the case.

Berthe took a deep breath and then knocked on the door with her gloved hand. At first there was no response. She knocked again, a trifle louder this time. What if she were wrong? Would she have to knock on the door of every room in the Hotel Metropole?

She heard a stirring inside the room, the scratch of a chair being pushed back on parquet. In another instant the door opened, revealing the tall, thin visage of Baron Arthur von Suttner, who was dressed impeccably in morning coat, wing collar and tie. A tall man, he stooped in the doorway, his thinning reddish-blond hair neatly coiffed. His long waxed moustaches seemed to bristle as he looked at her with grey-green eyes that held both suspicion and disdain.

'I thought you might be the chambermaid,' he said.

'Who is it, Uncle?' a female voice inquired from within.

'Good day, Baron,' Berthe said. 'I have come with urgent news for you. May I come in?'

'This is rather irregular,' he said, clearly not knowing what to make of Berthe. 'Who are you, young lady? And why have you come to our room?'

Berthe heard the squeak of wheels coming from around the corner of the corridor. The chambermaid was clearly about her work. Berthe did not want to complicate matters with her presence.

'All will be revealed,' she said. 'I bring vital urgent news for you.'

'Is it Frau von Suttner? Has something happened to my wife?'

'Allow me to come in, and I will share what I know with you.'

She did not wait for a response, but simply bustled in past the astonished baron.

'It is as we suspected,' Gross said, slapping down a sheaf of papers on Werthen's desk. 'The Marsh test was positive. Von Ebersdorf died of arsenic poisoning, not bad shellfish.'

'In all of this one thing is clear, at least. We are talking about murder.'

'Three murders,' Gross added, taking a seat opposite Werthen.

'But of widely different *modus operandi*.'

'Ah, Werthen, you take a page out of my book on criminal investigation. *Every deed is an outcome of the character of the doer.* I hope I quote myself correctly.'

'I am sure you do, Gross.'

'But you recall, also from that book, my theory of the staged crime scene? In some cases the perpetrator wishes to confuse the investigators by purposely changing the evidence, adding clues that lead nowhere.'

'So von Ebersdorf's killer and that of Mitzi and Fanny could be one and the same, but simply chose poison for the Count to throw off investigators.'

'Precisely.'

'Thus, we either have two killers or one,' Werthen said. 'The three murders are connected or, by the wildest improbability, a matter of coincidence.'

'We continue to knock our heads against the wall of coincidence. We must also remember, however, that even if the crimes are linked, they may not be connected.'

'You might just as well be spouting *haiku* now, Gross.'

'A convergence despite different motives.'

'Franz Ferdinand implied that the Intelligence Bureau of the General Staff could have had a hand in von Ebersdorf's death.'

'In fact the Archduke has been as good as his word, now it has been established that it was murder. He has dispatched the long-suffering Duncan to take up guard across the street from this office. I saw him upon entering.'

'More than an implication, then?' Werthen said, feeling a sudden tightness in his stomach. 'It would appear that all three are the victims of an absurd power struggle between rival intelligence agencies?'

'I am more comfortable calling them what they really are, the espionage arms of the government. I have witnessed little sign of intelligence thus far.'

'That does not answer my question,' Werthen replied.

'It's one possibility,' Gross allowed. 'In such a scenario we have Fräulein Mitzi recruited by the General Staff. But how?'

'Perhaps someone knew of her predicament, of the situation with her uncle. Or more importantly that she was working in a bordello. And then threatened to tell her parents if she did not cooperate?'

'Plausible,' Gross allowed. 'Or simply paid her for the services.'

Werthen thought about this for a moment. It simply did not fit the mental picture of Fräulein Mitzi he had built up.

Gross did not wait for a reply, 'Recruited her to do what . . .?'

This was an easier one for Werthen to answer. 'Gather secrets from someone in the Foreign Office. Compromise them, make them look like amateurs.'

'Yes, good.' Gross was beginning to enjoy this. 'But our man from the Foreign Office, von Ebersdorf – who perhaps talked more than he should have done to a sweet young thing – somehow discovers this and kills the informant, the unfortunate Fräulein Mitzi.'

'And the General Staff retaliates by killing von Ebersdorf,' Werthen added.

'Which leaves us with Fräulein Fanny. You see the problem of course? If von Ebersdorf was the killer in the first instance, he was clearly not around to commit the third murder.'

'He himself or his minions? A man like von Ebersdorf is surely not going to bloody his own hands.'

'Or his minions,' Gross allowed. 'Still, why the need to kill the second girl?'

'She knew what Mitzi knew. They were room-mates. Perhaps they shared more than she let on when I first interviewed her. Perhaps she tried to sell her information to the wrong person.'

'In which case the score is not even, is it?'

It took Werthen a moment to understand what Gross meant. 'Yes, right. If this theory is correct, it means there may still be a retaliation for the murder of Fräulein Fanny.'

Gross nodded, solemnly. 'The stakes would seem to be rising.'

'Who is this woman, Uncle?'

Berthe was happy to see the couple were still attired. In fact it rather looked as if they had been reading together; a book lay open on the table in the middle of the room. The bed had not been turned down.

'I have no idea,' Baron von Suttner said. Then to Berthe, 'I suggest you leave immediately or I shall call the police.'

'There are those who know of your assignations,' Berthe blurted out.

'It's your wife!' the young Marie shrieked. 'She hounds us everywhere we go.'

'No,' Berthe said firmly. 'I have come upon information that one of this country's intelligence services is following you. In fact, you can see the man just outside your window.'

'Who are you?' insisted the young woman.

'Don't move the curtains,' Berthe advised. 'Look from the corner of the window. He is below, just by the lamppost across the street from this hotel. Wearing a boater and a summer suit.'

'It's a trick,' Marie hissed. 'How could anyone but your wife know about our trips to Vienna?'

Berthe turned a stern eye on the young woman. 'You told them.'

'You're mad!'

Meanwhile, the Baron edged towards the window, peering below. 'He is there.'

'Which proves nothing,' Marie said. 'It is probably this woman's accomplice. They have come to extort money from us.'

Marie faced Berthe again. 'How could I have told anybody?'

'It was all there in your novel, *As Light Dawned*. The book your aunt so generously had published. The book you dedicated to her. All there for anybody to read: the thinly veiled *roman à clef* about a young woman's love for a much older man bound to a loveless marriage. About their passion for one another. You've set the dogs on yourselves. You've provided the fuel.'

'What interest would the intelligence services of this country have in us?' Baron von Suttner asked, but it was clear he already knew the answer.

'You don't believe this woman?' It was almost a shriek.

'Perhaps we should hear her out,' he said. 'Now you must identify yourself and apprise me of your interest in this matter.'

'My name is Berthe Meisner,' she said. 'I confess to being a great follower of your wife's work, and I have come here out of my own sense of duty.'

A partial lie, but she could hardly say that Frau von Suttner had hired her to follow her husband and niece. Karl had warned her about the dangers of getting too close to an investigation, of investing emotion rather than intellect, and now she was paying for it. Bertha von Suttner was her idol in so many ways; she did not want to disappoint her, nor did she want to expose the Baroness's fears to this horrid little niece.

'My husband is a lawyer who also is involved in private inquiries.'

'His name?' This from von Suttner.

'Werthen. Karl Werthen.'

'They do not even share a family name,' Marie said. 'Why should we believe her?'

But he ignored this outburst, ruminating. 'I have heard of your husband. He did some work for the Herbst family. A trust, I believe. They recommended him highly.'

She nodded at this acknowledgement. 'In the course of one of his investigations he discovered that an intelligence service has a dossier on your wife; and that they were following you in the hope of gathering incriminating evidence, something they could use to compromise your wife's peace work.'

'*Our* peace work,' he said.

'They must have read the novel, as they suspected there were trysts. And that is why I have come.'

'To gloat?' Marie said.

'Hardly. No, to offer a solution. An explanation for these trips to Vienna and the hiring of a hotel room.'

'And that would be?'

She took the Brownie camera out of her handbag. 'I would like to take some photos of your niece.'

'I know I put it down somewhere here,' Erika Metzinger said, looking with great attention under each table in the breakfast room.

'I still do not recall you, Fräulein. And I have a very good memory for faces.'

The concierge said this, but was not looking at her face at all. His inspection of her bosom made her blush.

'Perhaps someone else was at the desk at the time,' she finally managed to say. Over his shoulder she saw Berthe descend the stairs and head for the exit.

'It is doubtful.' He smirked as he said this. 'Was it for the night or the hour?'

'I beg your pardon?'

'The room. Were you a guest or . . .?' He left the rest unsaid.

'I am sure I do not understand what you are getting at. I seem to have wasted my time in this fruitless search.'

She began to leave, but he cut her off from the door, a sneer on his face as he drew close to her. 'Oh, I imagine you do, understand, Fräulein. Strict policy here. You share your income with the management. That would be me. I don't recall receiving any share from you. Perhaps we could strike a little bargain, you and I?'

He placed his right hand on her breast and she let out an audible gasp.

'An actress. How wonderful!' He moved in closer, his other hand now groping at her skirt.

A sudden wave of anger swept over her, replacing any fear she might have felt.

'You pig!' she shouted, then spat in his eye. As he wiped away the spit, she brought her right foot down and stabbed his instep with her heel. He howled in pain and reached for the injured foot. This gave her the opportunity to push him over; as he fell, he crashed into a table, upturning it on top of himself.

'You little vixen!' he cried, attempting to untangle himself from the table legs and cloth.

But she was out the door of the breakfast room before he could stand; and then flew out of the hotel, running for the fiaker that Bertha had waiting at the corner.

As she leaped aboard, she discovered a strange emotion flooding her body and then heard an odd sound issuing from her own throat. She was laughing like a gurgling drainpipe.

EIGHTEEN

Werthen had to get some work done today on the von Königstein will. Cases were piling up with both him and Fräulein Metzinger otherwise occupied. This was a fairly straightforward matter – the addition of a codicil stating that if any son married outside the aristocracy, he would be excluded from participation in the proceeds of the said will. This codicil was, of course, directed at the eldest son, Waldemar, who was widely known to be infatuated with an operetta singer from the Carlstheater.

Werthen had actually seen the young woman playing Zingra, the gypsy girl in Carl Michael Ziehrer's new operetta from last spring, *The Three Wishes*. Charming as a singer she was, but then one assumed the von Königsteins did not want a girl who plays gypsies as the mother of their heirs.

Even as Werthen was thus engaged, part of his mind was still playing over Berthe's latest request. On the whole, she had concocted an admirable plan for the von Suttner affair and had executed it almost perfectly. The 'almost' was reserved for the fact that violence had befallen Fräulein Metzinger. The man responsible needed a good thrashing, but that was not what Berthe was requesting. He would need to confer with Gross on her novel request to deal with the hotel concierge. It might put them further into debt *vis-à-vis* the Archduke. Gross needed a say in that. But all in all it seemed an appropriate solution.

He looked down at the half-finished codicil. He really must get this done. Focus, he counseled himself.

He was just finishing the codicil when Fräulein Metzinger – who was also devoting that day to the firm's legal business – tapped on his office door.

Poking her head in, she announced, 'A visitor, Herr Advokat.'

'I thought we had no appointments this morning.'

She raised her eyebrows as if shrugging. 'He doesn't have an appointment, but says it is rather urgent. You saw him once before, I believe.'

'Very well,' Werthen said, putting the cap on his pen and blotting what he had written thus far.

A tall young man in a black cassock with a cincture or sash around the waist stood in the doorway. His fair hair was disheveled, as if caught in a strong breeze.

Werthen stood, immediately recognizing him. 'Father Mickelsburg! How good to see you.'

It was a priest he had met on his previous case, tracking down the missing son of Karl Wittgenstein, the wealthy industrialist.

He moved around the desk to greet the priest, shaking his hand with real feeling.

'Herr Advokat. You are looking well.'

They stood hand in hand for a long moment.

Finally Werthen directed the priest to a chair.

'What brings you here, Father? Can't be a will at your age.'

'A good lawyer would recommend such a legal instrument for any age. One never knows when God will call.'

Werthen felt himself redden. The man was right, of course, but Werthen's playful *bonhomie* seemed to have been lost on the priest. He credited Father Mickelsburg with a sense of irony, but wondered at his literalness.

'In fact there are legal ramifications to my visit,' the priest said. 'I understand that you are investigating the death of a young woman named Waltraude Moos.'

Werthen looked at him blankly for a moment, then suddenly remembered the girl's real name.

'Ah yes, Fräulein Mitzi.'

Father Mickelsburg squinted at him.

'Her name at, um, her place—'

'Her professional name,' Father Mickelsburg said perfunctorily. 'There is no need for such prudishness with me, Herr Advokat. I seem to recall unburdening my soul to you last time we met. I am no stranger to the ways of the flesh, despite my cassock.'

'Why is this of interest to you, Father?' Werthen again felt the discomfort of addressing this younger man by such a title.

'A certain friend is connected with these investigations. We were at seminary together.'

'The girl's uncle,' Werthen said flatly, immediately making the connection. 'Father Hieronymus.'

The priest nodded.

'The man's a cad.'

Father Mickelsburg did not respond for a moment. Then said, 'A strong word, Advokat.'

'He took advantage of his own niece. He may have even killed her to cover up his misdeeds. Such a description is hardly strong enough, in my book.'

Mickelsburg slowly shook his head.

'You are the last one, I would think, who would want to cover up such practices,' Werthen added, feeling real emotion, and realizing he was making the very mistake he counseled his wife Berthe against: becoming too emotionally involved with an investigation. But he could still see the mother in tears at that tidy little farm in the Weinviertel, still hear the words of denial of the father, unwilling to accept the reality of his loss.

'Will you hear me out? Or are you now judge and jury in addition to private inquiry agent?'

There was the bite of irony he knew Father Mickelsburg to be capable of, and it brought him up short.

'Sorry, Father. I have been much involved with this case of late. But there is something you should know. I no longer have any official standing. The client dispensed with my services.'

'I see. But you sound as if you have not personally given up on the investigation. That you have more than a merely professional interest in the matter.'

'Yes.' Werthen said. 'The girl was badly used from many quarters. I admit to a certain empathy.'

'Have you discovered the person responsible?'

'No. And as I say, I am no longer officially on the case. After the death of the second girl, the police have finally taken over.'

'A second girl?'

'Sorry. You wouldn't know. I mean a second young woman from the same bordello, the Bower.'

'A second murder. Then it couldn't be Hieronymus, could it?'

'Why not? Perhaps she was blackmailing him about the affair with his niece.'

'Then you need to hear what I have to say. Will you do that?'

'Of course.'

'Not just listen to my words. I mean hear me with an open mind.'

Werthen wondered what kind of hold the corrupt Hieronymus could have over Father Mickelsburg. Nothing else could explain him coming to the aid of such a complete villain.

'Father Hieronymus is one of the most virtuous men I have ever known.' It was as if Father Mickelsburg were waiting for Werthen to protest. Greeted by silence, the priest continued. 'As I said, we were at seminary together, and we became close friends. Intimates, but not in the way you are thinking. He was always the one to help others who could not do their duties, to aid those struggling, be it with theological concepts or with their own self-doubts. He very much wanted to be sent to Africa once he was ordained, but the Church wanted him here. He is the sort of shining light that the hierarchy wants in a public position. But Hieronymus campaigned for several years and finally was sent to the Belgian Congo. He lasted only a matter of months. He was badly wounded in an attempt on his life. Hieronymus said things from the pulpit about the rubber-plantation owners' inhuman practices that they did not want to hear. He tried to expose the cruelty and hardship imposed on those workers, those poor children of God. He was brought back, badly wounded, and after recuperating was given a safe church where the bishops thought he could cause no trouble.'

Werthen had difficulty accepting this biography, remembering only the shifty eyes of the priest when confronted with his misdeeds regarding his niece.

'What happened to him, then?' Werthen said. 'To make him forget his vows and take advantage of a young woman, his own niece?'

'He tells me, and I believe him, that it was the young woman who made advances. Who actually came to his room one night, crawled under the covers, and began fondling him. He awoke in an excited state, but when he realized what was happening, he stopped her, made her go back to her room, and threatened to send her home in disgrace. She disappeared soon after, leaving behind a letter threatening to expose him, to lie about their so-called affair if he so much as contacted her parents. To his lasting regret, in this event Hieronymus was weak. Faced with such threats, he acquiesced.'

Werthen felt the ground slipping from under him, a vertigo of unrealized aspects gripping him. He managed to grab hold of one bit of flotsam.

'I don't suppose you have that letter?'

'Once I heard my friend's story and that you were the one interviewing him, I knew it was God's way of giving me a second chance for having let my other friend down. For not standing up to the world and being honest. Such a coincidence could not be other than divinely inspired.' When he met Father Mickelsburg previously, the priest had initially been less than forthcoming about his special relationship with a young journalist who was murdered. He had come to Werthen later to supply valuable information, but had obviously felt a great sense of guilt at attempting to keep this homosexual relationship secret.

Now Father Mickelsburg reached inside his cassock. took out a letter, and placed it on the desktop in front of Werthen.

Later, after the priest had departed and he was left alone with his own thoughts, Werthen remembered something the driver he hired in the Weinviertel, the man called Pratt, had said regarding the Moos girl: that she was the wild one, the one about whom stories were told in the village. He had dismissed this at the time as a product of rural conservatism and jealousies at play. But perhaps there was something in it.

Still, what did it matter? So the girl had a lusty nature. It changed nothing. Someone had brutally killed her.

Then Werthen began to wonder about other stories he had been told about Fräulein Mitzi – by Frau Mutzenbacher and Siegfried, by Salten, Altenberg and her one-time lover, Schnitzler. Were they depicting her as she really was, or were they hiding something? Something that could lead Werthen to her killer.

'And you believe Father Mickelsburg?'

'Yes, I do,' Werthen answered.

'In spite of the fact,' Berthe persisted, 'that he lied to you before?'

'It's different this time.'

'It often is,' Gross added.

They had gone out for dinner at Berthe's favorite restaurant. It was her birthday, and Werthen had been so preoccupied that he had forgotten it until Frau Blatschky reminded him that afternoon. The Frau had stayed on to serve as babysitter while he, Berthe and Gross dined at the Black Swan, an eatery resembling a French bistro, despite its name, which sounded more like a British public house than a Left Bank restaurant. The Black Swan had been a favorite of theirs for several years, but only lately had it been discovered by that class of Viennese who dined out in order that others could see them doing so.

In fact, Inspector Meindl, the diminutive chief of the Vienna Police Praesidium, had just left with his wife, who was a good seven or eight centimetres taller and fourteen or fifteen kilos heavier than him, but from a very well-placed family.

Meindl's presence had cast a pall over their celebrations, for he had given them the feeling that he knew exactly what they were discussing. Discovering it was Berthe's birthday, he had the waiter bring over a bottle of Schlumberger Sekt, and they had duly toasted his generosity. Meindl smiled back at them. He was the only man Werthen knew who could make a smile look threatening.

Thus, instead of being able to talk about the state of their various investigations during dinner, they had to wait for his departure. Meindl was no friend to private inquiry agents, fearing that they might outdo the investigative efforts of his own detectives. Werthen, Berthe, and Gross had proved this fear to be valid on more than one occasion.

Despite the fact that Gross had been the man's mentor as a young constable in Graz, Meindl had attempted to derail their investigations in the past and, Werthen assumed, would continue to do so. Meindl's career to date had been marked by the single-minded pursuit not of justice but of personal advancement.

Once the police chief was gone, they set aside their barely touched glasses of Sekt, ordered a bottle of French champagne instead, and toasted Berthe's health.

'I still think Father Mickelsburg's words should be taken with some degree of mistrust,' she said.

Werthen did not want to reassess his vision of Fräulein Mitzi as the badly wronged country girl, any more than Berthe did; however, there was some compelling evidence.

'I did a thorough hand-writing analysis this afternoon,' Werthen announced. 'We have the letter from Mitzi I discovered at the Bower, and the ones I was able to secure from her parents.' He turned his gaze to Gross. 'I followed your ten-point matching system, Gross, comparing them with the letter Father Mickelsburg turned over to me today.'

He paused.

'And?' Berthe said.

'It was a ten-point match.'

There followed a moment of silence. Then Werthen added, 'Which reminds me. We should get the letters from the parents translated. Do you think Baroness von Suttner would help out in this regard once more?'

'No doubt,' Berthe said.

'I'll have Fräulein Metzinger type a copy to send her. We need to keep the original in our files.'

'Have you told Inspector Drechsler of this development?' Gross suddenly asked, looking very pleased with himself.

'Actually, no,' Werthen said. 'I wanted to try to verify—'

'Yes, I am sure you do,' Gross interrupted. 'And what if it is impossible to verify this new information about Fräulein Mitzi with absolute certainty?'

Werthen visibly reddened.

'The police don't know about Father Hieronymus, do they?'

'Well, I haven't quite got around to delivering the file.'

'You mean the one in which we are keeping the original of Fräulein Mitzi's letter?' asked Berthe, now understanding Gross's line of questioning.

'When were you thinking of delivering the file, Karl?' she asked.

'Alright. You both know how I feel about this case.'

'The white knight,' Berthe said.

'Something along those lines.'

'And now there may be other sides to Fräulein Mitzi you intend to do so?'

'That may not be advisable, as they could pertain to another ongoing investigation,' Gross said, leaning back in his chair and placing both hands over his stomach. He eyed Werthen with his mentor's expression.

'What? Why are you smiling like that? You haven't shared your information from today, is that it? Out with it, Gross.'

'You recall I requested a list of extra kitchen helpers and sous-chefs laid on specially for the von Ebersdorf banquet? After all, the fact that he was the only one to suffer from tainted shellfish is an Alp too high to believe in. The autopsy shows he was the deliberate target of poisoning.'

'What else?' Berthe insisted.

'I've received a list of the temporary help. One name might interest you.'

He reached into his waistcoat pocket, withdrew a folded square of paper, spread it out on the table, and pushed it across to Werthen and Berthe.

Mid-list a name was circled: Mutzenbacher, Siegfried.

NINETEEN

They waited for him on the street. Werthen was familiar with Siegfried's daily schedule now, which included mid-morning shopping. They had no desire to beard the man inside the Bower, where his sister could be his protector.

It was 10:23 when Siegfried came out, blinking in the strong sunlight, an incongruous-looking shopping basket in each of his large hands. They let him leave the precincts of the Bower, following a full block behind him. Siegfried made his way slowly through the lanes away from the Danube Canal (which far too many visitors to the city mistook for the Danube itself), looking into the window of a vegetable shop here, a bakery there. When he had gone just beyond the cathedral of Stephansdom, they decided it was time to overtake him. He was again staring into the window of a bakery and, as they approached, Werthen could see that Siegfried was appreciating a display of freshly baked poppy-seed tarts arranged appealingly in linen-lined baskets. Werthen and Gross stood on each side of him, ostensibly admiring the display. He suddenly focused on their reflection and jerked to attention, suspicion in his eyes.

'Advokat Werthen. Odd meeting you like this.'

'Fine day for a walk,' Werthen said by way of reply. 'You haven't met my colleague, Doktor Gross.'

'Good day to you,' Gross said, nodding his head, his forefinger and thumb to the front brim of his bowler hat.

Siegfried said nothing, just squinted at Gross. There was towel lint, Werthen noticed, caught in the stubble just below his left ear. He had washed, but not shaved.

'I have to do my shopping,' Siegfried said, about to move off.

'I think it might be wise to talk with us first.'

'I've got nothing to talk to you about. You don't work for us anymore.'

'I either talk to you first or go directly to the police,' Werthen said.

Siegfried shrugged his shoulders. 'Fine. Go talk to them, then. They were friends, both of them, Fräulein Mitzi and Fanny. I've told you all I know.'

'Actually,' Gross said, his voice assuming the rich sonority it took on when giving evidence in court, 'it was in reference to a different matter. The death of Count von Ebersdorf.'

'*Der Alte?* My sister already explained why we said we didn't recognize the sketch. We protect the anonymity of our more esteemed clientele. I only saw him now and again at the Bower. They say he died of food poisoning.'

'He was not so old,' Gross said. 'And he didn't die because of bad shellfish.'

Siegfried began to lose his aggressive demeanor, chewing on the inside of his mouth and assessing the situation.

'A cup of coffee might be in order,' Werthen said. 'Don't you think so, Siegfried?'

He made no reply, but followed them as Werthen made his way to Himmelpfortgasse and his usual coffee-house, the Café Frauenhuber. Herr Otto, who was on duty, bade them a hearty good day.

'It's been too long since we've seen you, Advokat.'

To which Werthen smiled and said, 'Perhaps a corner table, Herr Otto? A bit of privacy.'

'But of course.' The headwaiter led them through a maze of marble-topped tables, around Thonet chairs and red-velvet benches to a banquette in the deepest corner of the establishment. A student had spread out his papers on the table, but Otto efficiently and politely informed the young man that the table was reserved, and would it not please the young gentleman to take the fine table nearer the window where the light was better?

The young gentleman was not overjoyed at the suggestion until Otto offered him a refill of his mocha.

Werthen had once proved the headwaiter innocent of petty theft at another establishment and had won the man's allegiance for ever. A handy thing in Vienna, the loyalty of the Herr Ober at a coffee-house.

Siegfried had watched the affair with interest. 'So that's the way you folks make your way in the world, is it?' he said after Otto had brought their drinks and left again.

'Not much different from how *you* folks make your way,' Gross rebutted. 'Connections, connections. They bind the world.'

They sat, Siegfried between them. His momentary silence had allowed him to regain some of his old bluster.

'So, what's this all about, then?'

'You had no contact with von Ebersdorf?' Werthen asked.

'He was a client. We were hardly pals.'

'He was Fräulein Mitzi's regular.'

'That's true.'

'Did she ever talk about him?'

'What was there to talk about? It was a business matter, not love.'

'You're certain of that?'

'What do you want from me?'

'The truth, for starters,' Gross interjected. 'You see, we have come across a bit of interesting information. It seems you were among the temporary help at the Hotel Excelsior the day of the banquet at which von Ebersdorf died.'

'So? I help out there a lot. I have dreams, you know. Ambitions. I don't always want to be herding women around the Bower. I want to become a chef some day. I learn on the job.'

'I would not put that particular day on your résumé, if I were you,' Gross said. 'Poison is hardly among the accepted culinary ingredients.'

'It was the shellfish. They all said so. Besides, I was just the sous-chef that day. One of several. What? Is the great Chef Marcel trying to shift the blame? He chose the shellfish.'

'Peculiar that nobody else was taken ill, don't you think?' Werthen asked.

'I didn't get paid to think. I just got the ingredients ready.'

'It was the fact that only Count von Ebersdorf was affected by the tainted shellfish that made me curious,' Gross said.

Siegfried looked back and forth between them, his eyes narrowing to slits, his incisors working the inside of his mouth again.

'What are you two getting at?'

'Count von Ebersdorf didn't die of food poisoning,' Gross said.

'Yes he did. They said so in the papers.'

'No. I rather think the man was poisoned by some enemy who was present at the hotel restaurant. Who had access to his food?'

'The man's in the ground. Pretty hard to prove that now.'

'Well, actually, Herr Mutzenbacher,' Gross began, 'that is not accurate. Last I saw of the poor man, he was on an autopsy table at the General Hospital.'

'That's impossible. I read about his funeral. It was weeks ago now.'

'Yes, to be sure.'

Werthen could see that Gross was toying with Siegfried now. Not exactly a cat with a mouse, but toying nonetheless. Hoping the man would panic, get flustered, offer up a tacit confession.

Siegfried must have felt this too, for suddenly it was as if a curtain were drawn over his face. He shut down, let his eyes go blank, said nothing.

'In point of fact,' Gross continued, 'the body was exhumed. Aren't you interested in knowing what we discovered?'

Siegfried made no reply.

'Poison,' Gross said. 'Arsenic poison. That was the cause of death. Whoever killed von Ebersdorf was clever enough to know that arsenic can mimic the effects of food poisoning, but was not clever enough to know that arsenic remains in the body for a very long time *post mortem*.'

There was continued silence from Siegfried.

'Talk with us or we go to the police with this information,' Werthen reminded him.

Still nothing. Then, after another instant, Siegfried suddenly stood.

'I have to be going now, gentlemen. Shopping to do. Hungry girls to feed at lunch.'

'If you are innocent, it is far better for you to talk to us now. Clear up any misunderstandings.'

He said nothing, picking up his empty baskets and waiting for Werthen to move off the red-velvet bench and allow him to leave.

'It's only a matter of time, you know,' Werthen said to him as he passed. 'So many working in the kitchen that day. Someone is sure to remember something. Seeing somebody tamper with the food, or mark a plate as being specially for von Ebersdorf. Some pharmacist is going to remember the person who purchased arsenic for poisoning vermin.'

But he slipped past Werthen without further comment.

They watched him leave the café. There was nothing they could do to stop him.

'That went well,' Gross said, stirring his half-empty cup of coffee.

It took them over ninety minutes to be allowed in for an audience. By that time, Gross's stomach was beginning to make rather disturbing sounds.

'The man treats us like we're his employees,' complained the ravenous criminologist.

'We are, Gross.'

'Never,' he said with a degree of passion uncommon for him before his first glass of Vetliner. 'We . . . Well, at least you, are a private inquiry agent. A free-lance in the most literal and knightly sense of the word. We choose what cases to investigate.'

'Do we earn money by so doing?'

'Hardly the point.'

But Werthen would not let him off. 'It *is* the point. We are paid for our services, sometimes quite handsomely. I would call that a form of employment.'

'And ergo, Franz Ferdinand is the boss and can keep his underlings waiting.'

At which point the Archduke himself came bustling into the antechamber, right hand outstretched, a concerned expression on his face.

'My dear sirs,' he said as he got to them, and shook first one hand and then the other. 'They have just told me you were waiting. I do beg your pardon.'

At which comment, Gross shot Werthen a self-satisfied look.

Franz Ferdinand cast a glance at an ormolu clock resting on the marble mantle of the room's one fireplace.

'You two have been waiting right through lunch. You must be famished.'

Werthen was about to voice a polite denial when Gross jumped in.

'I am hungry enough to eat the nether parts of a skunk, if you must know, your Highness.'

Franz Ferdinand let out a quite unmanly giggle at this comment. Werthen felt his own face reddening: Gross had to be light-headed from lack of nutrition to use such language in front of the Archduke.

'Well, we shall have to do something about that, shan't we? Cook came up with a very passable venison ragout for lunch. I wouldn't doubt there is a bite or two left.'

'That would be heavenly, your Highness,' Gross told him.

The Archduke tugged on the brocade pull by the fireplace, and a liveried servant appeared instantly, as if popping out of a rabbit hole. Franz Ferdinand gave orders brusquely, and the man hastened off.

'You can dine in my office, gentlemen. I assume you have news for me?'

He did not wait for an answer, but set off with a rapid clacking of boots on the parquet, out of the anteroom and down a long sun-filled corridor whose one wall was covered with oil paintings marking the high points of Habsburg history. On the other side of the corridor, a bank of tall windows gave out on to the magnificent gardens below, with Vienna in the distance, the spires of the churches the highest man-made structures visible. It was a scene that filled Werthen with a quiet pride in his city of residence, that made him want to explore its quiet squares and little-known lanes. They were in the Upper Belvedere today, the higher of the two palaces in these splendid grounds, the summer palace, as it was called. Franz Ferdinand maintained his shadow government in the Lower Belvedere, but in the warmer months would repair to the airier upper palace for relaxation.

They both had to hurry to keep up with the Archduke as he made his way along the corridor and around to the side of the palace, to a suite of rooms that seemed large enough to hold a court ball. Of this opulent space – its walls bearing tapestries and enormous oil paintings in the Makart style – the Archduke appeared to be using one small corner, which contained a modest desk and a comfortable-looking leather chair.

No sooner did they arrive in the room than a scurry of servants appeared carrying chairs, small side tables, and table settings for Werthen and Gross. These they set up near the Archduke's desk with all the expertise of stagehands at the Burgtheater.

Then came another bevy of servants carrying silver-domed chafing dishes, which, when their lids were opened, gave off a rich aroma that set Werthen's salivary glands on alert.

'Please eat,' Franz Ferdinand said. 'And then we will talk. I have a telegram to send to the Kaiser, but shall return presently.'

Neither Werthen nor Gross waited for further invitations, but tucked into the fare with gusto. The cook had paired the venison with an excellent vintage Côtes du Rhône Villages. Werthen would have taken the Archduke for an Austria-first sort, serving at his table perhaps a Blauburgunder from the Esterházy estates or from the countryside around Eisenstadt to the east of Vienna; he was happy, however, for Franz Ferdinand's lack of nationalistic chauvinism in this regard.

They were just finishing their repast when Franz Ferdinand returned, a serious expression on his face. Werthen wondered what he and the German Kaiser had been communicating about.

'Bad news, your Highness?' Gross said, never one to let protocol get in the way of his native curiosity.

Franz Ferdinand looked as if he was about to upbraid the criminologist for his effrontery. But then, squinting first at Gross and then at Werthen, he seemed to think better of it.

'Alarming news, perhaps. But not from the Kaiser. I just received a dispatch from a man we have in St Petersburg. He talks of rumors of a double agent in Vienna. Someone at the Bureau in the employ of the Russians.'

There was silence for a moment, and then the Archduke shrugged. 'Rumors. They come cheap.' He smiled, looking suddenly more relaxed as if the mere act of sharing this piece of information had unburdened him.

'So, gentlemen,' he said, sinking into his leather chair, 'what wonderful news do you have for me?'

'There have been developments, your Highness,' Gross said, taking the lead. 'You have of course received the autopsy report?'

Franz Ferdinand nodded.

'We may, in fact, have a suspect,' Gross said.

The Archduke sat up in his chair. 'Who?'

Werthen knew it was silly to try to withhold the name of the suspect from the Archduke. After all, although he had not actually seen him, Werthen was certain that Duncan had been dogging them every step of the way that morning and would know exactly who they had been talking to. Nor was there reason to withhold the name from their 'employer'. He therefore explained about Siegfried Mutzenbacher, and how Gross had discovered that he was among the extra staff brought in for the von Ebersdorf banquet. He also told the Archduke about the interview they had had with Siegfried that morning.

'But why him?' Franz Ferdinand asked. 'What motive would he have?'

Werthen had given this some thought. 'I assume it had something to do with the death of Fräulein Mitzi, the young prostitute Count von Ebersdorf was frequenting.'

'Not jealousy, surely?' the Archduke said.

'He was close to her, that I know,' Werthen began. 'How close—'

Gross interjected, 'Jealousy would hardly seem to be the motive, seeing that the Count was killed after the death of the young woman.'

'Could he have imagined the Count was somehow responsible for the girl's death?' Franz Ferdinand said.

'That is one possibility,' Werthen allowed. 'Herr Mutzenbacher is not being forthcoming. We may have to turn this over to the police now.'

Another nod from Franz Ferdinand. 'Your decision.'

'We would of course continue our private investigation on your behalf,' Gross said. 'If that is your wish.'

'Please,' the Archduke said. 'It would seem that my fears about Joachim may have been unfounded. His death seems to have had nothing to do with rivalries in the intelligence services, but rather with a tawdry domestic matter.'

'As I said,' Werthen replied, 'that is one possibility. And it would seem, a very strong one. But we ought to pursue other possibilities, as well.'

'Could this Siegfried Mutzenbacher have killed all three?' Franz Ferdinand suddenly asked.

Gross and Werthen both shrugged. Then Gross said, 'There is another possible avenue of inquiry, your Highness. The first victim, Fräulein Mitzi, seems now not to have been such a put-upon and exploited girl as was first thought. Indications are that she was quite experienced at manipulation herself.'

Franz Ferdinand sighed, then stood to signal the end of the meeting.

'Well, I trust you two to follow your instincts in this matter. I wish to see justice done. Please proceed.'

He made to ring a bell on his desk, to summon a servant to lead them out.

'If I may, your Highness, one more thing.'

Franz Ferdinand stilled his hand. 'Yes.'

'It is about that other matter. Baroness von Suttner.'

'What is it?'

'We need your help.'

They reached Werthen's office by mid-afternoon, only to find Inspector Drechsler waiting impatiently.

'We were about to contact you,' Werthen said. 'You saved me a phone call.'

Drechsler did not appear to be in a happy state. The cadaverous detective looked glum as death, his long hawk nose sniffing at this statement.

'I thought we had an arrangement,' he replied, disappointment sounding in his voice. 'An understanding. Now you make me look like a fool in front of the *Giftzwerg*.' By 'poison dwarf' he meant the diminutive Inspector Meindl.

'I assure you, Drechsler—' Gross began, but was cut off by the detective.

'You withheld information on a case we are investigating. That's a crime, you know.'

Werthen's mind began racing. Which information? He had promised to turn over his files on Fräulein Mitzi and had not done so yet. It suddenly angered him that Drechsler should be accusing him over that, when the police had dragged their feet with her murder for weeks.

'Lord knows how, but she has some powerful connections,' Drechsler said. 'Powerful enough to set that bag of gas Meindl on fire. He threatened to have me on the beat in Meidling if I was somehow involved.'

'Just what are you talking about?' Gross finally demanded.

They were still standing in the front office, with Fräulein Metzinger trying unsuccessfully to focus on the sheet in her typing machine.

'Let's go into your office,' said Drechsler. It was a command rather than a suggestion.

Once inside Werthen's office, with the door closed behind them, there was no lessening of the tension.

'How long have you known about the von Ebersdorf poisoning?' Drechsler asked.

So that was it, Werthen realized. The 'she' with powerful connections that Drechsler had just mentioned was becoming clearer.

'When did you learn of it?' Gross countered.

'Earlier this afternoon, if you must know.'

'We assumed copies of the autopsy would circulate to the appropriate authorities,' Gross said, though both he and Werthen knew this was stretching the truth to breaking point. The Archduke had arranged the exhumation and autopsy privately through the von Ebersdorf family. He had not mentioned sharing the information with the constabulary, and they had not asked whether he intended to do so.

'We can hardly be blamed for bureaucratic bumbling.'

'Who ordered it?' Drechsler demanded.

'The identity of our client must, perforce, remain private.'

'Damn it, man, you're playing with my career here! Meindl thinks that I'm withholding information from him. That I am in some sort of conspiracy to make him look like an incompetent fool.'

'He hardly needs help in that venture,' Gross said. This comment broke the tension somewhat.

'Look, Inspector,' Werthen quickly jumped in. 'I assume that Frau Mutzenbacher was the one who brought a complaint to Meindl?'

'You assume correctly.'

'She must have some of her clientele under her thumb,' Werthen went on. 'Including someone powerful enough to get Meindl to try to stop the investigation.'

'If memory serves me right, "persecution" was the word used,' the policeman noted.

'I assure you we only learned yesterday that Siegfried Mutzenbacher was working in the kitchen where the von Ebersdorf banquet was served. We know that von Ebersdorf was a customer at the Bower; and a steady client of Fräulein Mitzi, who was murdered. In my earlier investigations into her death I found that there was a connection between Siegfried and the girl, but whether it was platonic, as he claimed, or otherwise, is uncertain.'

'So you assume that his mere presence in the kitchen of the hotel means he poisoned von Ebersdorf?'

'Something like that,' Werthen allowed, though when stated so simplistically it did sound somewhat far-fetched.

'Sound reasoning,' Drechsler said without a trace of irony.

'You think so?' Werthen asked.

'I must apologize to you, Inspector Drechsler,' Gross said suddenly, sounding honestly contrite. 'It was my suggestion that we interview Herr Mutzenbacher directly. I'm sure you understand the eagerness and excitement there is when you think you are about to close a case. I promise you, had we gained a confession, we would have contacted you directly.'

'And now that you've muddied the waters with this Siegfried fellow, I get to clean up your mess. Is that it?'

Werthen and Gross exchanged looks, the latter shrugging as if to say it was time to play their trump.

'In the greatest confidence, Inspector, I will tell you this. Our current employer . . .' Another quick glance at Werthen. 'Is a man of great power in the empire. A word in his ear from us would put you in very good stead, that I can promise.'

Drechsler considered this for a moment. 'At court?'

Gross raised his hands as if to show that they were tied in matters of client secrecy. 'You could have a protector in him. That is all I can say.'

Werthen thought that was again straining the truth, but it seemed to mollify the detective.

'Meindl wants you off this case,' Drechsler said. 'It is now officially Police Praesidium business. That and the murders of the two women from the Bower.'

Gross was about to respond, but Werthen cut him off.

'We will confer with our client,' he said.

'Meanwhile I want the files from your earlier investigation of Fräulein Mitzi's death. Everything.'

Werthen nodded. Conciliation was what was needed now, not confrontation or even offers of compromise.

'She may not have been the poor victimized girl we took her for,' Werthen added, offering this information as a sign of goodwill.

'Really?'

'You'll see it in the files. But her tale of being forced into prostitution has some holes in it.'

TWENTY

He had followed them through the course of the day, but he was not the only one doing so. There was also a cornstalk of a man with a scar on his face that would frighten even a crucifix-worshipping nun.

He was a protector or a watcher. At first Schmidt wasn't sure which.

Not very effective at either, though, since he never noticed me, Schmidt figured.

The lawyer and his bulky friend had been busy indeed. Cornering that pimp Siegfried from the Bower. Schmidt did not like the look of that interview: Siegfried had walked away from the café like a man with a noose round his neck.

And yet what the hell did Siegfried know? What could he tell the lawyer and his rotund pal? Another loose end that needed tying up.

Then to the Belvedere, and he could only guess at their mission there, as well. He followed them in through the entrance at No. 6 Rennweg, through a passage in the lower palace and to the grounds behind. Schmidt was in luck, for the gardens were open to the public during the warm months. He followed at a distance, through the ornamental flower-beds, past fountains and statues and terraces, up the slope to the Upper Belvedere.

It was while setting up watch at the Belvedere that Schmidt determined the cornstalk man's function. He was a protector, for not long after the lawyer and his companion entered the upper palace the cornstalk man followed, giving one last glance behind him. But by then Schmidt had melted into the midday throng of other Viennese enjoying the gardens.

They stayed in there for a good two hours. Schmidt knew it was the town residence of Archduke Franz Ferdinand, but he couldn't imagine what business the heir apparent would have with a lawyer who dabbled in private inquiries and wills and trusts. He'd need to find out the identity of the bulky older fellow accompanying him, but he did not like the direction this was headed.

He made a mental checklist, on the assumption they had gone to meet with the Archduke; it seemed unlikely they were making a social call on one of the footmen. Schmidt knew about Franz Ferdinand's shadow government; his Russian controller had apprised him of advances that the Archduke had made to Tsar Nicholas, desiring to maintain peaceful relations, especially regarding their mutual interests in the Balkans. The Archduke, Schmidt knew, was kept abreast of intelligence matters via informants in both the Austrian Foreign Office's espionage wing and the Intelligence Bureau of the General Staff. But what if he wanted to have his own agents in the field?

More checklists. This Werthen had gone to see the parents of the prostitute. He had also talked with Siegfried from the Bower and imparted something serious enough to make the man wear a look like he was attending his own wake.

And now to the Archduke. Was it mere coincidence that this lawyer, apparently investigating the death of the prostitute from the Bower, was also somehow involved with the ambitious and impatient Archduke?

This had all the signs of a field agent meeting with his controller.

Schmidt discounted the fact that he had followed the lawyer to Arthur Schnitzler's residence three days ago. The mere thought of that confusion made Schmidt wince. Forstl! What a complete idiot. Called him to a meet earlier in the week in a panic that he, Schmidt, had failed in his mission to dissuade a blackmailer with whom Forstl had had a homosexual affair. Lording it over him as if he, Schmidt, had made the error. Until he told Forstl that he had handled the matter with Arthur Schnitzler.

Forstl had gaped at him like a mouth-breather. 'Schnitzel, you fool!' he shouted at him. 'Not Schnitzler.' At which Schmidt pulled out the small leather-covered notepad he carried for such matters, and found the page with the appropriate name and showed it to Forstl.

'This was the name you gave me,' he said, reining in the desire to break the man's neck there and then and be done with it. 'Arthur Schnitzler, the physician. There was a plaque on the man's building.'

A look of horror had crossed Forstl's face as he realized the error was his own, and quickly explained how at that time he had been preoccupied with the 'traitor' Schnitzler, the playwright who had betrayed the military with some damned theater piece. Schmidt couldn't have cared less about the theater or the arts, and had never heard of the dramatist. All that concerned him was that the blackmailer Forstl mentioned was endangering the mission and needed a small disincentive.

Now he knew that he had got the wrong man. It was another doctor – named Arthur Schnitzel – he needed to deal with. And given the delay, a simple disincentive would hardly be enough now. No longer would it simply be enough to scare the man off with a beating. From what Forstl said of his last meeting with this Schnitzel, extreme action was now necessary.

Nor did Forstl apologize for his error, or for blaming Schmidt. His parting shot was, 'And no more fingers!'

Schmidt filed this slight away for another time, when there would be a reckoning.

He had yet to deal with the Schnitzel matter, but had made contact of a sort. At least he had found the correct address this time, a tenement in Hernals, and had learned the man's habits and when he was most vulnerable.

Meanwhile, there were other loose ends to tie up, or that needed cauterizing. Including Advokat Werthen and his connection to the matter at the Bower. Forstl again. Endangering his role as double agent with an unauthorized operation.

There was plenty of time for these ruminations as Schmidt strolled through the grounds of the Belvedere this sunny afternoon. Time enough even to recall his early, heady student days in St Petersburg.

It was the thought of the playwright Schnitzler that triggered these memories, the fact that he had never heard of the man. There was a time when he would have done, when the arts was all he cared about. He, the simple village boy from the Livonian coast north of Riga. His family was from a long line of amber fishers, plying the shore waters of that coast marked with banks of pine trees and sand dunes on the Baltic Sea. For two centuries the Klavan family had worked those waters in search of what was known as scoopstone, because of the large scoop-shaped nets used to sweep along the bottom of the sea and gather the precious chunks of amber dislodged from the ocean floor by wild storms and fierce tidal action. By the time young Pietr had joined his father and two older brothers in the trade, they were using a broad-beamed rowing-boat with men lying over the side raking the sea bottom to dislodge the amber, which was then swept into large nets.

For the fact that he was no good at this trade – the motion of the water even close to shore always made him ill – he compensated with his passion for music. He had no idea where the gift came from, but in the evenings he would entertain the family in their homely reed-roofed whitewashed dwelling with melodies picked out on the old violin his favorite uncle had given him. There had been no history of musicians in the family, only sturdy amber fishermen, but he loved the feel of the wood on that simple instrument which his uncle had found left behind in a tavern. The local priest had given Pietr rudimentary lessons, showing him the fingering and the sweep of bow against string. He had begun playing when he was eight; by the time he was fifteen he could play Bach sonatas in the local church, to the amazement of all, the rich, sonorous tones filling the small chapel.

His beloved uncle took to calling him Wenno – one of the masters of the Livonian Brothers of the Sword, a thirteenth-century military order founded in the vicinity of Riga. Like the knights of the Teutonic Order, the Livonian Brothers defended the Church in the northern crusades against the pagan peoples of the Baltic region. Pietr's uncle was a romantic: he claimed that the Klavans were descendants of the Livonian Brothers, that they were knights who took to the sea. Pietr's father had little patience for such nonsense, but Pietr would listen to his uncle's tales of the glorious deeds of this fighting order. His childhood was marked by dreams of devoting his own life to heroic deeds and to the warm touch of the violin he soon came to master.

Thus, when a nobleman, Count von Girzwold, from Riga happened to visit their humble chapel one Sunday when Pietr was playing his favorite Bach violin partita, he was overcome with emotion hearing this simple peasant lad create such sweet sounds. He talked with Pietr after the service, encouraged him to play more. This nobleman was a strong believer in the ideas of Rousseau; in Pietr he saw a perfect example of natural talent, of 'the noble savage'. He talked with Pietr's parents, who stood in the man's presence and bowed respectfully while he talked.

But upon his departure they said no. No, they would not send their youngest son off to the urban dangers of St Petersburg or the temptations of the Conservatory. For that was what the nobleman had offered them, intercession in winning the boy a scholarship to that famous musical institution.

But the uncle argued otherwise. The lad is unfit for the amber trade; far better to give him an education, make him a man of the world. He could become a famous musician, bring fame to the Klavan name once again, as in the age of the Livonian Brothers.

At which the father scoffed; but in the end he relented, after the nobleman offered to reimburse the father for the lost labor of his son.

And so it was off to St Petersburg for young Pietr; and when leaving, his uncle slipped him a going-away gift, telling him to open it only when safely on the train. Later, as the train carried him along the coast towards Tallinn, he opened the package and discovered a beautiful knife with amber-encrusted grip and the name Wenno inlaid in silver on the bronze blade. He tucked the prized knife away in his violin case.

The first weeks in St Petersburg were miserable ones for Pietr, accustomed as he was to the rhythms of the country, not the city. He had never used a flush toilet before, never ridden a street car or seen an electric light. The modest room he was assigned in a widow's flat seemed like a palace compared to his family home, but there was no warmth at night, no simple cheer of sitting around the open fire and sharing stories of the day's events, or experiencing the slap-and-clap accompaniment of his family to the tunes with which he would entertain them.

And the other students at the Conservatory, most of whom came from the professional class or higher, treated the scholarship boy like a leper. When he auditioned for and won a place with Professor Auer, he thought their attitude would change. He was right: it got worse. Now they called him names not just behind his back but to his face. They accused him of being the token poor boy, better suited to playing the hurdy-gurdy. One in particular, Heimito von Kornung, said the most stinging words:

'You're an amber fisher not a musician, Klavan. Go back to your own kind.'

He poured himself into his studies to prove them wrong. Auer was a harsh master, focusing on both technique and interpretation. His criticisms came so fast and furious that sometimes Pietr wondered why he had accepted him as a pupil; he must be terrible to deserve such criticism. He broke down one day, while playing Tchaikovsky's Violin Concerto in D Major, and voiced this senti-ment. Auer, who sat across from him bow in hand, usually brooked no such emotional outbursts. But the older man looked at him kindly, with sparkling eyes.

'It's because you have greatness in you, Klavan. That is why I am so hard on you. You of all the students in this Conservatory are headed for a concert career. You need to be strong, supple. Learn to bend against criticism and not let it break you.'

From that day on, Pietr began to feel at home in St Petersburg and at the Conservatory.

But it was short-lived comfort.

One afternoon, as he was about to prepare for his lesson with Auer, he came upon Heimito von Kornung and three of his wealthy friends. They were in the cloakroom, huddled near his locker. They seemed to be having a great deal of fun, giggling like little girls. He approached to retrieve his violin, and then saw what was amusing them. They had opened his violin case and were plucking the embedded bits of amber out of the cherished knife his uncle had given him.

Red-hot rage overcame him and he let out an animal scream as he plunged into their midst and grappled with Heimito for the knife. The other took up a defensive posture, switching instantly from humorous vandalism to deadly intent. Pietr could see it in his eyes: Heimito wanted to kill him. And Pietr understood the urge, for he too wanted to do as much damage as he could to these animals.

Pietr had never been in a fight, but he had witnessed plenty between the men on pay-days when they had spent too much time at the local inn. As Heimito swooped at him with the blade, Pietr dodged and spun out of range, whipping off the jacket of his woollen suit and wrapping it round his left arm. He quickly surveyed the area for a weapon, but the only thing within reach was his violin. He grabbed it and began circling to the right, out of range of the knife. Heimito made a sudden lunge and Pietr was able to block his thrust with his left arm, though the blade penetrated the wool and sank into his forearm. But he ignored the pain and swung his violin into Heimito's left temple, stunning the larger boy, who stumbled backwards, tripping over a bench. Pietr was on him now, lashing out with the violin mercilessly, hearing the crack of wood, the ping of broken strings, but not caring.

The others pulled him off, holding him by the arms. He was panting like a wild animal. Heimito struggled to his feet, blood coursing down his face. His eyes were tiny slits of hatred as he came up to Pietr, who struggled to free himself.

'Hold him,' Heimito ordered his companions.

And then he grabbed Pietr's left hand, securing his little finger in a tight grip and bent it until it broke like a twig. The pain tore at Pietr, but he forced back the tears. That he did not show the pain served only to anger Heimito further. He took Pietr's right little finger in the same grip and broke that one as well.

A scream filled the small room, and Pietr only slowly realized it came from him.

'Now try playing the fiddle, amber man.' Heimito spat at him and then left the room. The others followed.

The affair was, of course, covered up, for Heimito's parents had power. The others accused Pietr of attacking them; and the administration, despite Auer's protests, took their side.

Pietr rode the train back to his little village in disgrace, the broken violin in its case, his injured fingers splinted and bandaged, the wound on his forearm hot and sore.

It took two weeks before he finally told his uncle what had happened.

'So you won't be a famous musician,' his uncle said with surprisingly little sympathy. 'Did you fight back?'

Pietr nodded. 'I bloodied him.' His only regret was that he had not killed Heimito.

'Good. In that case we will make a knight of you.'

It happened very quickly. His uncle had a word with Count von Girzwold, who used his connections in St Petersburg to obtain a place for Pietr in the officers' cadet school. It was there an instructor saw his potential: the chameleon who could be at home in the country or the city; the man of no distinguishing characteristics. A person of iron will, both ruthless and clever. Thus was born Schmidt, agent number 302.

Schmidt suddenly realized he had been standing by the same flower-bed for minutes on end, staring at the orange-red swirl of geraniums on the ground before him. He blinked hard, feeling sudden moisture in his eyes. The pollen must be getting to me, he told himself.

And then he saw his quarry, the lawyer and his older companion, leaving the Upper Belvedere and heading for the gate in the Rennweg. He did not follow immediately, however, waiting until the cornstalk man took up position behind them. Schmidt quickly took off his bowler hat and tossed it into a bin when no one was watching. He needed to alter his appearance in some way. Cornstalk had not noticed him yet, but Schmidt was a cautious man.

Then the tall watcher suddenly turned and scanned the gardens once again, his eyes flickering past Schmidt, with his changed appearance.

No more following today, Schmidt decided. Caution had kept him alive for many years now.

Besides, he had the pressing matter of Doktor Schnitzel to deal with.

His experiences at the St Petersburg Conservatory had closed Schmidt's mind to the arts. Thereafter, they had become dead for him. He avoided mention of or contact with artists of any kind.

But now he realized such a stance was impractical. The fact that he had not known of this playwright, Schnitzler, made him less effective as an agent. His personal history had impinged on his mission. And that was something he would not let happen again.

TWENTY-ONE

'**K**limt, it's marvelous! However did you finish it so quickly?' Berthe was in Klimt's studio near their flat in the Josefstädterstrasse. The oil painting rested against the single-ply wall of the small studio built in the courtyard of an old apartment house. A cat twined around her legs as she examined the portrait. The woman was seated, wearing a soft chiffon dress in a wonderful shade of light blue – Berthe was unsure what to call the color. Not sky blue; paler. And not baby blue. Somewhere in between. A graceful portrait. The face of Marie Louise von Suttner, the troublesome niece, stared back at her, quite lifelike. The very image she had captured with the Brownie camera.

'Waste not want not,' Klimt said, smiling. 'It is quite good, no? One would never know the identity of the actual sitter.'

Klimt gave Berthe a sheepish look. 'Her husband was not well pleased to discover his wife was sitting for me. Gossip, you know.' In other words, Berthe understood, Klimt had slept with the lady in question, then her husband had found out and cancelled the commission. Marie Louise's head had been superimposed upon the body of the original subject.

'Fortunate they have the same body type,' Berthe said.

'Do they?' Klimt glanced at the painting now, appreciating his own work, or perhaps regretting that he was unable to paint Marie Louise in the flesh. Quite literally, for it was said that Klimt painted his female sitters in the nude and then later painted on layers of clothing.

'This will serve the purpose perfectly, Klimt. You are a genius.'

'Yes, so I've been told. Now, how about some coffee and cake?'

No Prokop or Meier today, Werthen noticed, as he sounded the bell on Schnitzler's flat. Gross stood next to him, surveying the ornamental plasterwork over the door: putti draped in what appeared to be grapes.

Werthen heard the brass plate on the peephole on the other side of the door slide back and saw the lens go dark as an eye was put to it. Then came the rattle of unbolting and unchaining, and the playwright himself opened the door.

'Herr Advokat! How good to see you. I rather thought you had given up on my hopeless case.' He looked from Werthen to Gross with a question in his eyes.

Before Werthen could answer, Schnitzler rushed on. 'Ah, that must be it. I have been rather remiss in sending payment. I do apologize.' He continued to look at Gross as if trying to place him.

'I assure you, Herr Schnitzler, that is not the case. This is my colleague, Doktor Gross. If we may come in, I can explain the purpose of our visit.'

'Please,' Schnitzler stood aside, sweeping his left hand towards the hallway. 'I was just having coffee in the study. Perhaps you would like to join me?'

The walk from the Upper Belvedere to the Ninth District had done little to cut through the heavy meal they had enjoyed courtesy of Franz Ferdinand. 'That would be good,' Werthen said. As they entered the flat, the scent of hyacinths greeted them, from a bouquet in a crystal vase on a side table by the coat and hat rack.

'I am honored to be host to the eminent criminologist,' Schnitzler said, closing the door behind them.

'And I,' Gross said, turning to face him, 'am equally pleased to finally make the acquaintance of the famous playwright.'

'Hardly famous,' Schnitzler said. 'Outside Vienna, that is. But let me tell cook to bring more coffee. I was in my study, but we can . . .'

'The study would be fine,' Werthen said.

They followed Schnitzler as he quickly ducked into the kitchen to give instructions, and then led them past the sitting room where they had met previously and on to double doors deeper in the apartment. Schnitzler was moving well and seemed to have gotten over most of his injuries. Apparently he had also gotten over his fear of further attack, if the absence of Prokop and Meier signified.

They went into a large and rather dark room; heavy drapes partially concealed floor-to-ceiling windows, a massive Persian carpet covered much of the parquet, and a bear skin sat under a large desk in the center of the room, its teeth bared at Werthen. Two walls were littered with framed photographs of friends, theater bills, and lithographs of foreign capitals. Another wall was completely covered by a bookcase that held leather-bound volumes of German and French writers from Goethe to Balzac.

Before they had a chance to sit down, the door opened behind them and the cook, a shy little woman with the shadow of a moustache on her upper lip, brought in a porcelain coffee pot and matching cups. A ring-shaped *Gugelhupf* cake accompanied this. Gross patted his stomach as if readying it for battle.

'Thank you, Martha,' Schnitzler said as the cook set it down on the desk. 'We'll serve ourselves.'

'Very good,' she said in a raspy voice.

Gross and Werthen pulled straight-backed leather-seated chairs to the desk. Schnitzler had obviously been at work when they arrived; manuscript pages littered the desk.

'A new play?' Werthen asked.

'A novel, actually. I've been attempting it for years. Perhaps I should just content myself with theater pieces and short stories. Olga . . . That is Fräulein Gussman, my fiancée, advises as much.'

Werthen noticed that Schnitzler now referred to Fräulein Gussman as his intended. She must be a powerful young woman, indeed.

'I'm sure you must follow your own instincts in this, Herr Schnitzler,' Gross said. 'Only an artist knows an artist's mind. Wouldn't you agree?'

Gross was being rather fulsome, Werthen thought. Normally he berated bohemia for self-indulgence. Science was for him – besides the work of his beloved Brueghel the Elder, of course – the only true art. But in fact Gross was simply employing his own interviewing technique for witnesses who do not wish to speak the truth, as set down in his book *Criminal Investigation*: 'You must take the witness entirely out of the circumstances and ask something which he does not anticipate.'

There was a time in Werthen's life when that work was his bible.

'I do agree, Herr Doktor Gross. It is good to see a man of practicalities such as yourself in tune with the artist's psyche.'

Gross smiled blandly at this and accepted the cup of coffee Schnitzler poured for him as well as a not insignificant slice of the *Gugelhupf*. Werthen took the coffee but not the cake.

'So, gentlemen, what may I do for you?' Schnitzler said once they had taken initial sips.

Gross set his cup down. 'You can tell us the truth about Fräulein Mitzi.'

This made Schnitzler sit up straight in his chair. 'But I have.

What more is there to tell? It is not a pretty picture I have painted of myself.'

'But it is the picture Vienna knows you by,' Gross said. 'The roué who takes the virginity of the sweet young thing and then casts her aside when she falls in love with him. The subject of so many of your theater pieces.'

Schnitzler turned from Gross to Werthen. 'Advokat, what is your colleague getting at? I have been honest with you. Painfully so.'

'I think not, Herr Schnitzler,' Werthen replied. 'I think that perhaps you have been protecting your reputation as a debauchee and rake. We have reason to believe that Fräulein Mitzi was not quite the sweet young innocent you portray her as.'

'What does it matter? The girl is dead.'

'It matters in terms of a range of suspects,' Gross answered. 'And of motive. We need to know who stood to benefit from her death.'

'I did not kill her.'

'We are not accusing you, Herr Schnitzler,' Gross said calmly. 'But we must have the truth from you about the young woman.'

Schnitzler tapped his right forefinger on the desktop as if transmitting Morse code.

'Alright,' he said finally. 'The truth. But this must not reach Olga's ears.'

Neither Gross nor Werthen assured him of this. Another moment of silence ensued.

Schnitzler let out an exasperated sigh. Then began to tell them about Mitzi.

'She brought nothing but trouble. A regular little vixen. We met in the park, as I told you. She appeared to be such a sweet young thing. And acted the part as well – until I got her in bed. It was obvious she had been with a man before. She told me it was her uncle who had done it, who had ruined her. And I felt sorry for her. But then she threatened to go to Olga, to tell her of our affair. She demanded I marry her. Her! A common little thing from the country. I finally had to buy her off. Not cheap, either, I can tell you. But anything to get her out of my life.'

'Then she was not cast out on the streets penniless after leaving you?' Werthen said.

'On the contrary. She could well afford lodgings after depleting my savings. You know what she told me when she finally left? She laughed at me and said that she had chosen the name Mitzi—'

'I thought you had given her that pet name,' Werthen said.

Schnitzler shook his head. 'That's what I told you. To save face. In fact, she had studied me and learned that I had affairs with two women named Mitzi in the past. One of them my great love.' He sighed again.

Werthen knew the story. The Mitzi he was talking about had had a child, stillborn, by Schnitzler, and then died from sepsis.

'She used me. Played me for a fool. She was only ever in it for the money, I am sure.'

'Then why go to the Bower?' Gross asked.

'Search me,' Schnitzler said. 'But there must have been money involved.'

'And you discovered her there later?' Werthen asked.

'Yes. Just as I told you. That part was the truth. But I stayed away.'

'Yet you told your friend Altenberg about this sweet young thing,' Werthen pressed. 'Weren't you afraid she would do the same to him?'

'No, no. Peter is, well . . . Peter does not get involved with women in the same way. Besides, she threatened to disclose our affair if I did not send her a nice steady regular. Peter fitted that description, and I assumed he would enjoy her schoolgirl act.'

'So you see, Herr Schnitzler, how important it is we have a true picture of the victim,' Gross said.

'I don't understand . . .'

'Motive,' said Gross, in his prosecuting magistrate's voice. 'You've got heaps of motive. There must be others, as well.'

'I swear that I did not—' And then he stopped himself. 'If anybody had motive it would be that uncle of hers.'

'We have reason to believe that Father Hieronymus was also badly used by her.'

'I see,' he said, nodding his head. 'That would make sense. In that case, I think I might have made an error. I should never have let those two go.'

'Prokop and Meier, you mean?'

Schnitzler nodded at Werthen. 'I assumed that after two weeks the danger had passed. But . . .' He trailed off, looking towards the ceiling as if computing a maths problem. 'If they had still been in my employ, the man would never have got in to see me. When you rang, I thought he'd come back.'

'That who had come back?' said Werthen.

'The father. Mitzi's father. The man was insane with grief. Cook let him in unsuspectingly. He came here accusing me of ruining his daughter. Seemed truly out of his mind.'

'And what error did you make, Schnitzler?' Werthen demanded. 'What did you tell him?' But he had already guessed the answer.

'That he had the wrong man. It was the uncle he should be accosting, not me. The uncle who took her virginity.'

'Jesus,' Werthen said. 'How long ago was this?'

Schnitzler shook his head. 'An hour ago, maybe more. But at the time I thought that was the case. It was an honest mistake.'

'Was he armed?' Gross asked.

'He was menacing. Crazy.'

'We've got to get to the uncle,' Werthen said.

As they quickly made their way to the door, Schnitzler called out to them, 'An honest mistake.'

They were in luck; a fiaker drove by just as they came out of the apartment house. Werthen flagged it down, gave the driver the address, and promised a healthy tip if he could get them there as fast as possible. With Werthen's usual fiaker driver, Bachmann, at the reins, it had taken forty-five minutes to reach the parish church of St Johann near the Meidlinger Haupstrasse. This cabbie accomplished the journey in thirty, with Werthen and Gross holding on to leather grips with tightly clenched fists and bobbing back and forth on the seat as the horse's hooves sparked on the cobbles and the carriage rattled along.

Arriving at the church, Werthen gave the man a crown and did not bother waiting for change. Both he and Gross ran past the church and through the graveyard to the small hunting lodge at the back that served as the rectory. They had not spoken during the journey, but now Gross, in between deep breaths, said, 'I hope for that man's sake we are not too late.'

It was not clear which man he meant; for both it would indeed be a tragedy.

Reaching the rectory, Werthen had just gripped the brass hand-shaped knocker when the front door flew open. It was the aged housekeeper and her eyes looked wild.

'Oh, murder, murder! Please, you must help.'

She grabbed Werthen's arm and he could hear voices shouting from down the long hallway. He raced to the door of the study, Gross behind him. As they reached it, they heard a harsh scream and then a crash of furniture. Throwing open the door, Werthen saw Herr Moos, Mitzi's father. In his hand was the poker from the ceramic stove, held by the tip; the heavy brass handle at the other end was smeared in blood. His face was a mask of rage and he was about to strike again at the body at his feet, but the overturned chair was in his way, allowing Werthen the opportunity to grab the man's arm. But Moos was enraged, and his strength was magnified by it. He threw Werthen off like a child, and he fell back and over the desk.

As he picked himself up, he saw that Gross had now tried to grab the man, but he too was tossed aside like a rag doll. Neither he nor Gross was armed. He therefore looked for a weapon, and grabbed a chair by the desk, noticing as he did so the crumpled body of Father Hieronymus at Moos's feet, the man's thinning ash-blond hair a tangle of blood. There was no time to think. Moos was swinging the poker, for a second time, handle first, at the priest's head. Werthen parried the thrust with the chair, knocking the poker out of Moos's hand. The housekeeper stood screaming helplessly in the doorway.

'Murder! Murder! He's killed him!'

The screams seemed to finally get through to Moos, who looked quickly from the housekeeper to Werthen and then to the motionless body of his brother-in-law. He let out an animal growl, turned, and ran out of the room, knocking the old housekeeper down on the way out.

Gross followed, but Werthen knelt by the priest to see if he could help. One look told him that it was hopeless. The skull had not simply been fractured; it was pulverized, a mass of blood and bone shard. The priest's watery blue eyes stared up at him without focus. Werthen put a finger to the carotid artery; there was no pulse. He closed the eyelids.

Too late. For either of them.

Werthen got to his feet, then made sure the housekeeper was not injured. 'Do you have a telephone here?'

Her eyes were still round as silver crown pieces.

'A telephone,' he said in almost a shout.

A quavering finger pointed back down the hallway. He saw it now in the gloom, on a hall table. He quickly telephoned the gendarmerie's emergency number and reported the incident, then went to hunt for Gross.

Outside, beyond the church, a small crowd had gathered. Werthen headed towards it. As he approached, he could see the legs of a body sprawled on the sidewalk. No, he thought. Not Gross, too. His heart raced and he could barely breathe as he pushed through the crowd to get to his friend, all the time calling out 'Gross'.

Then, as he emerged from the throng, he saw Gross standing over the unconscious body of Herr Moos.

'Ah, Werthen. How good of you to come.'

'Gross, how were you able to—'

'Friend Duncan,' he said. 'He thought it best not to wait at the scene. I assume you telephoned the police.'

Werthen nodded. 'They're on their way.'

They both looked down at Moos, beginning now to stir on the sidewalk.

'I suggest we bind the fellow before he completely regains consciousness,' Gross said.

'Murder! Murder!'

The housekeeper came stumbling across the street, spreading her tale of doom and woe to the shocked crowd.

'Why bother with the police?' came a shout from the back of the crowd. 'We should do him in here and now.'

'And hang for it yourselves?' Gross said. 'Don't be idiotic. We no longer live in the jungle. That was this man's error,' he said, pointing at Moos. 'Now help us secure him until the police arrive.'

There was grumbling from those gathered, but finally a peddler of household wares produced some strong jute rope from his cart and they bound Moos's hands and feet.

Five minutes later a motorized police van arrived, followed by an ambulance.

The crowd stayed long enough to see the body of Father Hieronymus wheeled out, the sheet covering him stained red at the head.

Gross shook his head. 'That one death would have such far-reaching consequences,' he said, with a note of sadness.

Gross was right, Werthen knew. He only wondered when the repercussions of Mitzi's death would cease.

TWENTY-TWO

'**O**nce again, gentlemen, your meddling has caused untold harm to a police investigation.'

Officious, tiny Meindl, clad today in an impeccably tailored linen three-piece suit in a pale shade of moss green, sat behind his massive desk at the Police Praesidium, his neatly manicured hands clasped over his narrow chest, hissing out the words in the affected Schönbrunn accent of the upper classes. He was making a hash of the job, Werthen knew, and was sure that Gross, seated next to him, could give the man dialect coaching advice, for he had made a long study of such speech patterns as part of his suspect-identification research.

'That is a bit much,' Gross said, who had until now sat quietly, listening to the railings of the inspector, his former protégé. 'Perhaps in the matter of Herr Mutzenbacher we acted somewhat precipitously, but I fail to see how we are at fault in the unfortunate death of Father Hieronymus.'

Meindl adjusted his tortoiseshell pince-nez and shook his head. 'If you had shared the information of your investigations into the death of this young . . .' Meindl was searching for the *mot juste* to describe a prostitute.

'Fräulein Waltraude Moos,' Inspector Drechsler, seated behind them, offered. 'Otherwise known as Fräulein Mitzi.'

'Exactly,' Meindl said with an appreciative nod his way. 'Fräulein Moos. In that case we would surely have foreseen the possibilities of such an altercation.'

'Surely,' said Gross, with ironic emphasis.

'I was in the process of handing over the files,' Werthen said. 'I spoke with Drechsler about it only yesterday. But there was no time.'

'Quite. Time is something the good priest ran out of yesterday.'

Gross was growing impatient. 'And you have no leads to Siegfried Mutzenbacher?'

'The man's bolted,' Meindl said. 'What would you expect him to do, given your advance notice to him?'

But Gross would not be baited. 'His sister?'

'She says she knows nothing of his whereabouts. Only that he returned to her establishment at midday yesterday distraught. By the evening, he had simply disappeared, taking with him the weekly receipts, which were to be deposited today.'

'I assume,' said Gross, 'that you have distributed his likeness to all the appropriate agencies, railway stations, border police—'

'That is no longer your concern,' Meindl interrupted. 'I have been apprised of your powerful friend in this regard. He has been duly notified of the situation. I believe it is safe to say that the matter has been concluded. Not exactly successfully, but at least we now know where to lay blame. It will be up to other jurisdictions to return this killer.'

Meindl's pronouncement was at once obvious and cryptic. The implication, Werthen understood, was that Franz Ferdinand must have told the Police Praesidium that he and Gross were acting as the Archduke's agents. Gross had requested as much via Duncan earlier in the day, when they were summoned for an afternoon meeting with Meindl.

That much was clear. But when Meindl insisted that the matter had been concluded, Werthen felt a bit at sea.

Gross was equally unsure. He looked squarely at Meindl. 'What do you mean by "concluded"? You take Siegfried Mutzenbacher's flight as proof of his guilt in the murder of Count von Ebersdorf?'

'Yes. Among others.'

'You want to hang all the deaths on Siegfried?' Werthen said, amazed at the man's audacity.

Meindl leaned back in his chair, smiling at them like a lizard. '"Hang" is the apposite word here. For he certainly will hang once apprehended. But that is not our concern now. He has most likely taken himself off to Italy. The onus is now on the Italians to do the right thing.'

'How can you be certain of his destination?' Gross thundered.

'My dear Herr Doktor. It is a simple matter of deduction such as you yourself promote. Upon searching the man's room this morning, Inspector Drechsler came upon this.'

He proudly held up a dog-eared Italian phrase book, as if producing a gun still smoking at the barrel.

'And this proves what?' Gross demanded.

'Come now, Gross. The man was obviously polishing up his Italian. Ergo, Italy's where he would head in times of trouble.'

'Brilliant,' said Gross. 'In which case, however, why would he leave the phrase book behind? Or had he perfected his Italian already?'

Meindl scowled at this suggestion, placing the phrase book down on the desk.

'And your evidence for Siegfried's guilt in the murder of Fräulein Mitzi and Fräulein Fanny?'

'The psychological component must be reckoned with,' Meindl said. 'You yourself told Inspector Drechsler that Siegfried and Mitzi had a special relationship.'

'Special, not necessarily sexual,' Werthen added.

Meindl ignored this. 'And that the young lady in question was not the poor innocent country girl she appeared to be. In fact, she was a highly manipulative young woman. Who is to say she did not flaunt her relationship with von Ebersdorf? So that Siegfried snapped and killed her in a jealous rage, and then disposed of her lover, von Ebersdorf, as well?'

'And in this theory of events,' said Werthen, 'Fräulein Fanny was, I assume, blackmailing Siegfried, having seen or heard something incriminating.'

'Exactly, Advokat. And this is not a theory or conjecture, but represents the facts of the matter. We have a letter to prove it.'

'How handy of Siegfried to leave behind a confession,' Gross said.

'No, not from Herr Mutzenbacher.' Meindl looked beyond them to Inspector Drechsler. 'Perhaps you would care to inform the gentlemen, Inspector?'

Werthen and Gross turned to face Drechsler, who was looking more tired than usual.

'I found not only the phrase book in Herr Mutzenbacher's room, but also a letter addressed to Fräulein Mitzi. It seems unlikely it was sent through the mail. Instead, it was probably given to her during a session.'

'A session?' Gross said.

'Well, whatever it is one calls the time the girls at the Bower spend with their customers.'

'You mean it was from one of Mitzi's clients?'

'Yes, Advokat. It clearly was.'

'Von Ebersdorf?' Gross said.

Drechsler nodded. 'And it was clear the man was besotted with the girl. Spoke of wanting to run away with her.'

'You have shown this to handwriting experts?' Gross asked.

'Under way as we speak,' Meindl said. 'But it appears to be genuine.'

'Siegfried Mutzenbacher obviously discovered this love note,' Drechsler continued, 'and felt betrayed by Mitzi, setting in motion the entire tragic string of events.'

'So,' Meindl said imperiously, 'you see, gentlemen, that this case has been put to rest. A simple crime of passion in which, out of jealousy, Siegfried Mutzenbacher killed first Fräulein Mitzi and then the man he felt had cuckolded him. Fräulein Fanny sees the love letter from von Ebersdorf, puts two and two together, and tries to blackmail Siegfried, who kills her, as well. Your sponsor was satisfied with the results, I assure you. In future, I must insist that you confer with the police in such matters. I regret to say that your intervention has allowed a guilty man to remain free for the present, but I can also safely say that good, solid police investigative procedures have led to a successful culmination of the case.'

'Granted, it is not the optimum outcome,' Franz Ferdinand told them. 'It would have been much better to have had the man in custody.' He shook his head, disgusted. 'What was Joachim von Ebersdorf thinking of?'

Gross and Werthen exchanged glances. Clearly the Archduke was accepting Meindl's version of events.

They were meeting in the Lower Belvedere today, in Franz Ferdinand's war room, its walls covered with maps of each of the sections of Austria's far-flung empire. Stick pins with tiny red, yellow and green pennons decorated the maps, making them look like geographic pincushions. Werthen imagined these pins symbolized the deployment of the Imperial-Royal army along the borders of the empire.

'I would like to verify the handwriting of that note myself, your Highness,' Gross said.

'You do not trust Inspector Meindl?'

'Let us say simply that graphology is a complex skill.'

The Archduke nodded. 'It shall be done. Though let it be known that I am satisfied with the outcome. We will discover the whereabouts of Herr Mutzenbacher one fine day and then learn the complete truth about these events. But in the case of Count von Ebersdorf, it seems certain that Mutzenbacher was the culprit. I must thank both of you. A case neatly wrapped up.'

But he was only putting a polite face on it, Werthen knew. Siegfried was the key to it all, and they had let him slip away.

'I have deposited the agreed sum in your account,' Franz Ferdinand said, standing. 'And now . . .'

It was their cue to take their leave. They stood and made to bow, but the Archduke put out his hand and took each of theirs in turn.

'My thanks gentlemen. Oh, and Advokat, you can tell that clever wife of yours that her little favor has been accomplished. The hotel concierge was shipped off last night.'

'Thank you, your Highness. Berthe will be very pleased.'

As they left the grounds of the Belvedere, Werthen said, 'Very neat and tidy.'

'Yes,' Gross allowed. 'Everyone seems pleased.'

'What now?'

'Now, dear friend, after examining the note from Count von Ebersdorf and ascertaining its authenticity, I shall take my leave. I have to prepare for that interview in Prague.'

'You accept Meindl's solution, then?'

'I didn't say that. Merely that I am off to Prague in the morning. I think we have taken this matter as far as possible for the moment. Wouldn't you agree?'

It had been very close. Forstl had taken great pains to gain access to the top-secret files of the War Office. There was, of course, an overlap between his duties in intelligence and the Russia desk, but if discovered with the mobilization plans he would be hard put to explain it. And that is exactly what almost happened that afternoon. Just as he was pulling out the drawer with the plans, his nemesis at the Bureau, Captain Johann von Daum, strolled into the room, his arms filled with folders to be filed.

Forstl had to quickly close the one drawer and open another, dealing with Russian Army deployments, more his area of responsibility. Von Daum gave him one of his supercilious looks, but Forstl had bluffed his way through, taking out a file on the Köningsberg region.

'I was unaware you were certified for War Office files,' Captain Johann von Daum said.

'That's not surprising, Captain,' Forstl answered coolly. 'The clearance came through only two days ago. You might check with Colonel von Krahlich if . . .'

'Just a comment,' von Daum said. 'Just a comment. You have come a long way in a short time, Captain Forstl.'

He would love to see von Daum squirm. Perhaps he could be his next sacrificial lamb. Plant papers on him and then reveal him to be a double agent. That would be a fine day.

For now, Forstl tried to put the thoughts of the day out of his mind. He settled down in the depths of his bed, eager to sleep, eager to let the tension in his body slip away. He lay on his right side, curled somewhat, his favorite sleeping position. Never could sleep on his back. He slid his right arm under the pillow, feeling the muscles in his neck begin to relax.

But then his right hand hit a foreign object. Not part of the eiderdown pillow – something hard and angular.

He grasped the object. It appeared to be a box. He turned up the lamp on his bedside table, pulled the box out from under the pillow, and opened it without thinking.

His eyes grew large as he saw what was inside. A scream caught in his throat as he threw the box across the room.

A severed penis hit the wall and rolled to a stop under the dressing table.

PART THREE

TWENTY-THREE

'Does it always rain in June here?' Emile von Werthen was clearly put out by the weather in Laab im Walde. He'd brought along his butterfly net and collecting jars, and now stood like a disappointed child at the window, dressed in breeches and linen smock, watching the puddles forming in the courtyard of 'the farm'.

He presented a pitiful sight, and Werthen felt a sudden sympathy for his father. For the first time, he recognized that the man was vulnerable, and then Werthen remembered with something of a shock that his father was over sixty. He had taken to combing his thinning hair forward, rather in the style of a Roman senator; the tidy little moustache he sported looked strangely darker than before, obviously dyed. Once so tall and thin, he seemed diminished and had something of a stoop now.

As Emile von Werthen maintained his post at the rain-splattered window, gazing out wanly, butterfly net in hand, Werthen experienced a strange emotion – not dissimilar to the protective love he felt for his little daughter Frieda.

'The weather will surely clear up later this afternoon,' Frau von Werthen told her husband. 'Now come back to the table and eat your boiled egg.'

Emile von Werthen turned towards the breakfast table where Werthen, Berthe, Frieda and Frau von Werthen were seated.

'My god, I'd rather spend my day with the Lepidoptera than with such a gathering of humanity.'

Saying this, he stomped away from the window in stockinged feet and headed for the guest room at the back of the farmhouse.

Werthen could only shake his head. A hard man to love.

Werthen's parents had come to visit while their property in the Vienna Woods was being prepared for building work. His father had said he wanted to be there for the laying of the cornerstone. Werthen had given up trying to dissuade them from such a project and relented in his objections to having his parents so close at hand. However, scenes such as the one at the breakfast table made Werthen regret any such emotional weakness on his part.

As it turned out, the afternoon did not bring clear skies; instead, it saw the arrival of more visitors. Herr Meisner, Berthe's father, who had recently rented a small flat in Vienna, arrived in a covered fiaker. Emile von Werthen, who had returned to his post at the window, was the first to spot him.

'Well, I'll be . . .' he said. 'Looks like your father is coming to tea,' he called out to Berthe.

Busy in the kitchen making dough for the ravioli which they were to have for dinner, Berthe wiped a floured hand at a strand of hair that had fallen into her face, leaving a smudge of white on her cheek.

'He was supposed to come next weekend,' she said.

'Ah, doing the in-laws in shifts, are we?'

'Emile!' his wife, seated at the table doing needlework, gently chided her husband.

'Well, we have had our differences . . .' he began. And then said in amazement, 'Good lord, the man's got a woman in tow.'

Berthe hurried to the window in time to see her father gripping the hand of a tall, heavily cloaked woman descending the last step down from the carriage. Both were dressed for the weather, and put their heads down against a sudden gust of wind as they made their way across the muddy court towards the door.

Berthe had yet to meet her father's new friend and was amazed that he would bring her unannounced like this. She hurriedly took off her apron, after wiping her hands on it. Flustered, she looked round for some place to put it. Her father-in-law took it from her, smiling, and dabbed at her powdered cheek with a corner of it.

'A woman should look nice for her father,' he said with sudden tenderness.

This only served to fluster Berthe more. 'Could you get Karl?'

He nodded and headed for the study, where Werthen was catching up on some legal work he had brought with him for the weekend.

'Who is the woman, dear?' Frau von Werthen asked as Berthe moved to the door.

'I—' Berthe said, and then came a rapping at the door.

Berthe opened it to see her father in the company of Frau von Suttner.

'Oh,' Berthe said. 'Hello. How good to see you . . . both.'

Werthen, Berthe and Frau von Suttner gathered in the study, leaving the in-laws to fend for themselves.

Herr Meisner was staying at Berthe and Werthen's flat in Vienna while his own apartment was being readied. He had not given up his home in Linz, but intended to spend more time in Vienna, especially since making the acquaintance of a 'special friend'.

Frau von Suttner had come to the flat, looking for Berthe. After explaining the reason for her visit to Herr Meisner and receiving plaudits from him – as he was just as enthusiastic a fan of her work as Berthe – the two of them made the journey out to Laab im Walde together.

'I must apologize for bursting in on you like this,' Frau von Suttner said, now they were comfortably seated in the study. 'I just had to thank you.'

She fixed Berthe with her grey eyes, smiling.

'Well, it was just a silly misunderstanding,' Berthe said. 'Anybody could have cleared it up.'

Frau von Suttner shook her head. 'Please. I am fully grown. There is no need to continue the subterfuge. Arthur . . . Baron von Suttner is playing his part quite nicely. He has brought me on a luxury trip to Vienna for the weekend as a birthday celebration. But then of course you must know that.'

That part of it Berthe had not arranged. 'I assure you, Baroness . . .'

'I have already got a peek at the surprise present. My only concern is that Herr Klimt does not break the bank – we have those roof repairs to think of.'

Berthe's face reddened, realizing that her ploy had not fooled Frau von Suttner.

'It was done as a personal favour,' Berthe said.

'Yes,' the Baroness nodded, looking at Werthen. 'A former client, as I remember.'

'My first case,' Werthen said.

'The portrait is quite beautiful. Who was the original model?'

'Klimt has his little secrets,' Berthe replied.

Another smile crossed von Suttner's face. 'Don't be downcast. You have performed a wonderful service. Miracles, however, are not in your line of work. I know Arthur and the girl were carrying on. It tears at my heart, but I accept it. You have made a valiant effort to protect me from the truth, but as you see, I shall survive. I have kept a brave face for the two of them. They think I actually believe the story of them sneaking off to Vienna to have the great painter Klimt create a portrait of Marie for my birthday tomorrow. How clever you are!'

Again, Berthe felt her face grow red. 'I am sorry.'

'Do not be. You have done us a great service. You have kept my husband's indiscretions from damaging the peace movement, from possibly compromising my own whole-hearted involvement in it. That to me is a case successfully concluded. I just had to tell you this personally, from the bottom of my heart. Thank you, dear girl. I also wanted to give this to you.'

She handed Berthe a transcribed and translated version of the letters from Fräulein Mitzi that Werthen had taken from her parent's house in the Weinviertel.

They could not convince Frau von Suttner or Herr Meisner to stay. The fiaker was still waiting in the courtyard, but the driver had finally taken refuge in the kitchen, and Werthen's father was busily informing him of the saintly derivation of the name of his carriage.

'Fiacre was a seventh-century Irish monk, you see, my good man.'

The fiaker driver did not appear to have any saintly qualities, his tell-tale red, venous nose a tribute to Bacchus, not to Irish saints.

'A healer, in fact, who built a hospice for travelers in France. Later, the Hotel de Saint Fiacre in Paris rented out carriages, so the French gave the saint's name to rented carriages. And *voilà*, my good sir, you have the fiaker.'

The cabbie was not listening to this peroration. Instead, he asked Frau von Werthen for another cup of tea.

'And I wouldn't say no to a spot of slivowitz in it. Driving a carriage is a cold wet job today.'

After they had left and his parents had gone to their room for a nap (Frieda was just up from hers), Werthen asked Berthe about the one aspect of the case he did not understand. She had obviously charmed Klimt into doing his part, and had gotten Archduke Franz Ferdinand to have the hideous hotel deskman deported to his native Italy with a warning not to return – so the sole witness to the Baron's assignation with his niece was neatly taken care of. One thing, however, remained unclear to him.

'How did you convince the Baron to go along with this ruse? An appeal to his better self?'

'Something like that. But the niece was having none of it.'

Berthe was back to working the dough for the ravioli.

'Well?' he said.

'So I told him the truth. That he was being watched by agents for the state who wanted to embarrass his wife, to destroy the work that she . . . they . . . had accomplished over many years.'

'And that did the job?'

'With him. Not with the girl.'

The kitchen resounded with the thump of pummeled dough.

'Noodoo!' Frieda said, delightedly watching her mother work the dough.

'That's right, *Schatzi*,' Berthe said. 'Noodle.'

'And you said . . .'

Berthe turned from the dough to Werthen. 'That I would have the watcher on the street corner outside come up and arrest them for gross indecency if she did not agree. That seemed to get through to her.'

'Well done!' Werthen said, bringing a smile to her lips.

Werthen only then remembered the letters Frau von Suttner had brought with her and went back to the study to look at them.

The first one talked about Schnitzler and contained nothing of interest; and most of the second one was filled with flowery lies about the grand life the girl was living in Vienna. He checked the date; it had been sent during her time as a prostitute at the Bower.

But one phrase did stand out. 'You will all be so proud of me,' she wrote. 'I am working in secret but for the good of the country. You might say this is patriotic work!'

TWENTY-FOUR

'You are never satisfied, Gross,' Berthe said as they finished their coffee after a sumptuous Frau Blatschky feast of stuffed cabbage preceded by liver-dumpling soup and followed by *Kaiserschmarrn,* a kind of caramelized crêpe.

'Prague has the world's oldest university,' Werthen added.

'Yes, that is true,' Gross said, eying the dish of *Kaiserschmarrn* hungrily. 'But in a modern science like criminalistics, old is not especially good.'

'But you would be back in Europe again,' Berthe said. 'It certainly is an improvement on Czernowitz.'

'My dear lady, St Pölten would be an improvement on Czernowitz. And as for Europe, I believe you mean Central Europe. There is a difference.'

'Come now, Gross. You're just being obstinate. Prague is a lovely city. Berthe and I were there earlier in the spring. It's quite cosmopolitan and the cultural life is vibrant.'

Gross sighed. 'If offered the post, I suppose I would go. But you know, I have grown rather fond of my students in Czernowitz. We are making great strides forward in research.'

'I'm not listening to this anymore,' Berthe said. 'Stay in Czernowitz, then.'

'But there is my lady wife, Adele, to consider. She's not overly fond of life in a yurt.'

'It's hardly the steppes, Gross,' Werthen said. 'Have another glass of this lovely Moravian wine you have brought and cheer up.'

Gross had been gone only a week and a half, but Werthen had to admit he was glad to see him. Especially after the less than satisfactory visit from his parents over the weekend.

Gross filled his glass as requested and put it to his lips, breathing in the bouquet as he did so. But his contrived look of expectancy turned to disappointment before he had taken even one sip. He put the glass down with a sigh.

'It's not the school, you know,' he said finally. 'It's this matter of the Bower. We really cannot let it stand as it is.'

'I thought as much,' Werthen said. 'And I quite agree.'

Berthe said nothing, turning the stem of her wine glass reflectively, like a chess player determining the next move.

Werthen and Gross sat in eager anticipation, two gymnasium students waiting to hear the results of their *Matura* graduation exam. Each was silent; each waiting for the other to begin.

The tension was almost palpable. Berthe stopped turning her wine glass.

'For heaven's sake,' she said, exasperated. 'Gross, you go first.'

'Sensible woman. Yes, to be sure. I do come bearing information. I found time while in Prague to visit colleagues in the local

Police Praesidium. Do you remember me talking of Jan Sokol?'
But this question was rhetorical and he did not wait for a response.

'We met a dozen years ago at a criminalistics conference in Paris.
Just a detective inspector then, was Sokol. He's risen through the
ranks. He could go toe to toe with friend Meindl now.'

Werthen began to squirm with impatience, Berthe noted.

'Perhaps we could get to the information,' she suggested.

'Apologies,' Gross said, now turning to his wine with his usual
gusto. 'Well,' he wiped at his moustache with the knuckle of his
forefinger. 'Sokol and I had a fine chat. He quizzed me about my
recent cases – he has been following our successes, Werthen.'

'Penned so eloquently in your journal, *Archive for Criminology,*'
Berthe added with no little sarcasm.

'Yes, quite. But I should get to the point,' said Gross, puffing his
chest. 'Which is that when I informed Sokol of our recent case
involving the deaths of the two young women, he looked profoundly
shocked. "The same thing has been happening here!" he exclaimed.
Those were his very words.'

'The murder of young prostitutes?' Werthen said, unwrapping
his long legs, which he had managed to entwine to stop his right
leg from twitching.

Gross smiled. 'That's what I thought, too. However, Sokol was
referring not to the gender or profession of the victim, but to the
severing of the little finger of the left hand.'

He sat back in his chair, a look of satisfaction on his face at the
reaction he had provoked in both Werthen and Berthe.

He waited another half minute before plunging on. 'The victim
was a low-level officer in the Foreign Ministry. Suspicion fell on
one Herr Maarkovsky, a Polish importer of vodka with whom the
officer had lately been seen. Maarkovsky, of course, was nowhere
to be found for questioning; nor, upon further investigation, was his
supposed employer aware of his existence.'

'An assumed identity,' Werthen said in almost a whisper.

Gross nodded.

'I became curious,' Gross said. 'Similar *modus operandi* in crimes
in Vienna and Prague. Could there be others as well?'

He leaned back in his chair, looking as if he was once more about
to smile, but Berthe's voice brought him up short.

'No Cheshire-cat poses, Gross. What did you learn?' she demanded.
Werthen noticed that tonight she had drunk rather more than her
usual amount of wine.

'Werthen, you must cease feeding your lady wife red meat,' he said with a smile. 'It brings out aggression in her. To answer your question briefly, I have discovered three other similar cases. One in Berlin, one in Warsaw, and one in Zurich. Our friend Monsieur Auberty, investigating magistrate of the Direction Centrale de la Police Judiciaire in Geneva, was most helpful in this regard.'

Werthen knew exactly who Gross referred to: they had made use of Auberty's services in their first case together, looking into the Luccheni assassination of Empress Elisabeth.

'It seems Auberty is becoming something of a clearing-house for criminal proceedings throughout Europe. Quite informally as of now, but I can foresee the day when countries around the world will band together in some sort of official international policing arrangement to combat crime. Auberty has made the acquaintance of police officers throughout Europe at one conference or another. He is what the British might term a clubbable sort. He has a mind that works like a filing cabinet and he is a relentless correspondent. It was he who put me on to the other three murders involving severed little fingers.

'Five cases, then,' Werthen said.

'That we know of,' Gross added.

'Are there suspects in the others?' Berthe asked.

'Yes, suspects aplenty.' From the inside breast pocket of his jacket, Gross dug out the small leather notebook he always carried with him, opened it to the page that was marked by a faded crimson ribbon, and began reading. 'In Berlin, there was a certain Herr Erlanger, a Hungarian rail engineer who was the prime suspect; in Warsaw, it was a Herr de Koenig, the agent of a Dutch mining concern; in Zurich it was Axel Wouters, a Belgian rubber merchant. As with the mysterious Herr Maarkovsky, the person in each incident simply disappeared; and so did his professional connections, along with him. In short, no such person existed.'

'What about the victims?' Werthen said.

'Yes. That is the other important piece in the puzzle. In each case, the victim was involved in one way or another with government security or information agencies: either low-level clerks or external suppliers, and in one case even a high-ranking officer of a counter-espionage unit.'

Werthen was out of his chair now. 'Then what I have to show you may be more important than I originally thought.'

Werthen fetched the second letter from Fräulein Mitzi and its translation by Frau von Suttner from the study and placed the two pieces of paper side by side in front of Gross.

The criminalist's attention went immediately to the underlined parts of the translation.

'Patriotic work, she says. Hyperbole?' Gross remarked as he read.

'This is one of a series of letters sent to her parents, of course,' Werthen allowed. 'In another she made much of the literary tutelage she was supposedly receiving from Schnitzler. So, yes, it could be mere braggadocio, but—'

'But . . .?'

'This fits our earlier theories rather too neatly to disregard. It would be just like the girl to describe her spying on the Foreign Ministry as patriotic work.'

Gross made a murmuring sound. 'And what is this other bit here?'

All three looked to where Gross was pointing with his forefinger:

'*The well-tended Copse says I am a clever girl!*'

'Yes,' Werthen said. 'That caught my attention as well.'

'Her controller?' Berthe offered.

Werthen nodded. 'That was my first thought. Or perhaps her nickname for someone at the Bower. In fact I have written to Frau von Suttner to make sure about the translation, but she has yet to respond.'

'Do they have no telephones on her estate?' Gross said, suddenly impatient.

'In fact they don't,' Berthe said, remembering Frau von Suttner's earlier discussion about their economic state.

Gross sighed.

'So,' he muttered, 'here we sit mired in the nineteenth century while the rest of Europe buzzes along in the twentieth.'

'Central Europe,' Berthe reminded him.

'*Contrition*', that's what the painting would be called. It would take a master of the homely emotive detail such as Ferdinand Waldmüller to depict the filtered morning light through the breakfast-room window picking up the wisps of steam rising from the cups of coffee; the glint of light off white porcelain and polished silver; the down-turned eyes of the woman; the set of jaw and pout of lips.

However, to capture the nervous tap of fingernails on damask table cloth it would take one of the Lumière's moving-picture cameras.

'Was I too hard on him?' Berthe finally said. Still dressed in her blue robe and slippers, her hair done up in a bun, she ceased her finger-tapping exercise and tended to Frieda, who was busy spreading oatmeal on the surface of the wooden tray of her high chair.

'Gross needs a nudging like that from time to time,' Werthen said. 'Makes him remember where the boundaries of the classroom lie.'

'That's right, darling.' Berthe helped the child spoon the food back into her bowl.

She turned back to Werthen. 'It really is not like me. I mean, I might think such remarks, but I usually am able to control myself.'

'Not to worry.' He reached a hand to her shoulder, feeling the pull of desire at the warmth coming through her silk robe. Perhaps it had been the wine, but that was hard luck for Gross. Berthe's overindulgence had led to an amorous night for Werthen and his wife. Berthe's abandon in bed had been quite different from her abandonment of social graces with the criminologist. And Werthen was not complaining.

The jingling of the phone in the hall made him put such thoughts aside.

'Werthen.' Frieda shrieked and then broke into uncontrollable giggles. It was her name for the telephone, as that was the way Werthen answered calls, even at home, giving his surname when he picked up the receiver. Silly habit, he suddenly thought; the person making the call should know who is on the other end of the line. Shouldn't it be up to the caller to identify himself or herself first?

But the second round of jingling sent him out of his chair to intercept Frau Blatschky before she felt compelled to answer the 'infernal contraption,' as she still insisted on calling the telephone.

He was just in time to wave her off as she peeked out of the kitchen.

'Werthen,' he said, the receiver to his ear. There was an echoing sound to his voice as he spoke.

'Drechsler here. I might have something for you.'

'That is rather cryptic, Inspector.'

There was an awkward pause, as if Drechsler was unsure if it was his turn to speak or not. Then, 'Cryptic or not, would you care to come to my office this morning? I do not believe your time would be wasted. And Gross will surely find some interest in it.'

The connection went dead. Werthen held the receiver at arm's length, shaking his head at the instrument. Efficient, but an advancement in civilization?

TWENTY-FIVE

Gross was staying at the nearby Hotel zur Josefstadt, as he usually did when visiting Vienna, and Werthen was able to catch him just as he was finishing his not insubstantial breakfast of thick slices of farmer's bread, fresh butter, slabs of wurst and Emmenthaler cheese – plus, judging by the fragments of brown shell on the table, one or more hard-boiled eggs.

'The wife, by the way, sends apologies,' Werthen said as they were leaving. And indeed she had, giving Werthen explicit instructions as he was closing the door of their flat.

'Whatever for?' Gross said.

'She felt she was rather hard on you, prodding you to get on with the information you had.'

'And quite right she was, too. I enjoy a woman with spirit. Well, not every hour of the day, to be sure. But the occasional display of grit is a worthwhile attribute in the fairer sex.'

Werthen was beginning to regret imparting the apology.

Nothing more was said as they walked to the Police Praesidium on Schottenring. Drechsler had not spoken of an emergency situation, and it was most definitely the sort of fine morning that warranted strolling. Gross, however, was not in the mood for a pleasant stroll, but instead set off at a furious pace down the Josefstädterstrasse towards the Ring, making his way brusquely past early-morning shoppers and professional men on their way to their offices. The laboring class had already been at work for several hours.

Werthen kept pace with Gross at first, but slowed for a time when he again saw the military man making his way at a brisk clip down the other side of the street. He wondered once again about the man's life, and was about to tell Gross of his fictional fantasies regarding this officer from the General Staff. But Gross turned to him at that very moment.

'Stop dawdling, will you, Werthen? I have a feeling that Drechsler has something of the utmost importance to share with us.'

'Really, Gross. you can be tiresome at times.'

The criminalist squinted at him. 'At times?' he thundered.

His sudden outburst startled an old woman carrying a basket full of eggs. She shot Gross a withering look, which he ignored.

'You do me an injustice, Werthen,' he said, a sly smile on his face. 'I strive for continual annoyance.' At which he emitted a barking excuse for a laugh and charged along the sidewalk.

They arrived at the Police Praesidium at 9:15. They had to write their time of arrival in a guest book – an innovation obviously introduced by Meindl, who wanted to keep track of all the comings and goings in his fiefdom.

Drechsler was at his desk, coat off and sleeves rolled up, as they entered. He made to put on his jacket, but Gross insisted he remain as he was.

'We are at your service, Inspector,' Gross said, as they sat across the desk from Drechsler. The only window in the office was open, letting in a waft of sweet-smelling air off the nearby Danube Canal, along with the faint chatter of voices from the dockworkers and bargemen who worked there.

'There was a murder,' he began.

Gross sat up straighter in his chair, his hands clenched tightly in his lap. 'Do tell us,' he said.

'At first I thought nothing of it. But then, upon reflection, I thought to myself, well this might interest Doktor Gross and Advokat Werthen.'

By this time, Gross was physically, and not metaphorically, squirming in his seat. Werthen looked forward to seeing the criminologist get his own back.

But Gross held his tongue.

There was silence for a moment.

'Well, the long and short of it,' Drechsler finally began, 'is that a body was discovered yesterday at the Hernals Cemetery.'

'Hardly an unexpected place to find a corpse,' Gross quipped.

'Yes, I thought you might say something like that,' the hawk-nosed inspector retorted. 'This particular body, however, did not belong in the cemetery.'

'What? Not dead enough?'

To which Drechsler cast such a baleful look, that Gross muttered an apology.

'Please, do go on, Inspector,' Werthen added.

'Someone, most probably the killer, intended the body not to be found, for it was deposited in a freshly dug grave then covered with a layer of dirt. Now the interesting thing is, this particular grave was intended for an old gentleman who was at death's door. The family wanted the grave ready for when the man died. But the old gentleman has proved rather stubborn in regard to his hold on life. The grave has stood open for about two weeks. And only yesterday did the sexton discover an odor coming from it. Upon inspection, he discovered the body and alerted the local constabulary.'

Gross seemed to relax somewhat now. 'Interesting from a forensics viewpoint, but otherwise . . .'

'Yes, well Doktor, this is where you and your colleague may come in. The Hernals police proved to be on their toes, and quite quickly linked the dead body with a missing-person case that had been filed with them by a frantic bride. It seems, her husband, a newly minted medical doctor, had been called out on a home visit on the evening of May 30 and never returned. They made the connection between the date the man went missing and the time when the grave was dug, and thought it worth the chance to call the woman in for an identification.'

'The poor woman,' Gross said, uncharacteristically empathetic.

'Corpse wasn't as bad as all that. The nights have been cool. Gases yes, but the features are still intact. Eyes a bit sunken, of course, stomach distended, but recognizable. And after all, she is, or was, a doctor's wife.'

Werthen doubted that she accompanied her husband into the surgery, but held his tongue.

Drechsler sighed, a dramatic pause. 'In the event, it turned out to be the missing doctor. The lady was apparently quite distraught. We are making further inquiries. It was a clear case of murder by a professional. One stab wound to the heart, from the rear. No mucking about, no hesitation. A sure stroke through the victim's light overcoat and dress jacket.'

'And,' Gross said, 'this is of interest to us because . . .?'

'For two reasons. The doctor's name. Schnitzel. Arthur Schnitzel.'

Gross and Werthen exchanged looks, both minds traveling in the same direction: Arthur Schnitzel and Arthur Schnitzler.

'Seemed coincidental to me,' Drechsler said. 'Two men with such similar names, both doctors. One beaten up, the other murdered.'

'You mentioned a second reason,' Werthen said.

'Yes. And that is why I felt I had to call you. Too many coincidences.'

'Well, it can't be a missing little finger on the left hand,' Gross said. 'Otherwise you would have called yesterday. No need to ruminate on that.'

'You're quite right, Doktor Gross. But there was something missing.'

The way he said it made Werthen intuit his meaning. 'The man's penis?'

'Very good, Advokat. I am not sure what any of it means, but I thought you two should know about it.'

'Not one of those cases you care to explore?' said Gross.

'I have rather got my hands full lately. And if you remember, as far as Inspector Meindl is concerned, that other case is solved.'

'We think not,' Gross said, and then began to tell Drechsler of his discoveries in Prague; but the inspector held up a hand to stop him.

'The case is solved, Doktor Gross, if you fully understand my meaning. I do not want to have other information regarding it. But if you gentlemen care to pursue the matter. Well, it is a relatively free country, isn't it?'

The three men sat in silence for a moment.

Finally Gross broke the silence. 'It was good of you to share the information, Inspector. If necessary, you can explain away our visit . . .'

'Oh, I already have that in hand. I called the two of you in to further reprimand you for your obstruction in the matter of the death of Count von Ebersdorf. I assume you feel duly chastised?'

'Absolutely,' Werthen said, rising to leave.

Gross lingered for a moment. 'I was wondering,' he said. 'Is the body of the unfortunate Doktor Schnitzel available for inspection?'

Drechsler shrugged. 'As far as I know. But the cause of death is certain. Herr Todt himself examined it.'

'Ah, then it is at the central morgue?'

Drechsler nodded.

'One hopes they have not tidied it up too much. It could be of great benefit to forensic science if certain insects are still to be found among the hairs.'

Both Drechsler and Werthen were now staring at him.

'A simple matter of science,' Gross said. 'Not ghoulishness. We know this man died twelve days ago. This provides us with a time-line. Certain insects like to lay their eggs on fresh corpses. By finding those that take ten to twelve days to completely develop from larval form to mature insect, we could establish a valuable tool in determining time of death in future cases.'

Drechsler eyed Werthen. 'I told you Doktor Gross would find some interest in this.'

They arranged to meet at the Lepidoptera cabinet in the Court Natural History Museum. Schmidt had been very precise about the exact location, for the insect collection was the largest in the world and its cabinets spanned several rooms. They would meet in front of a relatively new addition to the collection: the largest known butterfly, Queen Alexandra's birdwing, *Ornithoptera alexandrae.*

Forstl, in civilian dress, was early. Schoolchildren abounded, seemingly as plentiful as the insects in the glass cases. It took Forstl back to his own schooldays in Lemberg, and he suddenly realized this must be the annual school-leaving field trip. His had been to the local freight station, where his father was the clerk. He had always hidden his father's lowly profession from the other boys in his class. Visiting with his entire class, he ignored his father's friendly glances as he explained to the noisy group the operation of the freight station. Afterwards, he had joined in the cruel jokes about the 'squat, bald toad' behind the counter. He laughed heartily along with the others when one of them, Mayerhof, had quipped that there was nothing very *good* about the man, punning on *Güter,* the German word for goods or freight. He still remembered the pun.

'It is beautiful, no?'

Schmidt stood behind him, his voice raised just enough for Forstl to hear.

'They have an amazing collection here,' the agent went on. 'Someday you should take it all in. Herr Rebel, the keeper of the Lepidoptera collection, is considered a genius in his discipline. A former lawyer, you know.'

Forstl did not know that, nor did he care for any of Schmidt's bizarre small talk today. He moved away from the crowds of children and from the cabinets to a velvet-cushioned bench under a window that gave out on to Maria Theresa Square, which separated the twin museums devoted to art and natural history. The red plush had faded to a shade of pink. They sat side by side. Schmidt was dressed in the same blue suit he wore for every occasion.

'You brought them?'

Forstl shook his head. 'There have been complications. Something else needs to be seen to first.'

Schmidt tensed at his side. 'Our friends in St Petersburg will not be pleased. They are most anxious to see the mobilization plans.'

'We are playing the long game here, I thought. I must establish my credentials. I have to become invaluable to Colonel von Krahlich. And now you want me to make him displeased? You tell me, which is the more important?'

'Does this have to do with the Bower again?'

'No,' Forstl replied. 'That was personal insurance. Von Ebersdorf, as you know, was meant to become the prime suspect in case there were rumors of a Russian double agent at work in Vienna. Loose lips of the chief of the Foreign Ministry's Russia desk when in bed with a whore. How was I to know the fool would fall in love with the girl?'

'Stop whining,' Schmidt said. 'I was the one who had to clean up that mess for you when the little whore wanted to run off with von Ebersdorf and when her friend demanded hush money for secrets they had shared.'

There was a moment of silence between them filled by the din of high, excited voices.

'Then what is this meet about?' Schmidt demanded.

Forstl reached into the inside pocket of his linen jacket and took out an envelope. Opening it, he pulled out a sheet of blue flimsy and handed it to Schmidt.

As Schmidt read the report, Forstl looked behind him out of the window to the statue of the Empress Maria Theresa in the little square below. More children were milling about its base, gazing up at the first female ruler of Austria. One child in tie and short pants traced the letters of the etched inscription on the base with a forefinger.

'So there was a blown operation,' Schmidt said, handing back the report. 'Who is this von Suttner anyway? And why should we care?'

'We should care because it is von Krahlich's project. He handed it to me several months ago after hearing rumors of the husband's dalliances with his niece. Apparently the wife, Bertha von Suttner, is influential among international pacifists. "Traitors" von Krahlich calls them.'

'So the love birds are caught *in flagrante* and this evidence is presented to the wife with an ultimatum – tone down the rhetoric or we make this public.'

'Along those lines,' Forstl said. 'But, as you see from my agent's report, the operation came to nothing. Just as he was about to spring the trap and confront Baron von Suttner and his niece in their room at the Hotel Metropole, my agent discovered that his chief witness, the concierge, was no longer there. Indeed, according to the agent, the whole affair had been covered up as a scheme to present the Baroness von Suttner with a birthday present of a portrait of her niece.'

Forstl pulled out a pair of photos from the same envelope, and handed one to Schmidt. It showed a tall, handsome woman – not pretty, but handsome – dressed in a rather unconventional loose-fitting dress. None of the wasp waist that most women of a certain station wore, nor the high-collared look preferred for daytime. Forstl thought the material was muslin, but tailored so that it clung to the body rather than ballooning out with bustles and hoops. She was standing in front of a bakery, eying the goods, a little girl standing at her side, dressed in a sailor suit, her podgy hand gripping her mother's.

'The woman in this photo, Berthe Meisner, was spotted at the Metropole twice. The second time my agent trailed her to her home. He avers that it was she who ruined the operation, who somehow convinced the lovers of the portrait ruse – that they were only in a Viennese hotel room to secretly have the niece's portrait painted for the Suttner woman's birthday.'

He now handed over the second photo, this one of a man, also tall in stature, caught mid-stride as he was walking along a city sidewalk, his long legs a blur of motion. Forstl thought he had seen this person before; there was something about the loose smile, the self-assured movement, the eyes that seemed to fix on and bore into whatever he scanned. A pleasant face, he thought. An intelligent one.

'This is the woman's husband—'

'Advokat Karl Werthen,' said Schmidt, taking Forstl by surprise. 'How do you know that?'

Schmidt quickly explained that he had seen the Advokat and an older man confront Siegfried Mutzenbacher, and had then followed them to Archduke Franz Ferdinand's headquarters at the Belvedere.

'You are becoming a costly asset,' Schmidt muttered, reflecting on how many deaths Forstl had already caused in order to protect his role as a Russian agent.

'How so?'

'I think these men are in the employ of the Archduke. Werthen isn't just a lawyer. He runs a private-inquiries firm that has handled several high-profile cases. I did a bit of homework on him in back issues of *Neue Freie Presse*. And his colleague is the eminent criminologist Hanns Gross.'

'Never heard of either of them,' Forstl said.

'That may be so, but my fear is they may soon hear of you.'

Forstl shook his head, not understanding.

'Triangulation, my friend. Simple triangulation. They already have two leads that could be traced back to your office – the Bower and this absurd action at the Hotel Metropole. One more lead, one more shoe to drop, and they should be able to fix you, as if in the sights of a rifle.'

Forstl suddenly stood up, straightening the crease in his trousers.

'Well then,' he said. 'I assume you know your next assignment. If our friends in St Petersburg want certain documents and care for a mutually beneficial long-term working relationship, then you should proceed quickly and take care of this threat.'

'A large "if", Captain Forstl. We shall see.'

'And I need no further mementoes. Is that clear?'

Forstl did not wait for an answer, but turned and made his way through the throngs of schoolchildren to the exit.

Schmidt did not follow. He sat on the bench thinking for some minutes, and then got up and went back to the Lepidoptera cabinets. He had paid his one-crown entry fee; he would enjoy the arthropod collection.

TWENTY-SIX

They made no progress on the matter for the next several days. Gross, however, was in a fine mood, delighted at the collection of larvae and insects he had gathered from the corpse of Herr Schnitzel.

Werthen and his family spent the weekend at the farmhouse in Laab im Walde. The weather was fine, and he was now able to see the green fuzz of the tennis lawn. Despite his complete neglect, the seeds had taken root and formed a large rectangle of delicate new pale green amid the profusion of tall grasses and wild flowers.

Frieda accompanied him and was now busily running her hand over the new grass.

'Sof,' she said.

'Yes, it is nice and soft, isn't it?' Werthen leaned over and ran his hand over the new shoots; they tickled his palm.

'Pwetty.'

He beamed at her. 'Not as pretty as you, though.'

She grabbed his leg, her grip surprisingly strong, and buried her little head in the folds of his corduroy breeches.

'Does it embarrass you to be told you're pretty?'

She lifted her head, peering up at him.

'Because you are going to spend a lot of time being embarrassed. You're a beautiful little girl, just like your mother.'

'Just like her mother how?' Berthe said as she approached them. 'Look at that! It has sprouted.'

'It certainly has,' Werthen agreed. 'Maybe we should continue to ignore it. It seems to like low maintenance.'

'Why do I get the feeling we are going to have a grass court?'

'Maybe it wouldn't be such a bad thing, after all. Exercise would do us all good.'

They returned late Sunday night to find a telegram from Gross requesting that they meet first thing in the morning at Werthen's office. The criminalist was his usual pedantic self, even in the abbreviated language of the telegram, demanding that they meet at eight sharp, and that Berthe accompany him.

'Whatever is he up to?' she said as they climbed into bed that night.

'One of his unveilings. I assume he has discovered some evidence and wants to present it in dramatic form.'

In the morning they left Frieda with Frau Blatschky and walked to the Habsburgergasse. It was one of those clear, warm mornings that made Werthen happy he lived in the city. Everything seemed alive and vibrant; as they passed through the Volksgarten, they saw a dog slip its leash and run after a family of ducks. The dog's owner, a well-dressed matron in her fifties, could only stand and clap her hands at her disobedient long-haired dachshund. The ducks escaped unharmed and a constabulary officer was able to regain control of the dog and keep it from further pranks.

'Better to have a child than a dog,' Werthen said, taking his wife's hand. 'No leashes.'

'Wait until suitors start knocking at the door,' she said, squeezing his hand as they walked.

By the time they arrived at the Habsburgergasse, the nearby businesses had already opened their shutters. The first gladioli were displayed in buckets on the street in front of Nestor's; a rack of used books in uniform leather binding stood in front of Waltrum's.

'There's Gross,' Berthe said, drawing his attention away from the shops. Gross stood at the entrance to Habsburgergasse 4, an expectant look on his face.

He began speaking as they approached.

'Well whatever it is that makes you command my presence first thing in the morning, I hope it is important. I did not even have time to finish my coffee.'

'Good morning to you, too, Gross,' Werthen said. 'But you were the one to command our presence.'

His smile was cut short at the booming sound of an explosion overhead. Shards of glass sprayed the sidewalk. Luckily, they were all wearing hats and the glass fell around them. One splinter lodged in Werthen's hand, which bled steadily, but he was initially too stunned to pay it any attention. Automatically, he reached protectively for Berthe and held her to him. Her breath came in quick bursts. Gross stood unharmed but with mouth wide open as if in mid-scream.

The street was suddenly filled with people gaping at the smoke pouring out of the windows two floors up at Habsburgergasse 4.

Looking up, Berthe cried out, 'Karl, it's from your office!'

Werthen was still partly in shock. He calmly picked the splinter of glass out of his hand and wrapped his handkerchief around the hand to staunch the bleeding. 'Gas leak?' he said hopefully, and then dashed up the stairs, the others behind him. The smell of cordite was heavy in the air as he got closer to his floor.

Not a gas leak, then.

The outer door to the office had been blown off its hinges. Smoke filled the room, his inner office was a blackened ruin. He rushed to Fräulein Metzinger's desk, his heart pounding, fearing what he might find. But there she was, cowering on the floor on hands and knees, her hair blown wild as if in a storm.

She looked up at him, like a frightened child. 'I dropped a paperclip,' she said. 'Just as Oskar was delivering the paper, earlier than usual. Dropped the clip and then bent down to retrieve it and the world exploded.'

She passed out in his arms.

At the door Frau Ignatz stood bewildered, searching the ruins. 'Oskar, my little brother Oskar. Where are you?'

'There are fragments of electric wire by the door to the inner office,' Inspector Drechsler said. 'As well as the remains of what Doktor Gross here informs us is a dry-cell battery.'

'In short,' Gross interrupted, 'someone set a primitive bomb to go off when your inner-office door was opened. It would function rather like a burglar alarm, in that opening the door would close the circuit, sending electric current from the dry-cell battery to this.'

Gross held a small piece of charred metal in his hand; and Werthen, from his experience in a case involving the composer Gustav Mahler, quickly made the connection.

'Part of a detonator.'

'Exactly,' Gross confirmed. 'Which triggered a small explosion, setting off the dynamite it was nestled in.'

'Poor Oskar,' said Berthe.

Gross did not respond to this, holding emotion at bay as long as he could. 'Fortunately, the charge must have been small. A couple of sticks at most. Otherwise, Fräulein Metzinger would be suffering from more than tinnitus.'

The secretary had, despite her objections, been taken to the hospital for observation. They were gathered around her desk in the damaged outer office. The inner office had been destroyed. Police were still scouring the building, looking for suspects. Frau Ignatz had been taken back to her rooms, under the care of a hospital matron.

Suddenly, as the shock began to wear off, Werthen felt the impact of Oskar's death. His fault, in a way, for having the poor man deliver the paper every morning. He vowed he would find whoever had done this.

'All the hallmarks of the Black Hand,' Drechsler said.

'Nonsense,' Gross spluttered. 'What have we to do with the Serbs?'

'I'm only rehearsing what Meindl is sure to say. A bombing means anarchists at work, or the Black Hand. That's how his mind works. You have a better explanation?'

They had not taken Drechsler into their confidence regarding the new information concerning the Bower killings – that similar types of crime had been recorded in several European cities.

'There is the von Ebersdorf matter,' Werthen extemporized. 'Perhaps we were getting too close to the truth there—'

'That case is, need I repeat myself, closed. Unless you have, in spite of my direct request to the opposite, reopened it on your own.'

'But this one is very clearly open,' Gross thundered. 'There is a man dead here. Frau Ignatz's brother. Bits of his body are still to be found in there.' He pointed a condemning forefinger at Werthen's office. 'I picked through his remains retrieving evidence of the bomb. This is homicide, Drechsler, not a warning shot fired across our bows.'

Drechlser sat quietly through Gross's tirade.

'Finished, are we?'

Gross turned his back on the inspector.

'I am not saying I won't investigate this barbaric act. It shakes me as much as it does you, this act of terror. To set off a blast like this in the heart of our city, it is unthinkable. And I will pursue whoever did it with all the powers at my command. I simply wanted to let you know what I will be up against at the Praesidium. Now if you gentlemen have any further information you are holding back from me . . .'

'Men,' Berthe suddenly spat out. 'I don't know what you are playing at. You treat this like some schoolyard competition.'

Werthen put out a hand to her shoulder, but she shrugged it off.

'We're all on the same side here,' she said. 'Tell him, Karl, or I will.'

'Frau Meisner—' Gross began.

But she cut him off. 'Doktor Gross! Somebody tell the inspector!'

'She's right,' Werthen said.

And so they told Drechsler about the renewed investigation.

Frau Ignatz was busily sweeping out the foyer as they descended the stairs. The hospital matron simply raised her eyes at them as if to say she could not stop the woman.

Werthen could understand the need to stay busy, delay the realization of her brother's death. Compassion was not an emotion he had experienced regarding Frau Ignatz in the past, but that was what was welling up in his chest now. He wanted to reach out to her.

But Gross beat him to it, though in his own peculiar manner

'Frau Ignatz,' the criminologist said. 'You will want to help, of course. There is no good time for such questions, but the sooner we have answers the sooner we will be able to track down the monster who perpetrated this outrage.'

She looked up at him from her sweeping, suddenly a frail old woman. She peered at him as if he were speaking a foreign tongue.

'Did you see anyone peculiar in the vicinity this morning or perhaps last night? Anything untoward about building security?'

Frau Ignatz continued to stare at him, as if he were a zoo exhibit. Berthe finally put her arm around the woman's bony shoulders.

'Let's go and have a cup of chamomile tea, shall we?'

The *Portier* made no protest as Berthe moved her away to her quarters nearby. Gross and Werthen were about to follow, but Berthe gave a curt shake of her head to ward them off.

Gross sighed as Berthe, Frau Ignatz and the hospital matron removed to the ground-floor *Portier* apartment.

'Your wife certainly is taking charge lately.'

'And we should both be thankful for it,' Werthen added.

'Yes, of course. No criticism intended. As I have said before—'

'You like a woman with spirit. Not too much of it, however.'

Gross was silent a moment. 'You should have that hand looked after.'

Werthen glanced at the bloodied handkerchief wrapped around his left hand. He shook his head.

'Like a bad dream.'

'It's the shock,' Gross said. 'Still affecting all of us. We need to concentrate. To think clearly. There was nothing random about this attack. It was planned to kill me, you and your wife. Neatly arranged with matching telegrams to bring us together. Which means that whoever did it has knowledge of our domiciles; has been following us, in fact. And this person also has basic knowledge of bomb construction. Which indicates a military background perhaps.'

'Or mining or land management, or a dozen other occupations that employ dynamite from time to time,' Werthen said.

'Motive?'

'Clearly to silence us. But regarding what? Von Ebersdorf or the Bower murders?'

'Or perhaps the two are indeed linked.'

They were silent for a time. Drechsler and his men continued to search the building for any signs of a break-in, but Werthen doubted they would find anything. They were dealing with a professional, of that he was sure. But even professionals might make mistakes, as this one had done about who would be the first person to go into Werthen's inner office. And yet nobody could have foretold that Oskar would, today of all days, be so eager to prove his worth as to go into the inner office and put the newspaper on the desk himself. Custom had it that he would leave the newspaper with Fräulein Metzinger, who would in turn hand it to Werthen upon his arrival at the office. Thus, Werthen should have been the first to open the inner-office door this morning, in the company of his wife and Gross. But, out of eagerness, Oskar had beaten them to it.

Gross was observing an officer inspecting the lock on the front door of the building; he obviously felt as Werthen did, for he shook his head in indignation. Then turning to Werthen, he said, 'One bright spot out of all of this.'

He paused, but Werthen did not feel like rising to the bait.

Finally Gross explained. 'At least we know our instincts about all this are correct. This is not something that has been neatly wrapped up and solved, as Inspector Meindl would like to aver. There is a killer out there. And knowing that he has failed, he will probably try again.'

Which gave Werthen a sudden idea. 'But does he know that? I mean, why don't we broadcast that the three of us were killed, and then we can work behind the scenes . . .'

But even as he said it, he realized the folly of the idea: whoever set off the explosion most likely witnessed it. 'Sorry,' he said, 'it's still the shock working on my analytical skills.'

'Not at all,' Gross said. 'But we must be on our guard now. And it is good that your wife convinced us to share our information with Drechsler. It provides a kind of insurance to us.'

At which point Berthe came out of the *Portier*'s lodge alone.

'She did see someone,' Berthe said. 'But was unable to describe him. Medium height, nothing distinguishing about his features. He wore a blue suit. That is all that stood out. He passed her on the stairs last evening and she thought he was visiting someone, that a tenant had let him in. But she had never seen him before.'

'Not much to go on,' Gross said. 'And yet, at the same time, much to go on. A nondescript man. One who blends so well he is not noticed. A worthy adversary.'

TWENTY-SEVEN

They were given police protection, a constabulary man stationed outside their apartment building on Josefstädterstrasse who took his mid-morning *Jause* break at a local gasthaus, then lunch at the same establishment from noon to one. For afternoon coffee at three, the man wandered down to the Café Eiles, two blocks away, and for dinner he returned to the gasthaus. He went off duty at seven. It would be fortunate if the villains operated on such a schedule, too, Werthen ruefully thought.

He therefore hired the two stalwarts Meier and Prokop, and placed them outside the apartment door on Josefstädterstrasse. Prokop had been delighted to see the Advokat enter their office: a wine bar near the Margarethen Gürtel underneath the tracks of the new *Stadtbahn.* Meier bore further evidence to their violent profession: his left ear was bandaged, and it appeared that the top of it had been misplaced.

'We're your men,' chimed Prokop, in his choirboy tenor, and nearly crushed Werthen's hand in a gentleman's agreement grip regarding the fee. His time at Schnitzler's had affected Prokop, it seemed, for when he appeared for work, along with the sullen Meier, he carried a small Samuel Fischer edition of the playwright's early theatre series, *Anatol,* about an idle young womanizing bachelor. Werthen felt something akin to shock seeing a book in Prokop's meaty hands; he had never imagined the man was literate, let alone that he might actually enjoy such light entertainment. From time to time, when he passed the pair of them in the hallway, he would find Prokop reading a particularly piquant scene out loud, with Meier looking at first bored and then increasingly interested.

To ensure security, Gross moved into the flat, as well, taking over Werthen's study and sleeping on the leather chaise lounge. Werthen had taken to carrying a silver-tipped walking stick which had a sword concealed inside it; Gross employed the pair of Steyr automatic pistols that he normally travelled with. Young Frieda was quite excited by all the activity, running here and there in the flat to see what was afoot, and opening the door and playing peekaboo with Prokop from time to time.

Frau Blatschky was the only one displeased with the new arrangements.

'It's like feeding an army,' she said after a day of Gross living in and Meier and Prokop taking meals with the family. 'I am not a mess cook. And that Doktor Gross . . .'

'I thought you were fond of him,' Berthe said, attempting to console her.

'This is not about like or not like. He eats for two. Nothing stays around long enough in the kitchen to get stale except me!'

On the second day, Schmidt saw the scar-faced cornstalk man go into the apartment building. He had set up watch across the street from Werthen's Josefstädterstrasse home, invisible to the policeman on duty outside as well as to pedestrians. He was dressed as a chimney sweep, wearing a sandwich board announcing the services of the 'Soot Merchant', and carried a fistful of flyers, which no one took.

That was just as well, for the firm was mythical, its address a derelict warehouse in Ottakring. But it provided him with the anonymity he needed to watch the comings and goings at Advokat Werthen's flat. The policeman was no concern; the man took regular breaks during the day and was gone at night. Schmidt could easily enter the building in the middle of the night, or even at midday, and kill the entire family and the fatuous Doktor Gross.

But the lawyer was obviously no fool: Schmidt watched the arrival of the two strong-arm men and knew this would complicate matters. They looked thick as a plank, but the numbers were now badly against him.

And now there was that cornstalk, the Archduke's man. These were not good odds. Forstl was indeed becoming a very expensive commodity.

'What brings you to us, Duncan?' Werthen asked as they settled in his study. Gross had made himself at home, sitting in Werthen's chair behind the desk. He and Duncan sat across from him.

'The Archduke wishes to express his concern,' the Scot said in a German that was grammatically precise but had the ring of the Highlands to it. Werthen strained to understand, but Gross's ear picked it up at first utterance.

'Please convey our thanks for his concern,' Gross said. 'We have taken certain precautions, as I am sure you noticed.'

Duncan smiled at this, an expression of scepticism rather than mirth.

'The two in the hall are the literary type, it seems.'

In fact, Duncan had made it to the door of the flat before Prokop and Meier, deep in the misadventures of Anatol, awoke from their fictional miasma. And the policeman on duty on the street had not noticed him enter the building, being too busy chatting to the young *Portier* next door who was sweeping the sidewalk in front of her building.

'Have you come to offer your services once again?' Werthen asked, hoping that was the case.

Duncan tilted his head, as if giving the notion some thought.

'The Archduke indicated that I could use my own discretion in that, but actually I have come with information. The Archduke wishes to tell you that there was something that might prove valuable in the case of Baroness von Suttner. You recall that we induced the night clerk from the Hotel Metropole to repatriate to Italy?'

Werthen and Gross nodded simultaneously.

'The man did supply one piece of interesting information. The telephone number he used to reach the person employing him. The Archduke has had the number traced and finds that it belongs to the Bureau.'

Gross and Werthen exchanged quick glances, each thinking the same: confirmation that it was Military Intelligence that had set up Frau von Suttner, and not the Foreign Office.

'More particularly,' Duncan added, 'it is the number of the Operations Section of the General Staff's Intelligence Bureau. The head of that section is one Captain Adelbert Forstl.'

'Forstl?' Gross repeated the name. 'I've come across that name recently. But where?'

He began drumming on the desk with his knuckles, as if to beat an answer out of the wood.

'It will come,' said the Scot philosophically. 'But there is something else you should know.'

He went to one side of the window, making sure that his silhouette was not showing, and peered at the street below.

'Ach, so he must have noticed.'

'Who?' Werthen said, following Duncan to the window.

'You had a watcher down there across the street. He was disguised as a chimney sweep wearing a sandwich board. But he seemed more interested in this building than in handing out the flyers he had.'

Werthen peered at the street below. 'I don't see him'

'No, you wouldn't. He's not there anymore. As I said, he must have noticed that I was aware of him. He's at least enough of a professional to know when to disappear.'

'Then he's still tracking us,' Werthen said, sick at the thought of once again putting his family in danger because of his work.

'Of course he is tracking us,' said Gross, still seated at the desk. 'I noticed him yesterday when he first appeared on the street.'

'And you didn't see fit to tell me?' Werthen said, unable to hide his outrage.

'I did not want you confronting the man. It is imperative for us to discover if he is working alone or in concert with others. I contacted Drechsler, and he was going to have two men dispatched today to follow our chimney sweep wherever he might go. I am afraid, however, that the arrival of friend Duncan has upset those plans and sent our man scurrying before Drechsler's men could be in place.'

'I apologize, Doktor Gross,' the Scot said.

Gross shook his head. 'There is no way you could have known.'

'But Gross,' Werthen persisted. 'I still feel you should have warned me. This is my home, in case you have forgotten.'

Gross ignored this remark, suddenly tapping his high forehead with a forefinger.

'Yes, that's it! I came across the name Forstl when investigating the past of the deceased Arthur Schnitzel. Schnitzel was in the medical corps before training as a doctor. And one of his officers wrote in an annual conduct report that he was a diligent orderly, but that there had been certain rumors about his attentions to a certain young lieutenant convalescing from a bout of pneumonia. Yes, that lieutenant's name was Forstl!'

'The same?' Werthen wondered aloud.

'That should be easy enough to determine,' Gross said.

Duncan suddenly muttered, 'Fools' names like fools' faces are often seen in public places.'

'I rather prefer another adage in this regard,' Gross said. And then dramatically intoned, 'No one is where he is by accident, and chance plays no part in God's plan.'

TWENTY-EIGHT

'**A**nd what does any of this have to do with me?'

The heavy drapes were open today, letting a slanting ray of sunlight into the room, the beam alive with dancing motes of dust. Schnitzler sat behind his desk, his face a mixture of incredulity and suspicion. No offer of coffee today.

'I simply thought you might want to know the full story behind your beating.'

Werthen smiled with false cheer as he spoke.

'The coincidence of the names, you see,' Gross added. 'And as Doktor Schnitzel was later found murdered, I might say you were quite lucky.'

'Luck,' Schnitzler said, laughing artificially, like a person with dyspepsia. 'A quaint idea.'

'You have not been quite honest with us, have you, Herr Schnitzler?'

Gross fixed the playwright with what one judge in Graz had dubbed his 'Meet your maker!' look.

'This is becoming rather tiresome, gentlemen. As I indicated last time we met, I had been protecting the fact that Mitzi played me. It rather hurts the ego to make such an admission, but there it is. And that is all there is to it. I am sorry my unthinking words to the girl's father led to such a tragic outcome, but that really is not my fault. It is as if Mitzi is still playing with us from the grave. And now, if you will forgive me, I have some final proofs to go through.'

'It is good that you only write plays, Herr Schnitzler, and don't act in them,' Gross said. 'You give an unconvincing performance.'

Werthen was still not sure what Gross was on about, but he had been adamant about visiting Schnitzler this morning. 'Tying up loose ends' he had called it, and had been as secretive and tenacious about it as a dachshund with a slipper.

'You would do well to unburden yourself,' Gross added.

'But as you point out, I am no longer in danger. I was not the target of the thug. It was merely a similarity in names.'

'But you were certain it was something else, weren't you?'

'My play . . . It angered some in the military.'

'Flummery and persiflage. I regret to inform you, Herr Schnitzler, that your words neither warrant nor command such a powerful response. But then, you already know that. No, it was something quite else that kept you from going to the police for protection. Something so secret it could be shared with no one.'

Gross suddenly clapped his hands together, making a surprisingly loud crack that made Schnitzler jerk in his chair.

'Out with it, man!'

Schnitzler looked confused, casting Werthen an almost pleading look.

'I am not your ally in this, Herr Schnitzler. Do as Doktor Gross says. Unburden yourself.'

Schnitzler let out a massive sigh that made him seem to shrink in his chair.

'You are a hard man, Doktor Gross.'

Gross beamed at this. 'So I have been told.'

'Alright. Though I cannot see how this will achieve anything other than to put me in a tight spot once again. But you are wrong about my words, Herr Doktor. They do have influence. My *Lieutenant Gustl* ruffled feathers at the War Ministry and at the Ballhausplatz, I can assure you. It cost me my commission in the reserves.'

Gross waved his right hand impatiently. 'Yes, quite. We know all this.'

'But you do not know that I tried to, how shall I say it, prove myself again to my former comrades in arms at the General Staff.'

'Ingratiate yourself, you mean,' Werthen added.

'If you will,' Schnitzler said with a shrug. 'I cannot for the life of me determine why I cared. To them, I am just another Jew trying to rise above my station. Perhaps they are right. You see I love my country, I loved serving it in a certain capacity . . .'

'Low-level espionage,' said Gross.

A slight tilt of Schnitzler's head; not a full nod, but neither was it a denial.

'I thought that my controller – my former controller, that is – might be interested in certain information I had stumbled on at a certain house of ill repute.'

'So that is how the thing began,' Gross said, clucking his tongue in disgust that he had not figured it out before.

'Yes,' Schnitzler said, sighing again.

'The Bower, you mean?' Werthen said.

'Of course he does,' said Gross, with something like irritation in his voice. 'It was the information that his former lover was now working as a prostitute and that her primary client . . .'

'Was von Ebersdorf,' Werthen added. 'And that could be used as a weapon in the power struggle between the Foreign Office and the Bureau.'

'I thought someone at the Bureau might make use of such information, yes,' Schnitzler said.

And now he looked almost in a panic. 'But wait. You can't think that had anything to do with her death can you?'

'And I submit that you can't imagine it did not,' Gross thundered at him. Then taking a deep breath, the criminologist continued in a rather more subdued tone of voice. 'After all, you put the girl in harm's way by involving her in deadly games between competing services. Perhaps it was the Foreign Office that decided she was a threat. Or perhaps her own handler at the Bureau. Whatever it was that induced her to participate – money, blackmail – was no longer effective as an incentive. She left a note that von Ebersdorf had fallen in love with her, wanted to marry her even. But she knew too much, she could not be left to tell tales. Careers hung in the balance.'

'And now who is playing the playwright?' Schnitzler scoffed. 'That is utter fantasy.'

Gross ignored this. 'What is the name of your controller?'

'Kohler. But that is not his real name. We both had operational names.'

'How did you contact him? Telephone, mail?'

Schnitzler smirked at the suggestion. 'Nothing quite so prosaic. No, meets were arranged by this.' Schnitzler reached into a drawer of his desk and withdrew a battered kid leather glove of a delicate size. He laid it on the desk for them both to see.

'Near the monument to Franz Grillparzer in the Volksgarten there is a stretch of wrought-iron fencing. If I required a meeting, I would place the glove on the third spearpoint finial from the left end.'

'Your choice of location, I assume,' Werthen said. 'A fellow playwright, Grillparzer.'

Schnitzler smiled wanly. 'I do not place myself at the same level, but yes. There was an element of homage in the choice of place. To passers-by it would appear simply to be a lost glove that someone had picked up off the ground and displayed in case the owner was searching for it. For Kohler, it meant that we would meet the following day at the usual time. He or one of his colleagues would check the park daily.'

'Somewhat baroque, don't you think?' Gross muttered. 'Why all the secrecy? After all, it is not as if you were trading in state secrets.'

'Well, I have my position to protect. It would hardly do for everyone to know that the firebrand playwright Schnitzler was cosying up to the secret services.'

Werthen had the feeling Schnitzler had enjoyed all the secrecy, the playing at spy games; it had appealed to his dramatic nature.

'One assumes your Herr Kohler returned the glove at each meeting,' Gross said.

'Correct.'

'And you have not been in contact with him since?'

Schnitzler shook his head.

'It must have failed to work then,' Werthen said, looking hard at Schnitzler.

'I don't follow you,' Schnitzler said.

'Your attempt at ingratiating yourself with your former masters. No more contact.'

'Well, I have not actually tried. After the attack, I thought—'

'Quite,' Gross interrupted. 'But you were wrong. Now I want the glove put in place one more time.'

'I have no need to meet with Kohler.'

'I realize that, Herr Schnitzler. But you will give us the opportunity of seeing who this mysterious contact is.'

'I couldn't do that. What would I say?'

'Nothing. You will not be there, but we will, in hiding. We will photograph him. That is all.'

'But the glove. They'll know it was me.'

'That, Herr Schnitzler, is your lookout. You are a creative man. I'm sure you can come up with some story to explain your absence. But if you refuse, my colleague Werthen here might just feel tempted to take up his pen again. He is a literary gentleman, or did you not know? Yes, several fine short stories.'

It was news to Werthen that Gross had even an inkling of his writing efforts. But Werthen suddenly realized where this was going.

'Quite right, Doktor Gross,' Werthen said. 'I am sure my friend Kraus would snap up a feuilleton on the espionage adventures of a certain unnamed playwright.'

Being no friend of Schnitzler and the other Jung Wien writers,

Karl Kraus would happily publish an exposé in his journal, *Die Fackel*.

'You wouldn't dare,' Schnitzler said. 'I would sue for defamation.'

'But you won't be named directly, Herr Schnitzler.' Gross picked the glove up off the desk and put it in his pocket. 'Now explain exactly where this fence is, and where and when you meet Herr Kohler.'

Out on the street again, Werthen had to squint in the fierce noontime sun. Duncan was at the entrance to the apartment building where they had left him. Franz Ferdinand had put the man at their disposal, and Werthen for one was glad of it. He and Gross were both armed, but Duncan provided a real sense of security.

The Scot followed a couple of paces behind them as they made their way once again to the Ringstrasse.

'That was a nice bluff you came up with, Gross.'

The criminologist took off his bowler as they walked, wiping the leather sweat-band with the handkerchief from his breast pocket. It was a warm day and Gross was dressed heavily for the season. Like many of his generation, he did not believe in lightweight summer suits, regarding them as frivolous.

'What bluff would that be, Werthen?'

'That I would place an article with Kraus exposing Schnitzler's activities.'

Gross replaced the bowler on his nearly bald pate and fastidiously folded the handkerchief as they walked, carefully placing it back in his breast pocket with a couple of centimetres of white showing.

'That was no bluff. If you wouldn't see to it, I would. The man needs to take some responsibility for his actions.'

Schmidt followed them at a discreet distance, wary of the tall, gaunt protector. He was carrying both a gun and a long blade, but it was insanity to contemplate an outrage in the middle of the day on a busy city street. The failed attempt at the law office had been bad enough, sparking headlines about anarchists and a reprimand from St Petersburg. But Schmidt would dearly love to finish this. One way or the other.

He followed the three men as they went into the Volksgarten, watching the heavily built one, the criminologist Gross, place a white kid glove on the finial on the wrought-iron fencing.

He knew immediately what they were up to – summoning a

controller. This was one of the oldest coded signs in the operation manuals. But what were they playing at? Whose controller? The logical deduction would be that it had directly to do with the playwright Schnitzler whom they had just visited. Schmidt considered it: a playwright would have easy access to international contacts. He could attend conferences abroad and openings of his plays without anyone batting an eyelid. Not a bad cover at all for a secret agent. But what could be the draw for one such as Arthur Schnitzler? Schmidt wondered.

Since making that mistake about names, Schmidt had studied Schnitzler, just as he had looked up Doktor Gross and Advokat Werthen in old editions of the Viennese newspapers. Schnitzler had recently caused something of a furore in Vienna with his play about a cowardly lieutenant, afraid even to challenge a baker to a duel. Not the best candidate for an agent, one would think, unless that play was in itself a form of cover.

Schmidt was all too familiar with the motivations for his agents. There were those who offered their services out of patriotic zeal. Usually their perceptions were so tainted that one could view their information only with great skepticism. Then there were those in it for a profit, whose reports were generally inflated as a result. And there were the reluctant agents, like Forstl, coerced into service through blackmail. They found a thousand reasons to drag their heels, resentful of their new masters and conflicted about their allegiances.

And me? Schmidt thought. The agent with something to prove, with a need for revenge. Was that Schnitzler's motivation, too?

Schmidt would find out.

He waited in place for two hours before contact was made. A fresh-faced young recruit, by the look of him, though dressed in civilian clothes. Looked barely old enough to put a razor to those apple cheeks. He walked by the glove twice before stopping on the third pass, looking over his shoulder but failing to notice Schmidt, now busily reading a newspaper on a nearby park bench. Schmidt kept watch through a small hole he had cut in the centerfold.

The youth quickly took the glove, tucked it into a pocket, and headed out of the park towards the Hofburg.

Schmidt followed him through interior courtyards to the main door of the War Ministry. With another quick glance over his shoulder, the agent entered.

More and more interesting, thought Schmidt.

TWENTY-NINE

I t was the solstice, and for Werthen the longest day of the year was dragging out interminably. Schnitzler had explained that someone checked the fence daily, late in the afternoon. If the glove was in place, then the meet would automatically be set for the next day, at two in the afternoon at the Grillparzer monument.

It was now ten past two. The glove was no longer in place, but that could mean anything, Werthen assumed. Some pedestrian might have taken it, or the controller. But if the latter, then why did no one appear? They should have had Schnitzler make the meeting. Was the controller one of the idle strollers in the park, waiting for Schnitzler to appear before he did so himself?

Werthen was about to suggest the same to Gross, when a man approached the monument. Clean-shaven, he carried himself like a soldier, though he was dressed in a linen suit and straw boater.

Werthen nodded at Berthe, who had taken up position under a nearby tree. She had the Brownie camera in her hands but she was not operating it, too busy staring at the man with a startled expression on her face. Werthen nodded at her to take the photo; they would not have another chance, for the man was beginning to look nervous.

Just as he thought this, the man abruptly turned and made his way out of the park. As planned, Werthen followed him, but professional training ultimately won out and Werthen lost him in the welter of interior courtyards at the Hofburg.

Gross and Berthe were waiting for him at the park.

'Did you get the photo?' Werthen asked.

Gross answered the question with another. 'You lost him?'

Werthen nodded, then looked at his wife.

'Oh, I took the photo. But there was no need.'

Werthen looked from Berthe to Gross, puzzled.

'It was the watcher from the Hotel Metropole,' Berthe said. 'And we know who he works for. His name is Captain Forstl and he is on the staff of the Bureau.'

Schmidt watched the farce with some amusement. He assumed that the lawyer had lost the agent. Schmidt would not have lost him.

But there was no need to follow; he already knew where the agent was headed.

And by the look of the animated discussion, it appeared that the lawyer's wife and the criminologist had recognized the agent while the lawyer was fruitlessly tailing the man.

It was also apparent from the slight bulge in the criminologist's right jacket pocket that he expected trouble, for he was armed and ready to defend himself.

Schmidt shook his head. This was not right. None of it. He had had enough of clearing up Forstl's messes. If this blew up now, it could easily be traced back to St Petersburg; Forstl would surely say anything, sell anyone, to save his own skin.

His masters had made it clear to Schmidt that they were not ready yet for an altercation with the Habsburgs. Not until they had built enough railway lines to mobilize their army – and that could take another decade. Russia possessed the largest army in Europe, but this would be no use unless they could deploy the troops in a timely manner.

Another disgusted shake of the head. Schmidt rose and turned his back to the lawyer and his wife and Gross before closing his newspaper. He headed for the nearest tram stop to travel to the telegraph office at the South Railway Station. He would need to send a coded message to St Petersburg. He did not want to make this decision on his own.

Later that evening, after Frieda had been put to bed, Berthe, Werthen and Gross gathered in the sitting room, husband and wife shoulder to shoulder on the leather couch, and Gross occupying one of the Biedermeier chairs. They had brandies in their hands, but no one had taken a sip.

'For me it is only too clear,' Berthe insisted. 'All the roads lead to this Captain Forstl.'

Gross blew air in derision. 'Bosh! We have merely accomplished a certain degree of triangulation. But detection is not trigonometry.'

'And there is nothing clearly linking Forstl to the Bower operation,' Werthen agreed. 'Schnitzler's suggestions may well have fallen on deaf ears at the Bureau after the scandal of *Lieutenant Gustl.*'

Berthe took a sip of her brandy. 'You say it yourself all the time, Gross. Too many coincidences. Sometimes you men cannot see the woods for the trees.'

Gross suddenly sat bolt upright in his chair, looking for all the world as if he had swallowed a partridge.

'Jesus, Mary and Joseph! That's it. I think you may have something there, Frau Meisner.'

'How do you mean, Gross?' Werthen said, setting down his glass on a side table, as if ready to apply a life-saving slap to the man's back.

'The letter,' he said, twirling his right forefinger through the air like a conductor. 'The one to the girl's father that includes the word "copse". That one, fetch it.'

Werthen was too tired to respond with irony to this impolite demand, but simply got up and went to his office, riffled through the drawers until he found the relevant documents, and returned to the sitting room. He could hear Frieda's regular breathing from her room as he passed it.

Gross was pacing about the room. He tore the papers out of Werthen's hands and placed them side by side: the one in the original Volapük, and the other Frau von Suttner's translation.

'It's this section,' Gross said, stabbing the paper with a forefinger. *'The well-tended Copse says I am a clever girl! I love my patriotic work*. That section is the key to it.'

'And it still makes no sense,' Werthen said.

'Assuming that it has been translated correctly,' Gross added.

'But how can we check—' Werthen stopped in mid-sentence, seeing what Gross was getting at.

Berthe, too, understood. 'Herr Moos!'

'Quite right,' Gross said. 'I would assume the man would be more than happy to aid us in our inquiries. I propose a visit to the Landesgericht prison tomorrow.'

'I'm afraid it will have to wait,' Werthen said.

'Why the devil should it?' Gross boomed.

'Because tomorrow is Saturday, and there are no visiting times on Saturday or Sunday.'

Gross merely harrumphed, as if Werthen himself had set the visiting hours at the prison.

On Monday morning Jakob Moos sat slump-shouldered on his bunk in the cell at the Liesel, the Landesgericht prison. Moos was being held in B block, for murder suspects.

The sallow-faced guard did not want to allow them into the cell at first, warning them that Moos had murdered a man with his bare hands.

'It was in a moment of rage,' Werthen replied. 'There was no premeditation.'

'It's still the noose for him, killing a priest,' the guard replied, sniffling as he took out his keys. 'And don't say I didn't warn you.' Another sniff, as if he was suffering from hay fever.

A call to Inspector Drechsler had allowed this visit but, to be honest, Werthen was not so sure about Moos. His one other meeting with the man had not gone well.

The prisoner sat hunched like a brooding bear, his massive fingers intertwined in his lap. He did not look up at the sound of the key in the lock, nor when Gross and Werthen entered. The guard remained outside the cell, his back turned to them, a snuffle emitting from him occasionally.

'Herr Moos,' Gross said, 'we need your help.'

The bowed head did not move. He was dressed in standard grey convict jacket and pants, both of them at least a size too small. The man's thick wrists and ankles showed. His hair had been shorn as if he were already convicted.

'It is in regard to your daughter, Waltraude,' Gross added.

This brought a low moan from Moos. Werthen was fearful that Gross might enrage the man after all.

'We are trying to discover who killed her. Won't you help us?'

The large hands flexed as if wringing the neck of a chicken.

Werthen tapped Gross's arm in warning, but the criminologist plunged on.

'I think I understand you, Herr Moos. Your daughter disappointed you. It is as if she was no longer your daughter before her cruel death. I have a son, you see, and we have been estranged for years.'

Werthen was shocked to hear Gross mention his only son, Otto. It was true, there was no love lost between father and son, but it was unlike the criminologist to mention his wayward son to a stranger.

'But were my son to be so brutally murdered, I would want vengeance, I assure you.' Gross spoke with real passion, Werthen thought. 'I would want the killer brought to justice. That is what any father would want, isn't it, Herr Moos?'

Moos suddenly stood upright, a movement so forceful it caught the attention of the guard who jolted himself into a semblance of action.

'What is it you want?' His voice thundered in the small cell; he towered over them.

Werthen stepped back a pace, but Gross held his ground. A tall man, Gross was not accustomed to looking up at others, but he had to do so with Moos.

'We need your assistance with this letter from your daughter.' Gross quickly drew out the letter in question, unfolding it for Moos.

The big man glanced at it for a moment, surprise on his face. 'Where did you get this?'

Werthen said, 'Your wife gave it to me when I visited your farm.'

Moos nodded his head. 'Yes, I remember you. The fancy man from the city come to tell us our Traudl was dead.'

But he said it in a resigned tone, slumping back on the bunk, the letter in his hands.

Werthen turned to the guard, shaking his head. The policeman put the truncheon he had drawn back in its sheath.

'I have underlined the passage we are concerned with, Herr Moos,' Gross gently explained.

A sudden smile crossed Moos's lined face. A strangled chuckle emitted from his mouth.

'What is it, Herr Moos?'

Moos looked up at the two of them, his eyes watering. 'She was always the bright one, our Traudl. The only one to really learn the language properly. So smart, she was. Such a waste.' He lowered his head, choking back a sob, the paper trembling in his hands.

They waited a moment, not wishing to hurry him. It was perhaps the first time he had actually allowed himself to grieve the loss of his daughter.

He looked up again, his jaw muscles working. 'We had a game, you see,' Moos explained. 'A little play with words, changing people's names into a sort of code. A silly childish game, really, but it was our private fun.'

'Is there a name here, Herr Moos?' Werthen asked. 'This passage has been translated as "the well-tended copse". But that makes no sense, of course.'

An actual laugh came from Moos now. 'To you folks, maybe not. But it is close.'

Then suspicion crossed his face. 'You think this name is important?'

'We think,' Gross said, 'that this is the person who . . .' Gross hesitated a moment, wondering how much detail to supply.

'The person responsible for leading Waltraude astray,' Werthen said, simplifying matters. 'And perhaps also her killer.'

Moos set his jaw again, nodding. 'Let's get it right then. Like I say, whoever tried to translate this got it right and wrong. It's this word here,' Moos pointed to the word *smafot* on the page, showing it to Gross and Werthen.

'That's made up. Traudl put together a couple of words in Volapük to get that. *Sma,* that means small; and *fot,* for woods or forest. So your translator got the small part right, as a copse is a small wood. Problem is *fot.* Volapük is an economical language and, like I say, *fot* can mean either woods or forest. In one meaning it is a wild forest or wood, but in another meaning we have forest like where you cut timber, like farming almost.'

'That's the "well-tended" part?' Werthen said.

Moos nodded. 'Like I say, right and wrong.'

'And your daughter meant "little forest"?' Gross said. '*Forstl.*'

'That's my guess. Mean anything to you?'

Gross sucked in air mightily. 'Oh yes, Herr Moos.'

'Wait. You don't think he's the one come visiting, do you?'

Werthen and Gross looked quizzical.

'Another man from the city. He came several days after you did,' he said, looking at Werthen. 'Acting like he was handing out samples of perfume. I gave him short shrift, sent him on his way. Him and his bottles of fancy-smelling whale vomit.'

'What did he look like?'

'What do all city folk look like? Dressed in their suits and hats, so you can't even see them.'

'Tall, short, slim, fat?' Werthen prompted.

'Oh, he was a man you would never notice,' Moos said. 'Neither tall nor short, thin or fat. Almost like he had no features. But he wasn't Austrian, I can tell you that. I'm a student of languages, and he spoke German like . . . Well, he didn't learn it from his mama. Too clear, like; too formal. Not just city formal, but from foreign parts.'

Werthen was immediately reminded of Frau Ignatz's description of the man in the stairwell at Habsburgergasse the night before the explosion; and Duncan's description of the man with the sandwich board outside their flat. Everyman; the man who blended into the background.

'But I did notice something about him. His hands. When he went to gather up the bottles of perfume he'd tried to give us, his little fingers were odd. He picked things up like a high-class woman drinking tea.' He mimicked holding a tea cup between thumb and forefinger, his little finger sticking out straight. 'But on both hands, like he couldn't use them properly. Like maybe they had been broken.'

'Do you remember the name of the perfume?' Gross asked.

Moos looked to the ceiling in an attempt at memory, then to his left and right. Finally, he shook his head. 'Can't say as I do. I think there was some writing on the bag he was carrying, but I didn't catch it. The only reason I noticed his fingers was because I had a friend once who had the same problem with a finger after breaking it. Just stiffened up on him.'

Moos looked down at the letter. 'She was a smart one, was our Traudl.'

He handed the letter back to Gross. 'You better keep this. It might be evidence.'

'You're right, Herr Moos. It might well be.'

'I appreciate your help,' he said after a moment's silence. 'You find the man who did this, right? He ruined our lives. All of us.'

As they were leaving the prison, Werthen was surprised to see two familiar faces approaching on the street. As they drew nearer, it seemed they remembered him, as well.

'Frau Moos,' Werthen said, lifting his hat to her. 'Good to see you, again.'

'Oh, it's the lawyer, isn't it? Wills and trusts?'

'And private inquiries,' Werthen added.

He turned to her companion, who disengaged his arm from that of Frau Moss.

'Herr Platt, if I remember correctly.'

'You do, you do,' the man replied. 'We've come to see poor Jakob.'

Werthen made speedy introductions all around, and then explained their visit to Jakob Moos.

'I am glad to hear he can help somehow,' Frau Moos said. 'He has been desolate since my brother . . .' She broke off, and soon was in tears.

'There, there, my dear lady,' Platt said, putting a protective arm around her and smiling at Werthen's look of astonishment. 'The lady's going to need a protector after her husband is gone,' Platt said *sotto voce* to Werthen. 'And that big farm to run all by herself. She'll need a man about the place.'

It was country logic, even though it seemed cold-blooded to Werthen.

He was about to comment, but thought better of it. Instead he asked, 'Do you remember another visitor from the city a few days after I was there? Herr Moos mentioned a perfume salesman.'

Frau Moos was dabbing her eyes, and managed a nod of assent.

'Aw that fellow,' Platt said. 'Told him Jakob would give him what for.'

'You gave him a ride from the station?'

'That I did. Not so much gave as, you know, got paid. Like with you. City man, city manners. Except that he claimed he was from the country, just like me. Well, who knows, maybe he was once.'

'Can you describe him?' Gross asked.

Platt looked at Frau Moos and they both shrugged. 'Wore a city suit,' Platt said, 'but it had a good deal of wear to it, I can say that much. Small, compact sort of fellow. Didn't seem the salesman type.'

'He tried to give me perfume, to cheer me up,' Frau Moos added.

'He knew about your loss?' Werthen asked.

She nodded.

'I told him,' Platt said. 'Thought he was from the city like you, come to talk about the matter.'

'And the perfume?' Gross said. 'Can either of you remember the name?'

Frau Moos looked suddenly sheepish.

'Frau Moos?' Gross said, with an edge to his voice.

She opened her handbag and pulled out a small sample bottle.

'I managed to put it in my apron before Jakob discovered the man. He would never allow me to wear perfume. I just wanted to see what it was like.'

Gross took the bottle and looked at the name on it: Heisl Parfumerie. Their address was also on the bottle, in Vienna's fourteenth district.

Gross made a note of this, then handed the bottle back to Frau Moos.

'No,' she said. 'You keep it. I wouldn't know what to do with it. And if it can lead to Traudl's killer . . .'

Gross nodded. 'Most wise.'

As they left, Platt winked in Werthen's direction.

THIRTY

It turned out the Heisl Parfumerie was in the telephone book, and it took only a few minutes calling from the nearest post office to verify that Heisl did not employ a salesman who had recently visited Buchberg. Indeed their only field man, Herr Theobald Vogel, was currently laid up with a summer cold that, *Gott sei dank*, was apparently not developing into pneumonia.

The telephonist on the other end was the chatty type, and Werthen was also able to ascertain that Herr Vogel's sample case had gone missing only a few months earlier.

Two minutes later, after learning that the secretary's brother had also once lost a suitcase on the Budapest express and that her nephew Wilhelm survived pneumonia last winter, Werthen was able to hang up the earpiece and open the door to the small, stuffy phone booth. Gross had meanwhile busied himself reading the customs regulations for shipping parcels to Serbia and Montenegro, on a nearby wall. He would, Werthen reflected, no doubt be able to quote from that material several months later. The man had a dome for a head, but still Werthen wondered where he found the space in his brain to store such information.

Werthen simply shook his head at Gross when the criminologist turned to face him.

'Looks like our man stole a samples case.'

Our man. There was no way of knowing who this man might be. Forstl himself? A minion of Forstl's? Somebody completely unconnected with Forstl? Nor of knowing of what deeds he was culpable.

As if reading his mind – and sometimes Werthen thought him capable of such a trick – Gross made a dismissive grunt.

'Our mystery man. What do we really know? Let's walk briskly and cogitate. I need a flow of blood through my body.'

Gross set off at a breakneck speed through the midday crush of pedestrians. Werthen struggled to keep up with him, as he was courteous enough not to barge through people; instead he sidestepped here and went into the gutter there, in an effort to keep up with his friend. Meanwhile, Gross, eyes forward and a determined set to his jaw, sailed through the pedestrians like a battleship on patrol.

Werthen suddenly realized that Gross was heading back to the Volksgarten. They crossed the Ring at the Parliament and entered the park. Gross sat down at one end of a bench, Werthen at the other.

'So,' Gross said, his voice sounding hearty after their energizing walk. 'Any thoughts?'

Werthen shared Gross's logic. The mystery man was either Forstl himself or someone working with him, or someone who had no connection with Forstl and the Bureau. Gross merely raised an eyebrow and murmured to himself.

'I suppose you have it figured out?'

'Just about,' Gross said with no little pride. 'Forstl is clearly our major suspect.'

'But you told Berthe—'

'I know what I told your lady wife, and what you also suggested. But we can't let the ladies steal the game from us, can we?'

'Surely not,' Werthen said. 'The empire would fall, the sun fail to rise.'

'Sarcasm is the poor man's substitute for humor, Werthen. Let us consider the facts. Captain Forstl appears to be at the center of a web of intrigue. The Bureau mounts a trap for Baron von Suttner in order to compromise his wife, and Forstl seems to be in charge of it; he establishes a spy in a brothel in order to discredit a high-level member of the Foreign Office. What else is the Captain up to? Murder most foul.'

He said this last loud enough to disturb a thin little lady knitting on a nearby bench. At the sound of the word 'murder,' she rose, tugged the leash of the white poodle sleeping at her feet, and moved to another bench, distant from the one occupied by Gross and Werthen.

The criminologist was oblivious to this disturbance. 'Not that he sullied his own hands with such things. No, clearly he did not.'

'So we are looking for his minion, as I suggested. But how can you be so sure?'

'Really, Werthen, your powers of deduction are failing you today. Do you forget that we have a series of similar murders throughout Central Europe? Captain Forstl was presumably not abroad when most of these murders took place. Easy enough to check, at any rate. Ergo, there is another man, who specializes in killing.'

'And what is his connection to Forstl? A hired killer?'

'An assassin, yes. Someone trained to take lives, someone cold and calculating enough to gain entrance to your office and plant a bomb. But, as we know, he is not infallible. An assassin, yes, but not one for hire to the general public. No, Werthen, I think we are dealing with an agent. An agent eager to cover any trail that might lead to Forstl. Which would explain Doktor Schnitzel's death. Let's say the barracks rumors about Forstl and Schnitzel were true, and perhaps the young doctor came looking for a "loan" to help set up his practice.'

'Extortion?'

'Yes, that's better, Werthen. So, after the misstep with Schnitzler, Schnitzel was disposed of. Just as Fräulein Mitzi and Fanny were before. Let us say the love-struck Mitzi wanted to end her work for Forstl—'

'Or more likely wanted more money,' Werthen interrupted.

'Quite,' Gross said without enthusiasm, 'or that she planned to run off with von Ebersdorf. We may never know the exact reason. And Fräulein Fanny perhaps knew of the arrangement and, following the death of Mitzi, wanted a gratuity to forget it. Again, a possible trail to Forstl is dealt with in the harshest manner. I understand why Schnitzel had to be silenced: he was potentially an embarrassment for an officer, a career ender, in fact. But the Bower operation? One imagines that was sanctioned by the Bureau, a chance to get one up on their rivals at the Foreign Office. So I ask myself, what trail was being covered up with the deaths of those two young women?'

'Perhaps it was not a sanctioned operation,' Werthen said.

'Ah, yes, Werthen. It is good to see you in fine fettle once again. See what a brisk walk can do for that piece of muscle between your ears? Not sanctioned, then. And what else about Forstl is not sanctioned?'

'You mean . . .'

'He was a double agent? Yes, that possibility comes to mind. Our Captain Forstl may be in the pay of a foreign power.'

'In which case the killer, the assassin, could be controlling Forstl, not simply working for him. He was able to hold the man's homosexuality over him, force him to work for a foreign government.' Werthen was growing excited at the implications.

'My God!' He suddenly remembered their last meeting with the Archduke and the troubling rumor about a possible Russian double agent at work in the Bureau.

Gross was smiling at Werthen's realization. 'Yes, Werthen, I assume you recall our conversation with Franz Ferdinand.'

'We have to stop him.'

'My dear friend, all we have so far is conjecture. Highly competent and intelligent conjecture, but merely a theory nonetheless. What we need is an experiment to test our theory.'

Neither Werthen nor Gross knew that Berthe and her friends were at that very moment undertaking such an experiment.

They had left Frau Ignatz with the *Portier* who looked after the building while they broke into Captain Forstl's apartment.

The scheme had been hatched quite spontaneously, the result of a casual comment and the conjoining of forces as if in a once-in-a-lifetime alignment of planets. First had come the visit of Frau Ignatz, whom Erika Metzinger had brought with her that morning. With the law office in ruins, Erika was working in Werthen's study until they could find new quarters. Erika, forever protecting strays of one sort or another, had now taken Frau Ignatz under her wing, for the poor woman was still grieving for her brother so cruelly killed in the bomb blast intended for Werthen, Berthe and Gross.

No sooner had Frau Ignatz been offered a cup of tea and was ensconced in a comfortable chair than Frau Blatschky announced another visitor. Berthe was pleased to see Frau von Suttner ushered into the sitting room. It turned out that the peace advocate had come to town to talk with her publisher about a new edition of *Lay Down Your Arms,* but in the event he had suddenly been taken ill and her trip was for naught.

'And then I thought, why not pay Frau Meisner a call and thank her once again for a job so well done. I must apologize for barging in like this unannounced. You must think me an awful bore.' She smiled in Frau Ignatz's direction.

'Not at all,' Berthe said with real sincerity. 'You are always welcome here, Frau von Suttner.'

They sat chatting for several minutes, reviewing the latest Viennese gossip and news. Frau Ignatz was not saying a peep, but taking it all in like a schoolgirl on an outing. At one point Berthe thought she actually caught an impish gleam in her eye when Frau von Suttner railed at that 'idiot Schönerer' and his 'Away from Rome' movement.

She was referring to Georg Ritter von Schönerer, the anti-Semitic, pan-German and anti-Catholic member of parliament who advocated that true Germans leave the Catholic church and convert to Protestantism. Twenty-one members of his nationalistic far-right party had recently gained seats in Parliament, and he and his political ideas were enjoying a resurgence in the newspapers.

'His poor sister,' Frau von Suttner added.

Berthe nodded. She too knew Alexandrine von Schönerer, the politician's younger sister and since 1889 director of the Theater an der Wien, one of the grand old theaters of the city.

Alexandrine was embarrassed by her brother's primitive political ideas and took every opportunity to distance herself from his anti-Semitism and anti-Catholicism.

Erika came into the sitting room, a brief in hand. 'Do you know where your husband has put the Wildganz file?' she asked and then noticed Frau von Suttner. 'I am sorry. I thought you were alone.'

Greetings were made, and the conversation ultimately got round to the reason for Erika working out of the Werthen flat.

'You mean the explosion that was written about in all the papers was at your office?' Frau von Suttner exclaimed once the full story had been divulged.

At the mention of the bomb, Frau Ignatz uttered a high keening sound that reminded Berthe of the pitiful noise she had once heard a baby elephant make at the Schönbrunn Zoo after its mother had died.

Berthe did not want to be so cruel as to explain to Frau von Suttner in front of Frau Ignatz about her brother Oskar. She glanced at Erika for assistance, but did not require it, for Frau Ignatz herself made the matter clear.

'My brother was killed in the blast,' she said. 'And if I ever get the killer in my hands, I will rip his eyes out.'

The matter of fact manner in which she uttered this threat sent a *frisson* through Berthe, but she knew she would feel the same if someone harmed Karl or Frieda.

'That day may not be so very far away,' Berthe said. And then to the barrage of questions this statement elicited, Berthe explained the course their investigation was taking and how one man's name kept cropping up – even as the person responsible for Baron von Suttner's attempted entrapment.

They had still not received a photograph that Inspector Drechsler had promised to send them to confirm Captain Forstl's identity; and Berthe was anxious to show it to Frau Ignatz as soon as it arrived to ascertain whether he was the man the *Portier* had seen in the stairwell at Habsburgergasse the night before the blast. But whether directly or indirectly responsible for the bombing, Captain

Forstl was responsible for a host of evil deeds. Of this, Berthe was sure.

'I would like to put him under the lens the way he has done to others,' she almost casually remarked.

This comment brought a moment of silence to the room as the women looked from one to the other. Erika was the first to react.

'So why don't we?'

They began discussing ways in which they might follow the captain, discover his secrets. But it was Frau Ignatz who took it to another level.

'We're not trained agents. He would surely spot us. I say we break into his apartment and go through the drawers.'

Berthe was amazed and almost shocked at the suggestion. Not that she opposed the idea, but she had had no idea Frau Ignatz possessed such *sang froid*. She could be a harridan when it came to her duties as a *Portier,* but what on earth would make her come up with such an idea?

'I read a story like that in an illustrated magazine once,' Frau Ignatz added.

'But do we even know where he lives?' Frau von Suttner asked, and by doing so tacitly joined in the conspiracy.

'Perhaps we will be lucky,' Berthe said, getting up and going into the foyer to the telephone table. A quick perusal of the directory showed her that luck was, indeed, with them. The man's flat was only a few streets away, in the Florianigasse.

Frau von Suttner was still unconvinced, but still asking the right questions.

'How would we get into his apartment?'

Erika looked a bit sheepish as she said, 'I think I might be able to help with that. Huck was only too happy to teach me some of his . . . skills.'

Huck was the nickname of the young street urchin whom Erika had wanted to adopt. He had tragically died last year in a case involving the Wittgenstein family. Breaking and entering, Berthe thought, might very well have been among the boy's skills.

'And I can chat up the *Portier,*' Frau Ignatz offered. 'Keep her busy while you women go about your business.'

Frau von Suttner suddenly clapped her hands together. 'Then what are we waiting for?'

And now, not half an hour later, Erika was delicately applying her hatpin to the lock on Captain Adelbert Forstl's apartment door.

Have we all gone crazy? Berthe suddenly asked herself. Too late now to stop.

He commanded himself to walk slowly, so as not to bring attention to himself as he made his way through the operations room. He had tucked the mobilization plans into his high boots, just in case.

Captain Forstl had finally complied with the orders of his masters in St Petersburg.

This should keep Schmidt off my back for a time, he thought ruefully. Now to get these papers into a safe place in his apartment.

Nothing suspicious about a man leaving the Bureau for lunch. He would hurry back to the Florianigasse, tuck the papers away in his desk, and then be back at his desk before his absence was even noticed. Tonight he would copy the papers and return the originals in the morning, before anyone noticed they were missing.

Outside, the midday sun and heat struck him, and he blinked in the glare for a time before his eyes dilated. Then he set off at a brisk pace for his apartment.

'My God, I wish I could afford one of these frocks.' Frau von Suttner felt the silk of one of the gowns in the dressing room off Forstl's bedroom. Berthe was surprised; she had thought the man was a bachelor, and said as much.

This brought a low laugh from Frau von Suttner. 'I doubt these belong to a woman.'

She lifted one dress from its hanger; it was so broad in the shoulder that it dwarfed the Baroness.

'You mean . . .?' Berthe felt her face going red.

'They call it transvestism,' Erika calmly explained. 'Men dressing as women and vice versa.'

Berthe had, of course, read about such things, but had never been presented with their reality. Then she remembered Gross's description of Forstl's rumored connection to Doktor Schnitzel. It all made sense now.

'Karl thought he might be trying to hide some such secret. Something that would compromise him.'

'There must be something else,' Erika said. 'Homosexuality is a crime, of course, but we are looking for something larger.'

Frau von Suttner had moved to a small table in the corner of the dressing room. A locked box sat on top of it.

'Can you apply your skills to this, Fräulein Metzinger?'

He began sweating into his tunic as he strode along Josefstädterstrasse. Perhaps he would have time for a quick wash and brush-up at his apartment. Quickly now, he prodded himself.

The plans hidden in his boot suddenly began to feel heavy and hot. He knew it was only his imagination, but nonetheless, he picked up pace as he neared the corner of Florianigasse.

As soon as Erika had performed another hatpin trick, Frau von Suttner slowly opened the box.

She was barely able to stifle a scream as she dropped the box and its contents on the parquet floor. It landed with a loud clatter, and several fleshy bits scattered about the floor.

For a moment the three women stood horrified.

'My God, it's a man's member!' Berthe hissed.

Erika was the first to regain her composure. 'And two little fingers. I do believe we have found the lodestone.'

Forstl had never been so happy to reach the apartment building on the Florianigasse. He was actually beginning to feel sick. All in my head, he kept telling himself. But he knew he could try to calm himself. The only thing that would make him feel better was to put these papers in a safe place.

He gave his mail box in the foyer a quick glance and noticed that there was a note indicating a package had been left with the *Portier.* He groaned to himself; he had no time to spare. But it might be something urgent from Schmidt: they sometimes made contact in this way. Instead of going directly to his apartment on the third floor, he stopped at Frau Novak's apartment in the mezzanine to collect the package.

He knocked at the door and could hear voices inside. When Frau Novak finally came to the door, Forstl could see the pinched face of another woman seated at the deal table in her kitchen. Some old friend he thought, come to share coffee. The woman's eyes seemed to brighten when Frau Novak addressed him by name and handed over the package. He looked at the return address. It was not important after all. Just a hat he had ordered from a milliner in Salzburg. Not even the thought of this lovely creation, with its nest of feathers, could take his mind off the damning papers stuck in his boot.

'Oh, but Captain Forstl, please do not run off,' Frau Novak's friend said as he was about to make his way up the stairs. 'I must ask you a question. You see I have a nephew who is interested in the military as a career. What branch would you recommend? Manfred is such a good young man. How would he serve his country best?'

'I am sure I do not know, Madam,' he said, irritation sounding in his voice. 'I know nothing about your nephew. It would be better for him to speak with a recruiter.'

'But you appear such an intelligent man and so young to have gone so far in the army. Surely you can spare an old lady a dram of advice?'

'The cavalry,' he said, exasperated. 'They get all the pretty women.'

Frau Novak looked shocked at the pronouncement, but her friend merely laughed. A high cackle that grated on his raw nerves.

'And a joker to boot,' the woman said.

'No,' Berthe said. 'We cannot take this with us. We have to leave it as evidence. Let the authorities discover it here. And leave the flat just as we found it, so that Captain Forstl is none the wiser.'

Frau von Suttner nodded at the wisdom of this.

'Quickly, though,' Erika said. She took a handkerchief from the waist of her skirt and picked up the grotesquely gray pieces of anatomy and returned them to their wooden box. She made sure it was locked and then placed the box back on the small table, careful to set it inside the rectangle of dust that had accumulated on the surface.

They hurriedly tidied up after themselves and were at the door when they heard footsteps on the stairs outside.

'Captain Forstl!'

He turned abruptly on the stairs just below his landing. It was the old lady from Frau Novak's. What now?

'Captain Forstl!'

'Yes. What is it?' His voice had a sharp edge.

'Your package,' she said, her voice echoing in the stairway. 'You forgot your package.'

They could hear Frau Ignatz's voice. She had said Forstl's name twice, as an obvious warning. Now or never, Berthe thought, opening the door as silently as she could and making sure the lock was in place before the three of them slipped out into the hallway, closing the door behind them.

There was nothing for it but to brazen their way down the stairs. If Forstl came up the last steps now and saw them moving towards the upper floors, he would surely know they had been in his apartment. Descending the stairs, however, there was no way for him to know where they had come from.

And it worked, Berthe was amazed to discover, as she passed the tall, thickset officer on the stairs. The three of them looked straight ahead as they passed him and Frau Ignatz, and quickly made their way to the vestibule and out on to the bright street.

Berthe breathed in a long draught of fresh air. None of them spoke as they waited several houses away for Frau Ignatz to appear. She did so several moments later and joined them.

'Well,' she said as she approached her friends. 'That was a waste of time.'

Berthe looked at her, puzzled.

'He is most definitely not the man I saw in the stairwell at Habsburgergasse the night before the explosion.'

'I think you will find it was far from a waste of time,' Erika told her, taking her arm as they hurried along the street to safety.

THIRTY-ONE

'**Y**ou could have been killed!'

'We did not really consider that,' Berthe said. Werthen had gone from relief to anger as she told him her story of discovery.

'And how are we supposed to get the authorities to search the man's premises?'

'You men will think of something, I am sure,' Berthe said, her voice sounding bolder than she felt. The adrenalin was wearing off, the moment of excitement passing, and she realized that Karl was right: they all could have been killed had Forstl caught them in his apartment.

Gross had remained silent throughout Berthe's recitation of events. Frau von Suttner and Frau Ignatz had left earlier, but Erika continued working in the study. She came in now as she heard raised voices.

'It was my fault, Advokat Werthen,' she said. 'I was the one who suggested we do something concrete.'

'Well, to be completely truthful,' said Berthe, regaining some of her former fearless giddiness, 'it was actually Frau Ignatz who suggested we break into the man's flat. She'd read stories about such endeavours.'

'Proves once again the danger of an education in the wrong hands,' Gross muttered.

Berthe finally said. 'I am sorry this has given you a fright, Karl. But you must stop wearing a funereal face, both of you.'

'It's the fruit of an illegal search,' Gross said. 'You broke into the man's apartment.'

'But you're the only ones to know that,' Berthe insisted, suddenly tired of having to apologize for breaking the case wide open.

Karl smiled at her, then turned to Gross.

'She's right, you know.' Then swinging back to Berthe, 'Not that I condone such an action, but we had apparently come to a standstill in the case. This puts the murders squarely on Forstl's shoulders.'

'But Frau Ignatz did tell us he was not the man she had seen on the stairs that evening,' Erika reminded them.

'And who is to say that was the man who set the lethal charge?' Werthen replied.

Gross made a sound somewhere between clearing his throat and moaning. Was he actually growling? Berthe wondered.

'May I point out the results of the investigative work your husband and I have done today?' Gross said this as if speaking to a classroom of first-year students.

'Point away,' Berthe said.

He quickly filled her and Erika in on the conversation with Moos.

'Then we know that Forstl was in charge of the Bower operation,' Berthe said. 'It all fits.'

'And what of this other man, the nondescript one who visited the Moos farm, who would also seem to fit the descriptions given by Frau Ignatz and the good Duncan? It would make sense that he is running Forstl for St Petersburg. And protecting him, keeping him undiscovered.'

'Then why that horrible collection in Forstl's flat?' Erika said.

'Ah, I was hoping you would ask about that,' Gross said, looking awfully pleased with himself. 'Now, a professional – and I assume our man, shall we call him Herr X, is a professional – would never keep such a collection. That is the sort of perverse action that bespeaks a neurosis. I do see a connection with such macabre ornaments and Herr X, however. The way the man holds his fingers . . . Moos was quite insistent about that. It indicates that the injuries to his little fingers were quite savagely applied. One does not like to make surmises on such scant facts . . .'

'Please, Doktor Gross,' Berthe interrupted. 'feel free to do so.'

Werthen shot her a look, but Gross was so wrapped up in his thoughts that he did not hear the sarcastic tone to her voice.

'Well, in point of fact, our Herr X might have suffered a most grievous injury that set him on the path of becoming an *agent provocateur*.'

'You are right, Gross,' Werthen said. 'Scant facts for such a surmise.'

Gross eyed Werthen with something very close to disdain. 'An agent must be among the fittest of the fit. Able to use brains and brawn. Able to kill with gun or knife, and even with his bare hands. Herr X appears to have a disability in that regard. It's doubtful whether an intelligence service would actively recruit such a man. Ergo, Herr X was able to overcome such a seeming disability by sheer force of will, perhaps inspired by the injuries done to him. To convince skeptical professionals that he could perform the tasks of a secret agent as well as, or better than, others.'

The three of them listened closely to Gross's argument.

'You have been giving this some thought,' Werthen said.

'You must become one with your nemesis in order to conquer him.'

'And what if Herr X is imaginary? And Forstl is the one responsible for all of this?' Berthe asked.

Gross did not bother with this question, but instead plunged on.

'There is one way to make Herr X become visible,' Gross said. 'It appears that his task is to protect Captain Forstl, to keep him from being exposed. If he were to suspect that Forstl was in imminent danger, he might come out from under his rock, might expose himself. He has been following us, of this I am sure. Watching our every step as we get ever closer to dropping the net on Forstl. That, Werthen, was what the bomb at your office was about. An attempt to stop our investigation before it reached the door of Forstl's office at the Bureau.'

'Not much of a professional,' Berthe said. 'Killing the wrong man.'

Gross nodded. 'Exactly, Frau Meisner. He should have known about the *Portier*'s brother, but time was running out. He could not undertake a meticulous operation. Urgency was his undoing. And I am counting on that for my plan, as well.'

*   *   *

They saw little of Gross the rest of that day. He kept to the study, displacing Fräulein Metzinger. The only communication Werthen or Berthe had was via Frau Blatschky, who complained mightily about the prodigious amounts of coffee being consumed by the criminologist.

Werthen knew this routine only too well from his days in Graz: Gross was removing himself from the distractions of society in order to concentrate all his formidable powers on this most challenging case. As with so much investigative work, Werthen was coming to understand, the real problem was not discovering who did it, but making sure they paid for their transgressions.

Before entering his ruminative hibernation, Gross issued a stern caveat: no one was to attempt to have the incriminating evidence hidden at Forstl's apartment 'discovered' by the police.

Berthe fumed at this directive. 'I risked my life to uncover that evidence and now he wants to give the man a chance to dispose of it.'

Werthen raised his eyebrows at this.

'What?' she said. 'It *was* dangerous. You said so yourself.'

Next morning, Gross deigned to breakfast with the mere mortals of the household. But Berthe was still with Frieda, so Werthen and Gross had the dining table to themselves.

'Have you got the solution, Gross?' Werthen asked as he passed the warmed milk for the coffee.

'Time will tell,' he said, pouring a trickle of milk into his steaming cup of coffee. There were fresh *Kipferls* today, and he plucked one of these predecessors to the croissant from the linen-lined basket and dunked it exuberantly into the coffee, leaving a brown trail dripping on the tablecloth as he maneuvered it to his mouth.

'I have but one request,' he said, reaching into his pocket and removing a small sheet of paper. On it the criminologist had written a telephone number and a paragraph of text.

'Ten minutes after I leave this morning, I want you to place a phone call to that number and relay the accompanying information to the person who answers the phone.'

Werthen quickly perused the note.

'You cannot be serious, Gross.'

'I am only too serious, my friend. Deadly serious.'

'But this is far too rash.'

'That is exactly what I am hoping.'

'And where exactly will you be while I am making this call?'

'Paying a long overdue visit.'

'This isn't a plan, it's a death wish.'

'Drama so early in the morning, Werthen. It is unbecoming.'

He rose suddenly before Werthen could proffer further arguments and passed out of the dining room just as Berthe was coming in, with Frieda in tow.

'Doktor Gross,' she said. 'We are honored by your presence.'

Gross shot her a sly smile. 'I am only sorry I cannot stay to converse over coffee. There is business to attend to.'

'Gross,' Werthen called to him, but it was no use. He heard the door of the flat open, and then close behind the criminologist.

The phone rang six times before it was finally picked up. Werthen looked at the script that Gross had provided, and immediately said 'I have something to tell you.'

A voice at the other end replied, 'Forstl, is that you?'

Werthen paused a moment, needing to extemporize. Obviously some colleague of Forstl's had answered his telephone; just as obviously this meant that Captain Forstl was not at the Bureau this morning.

Werthen coughed once into the mouthpiece and then automatically replied to the man's question, 'Yes.'

'Then you had better damn well get in here quick. The Colonel is about to explode. Somebody's been messing around in the vaults. The mobilization plans against Russia have been stolen. Do you hear me, Forstl?'

Werthen paused again. 'Yes. I will be there. Sick today. A summer cold.'

'Well, you don't sound like yourself. But this is no time for personal considerations.'

The receiver on the other end slammed down, then Werthen set his own down.

Berthe was standing by him in the hall. 'Well?'

'I think Gross is walking into a trap.'

He maneuvered past the *Portier* with ease, waiting for her to finish sweeping the sidewalk at the far end of the building and then slipped inside behind her. He knew where to find the apartment, from the story Werthen's wife had told them, and reached it without any curious residents passing him on the stairs.

Gross took deep breaths as he stood in front of the door, not because he was out of breath from climbing the stairs, but because he wanted to calm himself. He patted his jacket pocket automatically, and was reassured by the hard bulge of the Steyr pistol. He knew he might have to use the gun if, as he hoped, his message to Forstl – relayed by Werthen – brought the man's Russian controller out of the woodwork.

'*I have something to tell you,*' Gross had written. '*You are being watched. Your every move is tracked. We know about your memento mori collection, and your double agent status at the Bureau. We are coming for you.*'

Melodramatic, to be sure, Gross thought as he waited a moment longer outside the door. But it should prove effective, spurring not only Forstl but also his controller into action.

What had Werthen called it? Rash? Sometimes subtlety was insufficient to the moment, and Gross thought this was such a moment.

He reached inside his breast pocket and brought out the leather case containing his lock-picking tools. Arrayed on one side of the case was a set of skeleton keys; and on the other, more intricate L-shaped picks for a lock that proved more difficult and that would need its tumblers lifted one by one before the bolt could be slid back and the door opened. Gross was ready with the picks, for he assumed that a man like Forstl, acting as a double agent, would have at least a modern mortise lock in place – though it could not be difficult, as Werthen's secretary had managed the feat with a hatpin.

But, with his many years of experience in gathering evidence, Gross knew he should simply try the door first. It was amazing how many times a person forgot to lock the door when leaving in the morning.

He looked both ways along the corridor; there was no one about. He put his hand on the cool brass knob and twisted. The door opened. He hesitated. Luck or the unexpected?

Either way, there was no going back now.

A heavy brass smell assaulted his nostrils once he was inside the apartment, but Gross was sure this was not from the hardware on the door. The room was still in semi-darkness with the long drapes on the windows securely closed. A dim light shone from a room deeper in the flat.

Suddenly, more cool metal met his skin, but this time it felt like the barrel of a pistol biting into the back of his head.

'Move inside, Doktor Gross. Slowly. Do not reach for the pistol in your pocket or it will be your last action.'

'Tidying up, are you?' Gross said as the barrel dug deeper into his scalp, forcing him to move forward. The door closed behind them.

'Well, what did the pompous fool expect?' said Berthe, letting the note Gross had composed for Werthen drift from her hand to the parquet.

'This is hardly the time for recriminations. Forstl is most likely at his apartment now and it would seem that Gross is on his way there.'

'I'm sorry, Karl. I didn't mean to sound so shrewish, but sometimes Gross can be exasperating. He had a full night of cogitating and this is the best he could come up with? Stirring a nest of snakes?'

'He had to find a way to trap both Forstl and his controller. I assume this was it. With what you found in his apartment, Forstl would be the one to take the blame for everything. The controller would walk away free.'

'If there is a controller. I think we should call Inspector Drechsler.'

'I've got to go there. Warn Gross . . .'

'That is exactly why we need to call Drechsler. You are *not* going there alone.'

'I have read about you, Doktor Gross,' Schmidt said. 'You surprise me. This hardly seems your style.'

Gross was sitting on a straight-backed chair; his eyes had adjusted to the weak light in the flat. He looked closely at the small, compact man sitting across from him, gun in hand, examining him for any distinguishing characteristics. The only thing he could notice were the little fingers, sticking out stiffly from his hand. Gross's own pistol lay on the table next to the man.

'I am sorry to disappoint you, Herr . . .?'

The man simply nodded at him.

'But I badly wanted to talk with you.'

A smirk on the man's face. 'So you knew I would be here?'

'Eventually. Rather sooner than I had planned, I must admit.'

'And what is it that's so urgent for us to discuss?'

'Your murders, to begin with. You have been a busy man, Herr . . . I must call you something.'

'Schmidt will do.'

'Ah, the man of no name. Well, Herr Schmidt, you have been

active around the capitals of Central Europe. I have a litany of deaths attributable to you.'

Schmidt lost the smirk momentarily, to be replaced by a quizzical look.

'Your signature removal of the left little finger,' Gross added.

Schmidt nodded. 'Glad you noticed.'

'A bit of revenge for your own fingers, one assumes.'

This seemed to hit home. The muscle in his left jaw worked. 'You may assume whatever you want. I can only say I am grateful for your visit. It saves me the trouble of calling on you one final time.'

'And what business do you have with me, Herr Schmidt?'

'The same you have with me. Murder. You really should not pry so deeply into other people's affairs, you know. It shows a basic lack of courtesy.'

'I investigate murders, Herr Schmidt. If you do not want your affairs, as you call them, gone into, then I recommend you refrain from engaging in homicide.' He paused an instant. 'Herr Moos was correct about you, you know.'

'And who would this Moos fellow be?'

'You see that is the tragedy of such wholesale killing as you engage in. You even forget the names of your victims. Fräulein Mitzi's father. You paid him and his family a visit in the Weinviertel, I understand. Checking to see how much the family knew, I would assume. A man like you wants no loose ends that might start unraveling.'

'You said he was correct about me.'

'Well, in that your accent is neither Austrian nor German. No, there's a trace of the salt of the Baltic states about your speech, Herr Schmidt. And I see, by the sudden dilation of your eyes, I have hit home with that.'

'You're a smug one, aren't you? Very satisfied with yourself. I expect you know all about this matter.'

'You mean about you and your creature, Forstl? One must tire of cleaning up the messes of others. Especially when the others are so much less talented.'

'Please, Doktor Gross. None of your primitive psychological games. But yes, it is a tiresome business.'

He stood suddenly, an action abrupt enough to cause Gross to inhale deeply.

'Nothing to worry about . . . Not yet, at any rate, Doktor Gross.

But there is something you should see. Someone who would like to meet you.'

Werthen put the receiver back on its cradle.

'He's not there,' he told Berthe. 'The desk sergeant said Drechsler went out earlier this morning.'

They hovered over the telephone as if expecting it to make a decision for them.

'I've got to go there,' he finally said.

'No,' Berthe replied '*We've* got to go there.'

'There is no sense in putting both of us in harm's way,' he reasoned. 'Think of our daughter.'

'I am. But I am thinking of you, too, Karl. My husband. Now where is that cane of yours? The one with the blade inside.'

He knew it was useless to argue with her. 'I love you,' he said.

'Of course you do. So let's arm ourselves.'

'If only the Baroness von Suttner could hear you now.'

She pecked his cheek in response, grabbed the cane from the umbrella stand, and watched as he tucked Gross's second Steyr pistol into the waistband of his trousers. She hoped the criminologist had taken its twin with him for protection.

Berthe told Frau Blatschky that they would be back for lunch, then hurried into the nursery where Frieda was just waking up. She gave the child a kiss and a hug and told her that Frau Blatschky, Baba, would play with her this morning. This brought a radiant smile to Frieda's face, and she nuzzled her mother's hair for a moment.

Werthen and Berthe were just going out of the door when Fräulein Metzinger arrived, ready to reclaim the study and get some office work done. But when she saw the determined look on their faces and the swordstick in Berthe's hand, she knew something was afoot.

'You're going back there, aren't you?'

'Gross may have gotten himself into a bit of trouble,' Werthen explained quickly.

'I'm coming with you.'

'Not you too!' Werthen all but groaned.

'What if the door is locked, Advokat?' she said. 'Have you thought of that contingency?'

'Alright, alright.' He held out his hands in supplication. 'But let's be off now, before more reinforcements arrive.'

*   *   *

The scene before him explained the heavy brass smell he had noticed upon first entering the apartment.

Schmidt had turned on the gas light in the bathroom and it made the scene even more garish, the water in the bathtub a brilliant crimson against the whiteness of the porcelain and the alabaster of Forstl's skin. At least he assumed it was Forstl's corpse he was staring at. The wrists rested languorously on the edges of the tub, ribboned gashes were apparent on each. A cutthroat razor had been left on the tiled floor by the bathtub, to give it the appearance of having fallen from the dead man's hand.

'So you were just in the process of tying up further loose ends when I interrupted you,' Gross said, taking his eyes from the body.

'Indeed.' Schmidt smiled at him. 'And you know, your arrival is the most fortuitous event I could wish for.'

Schmidt pointed at him with the stiff little finger of his left hand, a flicker in his eye.

'Take your clothes off.'

Forstl's apartment was only minutes away, close to the baroque Palais Schönborn, which housed the supreme district court. He had taken part in trials there. Its gardens were now open to the public; Frieda often went there to play.

Werthen occupied his mind with these quotidian matters rather than face his fears about Gross. If Forstl was not at the Bureau this morning, that meant it was highly probable he was at his apartment. Would he be armed? Would his accomplice perhaps be with him? What had kept the man from his post at the Bureau? Should they look for a member of the constabulary on foot patrol and explain their fears?

To continue with these endless questions would sap him of courage, he knew. Thus, as they approached the apartment building in question, he told the women to get behind him and blindly charged up the stairs, quite unaware of Inspector Drechsler and two constabulary officers hiding behind a row of metal garbage bins deeper in the entrance.

He was up to the mezzanine before he heard Drechsler's voice calling to him.

'Werthen. Stop, man. You'll spoil everything.'

'Werthen?' Schmidt said, turning his ear to the shouting coming from the stairwell. 'Would that be your ally, Advokat Werthen, come to the rescue? And then whose is the other voice?'

Schmidt lifted the pistol level to Gross's eye, his forefinger tense on the trigger.

'You have arranged quite a little party, haven't you, Doktor Gross?'

Gross took a deep breath. He would not beg. That was beneath him.

The man's finger began to squeeze the trigger. Gross felt sweat roll down his spine.

Then Schmidt emitted a barking laugh and lowered the gun.

'This has been fun, Doktor Gross. We must do it again some time. Now into the wardrobe with you.'

Gross stood there dumbly for a moment.

'Now,' Schmidt hissed.

Gross did as he was told. He climbed into the cramped space, amid a welter of uniforms, and stumbled over a pair of knee-high boots. As he caught himself, the door swung to behind him and he heard the key turning in the lock. His hand fumbled into one of the boots and felt paper folded over on itself several times. He grasped this in a reflex action. From outside, came the sound of footsteps moving away. He thought he heard wood sliding on wood, but could not be sure. Then came a crash, which sounded like the apartment door flying open.

'Gross! Are you here?'

He let out a deep sigh. Werthen. His dear friend.

'In here!' he shouted. Then he was sorry he had done so, for it gave him no time to change.

'Where's the key?'

Drechsler's voice.

'The hell with the key. Kick the blasted thing in.'

Werthen at his most intemperate, Gross thought.

'Move back from the door if you can,' Werthen yelled. Then a rather massive boot was thrust through the thin paneling of the door, a constabulary boot by the look of it, and Gross was even more mortified.

The door was soon torn from its hinges and Gross blinked at the daylight, for another of the team had opened the drapes.

'Gross!' Werthen stood wide-eyed in shock, gaping at the criminologist who was dressed in a green-silk evening gown.

'Jesus, Mary and Joseph!' Drechsler muttered, running a hand through his thinning hair.

Two constables stood behind them, smirking at the sight.

To complete his mortification, Werthen's wife and secretary then entered the apartment.

Berthe took one look at Gross, tricked out in one of Forstl's evening gowns, smiled and said, 'You must introduce me to your dressmaker, Doktor Gross.'

THIRTY-TWO

Schmidt had gotten away, out of the bathroom window and across the neighboring roofs. There was no sign of him by the time they had figured out his escape route.

Drechsler arranged for all the train stations to be watched, but Werthen was almost certain they would not catch him. Austrian borders were porous to say the least. Besides the railways, there were any number of ways for Schmidt to flee. River barges plied the Danube to its furthest reaches; the man could hire a pony trap or even an automobile; simplest of all, he could simply walk across the border at any of thousands of places.

The inspector was the one to explain to Werthen that Gross had organized the trap for Forstl and his controller. Now in possession of photographic identification of Forstl, that morning Drechsler had been directed by Gross to await the man's return to his flat, stirred from the Bureau by Werthen's anonymous telephone message. He was to wait also for the arrival of another man – the controller whom Forstl would, it was hoped, summon as a result of Werthen's message. If no other person came within ten minutes of Forstl's arrival, then Drechsler and his men were to enter the apartment.

They had, of course, no way of knowing that both Forstl and Schmidt were already inside the flat when Gross arrived.

Werthen for his part was rather shocked to discover that the corpse in the bathtub – the same man smartly decked out in a captain's uniform in the photo in Drechsler's possession – was the military man he had so often seen in the morning walking along the Josefstädterstrasse towards the Inner City. Once again, Werthen was struck by the notion that Vienna was not a city at all, but rather a series of villages where no one was really anonymous.

Gross said little during the rest of the day, acting alternately like a chastised child and a Nietzschean *Übermensch* who did not deign to converse with mere mortals. Not even the fact that he had recovered the missing mobilization plans, hidden in Forstl's boot in the wardrobe, mollified him. Archduke Franz Ferdinand himself had called to congratulate Gross, but the criminologist had uttered a barely audible response.

'He obviously meant to make it look as if Forstl murdered you, his lover, and then took his own life,' Werthen offered at one point, hoping to make things better.

This was met by a gruff growl from Gross.

Berthe also tried to bury the hatchet, sincerely apologizing to Gross for her ironic comment about the dress he was wearing. He simply ignored her.

In the end, Frau Blatschky was the one to bring him round, cooking his favorite beef with onions, followed by a dessert of *Palatschinken,* crêpes stuffed with walnut paste and with a drizzling of chocolate sauce on top.

To celebrate and hasten his recovery, Werthen brought out a Château Margaux he had been saving for a special occasion.

She awoke with a start in the night and knew she was not alone. Suddenly a hand clamped over her mouth.

'There is just one thing I want to know,' the man called Schmidt said. 'And please do not attempt to scream or I will be forced to smother you with your own eiderdown.'

He could see her eyes, wide and white, in the gloom. 'Nod if you understand.'

She gave a brisk nod, not easily accomplished with his hand clamped over her mouth.

'I will take my hand away then. I mean you no harm. I have only come for information. Do you understand?'

Another nod, less panicked this time.

He took his hand away and she seemed to regain her composure, pulling the eiderdown up over her nightgown primly, as if she had not sold the body beneath those covers to legions.

'Who are you?' Frau Mutzenbacher demanded, her voice low but firm.

'Call me Schmidt.'

'Well, Herr Schmidt, what do you mean by breaking into my room this way? In fact, how did you get in here at all?'

'I am the one asking the questions. Time is short. I have come about your brother.'

'Siegfried?'

'Do you have others?'

She glared at Schmidt. 'What about him? I have no idea where he is off to.'

Schmidt slowly shook his head. 'That may suffice with the constabulary, but not with me. I leave no loose ends, and I think you know quite well where he is.'

'What concern is it of yours?'

The movement was so swift, she did not even see the knife until it was held only a centimetre or two from her left eye.

'I am the one asking the questions. Is that clear?'

She struggled with her fear, but finally gave in to it. 'Yes,' she whispered.

'Where is Siegfried?'

She paused, and the knife moved perceptibly closer to her eye. 'Do you want a matching scar for the one on the other side of your face?'

'He is dead.'

Schmidt said nothing in reply.

'Dead,' she whispered again.

'How?'

Another pause, and now there was a minute flick of the blade, a stinging sensation on her cheek, and she felt a warm trickle flow downward along her neck.

'I . . . I killed him.'

He laughed then. Not a real laugh, though, she registered. A sort of bitter chuckle.

'You're a real one, aren't you?' he said. 'Too bad we meet so late. We have much in common.'

He staunched her cut with the corner of the eiderdown.

This sudden concern scared Frau Mutzenbacher more than his threats with the knife.

'Tell me about it. He was your brother,' Schmidt said, 'but you killed him. Why?'

'He was going to bring ruin on this house. All my years of hard work, all my plans for retirement to Carinthia. They were going up in smoke because he killed this von Ebersdorf fellow. He was insane with jealousy.'

She felt tears coming to her eyes, remembering the deed. So easy. Siegfried had come running to her, begging for help, telling her how he had poisoned von Ebersdorf because he thought the Count had killed Mitzi. But she couldn't risk his being caught, could she? She gave him brandy to calm him; brandy laced with poison. He died quickly. She wrapped him in a rug, struggled to stuff his body into a storage trunk, and then hired a removal firm to transport the trunk to her little place in Carinthia before it began to stink. She followed several days later, a quick trip to bury the body.

'There's more, isn't there?'

It was as if he could see inside her very soul.

'Yes,' she said with a kind of ice-cold hatred. 'He deserved to die. He had an affair with my little Mitzi. The only person I ever loved, and he'd wanted to take her away from me. He could not keep his hands off her. My prize. My dearest.'

She had not cried in years, not since she was five and lost her virginity to a *bettgeher,* a man who rented bed space in her parents' meager flat in Ottakring. She had vowed after that incident never to cry again, never to weep but to get revenge.

But now she wept. She was not sure for whom.

When she finally regained self-control, the room was empty. The man called Schmidt had left as quietly as he had come.

EPILOGUE

The pleasant, rhythmic thwack of tennis balls filled the air. Fräulein Metzinger sat under the shade of the lone elm, refusing to join in, reminding Werthen none too gently that the vulcanized rubber used in the manufacture of these balls may have cost some African in the Belgian Congo his hand. Frau Ignatz, seated under the tree next to Fräulein Metzinger, clucked her agreement.

Other than that comment, the day had passed rather happily, Werthen thought.

Now, by the third week of July, the grass had grown nicely and Werthen was finding real satisfaction in tending it, watering the lawn by hand and mowing it with the special mower his father had given him. In fact, the last few weeks he had left town early on Friday to give himself and the family as much time as possible at the farmhouse in Laab im Walde. Werthen was also rediscovering the joy he had found as a boy in playing tennis; not the competitive part of it, but simply the joy of striking the ball well, feeling the racquet strings brush up and over the ball, and then watching the white orb spin over the net. Everything about lawn tennis was suddenly pleasing to Werthen: the greenness of the grass, the deep brown of the maple racquet, the pure whiteness of the ball.

'That was clearly out,' Gross said. He was acting as umpire and his wife, Adele, was assisting him on line calls. They were both taking the contest very seriously.

Werthen was teaming with Frau Juliani, the widow whom Berthe's father, Herr Meisner, was seeing. She hardly acted the role of demure widow, though; an outspoken and energetic little woman, to Werthen's surprise and delight she possessed a rather deft backhand. On the other side of the net, they faced the mixed-doubles team of Herr Meisner and Baroness von Suttner. Berthe had mysteriously bowed out of the game at the last minute, saying she needed a lie-down, which was quite unlike her.

'I'm not too sure of that call, Doktor Gross,' Herr von Werthen said from his sidelines seat. Werthen's father and mother were also in attendance, and Emile von Werthen seemed in fine spirits today – much better than on his previous visit to the farmhouse, when it had rained the entire weekend. He had been able to go butterfly-hunting this morning, even deigning to take Frieda along with him part of the time.

'Fine little lepidopterist she'll make,' he'd said upon returning, a touch of pride in his voice. Frieda now sat upon her grandfather's lap, as he questioned Gross's call.

Gross bristled at the suggestion that he could be wrong, but a placating touch by Adele made him resist the temptation to indulge in argument or condescension.

'Yes, well, it was on the far side of the court. I suppose you had a better view of it over there.'

Herr von Werthen nodded.

'Five–love,' Gross said.

Herr Meisner served for the second time. He had earlier demurred about his athletic ability, but he soon caught on to the game and was now sending a blistering ball in the direction of his paramour, whose return landed neatly at the feet of the Baroness, who netted her ball.

'Oh, I am sorry,' she said to her partner, but Herr Meisner was so overcome with competitive zeal that he simply made a harrumphing sound in reply. He had shaved off his long beard and looked at least ten years younger. Werthen was surprised at the transformation; and

Berthe had been shocked when she saw him *sans* whiskers. He had worn a beard all the years of her life.

Clearly, love had its own demands.

'Well played,' Werthen's mother called to Frau Juliani.

Looking about him, Werthen realized that everyone he cared about in the world was gathered at the farmhouse this beautiful Saturday. The soft heat of the afternoon even made him glad his parents were constructing their new residence nearby. Somehow the events of last month had mellowed him, had made him see how precious and short life is.

Berthe came out of the house, and watched the next few points as her father took his team to victory.

She came up to Werthen. 'That was good of you.'

'What?'

'Letting him win like that.'

He smiled, not knowing anyone would notice.

'I have something to tell you,' she said.

But at that moment his father said, 'Seems like you have visitors, son. And by the look of that automobile I would say important ones, as well.'

Werthen looked down the approach road to their farmhouse and saw the car moving along, leaving a funnel of dust in its wake. It looked very much like the vehicle they had ridden in when fetched to an audience with Archduke Franz Ferdinand. And if Werthen was not mistaken, that was the Archduke himself riding on the bench seat behind the driver, who would no doubt be Private Ferdinand Porsche. Next to the Archduke sat a beanpole of a man: Duncan, his personal bodyguard.

'You'd better tell me later,' Werthen said to Berthe. And then, still dressed in his tennis whites, together with Gross, attired rather more formally, went to the front of the farmhouse to greet them.

'Ask him to join us,' Herr von Werthen called to his son as he left. 'I've never met an Archduke, especially one nobody likes.'

'Emile,' his wife said in a chiding tone.

The others were chatting to one another about the surprise arrival as Werthen got out of earshot.

'What the devil do you think brings him here?' said Gross as they strolled towards the approaching vehicle.

Werthen did not care to speculate on what things might motivate royalty. He only hoped the Archduke was not about to cast a shadow over this perfect day.

Private Porsche thoughtfully pulled his automobile to a stop at a little distance from the house, so as not to engulf them in the dust trailing behind the vehicle. He and Duncan got down from the Lohner-Porsche and came towards them.

'Good day to you Duncan, Private Porsche.' Werthen nodded at each in turn. They made a humorous contrasting pair: the one tall and thin as a rail, the other a good deal shorter.

Private Porsche shot them a half salute and Duncan returned their greeting. Then, 'He wants to talk with the two of you,' the Scot said.

'Please, tell the Archduke that we would be more than happy to entertain him.'

Duncan shook his head. 'Not entertainment he's looking for, and he told me to apologize for barging in like this on your weekend, guests and all.' He nodded to the carriages parked nearby, and the people by the tennis court. 'Playing the game of kings, I see,' Duncan said, a sly smile on his face.

'We do not necessarily play it in a kingly manner,' Werthen said, 'but we do enjoy ourselves.'

'What's this about, Duncan?' Gross finally said.

'His Highness will tell you. He wants to meet with you at the motor vehicle.'

He said no more, and Werthen and Gross did as requested.

As they got near the automobile, Franz Ferdinand waved at them. 'Sorry to once again plague you on a Saturday, but I was in the vicinity and thought you might want to hear some information I've received. Please, no long faces, gentlemen. I will not keep you long. You may recall that I have an agent in place in St Petersburg?'

'The one who warned you about a double agent in the Bureau?' Gross said.

'Precisely. I received a communiqué from him this morning. It seems military intelligence in St Petersburg has been in a barking match with the Russian Foreign Office over the death of this double agent. Each accusing the other of incompetence, and looking for a scapegoat to save face. It appears they found one with the return of the man who was controlling their double agent.'

'Schmidt!' Gross said the name as if cursing.

'One would assume so,' said the Archduke. 'My agent merely noted that the controller running the double agent was appropriately chastised. I use his word: chastised.'

Werthen heard Gross emit a low growling sound.

'What are we to assume that means, your Highness?' Werthen asked.

Franz Ferdinand shrugged, a gesture that made him appear less than regal. 'Knowing the Russians, it would probably be either a bullet in the back of the head or a long vacation in Siberia. Either way, gentlemen, I don't think we will be plagued by the man in future. It would seem that, at long last, justice has been done. For quite the wrong reasons, but justice nonetheless.'

Gross suddenly stood tall, chest thrust out. 'It is good of you to bring this information, your Highness. A kind thought.'

Indeed, the news seemed to make Gross come alive again and to reassert his overbearing attitude. Werthen never thought he would entertain such a sentiment, but he had actually missed the Doktor Gross of old – supercilious, autocratic, officious.

They said their goodbyes, the Archduke politely declining an invitation to a cup of tea.

As they walked back to the lawn party, Gross sniffed once and then said, 'I could have told you that would happen to Schmidt. The man was a fool to return to his masters. My prediction exactly.'

It was good to have the old Gross back, Werthen thought.

Returning to the others, Werthen told the news first to Berthe, who seemed to breathe a sigh of relief, knowing Schmidt was no longer a threat. The bombing of Werthen's office was still uppermost in her mind. Meanwhile, Gross was entertaining the others with his own version of events.

'Now what was it you had to tell me?' Werthen asked his wife. 'Something about the law-office renovation?'

She put her mouth to his ear, whispering, and his smile turned into a sigh of love and happiness.

'You're sure?'

She nodded. 'It's been more than a month. You know how regular I am.'

He wanted to shout out for everyone to know. Instead, he took the cup of tea that Berthe handed to him.

Gross, finishing with his blandishments about Schmidt, turned to Werthen and saw such a blessed look of happiness on the man's face that he was indeed glad for his little bit of subterfuge at the news Franz Ferdinand had imparted. No need to spoil the nice tennis party.

Pure nonsense, of course, both the news and his feigned relief. For Schmidt was a survivor. He would never return to St Petersburg if he thought such a fate awaited him.

No. They would, Gross feared, hear more of Schmidt in the future.